BACKLASH

That's when I hear the scream. It slices through the morning air like a razor, cutting every conversation. Every face turns towards the mosque. Only when the scream dies do I register the fact that it's a woman's voice. One man unfreezes before the rest of us. He runs towards the door, then the crowd surges after him. I'm running with them.

The main prayer hall is through a set of doors straight ahead. To the right, stairs lead upwards. That's where I go. Towards the women's prayer hall.

I'm on the second flight now. At the top there's another set of doors. I crash them open and stumble forward.

The woman is standing next to a wooden screen on the right. She's draped in black – the full chador. Black cloth covering everything but her hands and a narrow strip above her veil. So all I can say about her is this: her eyes are wide with shock or fear and her hands are red with blood.

Born in Wales, Rod Duncan now lives in Leicester with his wife and children. *Backlash* is his first novel.

BACKLASH

Rod Duncan

POCKET
BOOKS

LONDON • SYDNEY • NEW YORK • TOKYO • SINGAPORE • TORONTO

First published in Great Britain by Simon & Schuster, 2003
This edition first published by Pocket Books, 2003
An imprint of Simon & Schuster UK
A Viacom company

1 3 5 7 9 10 8 6 4 2

Simon & Schuster UK Ltd
Africa House
64–78 Kingsway
London WC2B 6AH

www.simonsays.co.uk

Simon & Schuster Australia
Sydney

A CIP catalogue record for this book
is available from the British Library

ISBN 0 7434 5019 1

Typeset in Stone Serif by M Rules
Printed and bound in Great Britain
by Bookmarque Ltd, Croydon, Surrey

Some resent and others tolerate.
This novel is dedicated to those who embrace.

Acknowledgments

For a perfect blend of critical comment and generous encouragement, thanks go to David Hood, Bridget, Juliana, Siobhan, Lesley, Pam, Bead, Liz, Emma, Gwyneth, Margaret, Ros and the rest of LWC. For expert knowledge on Islam, policing, fire trucks and computer operating systems, thanks go to Khalid, Rob, Ian and Tim. And for their support and faith, my abiding gratitude goes to Stephanie, Hannah and Kate.

PART ONE

Chapter 1

It began with a stop and search. That's what they tell me. A couple of Asian lads outside the Waterfields Youth Club turned out to be carrying knives. So you've got two uniforms trying to disarm a couple of turban-wearing seventeen-year-olds. The youths don't cooperate, of course. And they're still warm from the evening karate class.

It gets ugly after that. Pepper spray. Handcuffs. The shouting draws in every hard case from the terraced streets around. By the time a Support Unit arrives, our boys in blue are separated from their patrol car and all but surrounded. They're glad when the van comes down the street to rescue them. Doubly glad that it's got a metal grille to shield the windscreen from the flying bottles.

You know how it is with a crowd like that on an August night. People do stuff they would never try if they were on their own. One person starts rocking the empty patrol car then there are two, then twenty. Then the car is on its roof and someone's messing around with a cigarette lighter.

Whoomf! You've got yourself a riot.

A car fire gives you two good explosions at least. That's my experience. One when the petrol in the engine goes up. The next, usually bigger, when the fuel tank blows. That brings in the fire brigade and more people to fill out the crowd.

There are people breaking up paving stones by this time. These are the veterans who've seen it all happen before. They know you have to prepare, just like the police do. The youngsters soon get up to speed, though, learning from their role models. A kid will throw a broken bottle at a fireman just as easy as an adult will.

The firemen have now been transformed into something they never signed up to be. They've become symbols of authority. They're white, like the police. They wear uniforms. That's enough for the hundreds who now make up the mob.

So, you've got a burned-out police car blocking one end of the street. A crowd of youths is trying to turn over a white transit van down the other end. And the fire crew suddenly realize they're in serious trouble. In a few seconds they're going to be trapped and their shiny red engine will be sending up fifty-foot flames into the night sky. Bang go the fire department's cash-flow projections for the next quarter.

They don't hang around chatting. The driver revs the engine and they're accelerating away, horn blaring. But the mob is still trying to block their path. They've got the transit on its side already, but there's still just enough space to get the fire engine through. The mob is rocking the van again, just about to roll it into the centre of the road. The fire engine has got only a couple of seconds to eat up the fifty yards that separate it from safety.

The driver floors the accelerator. He feels a sweat break out all over his body. His vision turns into a rifle sight. He can see only the gap between the ruined transit on one side and a line of parked cars on the other. He aims his twelve-ton vehicle. The van is toppling, but he's through. In his wing mirror he sees it crash over on to its roof. He's not

oking forward, so he doesn't see the ten-year-old boy who
ns into the road in front of him, a lump of smashed-up
aving stone in his hand.

It's only a broken arm, but the crowd doesn't know that
et. Someone has fetched the child's mother and sister.
hey're tearing their hair and wailing in the centre of the
rush. The ambulance can't get through the blockade,
hough somehow a TV crew has managed.

'My baby!' screams the mother.

The reporter has to shout to be heard. 'Who did this?'

The mother isn't listening, so youths in the crowd
nswer for her. 'It's the filth, i'n'it. The fucking police!'

Meanwhile, I'm cosied up on the couch, comforting
myself with a takeaway tandoori, when the Coen Brothers
movie I'm watching is interrupted by a newsflash.
Waterfields is burning. The pictures are being relayed live.
Men with scarves over their faces are smashing shop win-
ows and the crowd is screaming police brutality.

It's like an advert for looters. The reporter may as well be
aying, 'Free microwave ovens. All you can carry – get down
ere while stocks last.' If there were a couple of hundred
here before the newsflash, it's going to be a thousand
within an hour.

I put the foil carton to one side. It's a shame to waste a
erfectly good takeaway, for which a battery chicken has
made the ultimate sacrifice, but I'm suddenly feeling a bit
queasy.

Police reinforcements are being called up from all over
eicestershire by this time. They're unlocking the store-
ooms and getting out vanloads of shields and body-
rmour. Meanwhile, some of the more experienced rioters
re getting ready for the inevitable baton charge. They req-
uisition a crate of empty milk bottles from behind the

newsagent and start siphoning petrol with a short length
garden hose.

The ashes are still smoking the next morning when daw
breaks over the red-brick city. Weeping shopkeepers ha
begun to sweep up the shattered glass, and insuran
underwriters are blessing the exclusion for riot and war
the small print of their policy documents.

The two turbaned youths who started it all are still
custody. They're both Sikhs, of course. The top brass a
trying to figure out a way of releasing them without admi
ting that the arresting officers made a horrible mistake. I
religious law, all Sikh men have to carry a blade. They're n
supposed to be arrested for it. But some idiot must have fo
gotten to keep our enthusiastic beat bobbies up to speed.

That's when my presence is requested by the powers o
high. I'm Inspector Marjorie Akanbai, police communi
relations officer. Friends call me Mo.

'Mo. I want you in my office now!'

That's Superintendent Frank Shakespeare. My boss's bos
Sometimes known as The Bard. He calls to me through th
open door.

'Yes, sir.'

'Now!'

He would have had a rugby player's good looks when h
joined the force, twenty-something years ago. Since the
he's hit middle age. Or it's hit him. He's run too many a
night operations. Black coffee may keep you awake, but
doesn't stop the tired skin from sagging into hammock
below your eyes.

I step inside. 'Morning, sir.'

A huddle of other senior officers are on their way ou
I'm swimming with the big fish today. No one look

cheerful. I scan the group and notice the chief constable himself – outspoken champion of community policing and anti-racist initiatives, as seen on *Newsnight*. The top man flashes me his teeth in a brief shark smile.

The door closes behind him.

There isn't a mirror in the superintendent's office, or he'd have seen that his fringe is tufted up at the front where he's been running his hand through it. The hair is a rich chestnut brown – it used to be peppered with grey when I started working for him. That was a couple of years back. There's a Styrofoam cup on the desk. Black coffee. Half-empty.

'Didn't you teach them anything?'

He's talking about the men who arrested the two black-belts and thus triggered the riot. He reaches for the remains of his coffee and drains it in one. He hasn't made eye contact yet. 'We're supposed to have an understanding with the Sikh community!'

The morning hasn't got off to a good start. My guts don't feel too good after last night's takeaway, two years' worth of painstaking community relations work lie smoking in Waterfields, and to cap it all it seems that I'm the idiot who caused the riot in the first place.

'Sir . . .'

'They're talking about 7 million in damage.'

I guess he's just passing on the grief he's had from the chief constable. Even the chief isn't immune. He probably got a bollocking from the Home Secretary. The timing of this riot couldn't be worse for the government.

I say: 'The race-awareness training scheme would have been good.'

The superintendent runs a hand back through his hair, tufting it some more. We both know he was the one who refused my request for everyone working the Waterfields area to be put through the same professionally run course that my own team had gone through. It was something to do with the budget. Perhaps we should phone the Home Secretary and give him an earful.

'Well, it's a proper balls-up,' Shakespeare says, 'in more ways than one.'

'Yes sir.'

'The business community need to know we're on the case. But we don't want too many uniforms out there. Don't want it to look . . . well . . .'

'Like an occupying army?'

He casts the empty Styrofoam cup into the bin. 'Balance. That's what we're after.'

I nod and do a pretty good impression of someone who knows how to sort out a problem. 'Yes, sir.'

'I want you out there, Mo. You need to be seen. I need more officers with your . . . with your connections.'

What he wants to say is 'more officers with your skin colour', but sentences like that make him nervous. The force can't afford any more accusations of racism. Especially now.

'Get some snaps done for the *Crusader*.'

'Yes, sir.'

'Police talk to local people. Smiles and handshakes. That sort of thing.'

Shakespeare sees me as black, on account of my being a quarter West African. That was my dad's dad. But half the community leaders in Waterfields think of me as a white woman who's spent a few hours under the sunray lamp. Sure, my pale skin tone makes them uncomfortable, but it's the uniform that really makes me white.

*

So, there I am, flanked by my two sergeants – experienced men. They're well capable of getting us out of danger if open hostility were to flare up. Three uniforms feeling very conspicuous as we pick our way towards the youth club. The smell of burned rubber still hangs in the air near the blackened remains of the transit van. It's like I can feel the hostility radiating from the red-brick Victorian terraces on either side of the road.

I'm not sure yet of how to find the balance that the super talked about. First I have to get a feel for the mood on the streets. Find out which of the different communities are blaming the police and which are blaming each other.

I see this bearded Asian man outside the dead window of a corner shop. He leans on his shovel and watches us from under his eyebrows. I give him my best reassuring smile and nod. He just gets right back to work, clearing the drift of shattered safety glass from the pavement, dumping it into a wheely-bin. Scrape. Crunch. Scrape. Crunch. He's still looking at us, though, as we walk past.

There's the sound of someone hammering in the distance and a dog barking, but no sound of cars. No one is stupid enough to come into the war zone this morning. Except us, that is. And of the few people on the street, no one wants to risk being seen talking to the cops.

We get down the other end of the road and find the youth centre closed. Boards where windows should be. Unpainted plywood. Non-returnable screws.

I'm standing there outside the padlocked door, feeling like a fool. I'm not going to feel any better when I turn around and walk back the way we came. My two street-wise sergeants are looking embarrassed by the whole situation.

One of them, I have to tell you, is too damned handsome

for anyone's good. That's Sergeant John Greenway. He's a particular favourite of the two civilian secretaries in my unit. The other sergeant – Ivor Morris is his name – sports a moustache that would look more at home on the business end of a toilet brush. I'm not sure if it's the facial hair, but my female colleagues don't have so much difficulty treating *him* in a professional manner. As for me, their looks make no difference. Three days ago I gave up all interest in men.

Morris is inspecting the new security measures. He gives the door a prod with his foot.

'Well?' says Greenway at last.

I look from one to the other. 'Any suggestions?'

'Back to the station,' offers Greenway. 'Raise some of the locals by phone.'

Morris shrugs. He hasn't anything better to suggest.

It's usually me who takes the executive line on policing. Fax messages. Consultants. The graduate approach, they call it. Morris, particularly, has always looked more at ease reading a suspect his rights than when he has to make a phone call. But I guess we'd all feel more comfortable behind our desks this morning.

Then I hear the call to prayer. It's distant, though each Arabic syllable is clear in the still, morning air.

'Come on,' I say.

'Where we going?' asks Greenway.

'The Dean Street Mosque.'

Morris frowns.

'It's Friday,' I say. 'Everyone will be there.'

We go the long way round. Some streets look almost untouched. On others we have to negotiate an obstacle course of broken glass and fire-damaged shop furniture. We take it slowly. There's no point in arriving too soon. So

hen we do turn the corner on to Dean Street, they're
ready there – the crowd we haven't seen up till now.

Don't get me wrong: this isn't a representative sample of
e local community. Waterfields is as diverse as they come.
world in miniature. This crowd is all male. All Muslim.
ost have beards and traditional dress.

Sergeant Greenway whistles. 'Here we go then.'

If the riot were to start again, then Morris and Greenway
ould be the ones I'd want to have watching my back. But
the aftermath, with the community feeling battered and
ruised, I want to approach my once-supportive contacts in
umility. I've got this mental image of Gandhi in a loin-
oth going to negotiate with the British generals. Striding
own the road between Greenway and Morris would be
ore like arriving in a Centurion tank.

Time to ditch my escort.

There're a few trees down the other end of the road, at
e top end of a small park. Majestic Park, the locals call it.
hey don't get to see much greenery around here.

I point towards it. 'You guys go and check out the play-
round. Might find some youths hanging around there.'

'What you going to do, ma'am?'

'Talk to these people.'

'Better we stay together.'

'You won't be far.'

Morris gives me a troubled nod. 'Ma'am, in my experi-
nce . . . and I have walked the beat here for . . .'

'What can go wrong?'

For a few seconds I watch them walking away, then I turn
nd look at the crowd again. On the left side of the road is a
arge shoebox-like building. It's got a pole sticking up from
he flat roof with a pair of loudspeakers strapped to the top.
'his is your standard factory-cum-mosque conversion.

I step forward. The chatter of voices starts to die down
I approach. The crowd is silent by the time I'm in speaki
distance. I see someone I recognize. Anwar is his name. H
got a couple of garment factories in the Waterfields are
each churning out cheap leisurewear. A big chunk of t
money for the mosque came from his family. He acts a
kind of unofficial spokesman for one section of the Musli
community, and on the whole we get along pretty well.

He steps towards me. 'Inspector.'

'How's your business, Anwar?'

'One van burned.' He turns his palms towards the s
'No worse.'

I nod to indicate the crowd behind him. 'And t
others?'

'Shops are bad. They will survive, *inshallah*. But it is n
good. Like you see.'

The rest of the crowd has started speaking again, thoug
the voices are more hushed than before.

'Will it happen again tonight, inspector? Will the blac
attack our businesses again?'

That throws me for a moment. But I think Anwar is ju
probing. Testing me. 'It wasn't a race riot, Anwar. An
tonight will be better, I hope.'

He nods. '*Inshallah*.'

That's when I hear the scream. It slices through t
morning air like a razor, cutting every conversation. Eve
face turns towards the mosque. Only when the scream di
do I register the fact that it's a woman's voice. One ma
unfreezes before the rest of us. He runs towards the doc
then the crowd surges after him. I'm running with them.

I'm near the front when we get inside. To the left are t
washrooms and shoe-racks. The main prayer hall is throug
a set of doors straight ahead. To the right, stairs lea

upwards. That's where I go. Towards the women's prayer hall

I take the first three steps in one stride. Most of the men must be holding back from coming this way, or they're fanning out to search the other rooms of the building. Anwar is still with me, though. I file away my gratitude till later. I'm on the second flight now, and I can hear his footsteps following. At the top there's another washroom and shoe-rack. Another set of doors. I crash them open and stumble forward into the women's prayer hall. It's large. Empty. Six square pillars support the ceiling. Frosted windows line the walls on either side.

The woman is standing next to a wooden screen on the right. She's draped in black – the full chador. Black cloth covering everything but her hands and a narrow strip above her veil. So all I can say about her is this: her eyes are wide with shock or fear and her hands are red with blood.

Chapter 2

What's the point of a psychology degree and all that race relations training if you're dealing with a stiff? 'How do you feel about what's just happened to you?' Silence. I don't do bodies. That's what I'm getting at. I'm strictly a living people's police officer.

I fast-tracked through my two beat years with a fair share of the excitement. But however high, drunk, violent or abusive the people I dealt with, they were all alive. Sure, some were unresponsive. It's just that I could always have the vague hope they might snap out of it and shout at me – which would at least prove they were still breathing.

So there I am in the women's prayer hall, exhibiting all the symptoms of shock that I was supposed to have studied at university. My hands are trembling slightly. Part of my mind has gone into overdrive, taking in details and working out what needs to be done. But the strangest thing is the way the other part of my mind has gone off into a far corner of the room to sulk and is watching everything from a safe distance. Dissociation – that's what they taught us to call it at university.

The woman who found the thing has gone considerably beyond my stage of disturbance. We're talking serious trauma here. She's in a state of semi-collapse, kept standing only because of the way her elbow has come to rest on one of the old iron radiators. But it's the low whimpering that makes the scene so unnervingly creepy. She needs hospital. Sooner the better.

Then there's the body. It's lying under a length of black fabric, behind the wooden screen and just under a window. The blood has spread out over the tile-effect vinyl flooring, pooling in slight dips to make a disturbingly symmetrical pattern of puddles, shockingly dark. It reminds me of an ink-blot test. I'm never going to be able to take one of those again without giving the psychoanalyst something to think about.

And it's now, in this detached state, with Anwar running into the prayer hall in slow-mo, that it strikes me how blood doesn't show up on black. The hysterical woman is wet with the stuff – I can see that now. It glistens in the fabric of her chador. But it's only on her hands, where the skin is exposed, that it shows up red. The same goes for the cloth on the floor. If it'd been white, we'd have been looking at a scene from a slash-'em-up movie. As it is, all I can see is a faint tone change where the cloth has been soaked. It's not even wet any more. And that tells me another thing: the body has been lying there long enough for the blood to dry out in places. The woman must have got her soaking from one of the puddles.

Anwar is kneeling next to a dark pool. '*N'aoozubillah.*' He voices the word under his breath.

'Don't touch,' I say.

I'm looking at the cloth-muffled bundle, trying to decipher it. Which part is head, which part feet? But the form seems strange, and I feel a sudden fear that the body might have been in some way mutilated, dismembered and rearranged. I'm feeling nauseous again. I turn my back on the blood.

I see a crowd of men at the door. A few have followed

Anwar into the room and are venturing towards us. I shake my head and somehow manage to say: 'Stay back.' They look relieved.

I'm way out of my depth here, and wishing there was someone to tell *me* to stay back. Like I said, I don't do bodies.

That's when my head clears, and I suddenly know what to do. There are two victims in the room. One is beyond help – whoever it is has already spilled their full eight pints. The other is traumatized, crumpling on to the floor near the radiator. If she doesn't get the right kind of support over the next few hours and days, she could be facing months or years of psychological damage. I step around the blood, pull her to her feet and wrap my arms around her. I'm running on instinct here.

The woman is still whimpering, but I feel her muscles start to relax as I hug her close. I look at Anwar over her shoulder.

'Get everyone out,' I say. The scene-of-crime people should thank me for that, at least. 'Keep them downstairs.'

Then, in a step-at-a-time slow dance, I sidle her away from the body.

'It's all right,' I hear myself saying, though I have no idea if she understands any English, or even if my words are getting through to her mind. 'It's all right. It *is* all right.'

We're across the room, sitting with our backs to the wall, her head on my shoulder, waiting for the professionals to arrive. It feels like an hour has passed since the scream, though I know it should be measured in seconds. She needs help, and I feel queasy with that responsibility.

Then a tear falls from the woman's face and splashes on to the back of my hand. She shakes her head. 'So sorry,' she says. I hold her closer. There are sirens approaching outside the building. The tension is draining from me. I feel a tear running down my own face now. The tear brings a wash of relief, and suddenly my eyes are streaming.

I usually kick walls when I'm upset – or swear. I'm not a weepy person. And I'm not even feeling sad right now. It's just that I can't stop crying. We're talking Niagara after a major storm. The woman is gripping my hand, trying to comfort me.

'You all right?' she asks.

But I can't answer for sobbing.

It's at this precise moment, damn-it-all-to-hell-and-back, that my long-awaited sergeants burst through the door.

Greenway is first in. His eyes fix on my blood-smeared hands. 'My God!'

Morris has pushed past him. He's running across the hall towards me.

I point to the body. 'There.'

'Mo?' He slows, follows my finger with his eyes. Then he sees it.

I say: 'I'm OK.'

He swears under his breath, walks to the body, crouches, lifts one edge of the black cloth. There's a puzzled expression on his face, as if he can't resolve what he's seeing. His mouth opens then closes again. He lets the cloth fall back but remains crouching. Then, after a moment, he lifts it again and has another look. This time he lets it drop more quickly. He stands and walks back towards me, shaking his head. 'Did you look?'

'I . . .' I shake my head.

Greenway is calling in our status on his radio. He sees Morris's expression and stops mid-sentence. 'Ambulance?'

Morris shakes his head. 'Unless you're in need, ma'am?'

I've got my shock reaction under control by this time. 'This woman needs to see a doctor,' I say.

She tightens her grip on my hand.

'A medic for the woman,' Morris says. 'And . . .'

'And what?'

'And either a vet or a butcher.'

He can't hide his grin now. He opens his mouth to speak and suddenly the torn fragments of the puzzle arrange themselves into a complete picture in my head. I know what is happening. I wave my hand trying to stop him, but the words don't come out of my mouth quickly enough.

'What you have under that cloth,' he says, 'is a rather bloody and freshly butchered pig.'

The woman goes rigid against my shoulder. She opens her mouth and lets out a scream, sickening and jagged.

I've got to rewind here – two years back to when I was working up in Yorkshire. It was a mixed-up time for me. I'd just been promoted and I'd lost my dad to cancer all in the space of three months. Then trouble started on the streets – and it was my responsibility to sort it out.

There was a poster shop right in the middle of my patch. Wall coverings for teen bedrooms and damp bedsits. Boy bands and actresses. They also sold a line of A3 motto pictures, fluffy animals mostly. Among the images on the rack were several of pigs. Cute, if you like that kind of thing.

Taste is a strange thing. Personally, I'm grossed out by the idea of eyeballs – a culinary delicacy in some parts of the world. For many Muslims the most impure and stomach-churning thing is the pig. It's more than unclean. There's something blasphemous about it as well. *Haram* is the word they use. There's no English translation.

I don't know how it happened, but word got round the Muslim community that the poster shop was selling immoral pictures. A hate campaign started, beginning with anonymous letters and paint-spray graffiti. Then someone put a brick through the window in the night.

It turned out that the shop owner was a devotee of a guru who preached a particularly militant brand of Hinduism back in India. Never let go of Kashmir. Pull down mosques on Hindu holy sites. That kind of stuff. Some of the guru's philosophy must have rubbed off on the shopkeeper. He could easily have taken down the pig pictures for a month or two until everything had settled down. Instead he put them in his most prominent display and had grilles fitted to cover the window at night. Wanting to paint his attackers as hypocrites, he also displayed a quotation from the Holy Koran, urging tolerance and compassion.

That's when the race relations unit of the city council got dragged in. There was an official complaint. The shopkeeper was accused of blaspheming against Islam by putting pages from the sacred scriptures next to these *haram* images. The council came to consult our race crime experts. Nothing doing there. No legal action could be taken because blasphemy only counts as a crime if it's against Christianity.

The city council's Race Relations Unit didn't know what to do either. One ethnic minority was putting out the windows of another ethnic minority. Who was the victim? So they made soothing noises to both sides and issued a public statement, reaffirming the city council's commitment to equal opportunities.

Meanwhile, the shopkeeper was calling for help from his own community. Some of the more militant Hindus came to his aid. Volunteers guarded the shop around the clock. They set up a phone tree to bring in reinforcements at any time of day or night. It looked like we were a few days away from our very own street war.

It was a crazy situation. A few dozen hotheads were pushing two whole communities towards a conflict that no one really wanted. I pulled a few strings and got the head of one of the big Swaminarayan Hindu temples to meet up with a couple of the local Muslim leaders. They made a joint statement calling on everyone to back down.

If it hadn't been so close to Christmas, I don't think it would have worked. But no one wants to have running street battles when it's cold and raining. Calm returned to the streets. I got all kinds of commendations from on high. My name was mentioned in dispatches. Then a community relations job came up in Leicester – my home town. I went for it. And after my recent successes they couldn't refuse me. The job fell into my lap, and I came home to take up the Waterfields job.

Only after leaving Yorkshire did I learn that someone from the city council had whispered reassurance into the ears of a few of the Muslim community leaders there. It was a couple of months later that the militant shopkeeper finally got the result of a long-running dispute he'd been having with the local planning department. The decision went against him, and he had to close the shop.

All of which goes to show how little I know about what's really going on below the surface. And I'm supposed to be the expert.

Back to the women's prayer hall of the Dean Street Mosque. I was comforting the lady in the chador. Sergeant Morris was just about to reveal all, and I'd only that moment guessed what was going on. What I should have done was shout at him to keep quiet.

The woman next to me thought it was bad enough to be soaked in *human* blood. It takes a minute before she stops

screaming, and another eight before the ambulance arrives
to stretcher her away.

Anwar steps into the hall and hands me a headscarf.
'Cover your hair,' he says.

I nod. 'Sorry. I . . .'

'No matter.' He points to my feet. 'This also.'

I notice that he's remembered to bare his own feet. I slip
my shoes off and start to apologize.

He holds up a hand to stop me. 'No matter,' he says
again, though he doesn't look happy. 'You must go now.'

He's right. There's nothing more for me to do. The room
is taped off already, awaiting a scene-of-crime team. And no
one is going to talk to me looking as I am. So I walk down
the steps, shoes in my hands, and out of the front door. I
stand there in the morning sunshine, covered in pig's
blood, and I suddenly realize I've other things to worry
about than my dry-cleaning bill. There, in front of me, is a
crowd of perhaps a thousand Muslim men and boys. And
judging by their faces, they're about half a degree below
boiling point.

I want to run back into the mosque. Instead I step
towards the encircling wall of bodies. No one moves. I keep
my face forward, looking through to the other side.
Another step and the nearest men start to back away. Then
I'm in among them, and the sea is parting.

Chapter 3

Three things are waiting on my desk when I eventually get cleaned up and return to the cop shop. The first is a letter from my miserable, pathetic, useless, and, as of three days ago, ex-partner. This I drop in the waste-bin, unopened. Then there are half a pound of pork sausages and a packet of tissues – the kind that have a lemon-scented balm to soothe the skin around your nose. How thoughtful.

It's a macho world in the police force. I guess it has to be. We joke about the horrors we see. No one is allowed to show how much they're shaken up inside. It's a kind of unwritten rule. Coincidentally, it's the exact opposite of everything I was ever taught about keeping psychologically healthy.

I'm staring at the sausages, then it comes to me that I haven't had any lunch. In fact, I haven't chewed on anything since last night's tandoori – unless you count the stuff that passes for coffee in this place. I'm beginning to suspect that the chicken was off. I am hungry – though I think I'd throw up if I actually tried to eat anything. I check the date on the sausages anyway.

'Thanks, guys!' I shout, holding the packet up for all to see through the glass windows of my partitioned office. 'That's tonight's tea sorted.' Never let them know when they get under your skin. That's another of our rules. Worth remembering if you want to get on in this place.

There's a small explosion of laughter from behind a computer monitor somewhere in the outer office. It's one of my six constables. I can't make out which.

I take a deep breath, push the door closed with my foot and reach for the phone. I should really take time to figure out what I'm going to say. But the truth is, I don't have any answers. He picks up on the second ring.

'Superintendent.'

'Mo. Heard you had some trouble this morning.'

The whole of the Leicestershire police force probably knows by now.

'Yes, sir. And there's going to be more.'

'Hold on . . .'

There is a pause. I rub the telephone cable between finger and thumb. There are background voices on the other end of the line. Then there's a distant clunk – probably a door closing, and Superintendent Shakespeare is back with me.

'Sorry about that, Mo. You were saying?'

'The Muslim community, sir . . .'

'You should know,' he says, 'that it's going to be very different tonight. We're prepared.'

The super learned his trade on the toughest of the city's streets. And he had a nose for the job. Could always sense when something was about to happen. His arrest record proved that. But things have changed. Twenty years ago half the people in Waterfields were white.

'There's going to be low-key surveillance,' he says, 'of all the flash-points. And we'll have Support Units in place. We can be in there and breaking up trouble before it has a chance to get going.'

I wrap my finger in the telephone cable. 'This is something different, sir. The Muslim community. They're outraged by what happened today. Rightly so.'

He clears his throat. 'Mo . . .'

'They *need* to know we're taking it seriously.'

'It must have been very . . . well, upsetting for them. You too. But it's out of our jurisdiction. We've got to hand this one over to Race Crime. It's CID's property from here on.'

I give my jaw muscles a quick work-out grinding some more tooth enamel.

Don't get me wrong. I have a lot of respect for what the Race Crime Unit do. Whatever personal grudges I may have, I'll admit that they know more about organized racism than anyone else. But they don't understand the community dynamics in Waterfields.

'Sir.' I can hear the pitch of my voice getting higher. 'If the Muslim community don't think we're serious . . . I'm just worried some of them might try to take the law into their own hands.'

There's more background noise on the other end of the line. 'Hold on a moment,' he says. Then it goes quiet, like he's got his hand over the mouthpiece. I untangle my finger from the cable and rub at a coffee stain on my desk. There are a couple of constables carrying papers around in the outer office. I wrap my finger in the cable again. Then he's back.

'Sorry about that, Mo.'

'Sir, I think . . .'

'It's out of our hands,' he says. There's a note of finality in his voice. 'I expect the Race Crime Unit will . . . when they get round to it . . . they'll want to interview you.'

I feel my stomach clench. Interviewed. That's the last thing I want to face right now. I try to swallow, but somehow my throat won't cooperate.

'Mo. Everything that happened . . . Have you made an appointment with the counsellor?'

'I . . . no. No need.'

'Good.' He's glad to get that out of the way. Counselling is always offered these days – something to do with lawsuits and post-traumatic stress. No one ever accepts, of course.

'Now,' he grunts. 'This afternoon. Start to make arrangements with the schools. We'll need people out doing the Monday morning assemblies. Find out where that kid . . . the one who ran out in front of the fire engine . . .'

'Roddy Wellan, sir.'

'Indeed. Find out which school he goes to.'

'What about the Dean Street Mosque?'

'And the *Crusader*, Mo. Had those pictures taken yet?'

'I . . . no. But I think . . .'

'It's important. Take Sergeant Patel with you. Try to get someone prominent . . . one of the local community leaders. A handshake outside the Afro-Caribbean Centre. It's the symbolism we're after.'

I take a deep breath. One last attempt to avoid disaster. 'It's Friday . . .'

'I'll twist some arms, try to get your picture in the Saturday edition.'

'I mean the mosques, sir. They'll be full tonight after sunset. That means crowds of Muslim men. Thousands. All angry.'

'We *are* prepared, inspector,' he says, formality cooling his voice. 'Everything that can be done is being done.'

'Yes, sir.'

'Steer clear of Dean Street, inspector.'

The phone clicks quietly as he hangs up. I count to ten, like my mother always tells me. It never works for her either. I swivel to face the computer and stab the power button with my finger. I clench my teeth, waiting for it to boot up. It makes an optimistic chiming sound, which adds another inch of mercury to my blood pressure.

The first paragraph of my memo to the chief constable comes out, fast and angry. The keyboard rattles like a machine gun. By the second paragraph I've got my feelings almost under control. By the third I'm staring to have doubts. I save it, then sit looking at the screen for a few moments. In a flash of anxiety, I click 'select all' then hit the delete key. The computer doesn't even ask me if I'm sure. I stare at the blank page for a few seconds then start to type again – this time the memo is addressed to Superintendent Shakespeare.

I just wanted to thank you for your support earlier today.

I read the lie silently, wondering how I can live with myself.

I will get the photographs sorted this afternoon. The school visits are also in hand, I'll try to do Roddy Wellan's school myself.

Perhaps I should add another bland layer, but right now I can't think of anything else pleasant to say. Instead I get right down to the meat and mustard in this particular sandwich.

Thanks for listening to my warning about tension in the Muslim community – i.e. the danger they might believe that the police are not following their case seriously enough and so take the law into their own hands. I will leave the matter to the Race Crime Unit as you have instructed, though I must admit that I'd prefer Community Relations to be involved.

A few more lines of padding on the other side and the

memo is finished. If older, wiser members of the Muslim community don't manage to control the young hotheads, then we might be in for an unpleasant night. The super needs to know that. Having it in writing should make him think twice.

It seems strange to be worrying about this kind of thing here in Leicester. We've always been the model of inter-racial harmony that other cities have tried to follow. All this disturbance has come at exactly the wrong time – what with the Multiculturalism Conference only a couple of weeks away.

I click 'save' again, then fire off two copies to the printer – one for Superintendent Shakespeare, the second to slip into my emergency, complete-job-meltdown file. It's an insurance policy, one I'm still thinking I'll never have to use. I push the filing cabinet drawer. It rolls closed with a satisfying clunk. Done.

I'm walking away, through the main outer office, along the corridor, past the water cooler and up a flight of stairs. I drop the memo in my super's pigeonhole then go back down the stairwell, all the way to the ground floor and out into the car park, via two sets of swipecard-controlled security doors. I've got the keys to my Audi in my hand, when it hits me. Thud. It's Friday. The cleaners do my office on Friday.

I run back across the car park, accelerate up the stairs, then slow myself deliberately as I walk back into the Community Relations Office.

'Forget something?' asks Leah, one of the civilian secretaries.

I smile tightly. 'You know how it is.'

I'm in my fish-tank office now. I reach into the bin and pull out the unopened letter from my ex-partner. It's still scrumpled from when I dropped it in there half an hour ago. I crush it some more inside my fist. This is one document I definitely don't want the cleaners to find. I'll dispose of it at home.

'Off anywhere nice this weekend?' calls Leah from the outer office.

'Me? No. No. No. I'm going to . . .'

'Only they're saying it's going to be a scorcher.'

'Are they? Right. Good. Good.' I stand up.

'You working the weekend then?'

I nod as I pass her on my way out. 'I'm off Sunday, though,' I say.

'Have a good one then,' Leah calls after me.

'I'm sure I will,' I say. Damn. But this lying is a hard habit to break.

The riot started at a quarter-past nine in the evening with the first stone flying through the air. More stones followed. Then fire. This is what the preliminary report will say when it lands on the chief constable's desk. It's not true, though. You have to rewind the tape a fair few turns to find where the trouble really began.

While Sergeant Patel and I were out being photographed for the local rag, the Race Crime Unit were setting up their investigation. That meant sealing off sections of the mosque – the womens' prayer hall, the rear yard, the fire escape. They struggle through language problems to interview a couple of people, then sit around waiting for a scene-of-crime team to show up.

Scene-of-crime teams are in short supply on this particular day. Under cover of the looting and burning of the night before, persons unknown have pulled off a series of factory raids. Leisurewear. Enough to fill two forty-foot trucks. Whoever said crime doesn't pay?

What's a dead pig compared with £100,000-worth of
stolen goods? That's how the person coordinating things
back at the station must see it, because the mosque case
keeps slipping down the list of priorities. At three in the
afternoon it becomes obvious that forensic work isn't going
to begin until the following day. The last member of the
Scene Unit heads back to the shop a shade too early.

When the men start to arrive for mid-afternoon prayers,
there are no policemen in sight. A whisper goes around
that the blasphemous object is still lying upstairs – just
above their heads. It has been left. They're not allowed to
remove it themselves. The police have forbidden it.

The men return to the factories, carrying the story with
them. They tell their Muslim co-workers – men who pray at
different mosques throughout the Waterfields area. The
afternoon clicks slowly on. Weaving machines crash and
rattle. Flies buzz. Resentment incubates in the heat. And at
some stage an individual makes a phone call to his contact
in London.

Our lot haven't been idle, though. As well as investigating the factory raids and working their way through a
mountain of crime reports filed by people who still believe
that their insurance companies might pay out, they are
making preparations for the night. They deploy mobile surveillance equipment. Cameras and transmitters small
enough to fit into a suitcase. Cameras in upstairs rooms, on
flat roofs, in unmarked vans. In the control room they keep
lookout on all the potential trouble spots. The boarded-up
youth club. The length of West Park Road from the Majestic
Hotel all the way to Waterfields Community College.

From early evening, Tactical Support Unit vans start
taking up positions just outside the danger zone. Policemen
sweat in their riot gear. Controllers watch video screens,

looking for any sign of an angry mob starting to form.

As for me, I'm in my kitchen, which I've only just g
round to clearing up from breakfast. I've got half an e
tuned to BBC Radio Leicester and the other half tuned
the occasional traffic on my police radio.

The unopened letter from my ex-partner is now in t
swing-bin, covered in the uneaten remains of my Weetabi
There's a kind of poetry in that, which I'm thinking
should feel good about. I'm perched on a stool, eating
slice of Marmite on toast in lieu of dinner. It's staying dow
which is another reason to celebrate.

Just after sunset, my police radio crackles and I hear a
order going out to three of the TSUs to intercept a gang
twenty men who are advancing along West Park Road
stop chewing and look up at the wall clock. Eight for
The second hand ticks around the face. At eight forty-o
the radio crackles again with an order for the vehicles
return to their starting point. The men are Muslims, hea
ing towards the Dean Street Mosque. I swallow. Someone
the control room is thinking straight. I allow myself
believe that the coded warning in my memo might
having some effect after all.

More messages about the mosque follow. Crowds of me
are gathering. Police units are to stay clear. The crowds a
getting big – much bigger than usual. Men from oth
mosques are converging on Dean Street. Police units are
stay well back. The street empties as the men go inside
pray. The control room is doing just fine.

It's ten past nine when I hear a report of a group
youths – some black, some white – loitering around the edg
of Majestic Park. Control room sends one TSU to move the
on. When it gets there it finds that more youths were stand
ing unseen among the trees. Far too many for a single un

to handle. Danger. Three more TSU vans hurtle towards the park. Blues and twos. But there's no way for them to get through Dean Street. A crowd of some two thousand men and boys has now spilled out of the mosque on to the road. The van drivers shout for them to clear out of the way. But there's one group in the crowd who've travelled up to Leicester specially for this moment. A group more political than religious – though they probably wouldn't see the distinction. They now take their chance, stepping in front of the vans, linking arms to form a human barricade.

The vans are stuck. Somewhere up ahead, police officers are in need of help. But there's no way forward. They try to reverse, but the radicals are surrounding them now. One of the men punches his fist into the air and shouts.

'In-fid-els! In-fid-els! In-fid-els!'

Some of the crowd take up the chant. Then stones start clattering on the outside of the van.

It's nine fifteen.

The harder the trapped police officers swing their batons, the faster the group of radicals grows. There were only ten or twenty to start with – a couple of mini-bus loads. Within a minute a hundred young men have joined them. Anwar and others are trying to call them off, but their voices are drowned out by the clamour of the growing mob.

More TSUs are already arriving in support. Officers in full riot gear leap out of the vans and hurry into formation, a thin blue line across the width of Dean Street. Shields and batons. All the briefings are forgotten now. All the lectures on cultural sensitivity, all the anti-racist programmes. It's white men in helmets and visors against Asians carrying sharp rocks. We've got ourselves our very own *intifada*.

It takes me a long time to get to sleep. It's too hot – even with just a sheet. I wake in the night feeling clammy and hungry. I check the local radio for news, but it's playing the kind of bland mush that passes for music at three in the morning. After a handful of raisins from the jar in the kitchen, I'm feeling like I can't eat any more, so I head back to bed.

I'm woken by a clatter from the letterbox. The curtains are bright with sunlight and I'm feeling hungry again. I pick up the *Crusader* from the doormat and hobble stiffly across to the kettle.

Coffee. A triangle of toast. More coffee.

I unfold the paper and my stomach contracts into a ball of lead. There on the front page are two large photographs. On one side, a burning police van. And on the other – all smiles and complacency – me pressing the flesh with a local councillor. Two words make up the stinging banner headline. 'Pig's Ear.'

God, but the *Crusader*'s sub-editor must be feeling pleased with herself.

Chapter 4

'Everyone up!'

A ripple of nervous excitement spreads across the hall of St Catherine's School. Chair legs scrape and screech as three hundred and fifty children get to their feet. The teachers sitting around the outside of the room exchange uneasy glances. They are the last ones to stand. It's prayer, not drill from a police officer that should be starting their Monday morning assembly.

'Now,' I say. 'We're going to play a little game.'

More unease from the teachers. Giggles from the children.

'I'll go through it very simply to start with, so you get the idea. Are you ready?'

Nods and murmurs.

'You're sure you're ready?'

Calls of 'yes'.

'Here we go then. You can stay standing if—' I let the moment hang '—if you are a boy. Everyone else sit now!'

Boys and girls hover, caught in indecision. One girl sits. Her friends follow. Then all the girls are dropping to their seats, together with one or two confused boys. Children are laughing. Several male teachers bob down and up a couple of times before deciding that they are 'boys' no more.

OK, I know I haven't taught them anything about law and order yet. But this part is important.

'Everyone stand.'

The children are quicker on their feet this time. The teachers look less concerned than they did.

'Stay standing if—' I can stretch the pause longer now that I have their attention. '—if you are nine years old.'

They're getting the hang of it. Fewer mistakes. I don't catch any of the teachers out.

'Good. Very good.'

The head teacher, Mr Dunbar, smiles. He has not been taking part in the game, though he seems pleased that everyone else has. He's a roundish man. White, of course. Though 'white' seems an odd way to describe someone with such glowing cheeks. He sits, arms folded, behind a desk on one side of the stage.

Strangely, most of the children in St Catherine's School are also white. I visited another school this morning, serving exactly the same Waterfields catchment area, and that was ninety-five per cent Asian.

'Right,' I say. 'Everyone stand again. Now I'm going to make it more difficult. You can remain standing if . . . you've ever had anything stolen from you.'

I've done this assembly trick many times, and I always get the same result. The teachers smile because they can see where I'm leading, at last. The children are still treating it as a game, reacting as quickly as they can to the question. It's only after the giggling dies down that they start looking around. And this is the moment of impact. They see that around three-quarters of the children are still on their feet.

I clap my hands to draw their attention back to me. They fall silent almost immediately. 'Most of you have had something stolen? You can sit down now if you felt happy when it happened.'

No one sits.

I point to a girl on the front row. 'What did you have stolen?'

She breaks into a wide grin. 'Me, miss?'

'Yes.'

'It's last Christmas, yeah? They kicked in the back door. Took the Nintendo. Still wrapped 'n' everything.'

I choose a boy this time. 'What about you?'

'My crisps, miss. Someone nicked 'em from my lunchbox.'

Lots of the children around him laugh.

'A crime at school?' I frown, as if taking it very seriously. 'Then the person who did it must be in this room right now. Everyone sit down so I can see all your faces.'

They sit and I look from row to row as if searching for the public enemy.

'Do you think I'll be needing these?' I take out a pair of steel handcuffs from my box of goodies.

The children are wide-eyed, sitting on the edge of their seats.

A boy's voice shouts out: 'Lock 'im up, miss.'

Several of the teachers stand up and scan the room, trying to identify the culprit.

'Crime hurts,' I say. 'It hurts us all. Whose job is it to catch the criminals?'

Some of them shout, 'You, miss,' others shout, 'The police.'

'No. I can't do it on my own. You have to help me. Can you do that?'

Cries of 'yes!'

'Good. If you see someone stealing, you need to tell a police officer or a teacher. And you mustn't be copying them. You know what's right and wrong. Make your own

choices. You can always come and talk to police offic
like me – even if it's just that something's worrying you.

There are a few faces in today's audience that I recogni
Vandalism. Shoplifting. Small beer. If he wasn't still
home with his arm in plaster, little Roddy Wellan would
among them. He's the little angel who tried to throw
lump of concrete at a fire engine. This is his school.
shame he missed my performance.

I round up my spiel and hand over to the head teach
He makes a few announcements, then there's a final hym
accompanied by the music teacher on the piano. I
Dunbar puffs out his rounded chest and sings. His voice
a surprisingly rich tenor.

I mumble the words as I look at the faces of the childr
From this distance I feel perfectly comfortable with then

Mr Dunbar smiles benevolently as he leads me back to I
study. 'Very good. Very good. You really should have beer
teacher.'

'I don't think so.'

'No?' He opens the door to his study then turns to lo
at me. 'Get yourself a PGCE and I'll give you a job any tim
You have natural talent. Not that you need a job, of cours
He laughs.

'Assemblies are fine,' I say. 'But I don't think I'd be ve
good one to one.'

'You'd quickly get used to it. Think of them as small ve
sions of adults and you'd be fine.'

We step through the door. The room has an almost co
feeling. A desk, some comfortable chairs, a trophy cabin
There's an open door to the right, a secretary's offi
beyond. Through the window I can see the playground,
high boundary fence and the neighbouring West Pa

Junior School – the state-run operation where I spoke earlier in the day.

'I'm very glad,' Mr Dunbar is saying, 'really very glad that you came. The children . . . what happened to Roddy Wellan was a shock to them all.' He taps his fingertips together. 'I take it there will be no . . . how to say it . . . no *action* taken against the child?'

I look back to the head teacher and shake my head. 'He didn't do anything wrong. The fire engine hit him before he had a chance.'

'Good. Good. It's just that the governors . . . you know what they can be like . . .'

I don't. But I smile anyway. 'I've come across Roddy before. The Wellans are a difficult family. Didn't know they were Roman Catholic, though.'

'Oh, they're not. Being a Catholic school doesn't mean we turn anyone away on the basis of their religion. We have agnostics. Jews. Protestants even.'

'Muslims?'

'They're welcome, of course.'

'Sikhs, Hindus?'

'We do have some, yes. But the Asian parents prefer . . . it's not our choice, you see . . . they prefer West Park Junior.'

He looks slightly embarrassed. I can't think of anything to offer that wouldn't involve dynamiting the fence that divides the two schools. And I'm not sure he'd take too kindly to the idea.

Two of my Monday appointments can be ticked off the list. Unfortunately, the one remaining is the one I've been dreading since Friday. Paresh of the Race Crime Unit. As of last Wednesday, the man I least want to see.

I spent much of the weekend on the phone to people

I've met in the course of my two years in Waterfields. Most were embarrassed. It's like I was reminding them of the mistake they'd made in trusting me once. A few were openly hostile.

But, in spite of all the anti-police feeling, in spite of the heat-wave, there wasn't any more street fighting on Saturday or Sunday. That doesn't mean that nothing's been happening. Police officers worked round the clock to keep the balancing act going. Enough of a uniformed presence to deter, not so much as to provoke.

And the criminal world keeps on making work for us. A pensioner has gone missing over the weekend. Foul play suspected. The factory raids don't look like being solved. And we've had a rash of mobile phone thefts reported.

I walk from the school gate and down the road to the place where I left the car. I'm about to turn the ignition key when I get a sudden pang of foreboding. It's irrational. I'm not even sure where the feeling comes from. But I draw back my hand, get out on to the pavement and walk around the vehicle looking at the tyres, the paintwork. It all seems fine. Feeling self-conscious, I kneel, get my head down low and peer at the underside. I'm not sure what I'm looking for, or how I'd recognize it, but there's nothing to see.

I get back in, blushing, turn the key and drive away.

Paranoia. My mother would definitely blame it on a lack of breakfast. Get some more food down you, she'd say. Then you'll stop worrying. She'd be right. I'm hungry, like I haven't had a proper meal in days – which I haven't. The hunger's probably a good sign. I'm getting over the food poisoning at last. I promise myself a Mars bar from the vending machine before I face Paresh.

Then I notice the car following me.

At least I think that's what it's doing. It's pale green. An estate, by the look of it – though it's too far back for me to tell what make it is. I first noticed it as I drove towards Majestic Park. That was three turns back. It's still with me. I ease off the accelerator a little, change down to third. The speedometer needle falls back to twenty-five.

I watch the green estate getting closer in the rear-view. It's a Ford, I think. The gap closes. Then it starts to open up again. The car drops back to the same distance as before, matching my speed. That doesn't prove anything, of course. What driver in his right mind overtakes a police car on a city road?

So I try it the other way, pressing down the accelerator, watching the needle creep up to forty. He drops back. We're out of Waterfields by this time, heading into the city centre. Within a minute he's gone.

Definitely paranoia. I'll go straight to the vending machine.

We sit facing each other across the interview room table. Paresh is large for an Asian. Broad-shouldered but not heavy. He has a narrow nose and high cheekbones. More male model than police officer. Shame he missed his calling.

'Thanks for coming,' he says. 'For the record, I must tell you the interview's being taped.'

'Noted.'

He gives his own name, as if I didn't know, the date and time. Everything by the book. I'm not impressed by this unnecessary formality – especially after everything that's gone between us. But I guess he knows I can't kick him where it hurts if there's a tape running. Or he hopes I can't. The tape machine, a rectangular desk and three chairs are the only things in the room. The one empty chair is next to Paresh – as if an invisible bodyguard is sitting there for his security.

He clears his throat. 'You are?'

'Mo,' I say.

'Please. For the tape.'

I shift my chair back an inch further from the table, making the legs screech on the plastic floor tiles. 'Inspector Marjorie Akanbai.'

'And you were outside the Dean Street Mosque on Friday morning . . . that's 16 August?'

I nod.

'For the tape . . .'

'Yes.' The word comes out as a hiss.

'Interview suspended at . . . 10.38.' He reaches out and jabs the stop button on the tape machine. 'Look,' he says. 'I didn't want this any more than you.' He's avoiding eye contact. 'But hell, Mo, you're not making it any easier!'

I start counting to ten but give up on three. 'Easier? Easier! What the fuck were you doing yesterday? Two years I've been working with those people. Two years! And you didn't bother to leave an officer at the mosque?'

He holds up his hands as if stopping an oncoming truck. His eyes are still downcast, though. This truck's headlights are on full beam. 'We're sorry. Really. *I'm* sorry. But it's happened.'

'Bloody right it's happened!'

'And now we're trying to clear up the mess.'

'What about the mess in the prayer hall? You cleaned *that* up yet?'

'The forensic team couldn't . . . Saturday morning was the earliest they could do it.'

The headlights have turned into laser beams now. If

looks could kill, no one would be happier than me. 'And did you bother to explain your little timetable problem to the victims? A pool of pig's blood. De-prioritized?' I hit the flat of my palm against the desk.

He rubs his scalp with his fingers. This whole thing is getting to him big time. As it damned well should. I fold my arms tight across my chest. My jaw muscles ache with all the overtime they're putting in.

In the corridor outside someone is walking past, whistling the theme tune from *The Good, the Bad and the Ugly*. It seems kind of appropriate. It's a good thing we don't carry firearms in this country.

'What makes you think it's pig's blood?' Paresh asks at last, his voice very quiet.

That throws me for a moment. I'd assumed. Damn.

'It wasn't killed where you found it,' he says, warming to his theme, though still not looking at me straight. 'Humane killer. Standard abattoir issue.' He taps the side of his own head.

'So?'

'They bleed the carcass . . . the abattoir. The blood must have been brought in some kind of container, poured out on the floor.'

I'm still feeling a little delicate, and not at all sure I want to know all the detail. But I ask anyway. 'Why do it like that? And why cover it with a cloth?'

Paresh shrugs. 'The lab reports are due tomorrow. Till then we don't even know it's pig's blood.'

He looks across at the tape machine. 'Look,' he says, 'I've got to ask these questions. I'm sorry.' He clicks the start button. 'Interview recommences at . . . 10.40.

'Please explain what happened next.'

So I tell him. I've got no choice, really. The scream. The

pool of blood. I have to refer to my notebook for the names of people I spotted in the crowd. Anwar, a couple of his cousins. Members of other influential families who saw it all. I tell him about the woman in the chador, about how she needed to be sedated. Though I don't bother to mention my own reaction to the shock. He must know about that already. They've probably been having a good laugh about it over at the Race Crime Unit.

'Why didn't you warn someone?' he says at last. 'The risk that the Muslims might riot? You were in Waterfields. You could have told us in person if you'd wanted to.'

I can hear the tape going around inside the machine. 'I was ordered away from the mosque. And it wasn't the whole community who rioted – just a small part. Outsiders, mostly.'

He's leaning forward in his chair – almost as much as I'm leaning back in mine. 'Did you give any warnings to anyone?'

I'm trying to figure out what's going on. These questions aren't anything to do with the investigation. 'Yes,' I say. 'Verbal warnings and written. To Superintendent Shakespeare.'

A sigh comes out of him and his shoulders drop. He nods. 'You may be interested to know,' he says, 'that the warning never reached the Race Crime Unit.'

That's it. The real purpose of the interview. One little snippet of information is now on official record.

Timing is everything, they say. Bad timing in this case. In a couple of weeks Leicester is hosting 'Multiculturalism in the Twenty-first Century' – a big government conference. The great and the good will be talking up the new multi-ethnic Britain. Our riots will be a cause of serious embarrassment to several senior politicians. That means an inquiry – to deflect attention. Paresh is just doing what every other police officer, politician and community leader is probably doing right now – saving his skin. When the inquiry happens, this tape will be brought out and played. If it wasn't for our recent history, I might even think that he was trying to protect *me* as well.

'Interview concludes at . . . 11.15.' He clicks the tape off.

I stand, letting my chair legs scrape again. 'I'll need to talk to people at the mosque,' I say. 'Keep me briefed of your investigation.'

He looks up, straight at me for the first time. 'I'm . . .'

'What?'

'I'm just sorry. That's all.'

I'm reaching for the door handle when he says what's been on his mind all through the interview. 'The letter . . . I put it on your desk. You did read it?'

'Yes.'

OK. It's a lie. So shoot me. But there wasn't time to think. I'm in the corridor, marching away. But I still catch his last words.

'I'm glad,' he says. 'At least now you can understand.'

Damn the man.

I feel guilty about the lie and curious about the letter. Paresh always did get me confused about my emotions. I should be glad to be rid of him, but at that moment all I can feel is anxiety – because his precautions look a hell of a lot more well thought through than mine. I can't remember the exact wording in my memo to the super. And I'm suddenly not at all sure I've made it explicit enough to count as a written warning.

I try to look relaxed yet efficient as I walk back towards my office. An inspector. Not an over-promoted graduate. I march down the corridor, telling myself not to appear self-conscious, yet aware of every footfall on the grey carpet. The outer office is empty. Thank God. I close the door behind me, open my filing cabinet. The drawer rolls out with a dull rumble. I just need to check it. To touch the paper and feel sure of the security it gives me. I pull out my job-meltdown file and reach inside. But the memo isn't there.

Chapter 5

Cornwell Street. It's a strip of tarmac with garment factories on either side. Tall buildings. Red brick. The skyline is all chimneys and saw-blade roofs. Huge Victorian mills divided into a rat-run of knitwear manufacturers, fabric printers and finishers – all linked by fire escapes, corridors and overhead conveyor belts. It isn't pretty.

It's early evening. The air is starting to cool, thank God, but the red-brick walls are still radiating heat. The loading bay next to me stands open. I can see rolls of cloth piled high just inside and stacks of bright-blue plastic oil drums. A group of women in saris are standing on the other side of the road. Gujarati gossip in the last triangle of sunshine. I catch them watching me as I turn. They look away. I cut through between the buildings to a large courtyard. There are tall factories on three sides. The fourth side is a high wall, garnished with swirling loops of razor wire. Strands of shredded polythene dangle from some of the rusty blades.

I find the name I'm looking for among a cluster of signboards fixed to the wall next to a ground-floor entrance. Azzam Garment Finishers. Anwar's setup. I push open the doors and step inside.

One wall of the factory is lined with industrial washing machines and tumble dryers. The rest of the room is set out with garment presses. Rows and columns. One operator works behind each. The ceiling is all air ducts and strip lights. Banghara music blares from a loudspeaker on the wall – heavily distorted but loud enough for the beat to be heard over the hiss and rumble of presses and dryers.

Anwar's office. I can see him now, standing behind the glass. He's got a partitioned shoebox in the corner of the main room. A bodged-up fish tank. It's a little bigger than mine, but piles of cardboard boxes take up most of the space inside. He sees me and nods in recognition. He doesn't come out, though, so I go in.

'Inspector.' He isn't smiling.

'You left a message,' I say.

He shakes his head. 'I didn't mean for you to come.'

'If you don't want to talk . . .'

I'm trying to figure if he's embarrassed that his fellow Muslims torched a few police vans, or if he's angry that the police gave them the excuse. Perhaps it's both.

He shakes his head. 'This is not good to meet here.'

'Anwar . . . I'm sorry about what happened.'

He looks at his desk, as if the piles of papers and spike of receipts might provide an answer to the questions boiling away inside him. Then he looks back to me and nods. 'Yes,' he says. 'Sorry.'

He reaches on top of one of the filing cabinets and retrieves a copy of today's *Crusader*. He opens it at page three and passes it over. It's my picture again. Not quite so big this time, but looking just as complacent. 'Riot Officer Slammed.'

'You see this?' he says.

'No.'

'Read.'

I scan the page. Some reporter has gone and quizzed the head of the Waterfields Youth Club – together with a couple of people from the Caribbean Centre. None of them has anything good to say about the police handling of the riots. The worst thing about the article is the headline itself. I'm now the 'Riot Officer'. That's going to be a hard one to shake off.

There's another article further down the page. 'Conference Plan Turmoil'. I know this isn't the bit that Anwar was showing me. It's got a smaller headline, but it looks more significant.

Government plans to hold a major conference in the city are now in turmoil. 'We've got to shelve it,' said a source close to the Home Secretary. 'How can we sit around talking about the multicultural society, when the streets just outside are still smoking?'

The paper has picked up on only half the story. The plan, secret as yet, is to stage a walkabout for the conference delegates – in Majestic Park, right in the centre of Waterfields. Politicians pressing the flesh. Posing for the cameras. The Home Secretary isn't going to be a happy bunny if there are riots still going on. Even one Molotov cocktail could seriously ruin his day.

I drop the paper on the desk.

'You told me once,' I say, 'when we first met, that I could come to you for help if I ever needed it.'

He nods. 'Yes.'

'I need your help now.'

He doesn't answer me straightaway. Instead he pulls out a wooden chair, removes a pile of papers from it and gestures for me to sit.

'Tea?' he says.

The sudden change of tone throws me. 'I . . . no need. Really.'

'Yes. Hot day, *henna*.' He's reacting as if I've just told him I'm dying of thirst.

I sit down, still confused. 'I really don't . . .'

He raps a knuckle on the glass wall of the office and shouts an order in Gujarati.

The glass is behind me now. Everyone in the factory will be looking in my direction. I wonder if any of them were caught up in the riot – if any threw stones at the police. The back of my head is itching with all the anger I imagine I'm feeling from them. I don't want to raise a hand to scratch. Anwar pulls out another chair and sits facing me. He seems less on edge now that he's clicked into hospitality mode.

'Your family is well?' he asks.

'Thank you. Yes.'

'It is good.'

I want to talk about the riot, but this has to come first. 'Your family?'

His face is relaxing now. 'Yes. Good.'

'Your daughter – is she going to university next year?'

He nods. 'Study textile design. *Inshallah*.'

The tea arrives then. Two small, stainless-steel cups and a Thermos flask carried in on a stainless-steel tray by a nervous-looking girl in a punjabi suit. There is also a small cardboard box of Indian sweets. She clears a small space on the desk and puts the tray down before hurrying away. Anwar pours.

'Indian tea,' he says. 'Not like British Rail.'

I take the cup and nod.

'With spice and sugar and milk,' he says.

We raise our cups at the same time. Match each other sip for sip. I feel my heart-rate kick as the caffeine and sugar hit my system.

'Good?' he asks.

'Good.'

There's a pause while we sip some more. I glance at the clock on the wall. Steam presses hiss outside the office. The heat of the room and the tea are combining to make me sweat. The back of my head is still itching.

Anwar puts his empty cup down on the tray. I hold on to mine so he can't try to give me a refill. I don't think my system could take any more.

'They weren't from your mosque,' I say at last. 'It wasn't your fault. The ones who started it weren't even from Leicester. Someone bused them in just to make trouble.'

He shakes his head. 'You should not have done this way.'

'They ordered me not to go near Dean Street,' I tell him, 'or I would have done something.'

He looks down to the floor. 'Then this thing is not from you. But I have no choice.'

'We both have a problem. We can find a solution. Together.'

He shakes his head. 'Police fight Muslim. Muslim fight police. Some mosques complain.'

'But the trouble was outside your mosque, Anwar. Not theirs. No one else's complaints will matter.'

'Now our people go to their mosques. I . . .'

'I'm sorry,' I say. And I mean it. He's being undermined because of his moderation and tolerance.

'You understand?' he says. 'I can't do it. I tell you so you know. So you protect yourself, *henna*.'

'Can't do what, Anwar?'

'Can't stop my mosque making complaint.'

'Against the police?'

He nods. 'And against you.'

I don't know if it's the masala tea, but my heart is pounding fast enough to keep time with the banghara music outside. 'When . . . when will they put in the complaint?'

Anwar shakes his head. He says: 'You go inside the mosque with shoes. You go, hair uncovered. They make the complaint today. In morning. Already done.' Then he picks up the box of Indian sweets and hands it to me. 'Here. This for you.'

I walk out of the factory carrying the sweets, wondering if they are supposed to help the medicine go down. It's cooler outside now. The triangle of sunlight has gone from the other side of Cornwell Street. So have the women in saris. I think as I walk – about the riot outside the mosque. Then I think about all the things the police did. People made mistakes on both sides, but I can't really blame them. The only ones happy about it are the racists who dumped the pig in the women's prayer hall and the radicals who are siphoning off support from Anwar's moderate mosque. But if I can't blame anyone else, how come I feel like everyone else is blaming me?

There are five kids up ahead, playing football across the width of the road. Other than them, the place is deserted.

I don't feel like going back to the station after what I've just learned, so I don't stop when I reach the car. I keep on walking, thinking about Anwar. About the riot. About Paresh.

One of the boys up ahead mis-kicks the ball, sending it skimming down the road towards me. It hits the kerbstone and jumps up. I catch it one-handed. The kids look panicky. One runs. The others hesitate, then follow – all but one, who seems frozen by fear. I carry the ball back towards him.

He looks up at me, his body rigid and shivering slightly.

Wide grey eyes, pale skin, a mop of fair hair badly in need of a comb.

I force a smile. 'Yours?'

He doesn't answer.

'I won't bite,' I say.

The shiver in his arm turns into a jerky forward motion and he grabs the ball. After that he keeps his head angled down, though his eyes are darting around, taking in my feet and the lower part of my uniform. Then he sees the box of Indian sweets in my hand. After that his eyes keep flicking back to it.

According to police rules, I'm not allowed to interview children without someone else being present. Not that I'd want to. But this isn't an interview as such, and there's something about this boy that intrigues me. He looks different from the usual kids I see on the street around here. And I have half a feeling that I've seen him before somewhere.

'What do they call you?' I ask.

'Niko,' he mumbles.

I'm not sure I've heard him right. 'Nicky?'

He shakes his head and frowns. 'Niko.'

At least he's started talking. We'll both feel more comfortable if I can just put him at his ease.

He's a slight child. Thin arms, thin face.

'How old are you, Niko?'

'Eleven.'

From the size of him I would have guessed eight.

'Well,' I say, 'you're the only one brave enough to come and get the ball.'

His eyes look up to my face for the first time. 'I am,' he says. 'They think I'm not, but I am brave.'

'They? Who do you mean?'

He makes a vague gesture to the street around us. 'Them.'

I'm trying to puzzle this out when he throws me something even stranger. 'You ever kill anyone?'

'Kill?'

'In your police station?'

'No. Of course not.'

'You are a real police?'

'A police officer. Yes.'

He shakes his head as if he isn't convinced. I hold out the box of sweets towards him. He reaches to grab for one, then pulls back.

'I don't know which are good,' I say. 'Choose one for me as well.'

He screws up his face for a moment then rummages, pulling out two cream-coloured cubes. He watches me put mine in my mouth before mirroring my action.

OK, I shouldn't be getting into this conversation. But we are in a public place. And I'm sure I'm missing something obvious about the boy.

'Niko, have I seen you before?'

He frowns as he chews, then nods. 'At school. You said we can come and talk to you any time.'

That triggers the memory to click inside my head. 'Are you at St Catherine's?'

He doesn't answer. Instead he says: 'What kind of police are you?'

'A community officer. I help people to understand the police and help the police understand the people. That way everyone can help each other.'

He leans forward and nods as if we both now understand each other. 'OK. I help you then.'

His voice is much quieter now. Barely above a whisper.

I lean forward, bringing my head close to his.

'The Troubles,' he says, the phrase sounding strangely adult. 'Big problem. They don't understand.'

Presumably we're talking about the same 'they' as before. Everyone in the streets around. I know I'm not getting anywhere with this. But I'm curious about the boy, in spite of myself. I make a stab in the dark and say: 'You've seen things they haven't seen.' Then I take half a step back, so I can read his body language more easily.

'Yes.'

We're making eye contact now, which feels like progress.

'And that's why you understand.'

Again, 'Yes.'

'Why didn't they see as well?'

He raises his eyebrows as if surprised that I'd even ask. 'Different place. They can't see it.'

I'm still lost, but it feels like I've caught hold of the end of a thread.

'You remember what you saw, don't you, Niko.'

He nods, but his eyes drop to the tarmac again.

'Would you like them to understand?'

A vigorous nod this time. 'So they don't bring The Troubles here. Yes.'

I'm pulling in the thread, feeling less resistance with every question. But the closer I get to the end, the more I'm starting to worry about what I'll find. Perhaps I should stop. Give the boy a handful of sweets and send him on his way.

'If they'd been there,' I say, 'they'd understand already.'

'Yes.'

I can feel the skin on my upper arms prickling. 'Perhaps you could show them something to help them?'

His feet shift on the road and he looks up, first to me, then past me to the sky.

'What would you show them, Niko?'

His mouth stays closed and I'm thinking that the thread is broken. My skin is relaxing again. Then quite suddenly he says: 'Show them the dead people.' And I know I don't want to go any further. But Niko hasn't finished.

'Show them all the dead people in holes in the ground.'

'Niko?' I'm calling to him, but he's too far away to respond.

'Birds pecking. No eyes. Just blood.'

'Niko? Niko!'

'Running. And the men with gun and uniform. And . . .'

I reach out and take his hand. It is limp, very small in my own. Then I feel his grip tighten around my fingers.

'But you're safe now,' I say. 'It's all gone.'

He is crying. Silently. 'Now The Troubles come here.'

'No, they won't.'

'It started already. The letters come again. Tell us to go back to our country.'

'What letters?'

But I've pulled the thread too far and it's Niko that's unravelling. He turns, yanking his hand free, then starts to run.

Chapter 6

I'm lying full-length on the saggy sofa, telling myself not to get involved in the conversation, wondering why I came round here in the first place. I know the answer, of course. With Paresh suddenly a stranger, I've got no other shoulder to lean on except my mum's. Her name is Sal, and she's never held back from sharing her opinions.

'It's not as if they give me anything,' she shouts from the kitchen.

I listen to the clash of plates in the sink as she cleans a couple of mugs.

'I said,' Sal shouts again, 'it's not as if they give me anything.'

I close my eyes and take a deep breath. Time to disengage. I know I'm too tense to get into this kind of argument.

'They just spend it all on—' she pauses '—I don't even know what they spend it on!'

'Libraries,' I say, instantly regretting my weakness of character.

She pokes her head around the doorframe. Her round face is still beautiful, in spite of all the little wrinkles spreading from the corners of her deep-blue eyes. 'What's that supposed to mean?' she asks.

I say: 'They spend it on libraries.'

The kettle rumbles quietly as it starts to boil. She

disappears back into the kitchen, and I'm starting to think that I might be able to wriggle free. Then she says: 'I don't use the library. So they shouldn't get me to pay for it.'

'Sal . . .'

'People who use the library should pay.'

'Sal?'

'What?'

'I don't want to argue.'

'Well, you shouldn't have started then.'

She's back in the living room now, a mug of tea in each hand and a packet of biscuits under her arm. She shoos a cat off the coffee table and puts the mugs down. The cat springs up on to the couch, sniffs at my feet, then settles down to sleep. Sal is sitting in the armchair.

'I want biscuits, I pay for biscuits.' She opens the packet and pulls out a chocolate Hobnob to underline her point. 'They want books. Why should I pay for that too?'

She always did have an uncluttered view of politics.

'Waste of money, if you ask me.'

I'm telling myself to disengage, biting gently on my lower lip to stop myself speaking.

'And what kind of books are they buying with my money?'

Disengage. Disengage. I repeat the mantra inside my head.

'Crime books,' she says. 'Unhealthy rubbish by that David Hood. And horror stories.'

'I thought you didn't go to the library,' I say.

'Saw it on the TV.' She breaks a biscuit and posts one fragment into her mouth. 'It's my money they're wasting, you know.'

'They pay for the police,' I say. 'Some of my wages come from the council tax. And the Multiculturalism

Conference – you believe in that. I know you do. And . . . and the schools. The prisons.'

There's a pause. She crunches a biscuit. Then she says it. Quiet. But not so quiet that I can't hear. 'Bring back hanging. That way we wouldn't have to pay for all those prisoners.'

I'm on my feet before she's finished speaking. The cat's running for cover. 'Sal!'

She holds up her hands, as if the finger I'm pointing towards her were a gun.

'Sal!'

She says: 'Count to . . .'

'Ten!' I say, cutting her off.

She reaches for the packet of biscuits and holds it out in my direction.

I run a hand through my hair. 'That's the most outrageous . . . you know what I think about capital punishment.'

'Let's not argue,' she says.

There's a pause. Then I sit, but I keep my eyes down, fixed on the teacup rings on the tabletop. My shoulders are hunched up like some sulky teenager. I'm angry with myself. We always banter, but I can usually control myself better than that.

I pick up my mug and start to sip. Sal tries offering me a biscuit again. This time I take one.

'I'm sorry,' she says at last.

The cat pads back towards me and hops on to the couch, curling up in the hollow where I was just lying. It starts to purr.

'It's not you.' I run a hand through my hair. 'I'm just a little . . . you know.'

'PMT?' she asks.

It damned well feels like she's right. But it can't be that. 'Not due yet. Just washed out, I guess – from all this food poisoning thing.'

She puts her cup on the table, sits back in her chair and starts to look at me. No. It's more than that. I'm being examined.

Then she says: 'You're keeping regular then?'

I shrug, to show her I haven't a clue what she's on about.

'You know. Periods. You haven't missed one?'

'Sal!'

'Just asking.'

'Of course I haven't!'

My answer comes out sounding just that little bit too quick to my own ear. But Sal seems to accept it. She reaches out and strokes my knee. 'So long as you know I'm always here for you.'

I start nodding my head, then shake it. 'It's just all such a nightmare. I met this kid . . . he had some crazy story. Then all that stuff in the mosque. And the riots. That's the worst part. Now everyone's looking over their shoulders, trying to dodge the blame.'

'None of this is your fault, though,' she says.

I reach out to take another biscuit. 'Fault and blame don't always go together.'

'You want to talk about it?'

'No.' I take a bite of the chocolate Hobnob. 'It's just the Race Crime Unit. They messed up. They didn't know, I guess. But now . . .'

'Thought Paresh worked for Race Crime.'

I keep my mouth firmly closed.

Sal puts her head slightly on one side and looks at me. 'Oh,' she says at last. 'He's not your boyfriend any more?'

Damn, but sometimes I'd swear she can see into my

mind. How can anyone who reads the *Express* be so percep-
tive?

'Glad to be shot of him,' I say.

'He dumped you,' she says. It isn't a question.

'What does it matter!'

'I'm sorry.' She strokes my knee again. 'What happened?'
After a long moment, during which I haven't opened my
mouth, she shakes her head. 'Sorry. None of my business.'

'When did that ever stop you?'

'I thought you two were . . . well . . . thought he was
going to be the one.'

Damn. Damn. Damn.

I leave Sal and drive across to my own place so I can get
changed. I'm standing there, looking at my uniform, which
is hanging on the side of the wardrobe. I should be thinking
about the meeting that I'm about to attend. But it's Sal's
agenda that's making the gears grind in my head.

I'm going to be heading away from my home patch this
evening. The football stadium is a couple of miles beyond
the other side of Waterfields. Far enough that I won't know
the local people. And they won't know me. That decides it
for me – I put my uniform away and take out a business
suit. They'll think it's strange when I get to the meeting, but
they don't have to know my real reason.

The meeting is due to start at eight o'clock. I'm early
enough to go through with it. So I park the Audi in a side
road on Filbert Street, near the site where the football club
used to play. The Victorian terraces look just the same as
they do in Waterfields. But the balance of the races is different. Here whites are in a majority – just.

I check my face in the mirror then get out of the car and

start to walk. It's seven fifty by my watch. There's an out-of-hours chemist on the corner ahead of me. I slow down as I get closer. My heart is hammering away inside my chest and I'm thinking that I'm going to bottle out. But I push the door open and step inside. A bell chimes as it swings to.

There are other customers in here. A black guy with dreadlocks down to the small of his back. Holding his hand, a little girl in an orange tracksuit. There are a couple of glittery teens teetering on high heels near the bottles of hair colouring. I step further in, scanning the shelves. Toothbrushes. Baby food. Shampoo. Corn plasters.

There's an Asian man behind the till. A short-sleeved shirt, a tie and a benevolent smile. He watches me for a moment. 'Can I help you?'

'I . . . I'm not sure.'

I look across to the shelves behind the counter. Painkillers. Anti-fungal cream. Condoms lubricated with spermicide.

'What is it you're looking for?'

'Do you sell . . .'

'Yes?'

I move up closer and lower my voice. '. . . sell those home testing kits?'

'Pregnancy?' His voice is quieter too now, though not quiet enough.

'Those. Yes.'

One of the teenies is looking at me from under her fringe.

The pharmacist turns his back on me for a moment and takes a couple of different boxes from a high shelf. 'These are the only ones I have in stock now.' He places both on the glass counter and pushes one towards me. 'This is the cheapest. But they both do the same job.'

'Oh. Right.'

'I'll have another kind in next week.'

'Another . . .?'

'Don't worry. These are good.'

I nod and flash him the best smile I can manage.

Then he asks: 'Is it for you?'

'It's not that I . . . I've just been . . . you know . . . feeling . . .'

'I know,' he says. That should sound strange – coming from a man. It doesn't today.

'Well, I can't be,' I say. 'Not really.' I reach out and touch the nearest box, then draw my hand away.

'But you're wanting to buy one of these.' He's nodding slowly, an expression of gentle concern on his face. 'Some ladies want to buy these if they forget to take their pill – or have unprotected sex.'

I shake my head. 'No. Never.'

He frowns for a moment. 'If you're worried, you should see your doctor, isn't it?'

'Of course.'

'But,' he adds, 'even with protected sex, it's not one hundred per cent. You can still get pregnant. Sometimes.'

Chapter 7

The bell chimes as the door closes behind me. I gulp the evening air into my lungs. Deep breaths. Stay calm. More deep breaths. Now I'm feeling dizzy. Panic.

Slow the breathing. I'm hyperventilating, that's all. Get a grip. I always got Paresh to use a condom. He didn't like it, but he knew it was that or nothing. I should be safe. I have to be safe.

I'm walking down Burnmoor Street now. I can see the open ground ahead of me, where the houses stop. There's an electricity substation here. Huge transformers and steel pylons. And beyond them, the steel and glass splendour of the new stadium, so much higher than the Victorian ridge tiles and chimneypots. Shockingly modern in a landscape of decaying heavy industry.

As I walk, the briefcase feels heavy in my hand. It reminds me of what's inside it. And that makes me think of Paresh and the times we were alone together. Nights at my place – him always leaving to be home before morning. A few hours. God, but they were beautiful. All that holding back – the deliberate distance between our bodies when we were in public. As soon as the door closed and we were alone, it was all ripped away. But it is the moments of stillness that I remember most. The being pressed up against his warmth, bathing in his afterglow. Skin touching skin, one shade meeting another.

We had afternoons sometimes, with his car parked a safe distance from the front door. Never at his house, though. He had a thing about that. And always with a condom.

'Safe sex,' I told him. Not a complete guarantee, I did know that. But it's something like ninety-eight per cent.

Suddenly that doesn't seem so smart.

I find myself crossing Eastern Boulevard, walking into the front car park. The glass walls of the stadium are catching the evening sun. It's time to put Paresh out of my mind. I have to focus now. I'm heading for the main entrance. Plate-glass doors, plush blue carpet inside. The home of Leicester City Football Club – the Foxes. There's a young woman waiting for me in front of the reception desk. Very blonde, with a Barbie-smooth complexion. She flexes her mouth into a smile and says: 'Follow me.'

I allow myself to be led across the lobby, past a small trophy cabinet on my left. The lift doors close quietly behind us. We're almost standing close enough for her shoulder pads to touch mine. I'm just glad she isn't trying to engage me in conversation.

In my mind I can see the number ninety-eight displayed in neon. Ninety-eight per cent safe. I'm telling myself that those are pretty good odds. The other two per cent can wait. I'll worry about them later.

The doors slide open. We're on the top level now. There's an expanse of lounge bar to the left. Several groups of men are standing there chatting. Businessmen in suits. Some kind of conference, I guess. My guide leads me in the opposite direction.

I say: 'Have the others arrived yet?'

'You're the last one.'

She stops next to a large wooden door, knocks once, then opens it. She doesn't step inside herself.

They all stand when I enter the room.

'Inspector. Welcome. Welcome.'

That's the football club's representative speaking – an expansive man in an exquisite pinstripe suit. He shakes my hand. 'Akanbai, isn't it?'

'Yes.'

'Any relation to the footballer?'

'Different spelling,' I say.

I can see the disappointment on his face – even though the smile doesn't waver. He nods. 'Of course. Of course.' Then he starts guiding me around the group, introducing me to the other men.

'This is Marcel Bracknal from the Home Office.'

I smile. 'Pleased to meet you.'

'And representing the Local Government Management Board . . .'

I shake the second man's hand, note his name.

I move on to the Sikh man. A familiar face. 'Councillor . . .'

He beams at me. We've always got on pretty well.

'And from the Football Academy . . .'

The introductions are blurring. I know I'll never be able to remember everyone. More smiles. Then handshakes from three younger men – assistants, I suspect, to the two civil servants. These are not introduced by name – I'm glad of that.

It is only now that I start to take in the room. We are meeting in a large executive box overlooking the pitch. The fox-head logo appears everywhere. Small on the plush, blue back of each chair, and large in the middle of the blue carpet. One entire wall of the room is glass. Through it I can see the football pitch below. A rectangle of green – the only patch of any colour other than blue that I've seen since walking into the building. There is a huge fox's head printed into the seating just behind the far goal.

Mr Pinstripe guides me to a chair. The men sit a fraction of a second after me. I place my briefcase on the floor and rest my fingers on the edge of the polished wood of the conference table.

Marcel Bracknal, the Home Office man, coughs. 'Thank you for attending at such short notice,' he says. 'I'm truly sensitive to the inconvenience. But this meeting was made necessary by recent public order developments.'

There's an unreadable blandness about Bracknal's expression, as if he was talking about the price of beans rather than two riots and a bill for damage already topping 10 million.

'We have to ascertain,' he says, 'that the situation "on the ground", as it were, is under control.'

The city councillor interjects at this point. 'We've put a lot into the conference already. Too late to change.'

The conference. That's what this is all about. Multiculturalism in the Twenty-first Century. The main meetings are to be held right here at the stadium's conference suite. Then there will be side events around the city – at the Town Hall, in Waterfields. It was Leicester's good race relations record that brought the conference here. We're the most racially mixed community in England. I'm not saying everything's perfect, but the way the communities mix here has always been pretty damned good. Up till last weekend.

'A year's planning,' the councillor is saying . 'Thousands of man-hours.'

Bracknal raises one hand, as if he were the Pope bestowing a blessing. 'The minister has noted your contribution. But he is concerned that this city is becoming synonymous with a breakdown in public order. Gentlemen. There are ten days remaining. That still gives us time to focus our resources. I have been authorized to release certain details to you – to help you understand the importance of what we are doing here. But this is on the understanding that what I am about to say will not be made public.'

Nods from around the table. Signs of people waking up.

'Successive governments have tried to limit immigration. The demography of our ageing population makes this approach unsustainable.'

Bracknal must have picked up on the baffled looks from around the table because he elaborates. 'We need to bring in people of working age to keep the economy going. That means accelerating immigration rather than trying to limit it. It means positioning Britain as the multi-ethnic leader in Europe.'

Keeping out foreigners – I thought that had been government policy since 1067. Bracknal's blandness can't disguise the fact that he's talking about a monumental change.

'Because this policy shift is central to government thinking, the announcement will be made by the Prime Minister himself.'

The Sikh city councillor has raised his hand to attract Bracknal's attention. 'The PM – here?'

Bracknal tilts his head in a considered nod.

The councillor seems alarmed at the news. 'The walkabout in Majestic Park – he won't be joining the other conference delegates there, will he?'

Bracknal smiles with a slow flexing of one side of his mouth. 'The itinerary is still being reviewed. But in view of the media exposure that such an excursion would provide, it might be wise to factor in the Prime Minister's presence.'

The football club men are grinning from ear to ear. They can't believe they're being let in on the big secret – even if the Foxes are co-sponsors of the conference. I can't believe it either. The tabloid editors would kill for a story like this. I'm thinking that someone is bound to blab. Perhaps that's what this meeting is all about. The civil service doing what it does best – sabotaging the government's plans for change. I look around the table, wondering who is going to talk to the press. And – here's the second question – who's going to take the blame when the story hits the headlines?

As I'm churning this around in my mind, I notice that Bracknal has turned towards me. Everyone else is following his gaze.

'Superintendent Shakespeare has never been less than supportive of our project,' he says. 'I'm sorry he can't be with us tonight.'

'Me too,' I say, kicking myself for sounding far too enthusiastic.

Bracknal nods. 'But we have the pleasure of your charming company.'

The councillor shifts in his chair. There's a nervous expression on his face. He's seen people try to patronize me before. 'Mo is a very experienced officer,' he says quickly. 'Highly respected.'

'Then we shall all benefit from her report.'

That's my signal. I heft my briefcase on to my knee and spring the catches. 'I've got a summary of the investigation here,' I say. 'Should be one for everyone.'

In one movement I manage to extract my sheaf of papers and spill the newly acquired pregnancy test kit on to the floor. It lands half out of its paper bag near the feet of one of the unnamed junior civil servants. He picks it up and hands it back to me.

I stuff it back into the briefcase, hoping he didn't have time to read the packet.

'Please proceed,' says Bracknal.

'Yes . . . ah . . . right. If you could refer to the executive summary halfway down page one.'

I start guiding them through the bullet-points. First the public order issue. Estimated cost of damage. Numbers of complaints against the police. Numbers of arrests. It hadn't seemed so bad when I looked through it on my own. But after reading the first section aloud, I'm starting to get a pretty shrewd idea why Superintendent Shakespeare was suddenly busy this evening and unable to deliver the report in person.

'Have the instigators been identified?' Bracknal asks.

'Yes,' I say. 'Most of them.'

'And they were not local?'

I shake my head.

'If more troublemakers were to travel to the city,' he says, 'would we not expect similar levels of violence?'

I don't answer.

Bracknal waits for a second, then says: 'Perhaps we should move on to the second issue.'

So I give them my report on the race crime investigation. Man-hours used. Resources committed. No results, of course. Nothing concrete.

'Why did they leave the pig in the women's prayer hall?' asks the councillor.

He means the racists, not the police.

'We don't know. You might have thought they'd put it downstairs. That's where it'd be seen by most people. Or, if it was going to be upstairs, at least in the middle of the hall.'

'Perhaps,' says the councillor, 'they were scared off before they'd finished?'

'I don't think so. It was all arranged too neatly for that. The way the blood was poured over the floor.'

The men from the football club are sitting back in their chairs, keeping well out of this part of the meeting. Mr Pinstripe looks distinctly queasy. The Football Academy man is squirming where he sits.

Bracknal raises one eyebrow. 'Do you have some theory, inspector?'

'Nothing proved,' I say.

'But . . .?'

'But . . . the way it worked . . . Muslim men had been downstairs through two prayer sessions. One before dawn. A second in mid-morning. No women had been upstairs in all that time. The woman who found the thing was only up there to clean the place.'

'The women don't use their prayer hall?' asks Bracknal.

'It's not encouraged. The mullahs tell them that praying at home is more pious than going to the mosque. Whoever put the pig there could have expected it to stay undiscovered for days.'

I'm not only thinking about the way that meat putrefies in a hot room. The discovery of something so grossly impure – the knowledge that it's been there just above their heads for so many sessions of prayer – I think that would be far worse than finding it straightaway. I guess everyone else is imagining it too, because there's what feels like a long silence before Bracknal speaks.

'Is that all?'

'I guess.'

'Very well.'

But I know that it isn't all. I haven't voiced the obvious problem with my theory. Some people outside the Muslim community do know the detail of Islamic prayer practices.

But not the racist thugs. Everything about this feels too subtle for them.

'Inspector.'

Bracknal's voice makes me jump. 'Yes?'

'You have this report on disk?'

'I guess so . . .'

'Good. I'd like you to e-mail it to my office. I'll need to circulate it.'

Now it's the turn of the Football Academy man to make his report on the youth events that the club will be running in support of the conference. But I'm not listening. Bracknal's words are ping-ponging around inside my head. A copy of the report on paper. A copy on disk.

Disk.

My letter to Superintendent Shakespeare – the one that's gone missing from my file – there'll be a copy of that on disk as well. All I have to do is go into my office, fire up the computer and print it off.

I have to wait till after ten o'clock before the meeting ends and I can escape. It's dark now and I'm regretting leaving my car so far away. I run across the car park as fast as my shoes will allow, then across Eastern Boulevard and down the length of Burnmoor Street, my briefcase banging against my hip with every other stride. I turn on to Filbert Street. It's quiet here. Even the after-hours chemist is closed. My footfalls sound loud, conspicuous. I slow to a walk, then turn off down the side street towards my car.

It's only now that I hear the noise behind me. Someone else's footsteps. Softer than mine. Training shoes, perhaps. I don't start running. Nor do I look over my shoulder. Stand tall. Step strongly. Never look like a victim. I'm not far from safety now. My heels click on the pavement. The other footsteps aren't close enough to be a threat. But they're closer than they were. And quicker. I lengthen my stride, trying not to change the rhythm of my walking. Another few seconds and I'll be in my Audi. The keys are in my hand.

I'm ten paces away now. And I see the scrawl of racist graffiti paint-sprayed across the windscreen and bonnet. I'm suddenly feeling my heartbeat high up in my chest. I'm running forward, unlocking the door, jumping inside, slamming it closed. I'm jabbing the lock, fumbling with the ignition.

I see the man now – through the smears of graffiti on the windscreen. He's running towards me. Eighty, ninety kilos. Athletic. T-shirt and balaclava. White skin. I'm turning the key, pressing the accelerator. The engine coughs. He's next to the car. He doesn't shout. He just raises the hand without the knife and smashes it down on the glass. The car rocks with the impact.

I'm turning the key again. The engine won't start. There's a smell of petrol. I've flooded the carburettor. The man's elbow crashes against the window next to me. The glass hasn't broken.

I'm counting out loud. 'One. Two. Three.'

He leans his body away, then lashes out his foot in a side kick. He misses the glass. The car sways. He doesn't even grunt with the effort. The knife blade winks in the sodium light.

'Four. Five. Six.' My hand is on the ignition key – but I have to wait a few more seconds or the carburettor will flood even worse. I'm breathing in gasps. He's leaning back for another kick. 'Seven. Eight. Nine.'

Crash. The glass shatters.

'Ten.' I'm turning the key. The engine roars.

I'm starting to pull away. He's got a hand through the window. He grabs the steering wheel, turns it so I'm moving towards the lamppost. I'm bringing back my arm. Then I whip my elbow around. I can't see what it hits, but the impact feels solid. He's lost his grip and I'm away, wheel-spinning into second. Accelerating through third. Away around the corner.

Far enough. Then I jam on the brakes. Grab my mobile. Jab nine, nine, nine on the keypad, sure in my pounding heart that he'll be long gone before the first patrol car gets here. My hands are trembling now, as I sit waiting for the connection. Right in front of my face is one paint-sprayed word from the line of graffiti. It's mirror writing from this side of the glass, but clear enough in dripping red capitals.

KILL.

Chapter 8

Tuesday morning – the small hours. Sitting in a patrol car drinking black tea, syrupy with sugar. They tell me to go home, get some rest. But I'm not going until I've seen my Audi properly dealt with. It's gone three in the morning before the truck arrives to take it to the forensic garage. After that I let them drive me to the police station.

Dawn must still be an hour away. The building is empty. Almost.

I'm walking down the corridor towards the Community Relations Unit when I see Paresh coming the other way. He looks at me, breaks step. There's something in his face that I can't read. Is it guilt? Embarrassment? Relief? Then he's coming forward again. His arms extended towards me. Open.

I should turn. Run away.

We're moving together like planets caught in each other's gravitational field. My hand is reaching for his. Our fingers touch, then clasp. My face is tingling. My lips. But I don't stop walking. I mustn't stop walking. I step, conscious of each movement, one foot in front of the other. He turns with me as I pass. My hand is out behind me. Arm stretched. Grip slipping. Then he lets go.

I don't look back.

There's a soft, grey light filtering through the blinds in my office. I sit in the semi-gloom, with my forehead on the desk and my eyes closed. I don't want to move. I don't want to think. But I do think.

Why did Paresh come to me? How did he know I'd be here? I lift my head slightly then knock it down on the desk. If I hadn't been so shaken up I'd have seen it straightaway. Paresh leads the Race Crime Unit. He'd be informed of any serious race attack. He would be phoned, in the middle of the night if necessary. He came to interview me about the assault. That's all.

I sit up and scratch my scalp. I thought I'd felt something from him back there in the corridor. A breath of the emotions I used to feel. It frightened me. Now I'm thinking he came to me out of professional interest alone, and I'm bereft.

It was a year ago that it started between him and me. We'd been flirting on and off for a few weeks. He gave me a lift home that evening. I moved to kiss him good night – a peck on the cheek. I missed my target and neither of us pulled away.

I didn't worry that things would get complicated. Just like my previous relationships, it wasn't going to last beyond a month or two. No deeper than skin. So I went along with Paresh's suggestion and kept it a secret. Back then it seemed a small deception.

Perhaps it was the secrecy that made the relationship different. For one thing, we had to keep so separate when we were with other people. A painful distance. But when we were alone together the illicitness became the oxygen that fed our fire. And though I couldn't say when the change happened, there came a time when I knew my feelings for him were stronger than anything I'd experienced before.

Men had never distracted me from the important things

in life. Education. Career. Proving to the world that it was wrong about me. I still don't know if it was Paresh that was different from the other men – or if I had changed. All I'm sure about is my own grief now that it's over. My impossible wish to have my loss acknowledged by the people around me.

I get up and open the blinds. There are a few wisps of cloud near the horizon, lit pink against the pale sky. There are pigeons roosting on the guttering opposite. A line of birds, perfectly spaced.

I've got the pregnancy test kit in my briefcase. I could use it now. Get it over with. There's a ladies' toilet a dozen paces away down the corridor. But now I'm thinking about it, there's no way I could be in that kind of trouble. If something had gone wrong, if the condom had burst – we'd know about it. At the very least, he would have known about it when he came to take the thing off.

'Get a grip,' I say under my breath.

I had a job to do when I left the stadium. The memo to Superintendent Shakespeare. The missing sheet of paper. I go back to the desk, move my chair across to the computer. I sit for a moment, looking at specks of dust on the blank screen, then pull myself together and click the power button.

It's one of those new machines. I can't remember the number of gigahertz, but it sounded impressive when Bob, the computer manager, introduced me to it a couple of months back.

'It's idiot-proof,' he said. Being a civilian, he doesn't have to be so careful how he talks. He's not a higher or lower rank than anyone else. I like that.

'Just turn it on,' he said, 'and it'll get itself ready for you to use.'

Great.

Except that this time it doesn't happen. Instead of the attractive screen that I'm used to – showing a picture of sunflowers by Vincent van Gogh – there's an unfriendly message printed in capital letters, telling me that the system wasn't shut down properly last time I used it. Some of my data may be corrupted. Not the kind of thing I want to read before breakfast.

I press 'enter' and it starts fixing the problem. I'm scratching at my scalp again, trying to figure out what I did wrong, worrying about what I might have damaged.

The computer takes only a few seconds to finish its task. I guess that's why I needed so many gigahertz – to fix all the gigabites of hard disk when I mess things up. Thankfully, everything's fine this time. Except that I'm left with a niggling doubt. I'm sure I did shut the system down correctly last time I used it. I always do. But the screen looks friendly again, and I'm feeling irrationally grateful to my computer for being so clever.

There's more light in the room now. I glance at the window. Outside, the sky has deepened to blue and the clouds have turned from pink to gold. Somewhere in the building a door slams.

I type in my password and start looking for the memo.

I always imagine the files on my computer's hard drive as if they are printed on paper. Don't get me wrong, I do know they're just a magnetic record of my work. Ones and noughts. But when I look at the computer screen I see tiny pictures of sheets of paper. Just like a real desktop – except that it's neatly arranged.

I put my finger on to the glass and start tracing down the columns of files. I'm halfway down the second when a horrible thought pops into my head. If someone could steal the hard copy of my memo from my office, they could just as easily delete the digital version from my hard drive. Halfway down the third column and I'm panicking. Skimming. By the fourth column I can feel the back of my neck prickling with sweat.

Stop. Take a deep breath.

I'm going about this the wrong way. I click the button that enables me to see my documents arranged in date, rather than alphabetical, order. The all-important memo should now be displayed somewhere towards the top of the list.

Two emotions hit me at the same time. The first is relief, because I find it straightaway. My memo is still on the hard drive. The second emotion is curiosity, because the document has appeared at the very head of the list, in first place – which it shouldn't have done, because I've written three or four letters since then.

I open the document, read it from the screen, fearing that it might have been doctored in some way. But nothing seems to have been changed, so I close it again.

There's a way to get the computer to let you see the date and time that you created each of your documents. Bob showed me once. I screw up my face trying to remember exactly how.

That's when I hear a noise just outside my office. I turn sharply, jabbing the power button on my monitor as I do so. Making the screen blank.

'How long 've you been there?'

Paresh shakes his head and steps through the door. 'I'm sorry,' he says. 'Sorry about before . . .'

I don't know if he means what happened in the corridor or further back. I don't ask.

'You look awful,' he says.

'Thanks.'

He sighs. 'I'm trying to be nice.'

'It takes practice,' I say. 'Don't strain yourself.'

'Touché.'

We both take a moment to examine different aspects of the office décor. I'm looking at a small coffee stain on my desk. He seems to have a sudden fascination for the recessed strip lighting in the ceiling.

'Look,' he says at last, 'I've got a copy of the sergeant's notes from the scene. You did initial them, but I will need a more formal statement . . . when you can manage one. You know the way it works. But . . .'

'What?'

'Well, I'd like to know what you think about it . . . not just as a witness. As a police officer.'

'CID wants advice from a uniformed officer?'

He puts on his wounded puppy expression. 'Spare me *that*. Please.'

'Well,' I say. 'What is it I can tell you that you don't already know?'

He shrugs.

'Any sign of the attacker?' I ask.

'Not yet.'

'Any witnesses?'

He shakes his head. 'We're starting a door to door after 10am. Most people should be up by then.'

'What about fingerprints? The car windscreen?'

'They've taken your car to the forensic garage. It'll still be a few days before we get any results. But don't hold your breath.'

'He must have followed me,' I say. 'From Sal's house.'

Paresh doesn't look convinced. 'Why not follow you from the football stadium?'

'No one knew about the meeting.'

'No one?'

'Look,' I say. 'You asked for my advice!'

'OK, OK. We'll knock on some doors. Search the gardens.'

All this time he's been propping up the doorframe. Now he steps inside and casts around for a chair. There isn't one.

'Any similar attacks recently?' I ask.

'Recently? No. The last incident on our books was the Dean Street Mosque. And you know all about that.'

I think about this. There's the whine of the lift winches somewhere in the distance. Then it stops.

'So,' I say at last, 'I'm the connection.'

Paresh looks at the carpet and shrugs. He seems glad that I'm the one who came out and stated the obvious. 'Except,' he says, 'that you discovered the first crime and you were the victim in the second.'

'The newspaper,' I say. 'It printed my name. My picture. It connected me with the first crime.'

Paresh is looking right at me now. I get the feeling that he's encouraging me to go down a road that he's already explored. I'm not at all sure I want to find out what's at the end of it.

'What about the first crime?' he says. 'What was it designed to achieve?'

'Outrage in the Muslim community?'

He nods. 'Leading to riots. Asians against the police.'

'So? Where does that get anyone?'

'We have had that kind of attack in the past – deliberate incitement. Carefully thought-out crimes. Some in other parts of the East Midlands. Remember when those Muslim graves got desecrated? It was what . . . eight months ago? Then a Somali family got firebombed last year. We've catalogued seven different events in this category over a period of five years. Different targets, but all with the same . . .' he searches for a word.

'Flavour?'

He nods. 'Preplanned hate crimes. Always theatrical. Like the end result was arranged to make a good photograph.'

'The pig in the mosque. That I can see as theatre. But my attack?'

'We don't know how he'd have arranged it if . . .'

'If he'd got me?'

Paresh walks over to the window. He's looking down towards the car park. 'Sometimes I envy you.'

'*You* envy *me*?'

'Sometimes. Building communities has to be easier than looking into the minds of the white supremacists who do this kind of thing.'

'Give me a break, Paresh!'

He turns to face me. 'What?'

'Your job is easy. Goodies and baddies. Mine is every shade of grey. It's not just friction between the different races. It's different castes. Different generations. We've got religious communities out there with grudges that go back thousands of years.'

He shakes his head. 'White racism is a religion. That's what you don't understand. You haven't met the sickos I deal with. They're fanatics. They've got the future mapped out already like some kind of warped prophetic vision.'

Paresh turns his back on me again and stares out at the pink sky. I guess that not having to look at me makes the interview easier for him to cope with.

'You want to hear their creed?' he says.

'No.'

'This isn't a game.'

'I'm the one who's been attacked!'

'I'm sorry.'

I want to go and hit the man, but I stay seated. And I wish he'd let me see his eyes. I need to know what's going on inside him – under his skin. He must take my silence as consent, because after a moment he starts talking again.

'The vision they have is this. The blacks, Asians and Jews will attack the white community. Rape and pillage. The white race will unite in response. A violent backlash – led by the racist gangs, of course. There'll be a war. White peoples – the English, the Germans, the Serbs – against all the rest. The non-whites get driven out or slaughtered. They get a "racially pure" homeland, permanently and firmly under their own leadership.'

I have heard this kind of thing before. The ideology of the Balkans. But it's always seemed like it belongs in a different place or time.

'They can't seriously believe it,' I say. 'Not any more.'

Paresh turns towards me at last, and I notice for the first time how drawn and tired his face seems. 'They seriously believe they're going to be running the country in the next couple of years – yes.'

I shake my head. 'Are they stupid?'

'It takes a genius to prove that one and one make three.'

'But the different communities,' I say, 'they do live together. Here in Leicester more than anywhere else.'

'That makes us the obvious target. If they can cause trouble here, then the rest of the country will follow.'

'No way.'

'You said yourself. Friction between the races. Grudges between religions. All it needs is a spark to light the fuse.'

'Friction, yes. But not race war.'

He sighs. 'I've never met anyone who really believes in

the whole "community of communities" thing like you do. You've got a vision of where you want society to go. Unity in diversity. Mixing and blending. But the racists have a different vision.'

There's a long pause after that. I don't want to be the one to break the silence, but I do anyway. 'I need some coffee.'

He shakes his head. 'There's more. These people, whoever they are. They're not going to stop unless we catch them. I told you we've had seven similar attacks in five years – we're assuming it's all the work of the same group.'

'Yes.'

'Five of them were in the last three years. Three in the last eighteen months. That's not counting what happened to you. This group is getting bolder. There'll be more attacks. You ever heard of ZOG?'

I shrug.

'Zionist Occupation Government. It's what the white supremacists call the authorities. Anything to do with government is a target – including us, the police. But the people they hate the most—' he swallows '—are people of mixed race. You undermine their whole philosophy – just by existing. And that makes you a double target – especially when you get your picture on the cover of the newspaper.'

'Shit.'

'You need to get out of the city,' he says. 'At least for a few months. A temporary transfer.'

I'm shaking my head even before he's finished speaking. 'Ethnic cleansing. That's what they call it. And I'm not going anywhere.'

Chapter 9

Six in the morning. They don't run a night shift so the factory will have been quiet for eight hours. The workers troop inside, probably more asleep than awake. Someone flicks the switches and three lines of strip lights flicker into life. Fans start moving air through the ventilation system.

Hussayn. He's the man with the keys. From what I can work out, he can't have had much sleep. It would have been impossible, what with all the coming and going in the night. Phone calls. A trip to the local police station. An interview. The police asking the standard 'missing person' questions. It's never easy.

'Has it happened before?'

'Never.'

'Were any bags taken?'

'Bags?'

'Suitcases.'

'I don't understand.'

'Did he see any other women?'

It must have been a long night for Hussayn.

So he walks down the first line of machines, trying to keep himself sharp and awake. He checks that each operator has all the supplies he or she will need. People are loading denim jeans into the washing machines already. Steam presses start to hiss. He walks down the second line, then the third. Everything is in order. A few latecomers are hurrying in through the door. He won't dock them any pay, though he'll remember the names for future reference. The inspection is over.

He's about to go back to his office when he sees a dark patch on the floor next to the fire escape. Machine oil, he thinks. He walks over to it, bends down. There's something else wrong here, a movement of air where it should be still, a crack of light showing that the fire exit isn't firmly shut.

He pushes the door, steps out on to the iron grille. That's when he sees the body. It is hanging by its bound wrists from the fire escape level above, twisting slowly on a short length of cable. There is blood on the clothing. The mouth is gagged with black insulating tape, the eyes dull and lifeless.

It should be obvious, of course, but Hussayn probably can't take it in. A missing person. A dead body. The two won't connect in his mind. The missing person – a human being, a living, breathing member of the family. The corpse – useless, still, empty.

Then someone behind him screams and he finally understands. He throws up, adding to the confusion that the scene-of-crime team will find when they arrive. He uses his mobile to call the emergency services. To their credit, the first police officers arrive in under six minutes.

It's my day off. I'm supposed to be at home taking a well-earned rest. No one thinks to check, so no one finds out that I'm in my office, taking the name of Microsoft in vain.

All those gigahertz aren't helping my computer to have any kind of common sense. All I want to do is find out why it's listing my files in the wrong order. I've tried looking in the file menu. I've tried the help menu. I've learned more than I ever wanted to know about date fields and mail merge. I've tried picking up the keyboard and threatening to throw it in the bin. None of this has helped.

It's not eight thirty yet, but outside my office there's a hum of activity. The lift winches have been whining. Doors have slammed. People have been hurrying up and down the corridor. I have heard the noises, but they haven't seemed important.

I've been focused. Only now, as fatigue builds up, do I start to lose my sharpness. I sit back in my chair and rub my hands over my face. Time to give up. Bob can help me with it tomorrow. Time perhaps to drop in at the supermarket on my way home. Croissants and chocolate before bed.

But all this – the computer puzzle, the feel-good food – it's all a way of avoiding the issue that I'm scared to face. Somewhere inside my head, I do know what I'm doing.

I close my eyes and yawn. Computer off. Coffee cup in bin. Stretch. Stand. Pick up my briefcase. I hear the contents moving inside it. The pregnancy test kit. I feel queasy for a moment. I step towards the door.

The pregnancy test kit. The memo. It's all bouncing around in my mind. I go for the less disturbing of the two thoughts and lock on to it again. There's an idea niggling at me – that I should check the file again. It's completely illogical, but easier than thinking about other things.

I step back inside my office, pull the drawer of the filing cabinet open, reach into my emergency-job-meltdown pack. I tell myself how pointless the exercise is as I finger through the documents, looking for the sheet of paper that I know can't be there.

But it is.

I pull it out. *Thanks for listening to my warning about tension in the Muslim community – i.e. the danger they might believe that the police are not following their case seriously . . .*

I'm holding on to the doorframe with one hand, my face screwed up. The document *was* missing. I'm sure. At least, I *thought* I was sure. But I can't have been completely certain or I wouldn't have bothered to check the file again.

I'm standing in the doorway, rereading the memo, lost somewhere deep in the back of my own mind. Then someone calls me from down the corridor.

'Inspector?'

I turn and see a CID sergeant looking in my direction. 'Yes?'

He looks embarrassed. 'The duty roster . . . I'm sorry, ma'am. We didn't think you were here.'

'Well,' I say, 'now you know I am.'

'We called your home number . . .'

My mind is still on the puzzle of my reappearing file, and the sergeant is stopping me thinking clearly. I turn to look at him 'Is there some problem?'

'The murder,' he says. 'You do know about it?'

Murder. The word seeps into my awareness. I shake my head.

'Thought you . . . seeing as you're out of uniform . . . someone must have called you in.'

'What murder?'

'Some Asian bloke. It's real nasty.'

'Who?'

He's looking at the carpet. 'A foreign name. An-something. Only he's got a factory in Waterfields. They said you should be kept up to speed – seeing as it's on your patch.'

I feel a rush of fear, a sensation almost painful, which surges from the knot of my stomach up to my chest then to my throat. 'Anwar.'

The sergeant is nodding. 'Anwar,' he says. 'Yeah. That's the one.'

Even if I didn't know the place, there'd be no difficulty in finding the murder scene. It's a quiet morning. Or it would be if it wasn't for all the police activity. I count five patrol cars and two vans. Enough blue and white incident tape to wrap a building. It's stretched around the main entrance, around the fire escape and a big section of the car park. They've taped off an area of the road as well. A wide circle around a dark-blue Toyota transit. Uniformed policemen are moving across the area in a line. Shoulder to shoulder. Heads bowed.

There are a couple of reporters by the edge of the tape cordon. A man and a woman. They're both scribbling in their notebooks. Probably reworking the old phrases from the hack's book of murder-speak: 'fingertip search', 'anxious to interview' and the old favourite, 'senseless attack'.

The woman sees me.

Damn.

I'm smiling as she breaks away from her colleague and walks towards me. 'Diana. How nice . . .'

'Mo. No hard feelings.'

The *Crusader*'s crime reporter is a woman of indeterminable age. But if Max Factor really kept people young, I'd say she'd probably live for ever. There is a jerky energy about her, but that must be from all the cigarettes and coffee.

I look around for someone I have to go and speak to. There isn't anyone.

'The headlines,' she says, 'and the way they used your picture. It wasn't fair.' She nods her head, laying on the sincerity even thicker than her foundation. 'I wrote the text. But I never thought they'd use it like that.'

Unfortunately, I have to swallow all the sharp words that offer themselves in my mind. The chief constable reads Diana's column. My smile muscles feel like concrete. Quick-setting. I have to say something or they'll start to crack. 'Who's your friend?' I nod towards the other reporter, still standing by the incident tape.

'Him? No one.' She leans towards me and I get an unwelcome reminder of her tobacco habit. 'Some jerk-off from London.'

'Which paper?'

She shrugs. 'Freelancer.'

'From London? Quick off the mark.'

She flashes me a smile. 'One sniff of a corpse and they fly in. Vultures, aren't they? No commitment to the community.' She glances around, as if looking to see if there's anything more interesting happening yet. 'So,' she says. 'Anwar. It's a shock, yes?'

I nod. And I mean it.

'You knew him?'

'A little. But you know I really can't comment about—'

'It must make things very complicated,' she says, 'what with him having just made that complaint. Yesterday, wasn't it?'

I'm about to answer back, but I know that whatever I say will be used against me. And I'm wondering how it was she got to hear about the complaint so quickly. The Muslim community aren't usually so quick off the mark when it comes to using the media. I've got this horrible feeling that I'll find out more when I see the *Crusader* tomorrow.

'Look,' I say. 'The murder. It's a real shock, just like you said. But right now I don't know anything. I'll get back to you when there's something to tell. OK?'

Diana opens her mouth to tell me it isn't, but I'm

moving already, heading for the nearest cordon. I duck under the incident tape and head inside.

I walked into this building yesterday. Somehow it seems much longer ago than that. This time the machines are silent. There are no voices shouting to be heard. No bang-hara music. The double doors are open, wedged with chocks of wood. I step inside. I'm about to enter the room when a scene-of-crime officer steps across to bar my way. The white, one-piece outer suit makes him look like an astronaut. Figure muffled. Androgynous.

'You are?'

'Inspector Marjorie Akanbai. Community Relations.' I pull out my ID and hold it up for him to see.

He frowns at my civvies but jots my name in his notebook anyway. Then he points to a box of protective clothing. 'Feet and hands, please.'

I put on the white plastic overshoes and tight rubber gloves, then step inside.

There are two more SOCOs over on the far side of the factory room. One is crouched down on the floor. The other stands in the fire escape doorway. A blue–white flash jerks my attention over to the side office where I sat with Anwar some fourteen hours ago. Another officer is aiming a camera at the desk. Flash. Flash. Flash.

'Marjorie?'

The voice makes me jump. I turn to see the plain-clothes officer standing behind me. She has the kind of face that they might use to advertise instant coffee. Moderately attractive, but not threatening. Straight brown hair, blue eyes. Pleasant. But I know from experience that she can turn the expression to steel when she wants to.

She gives me a manicured handshake, her grip gentle.

'Alison,' I say.

'Glad they found you.'

'I was at the station.'

Detective Superintendent Alison Walker is another fast-tracker like me. When I joined the force, straight out of university, they told me that there was nothing to stop me becoming chief constable one day. Back then that was exactly what I wanted. But when I met Alison I changed my mind. She has the kind of single-minded focus that really will take her to the top. I'd never be able to compete with that.

She also has this solidarity thing going among the senior female officers. Watch out for each other because all men are set against us. Something like that. She's always been particularly warm towards me. But that's probably because she knows I'm not a threat to her. In a straight race between female solidarity and her own career prospects, I wouldn't put any money on the sisterhood.

She glances at my clothes, then over towards the fire escape. 'The pathologist has the body already. The victim . . .'

'Anwar,' I say.

Her eyes flick to me. 'Yes.'

'They respected him.'

'Who's they?'

'The Muslim community. His word meant something. And he was . . .' I want to use the word 'moderate', but there was nothing middle of the road about the man. He was completely true to his religious faith. He did what he believed was right. And many times I found myself agreeing with him. Instead, I say: 'When they built the Dean Street Mosque, he made them have a women's prayer hall. They wouldn't have had women in the building if it wasn't for him.'

The superintendent narrows her eyes. 'That was generous of him.' If sarcasm was an offensive weapon, her mouth would have to be licensed.

'You've got to see it from his background,' I say. 'They had to wait an extra year until they collected enough money to convert the whole building. All because he wanted women to be able to use the mosque. People were angry with him.'

She shrugs. 'OK. So he made enemies?'

'No one's ever . . . not to me . . . ever said a word against him. Just his ideas.'

There's a pause. And I'm trying to put it all together – the events of the last few days. 'Where was he attacked?'

'The van outside,' she says. 'Looks like that's where it started. There's blood around the driver's seat. Then he got brought back up here. Somewhere along the way he got gagged and tied. The bastards hung him out there,' she points to the fire escape. 'Let him bleed to death.'

Alison pauses and her words sink in. It is a few moments before I manage to speak, and then only in a whisper. 'I was with him yesterday.'

She turns back to me. 'I'm sorry.'

'He was a . . . a good man.'

'I didn't realize you . . .'

'No. I didn't know him that well.' I shake my head.

'You're OK with all this?'

I say, 'Yes,' though I don't feel so good. 'What time did he . . .'

She touches one gloved finger to her chin. 'You know what pathologists are like. Dr Loné said he'd need the air temperature at the time of death, cooling rates through the night, humidity. Should be keeping the Meteorological Office busy today.'

'Not even an off-the-record guess?'

'Off the record he told me 4 a.m. – give or take. But don't tell him I told you. He made me promise.'

While she's speaking, one of the scene-of-crime officers has been hurrying across the room towards us from the fire escape. He's pulled down his mask, so I can see a hint of a smile touching one side of his mouth. He nods once towards me then quickly turns to Alison. 'We've got something. A trail of very small bloodstains on the floor. Sub-millimetre size. Been walked on the sole of someone's shoe, by the look of it. They're just specks, nothing to make a usable print. But—' the smile strengthens '—just as a long shot I dusted the floor area around the stains. Still nothing.'

I can feel Alison bristling with impatience next to me. 'Well?'

'So I tried the UV lamp under a blackout cloth.'

'Yes?'

'Two sets of latent footprints, fluorescing like the Skegness illuminations. Beauties. Both men, I'd guess.'

'Linked to the blood – you're sure?'

He nods. 'Indisputable.'

The SOCO heads back to set up a camera and record his triumph.

The superintendent puts a hand on my forearm. 'I want your help on this one, Marjorie. I'm going to be putting together an investigation team – including Race Crime. But we're going to be trampling all over Waterfields. After the riots it's going to look like an invasion army . . .'

That phrase again. I could do with less of the war language.

'. . . we need your community relations input. I've got a meeting with the chief constable later today. I'll have a word . . .'

'Alison . . .'

'Yes?'

'There's something you should know.'

She takes her hand off my forearm, nods attentively.

'Anwar . . . the victim . . . he made a complaint yesterday, about the police. About me.'

Alison is still smiling, but her face has lost its fluidity, the sincerity frozen over.

She says: 'That complicates matters.' She moistens her lips. I can see the gears turning in her head. 'You've got to get off this crime scene. Get out of here. And for God's sake don't go telling anyone you've been here.'

She's bundling me towards the door. I'm trying to understand what is happening. And I'm remembering all the people who've already seen me here.

Chapter 10

DS Alison Walker may now see me as untouchable, but in other quarters my status has shot up. There's nothing like an attack from the outside to silence doubters from within. Two attacks are even better.

Sergeant Ivor Morris has just smiled at me. I counted three times in the last half-hour. That would be remarkable enough, but I've also caught him giving me silent nods of approval. I'm telling myself not to get used to it.

'Where do you keep the keys for this one? At night, I mean.'

'Kitchen,' I say. 'On a nail in the wall.'

He's bent low, examining the lock. Then he prods the sheet of plywood reinforcing that's just been fixed over the lowest door panel. 'How long are these screws? They've got to be at least . . .'

'Will you stop fussing, Ivor.'

He stands, shaking his head. 'You have to take this seriously, ma'am. There's a murderer out there.'

'Two,' I say. 'And you're off duty. You can drop the ma'am.'

'The panic button . . .' he says.

'In the living room when I'm downstairs. Other times in the bedroom. They went through all this when they gave the thing to me. I press the button, it sends out a radio signal and an alarm goes off at the station. Simple as that.'

Ivor steps through to the living room and brushes the side of the panic button with a finger. It looks mundane, like a mobile phone, but I'm well aware of its importance. He straightens himself and stares out of the French windows. 'I don't like it.'

'I never was much of a gardener,' I say, though I think my attempt at humour is lost on him.

'High hedges. Stand out there at night, no one's going to see you. And this,' he tuts as he taps the mock-Victorian frame. 'Anyone knows his business will be through here in a few seconds.'

I'm still not sure if it's the physical assault or Anwar's complaint that's made him so supportive. Either way, my recent experiences must be equivalent to several extra years on the beat as far as he's concerned. He's gone from having a fast-track embarrassment for a line manager to having someone who he actually feels proud of. Scary.

'You heard about your car?' he asks. This is the first mention of anything other than the security of my suburban semi. He doesn't wait for me to answer. 'They've lifted a good set of fingerprints from your steering wheel. And they found blood on the driver-side door. When you hit him, ma'am, it must have been a hell of a whack – looks like you rammed his forearm down into the broken glass.' He grins.

This is all news to me.

'Who told you?'

Ivor looks down at his shoes. 'I . . . know someone.'

'Who?'

'At the forensic garage.'

I file that information away for future reference.

'Get out of here, Sergeant Morris,' I say. 'Go home. Get a good night's sleep. The fun begins tomorrow.'

'OK,' he says. 'See you in Room 3.'

He goes then. Reluctantly, I think.

I watch him drive away into the dusk, then go to fix myself a bowl of cereal and a few slices of lime marmalade on toast. The feeding frenzy dies as quickly as it started. I'm left with a half-chewed morsel in my mouth, which I'm not at all sure I can swallow. I spit it into the kitchen bin, then go to the sink and swill with tapwater. The queasiness recedes slowly.

This has gone on too long for it to be food poisoning. I can't go on blaming the Indian takeaway. A stomach bug, perhaps. My briefcase is in the hallway next to the radiator. I stare at it, trying to psyche myself up. Then I step through and click the catches.

The test kit comes complete with a tiny plastic cup and a set of instructions that tell me to collect a mid-stream sample. The sample cup doesn't look very practical, so I take a large yoghurt carton from the cupboard under the kitchen sink and head upstairs to the bathroom. I try telling myself to relax. I put the cold tap on and leave it trickling into the sink. But after five minutes I still haven't managed to produce a drop. So I stuff the test kit into the cupboard, leave the yoghurt carton on top of the toilet cistern and go back downstairs.

It's dark outside now, and I can see my reflection in the black glass of the kitchen window. I can't see a thing outside. Just like Ivor said. Perhaps it's sometimes better not to know what's on the other side of the glass.

Then I think of someone else who doesn't have a clue what's outside her own window. And I think of my conversation with Paresh. Suddenly worried, I pick up the phone and dial. It rings seven times before I hear the click and her voice comes on the other end of the line.

'Hello?'

'Are you all right?' It's a stupid way to start a conversation, I know.

'Of course. Why shouldn't I be?'

'I was worried.'

'You know what? I was just thinking about you.' She always says that when I phone.

'Sal, you want to come over and stay the night?' There's a pause. 'Why should I?'

'It's just . . . you know . . . the attack and everything. He must have followed me from your place.'

'You're frightened?' she asks.

'Me? No. I thought you might . . .'

She doesn't let me finish. 'No need to worry about me. I did well enough before having a policewoman as a daughter.'

Change tack. That's what I should do. That would be the wise thing. But outrageous statements like that demand to be challenged. 'Before you had a police *officer* for a daughter, Dad was still around.'

There's silence on the other end of the line and I know I've made a mistake. I can almost hear the counting in Sal's mind. She can only have got to five by the time she bites back. 'Don't you bring your father into this!'

'I'm sorry.'

'He was a good man. A better man than . . .'

'I didn't say he wasn't.'

'. . . better than all the . . . you know how much he loved you? Sat up all night nursing you when you were sick.'

I usually like to think of myself as brighter than average. IQ of one hundred and forty when we tested each other at university. For what that's worth. But get me into an argument with my mum and it all goes down the toilet, intelligence, psychology training, everything. It's only at this moment, almost at the point of no return, that I realize how futile it is for me to offer help. I might as well be telling her that she's incapable of looking after herself, since Dad died.

'. . . we were fine then, and I'm still . . . I'm still fine now. If I can manage . . .'

'Sal . . .'

'. . . If I can manage to . . .'

'I'm not feeling well.'

'You're . . .'

'Feeling sick.'

'Where does it hurt, chick?' Her change in tone is so sudden it's almost funny.

'In my tummy.' I'll hate myself for this in the morning. 'And I'm frightened.'

There's the briefest of pauses, then: 'Stay just where you are. I'm coming round. I'll call a taxi.'

Wednesday morning in Room 3. They call it a 'shared space'. That means no one has the responsibility for making it look any better than it did when they put up this section of the police station back in the late 1970s. It also means that everyone gets to suffer it at some time or other.

My usual contact with Room 3 is when I speak to groups of further education students. They fidget in rows of grey plastic bucket seats, squinting against the flicker of one dodgy strip light. There's always one. I stand at the front delivering the good news about recent advances in community policing, wishing all the while for an external window to reassure me of the existence of the sky.

Today I'm one of the ones in the audience, sitting near the fire escape at the back of the room. Paresh and his team are near the front, mixed in with all the other CID crowd.

We've got civilians here as well – a recording secretary sitting to one side of the top table. The public information officer stands next to the door.

Sergeant Ivor Morris has just taken the seat next to me. He drops this morning's *Crusader* on my lap. 'Seen this?'

'Do I want to?'

'No.'

'Tell me then.'

'There's a picture of you in Cornwell Street. "Riot Officer at Murder Scene". Inside pages somewhere.'

'Hell.' I push the paper back into his hands. 'Take it.'

'And . . .' he says.

'And what?'

'And "Murdered Man Slammed Police" – naming you again. And . . .'

'Not more?'

'The editorial. "Who Inspects the Inspectors?"'

I'm just thinking that things can't get any worse when Superintendent Alison Walker sweeps into the room. Some unseen hand closes the door behind her. She waits for the shuffling to die down.

'Thanks for coming,' she says, which is polite of her because none of us had any choice in the matter. 'I won't make this any longer than it has to be. You all know the background by now. The murder of Anwar Khaliq.'

She stands there looking at us, born to lead. She could get one of her officers to do the briefing, but it looks like she's enjoying the platform too much to give it up just yet.

'The last reported sighting of the victim was by a nephew, Hussayn Khaliq, who claims to have seen his uncle driving away from the factory in a blue Toyota van. That was just after they closed up on Monday night. Hussayn says that he drove directly to his own home and went to bed. The victim's wife phoned Hussayn's house at one in the morning saying he hadn't come home. They say they phoned around the hospitals before contacting the police.'

One of the detectives on the front row raises his hand. 'Ma'am, I've just confirmed the phone calls. It all checks out.'

The superintendent gives him a curt nod. 'And so far forensics are bearing out our initial impressions. He was attacked by someone sitting in the passenger seat of the van. Five shallow knife slashes on the left arm. He returned to the factory, presumably under duress. Left the van outside the front. Entered by the main front door using his keys. He was bound, gagged and beaten and slashed again with the knife a few times – though we don't know the order those happened in. Then they took him out onto the fire escape, strung him up by a length of telephone cable and left him. He bled to death some time between one fifteen and four fifteen Tuesday morning.'

She pauses for effect. No one breaks the silence.

'We know that more than one person was at the scene. The good news is that they left two sets of latent footprints. Match the shoes and we'll be halfway home on this one.'

Paresh raises a hand and asks the question that must have been on everyone's mind. 'Are we looking at this as a punishment beating that went wrong or a premeditated murder?'

Alison nods. 'Can't be sure. The wounds on his arm were slashes, long cuts but shallow. None of them would have bled much. But there's a single stab wound in his calf that nicked a minor artery. From the blood distribution, it looks like this one happened in the factory. We've got a pool of blood just inside the fire escape door, together with the much larger pool on the ground directly below the place where he was hanging. So . . . it looks like they just wanted to scare him. A paramilitary-style punishment beating.'

A murmur goes around the room. None of us likes the story. Even if we manage to catch the killers, they'll try to get off on a manslaughter charge.

Another of the CID boys at the front raises his hand. 'What about the Dean Street Mosque, ma'am?'

The superintendent gestures to Paresh. 'That's still in the hands of Race Crime. It's a separate investigation.'

'No,' I say, blurting out my thought a shade too loudly. A couple of people turn in my direction.

Alison looks at me. 'Inspector?'

I stand up. 'The same man was attacked twice in three days. I don't . . .'

She raises a hand to stop me. 'Parallel investigations,' she says.

'But . . .'

'Close – but – separate.' Each word is edged with steel. 'Two investigations. Shared data. Joint briefings. But until we find an explicit connection they will remain separate.'

I lower myself back into my seat. There's a very uneasy pause, then she turns to Paresh and smiles. 'Bring us up to speed, will you.'

He gets to his feet and stands next to her. He doesn't look comfortable. 'The . . . uh . . . the attack on the mosque happened between ten fifteen on Thursday night and six twenty on Friday morning. They broke in through the fire escape . . .'

Someone in the audience coughs. 'They?'

'They. Yes. The pig weighs seventy-six kilos in total. To carry it there, even in pieces . . .' He shrugs. 'They came over a six-foot wall at the back of the property.'

I put up my hand. 'What about forensics? We've got the

latent footprints from the factory. If we could match them . . .'

Paresh is squirming where he stands. Either it's something I've just said, or he suddenly needs to use the toilet. The superintendent comes to his aid. 'No footprints were found at the mosque,' she says.

I puzzle over this for a moment. 'Did they look?'

'The SOCOs had no way of knowing there was going to be a murder.'

Another officer has put up his hand and is asking a question. I'm not even hearing the words. The truth is percolating through my mind. The scene-of-crime officers were being rushed from place to place that day, doing enough overtime to bankrupt the department. What was a pig in a converted factory building to them? No one bothered looking for latent footprints. I'm just wondering if enough small mistakes put together can make an institution racist, when Paresh's voice brings me back to the present.

'We now think that it wasn't butchered at an abattoir,' he says. 'Apparently the pattern of cuts would have been different. But it was slaughtered with a professional bit of kit called a humane killer. This looks like the best lead so far. We're thinking agricultural workers. Cross-referencing this with the database of known racist offenders and their contacts.'

That's the highlight as far as I'm concerned. He does mention the attack on my car – though it's more by way of a warning. 'We can't say it's connected,' he says. 'But there's some dangerous people out there. Don't take any risks.'

After that the briefing gets rather dry. Alison talks staff numbers and overtime. Specific timetables for action by different teams. Measurable outcomes. Management-speak.

'We need a door to door,' she is saying, 'all around the factory area.'

One of the sergeants raises a hand. 'It's not gunna be easy, not after the riots. Any chance of Mo's team giving us a hand smoothing the waters?'

'Community relations officers will be helping.'

There's something in the way she put her answer together that has my instant attention. But I don't have time to consider it in detail because she immediately throws out another stunner.

'Remember,' she says, 'we are alert to the possibility that the killing was a race crime. All leads are being followed. But at this time we have no reason for connecting it with the mosque. This is the official line. Anyone who says anything else in public will be answering to me.'

That's it. Everyone troops towards the door. There's a huddle of bodies all trying to get out at the same time. I stay seated, watching. The superintendent is still talking to Paresh. The room empties.

I get up and walk over to her. 'Ma'am?' Somehow I don't feel able to call her 'Alison' today.

'Yes?'

'Who should I liaise with about the investigation?'

She nods. 'Marjorie. It's not really that simple.'

Paresh steps away and busies himself collecting his papers.

'Why not?'

'The complaint against you. Your personal involvement . . . we don't want to leave any wrong impressions.'

'But you just said community relations officers could take part.' My voice comes out louder than I intended it to.

'Superintendent Shakespeare has cleared this already. Thought he'd have talked to you about it.'

'Cleared?'

'Some of your officers will be helping, but . . .'

'But not me? You're taking my officers and pushing me off to the side?'

Paresh has his papers under his arm now. He's shifting his weight from foot to foot. 'It's just for the duration,' he says. 'I mean . . .. they'll finish investigating the complaint and . . .'

I guess he means to help me back off from a dangerous conversation. You'd have thought he'd know me better than that after all we've been through.

'You're in on this as well!' I glare at him. 'Sidelining me!'

'Marjorie.' The superintendent reaches her hand out to touch my arm. I pull away. My eyes are locked with hers.

'Yes, ma'am?'

'Be careful, Marjorie.'

We're standing there, trying to out-stare each other, with Paresh to one side, looking like he's desperate to be somewhere else, when in swims the big fish himself.

'Chief constable,' says Alison, suddenly sweet.

He has a thin face with dark, widely spaced eyes. His teeth show when he smiles, white as broken seashells. He nods his narrow head, a gesture that seems to include all of us equally.

'Can't be long,' he says. 'Meeting at County Hall.'

Strange thing with the Chief: he never seems to be trying to assert his authority. I guess he doesn't have to. He and the Home Secretary are buddies from their Oxford days.

'Difficult situation,' he says.

We all nod, not having to fake the sincerity this time.

'First we have public disorder and now this.' He turns to me. 'Sorry about your trouble the other night. Truly.'

I shrug it off, but feel an unexpected glow of gratitude for the warmth of his concern.

'Any chance of an identification?'

Alison gets her answer in before I can speak. 'No chance, sir. He was wearing a balaclava.'

'It's an attack on all of us,' says the chief. 'And it comes at a sensitive time. The conference. Government sensitivities.'

Alison makes a noise of agreement.

'Racism. We expect to find it outside the force.' He looks at Paresh. 'That's why I set up your unit. Got to be seen fighting the problem. This city, the most diverse in the region. A community of communities. We've put in years of effort to build up trust. And it's worked – to a point.'

'That's thanks to your leadership,' says Alison.

Paresh nods.

'But racism within the force – what about that?'

He looks from face to face as if waiting for an answer. It would take an idiot to speak without knowing what line the chief is about to take.

'It exists,' I say. They're all looking at me now, waiting for an explanation. I feel myself blushing. 'Of course it exists. We're human. We've all got prejudices – but no worse than any other section of society.'

There's a pause. Then the chief constable nods. 'This is what we need. Honesty. Internally, yes. We need to examine ourselves in this way. But externally – this is what we have to worry about. It's a problem of politics. We're not just police officers responding to the situation. We take a course of action. We make a statement. We change the world outside these walls. No action is neutral.'

I can see the other two out of the corner of my eye. Alison is still nodding, though her fixed smile tells me she hasn't worked out where the chief is going with this argument. Nor have I.

'Here's the problem,' he says. 'One ethnic community makes a complaint. Do we take it seriously? Of course. Do we perhaps suspend the officer? The officer in question is non-white. If we treat her harshly, we alienate another section of the community. Suspicions of police racism vindicated either way. What do we do?'

Not even I'm stupid enough to offer an answer here. Nor is Alison.

'Have an investigation,' says Paresh, 'but keep her working in her job.'

The chief constable shows his teeth for a moment. A smile, I think. 'Good,' he says. 'And a public statement of support for Inspector Akanbai. A news conference perhaps. No way she can be an identifying witness – so no reason to keep her from being part of the investigation.'

DS Alison Walker is nodding, as if she's just had her own ideas confirmed from above. Paresh is looking at the toes of his shoes. I guess he knows she'll make him suffer for what he's just done.

As for me, I'm not so sure the big fish has got it right this time. My attacker *was* wearing a balaclava – that much is true. But I still think I might know him again. Not from a photograph. It was the way he moved that made him different.

The chief constable holds out his hand to me. I take it.

'We need your input,' he says. 'Now more than ever.'

Then he releases my hand and leaves. The three of us are standing together in the empty lecture room, curling our toes in embarrassment at each other's company.

'Well,' says Paresh. 'I think . . .'

But Alison turns to go. 'Do excuse me.' Then she marches out of the room.

Paresh looks at me and then nods towards the door. 'I'd better . . . you know . . .'

'Sure,' I say, as I watch him follow after his boss. 'I know.'

He gets to the exit then turns. 'Be careful, Mo.'

Chapter 11

'Want something to keep you awake?'

I hear the sergeant unscrewing the top of the Thermos. There's the trickle of liquid pouring into a plastic cup. 'Should give you a kick,' he says.

I reach to the front of the van and take it from his hand. It's hard to move here in the back, crammed together shoulder to shoulder. Padded out with body armour.

'Jolt fluid,' says the sergeant, making a sound halfway between a grunt and a snigger. 'Night duty special issue. Double the caffeine. Double the sugar.'

I cradle it in my hands and breathe the coffee steam. Even a sniff is enough to set my heart off on a hundred-metre dash. I take a sip of the syrupy liquid and screw up my face. 'How do you drink this stuff?'

A chuckle of approval comes from the officers on either side of me. The honour of the team has been satisfied.

We've been sitting here in the gloom for more than half an hour now, parked on an access road in the industrial estate. Waiting for something. No one's told me what, and I haven't asked. No point in exposing my ignorance during an operation in which I'm just an observer.

I could have sat in the front, of course. I'm now regretting my impulsive decision to muck in with the rest of them. When we climbed in and took our places – that was back at the central police station – they'd showed me the deference due to my rank. But you can't keep up that kind of pretence for long when you're nose to nose across the width of a van, breathing the same stale air, suffering the same muscle cramps. There's no 'ma'am' here.

A radio crackles. The voice on the other end, a woman, gives a curt instruction. The driver starts the engine. I knock back the remains of the coffee, scalding my throat in the process. We're moving. Down to the end of the road, around a tight circle. Then across Henley Rise and straight on to the Martin's Hill council estate, notorious home territory of the Martin's Hill Scalpers.

A first speed-bump, throwing us off our benches for a moment. It's not a race, but there's a kind of focused determination to the driving. A second bump. Slowing now. Stopping. A burst of static. The sergeant reporting that we're in position.

Then we're back to the waiting game again. I've decided now that this kind of operation is no different from most of policing. Hours and days of mind-numbing boredom, punctuated by short bursts of fear and adrenaline.

Through the tinted window of the van I can see a row of identical council houses. Semi-detached pairs. Set back from the wide road behind standard-issue wooden fences. There's a stripped-down motorbike in one garden, an old iron bed frame in another. The house opposite where we're parked is boarded up, the brickwork above windows and door stained black.

The whole estate was put up just after the war. Solidly built to house the solid folk who were going to rebuild the nation. This is what my social psychology lecturer used to tell me. Decaying Victorian terraces were going to be phased out. Everyone could aspire to a semi-detached middle-class life. He always saw things in terms of class.

Ugandan Asians moved into the terraces as fast as the white working class moved out. The least desirable property, the lowest pay, the hardest jobs. The new immigrants took it all on. And through a mixture of good business instinct and hard graft they got the local economy moving again. The Victorian terraces were on their way up. But the white housing estates were already going down the drain. When manufacturing industry collapsed in the 1980s and we got to ten per cent unemployment nationwide, more than half the families in Martin's Hill were on the dole.

It was one of my lecturer's pet subjects. He even wrote a paper on it: 'Social Housing and the Death of Society.' All I can say is that police officers don't like going into the Martin's Hill estate on foot.

'Everyone ready?' asks the sergeant.

There are a few nods and affirmative grunts from around the van.

Having been conspicuously unable to urinate into an empty plastic yoghurt pot before leaving the house this evening, I'm now aware of a growing need to empty my bladder. The man at my left shoulder stretches his arms. Someone reaches down and tests the weight of the battering ram that lies on the floor just in front of my feet. I try to stretch my legs, straighten my abdomen, relieve the pressure.

Then the radio crackles again. 'It's a go, go, go!'

The back doors open. I'm scrambling out behind the men with the ram. There's cold night air in my face. My feet hit the concrete road, jarring my knees. And we're running, as light-footed as we can manage on stiff limbs. Down the pavement. Around the corner.

I see Paresh now, coming the other way. He's moving swiftly, followed by three officers, two of them women. We converge at number 17, home of Vince the Prince. None of us speaks.

The gate is open already. Three men jump over a couple of bulging bin-bags and run down the side of the house. The two with the ram are at the front door. They raise it level with the lock, then swing it forward. Thud. The door shudders. A dog starts barking, going crazy out the back somewhere. Another swing. Another booming thud. Louder this time. The men are grunting with the effort. A third swing. A splintering crash and the wood of the doorframe splits.

We're in. Paresh ahead of me. 'Police!' he shouts. He's climbing, three stairs at a time, leading the way. 'Inspector Paresh Gupta. I have a warrant to search these premises.'

I stay by the front door with one of the ram carriers.

There are shouts from the upstairs landing. A man yelling in rage. A woman screaming. A crash as someone falls.

The sergeant comes running through from the back of the house. 'Ground floor clear,' he shouts, then pounds up the stairs, followed by the two female officers. There's one more really loud yell, impotent rage this time, and it's over.

I hear Paresh's voice from the landing above. He's out of breath. 'These premises are being searched because of information received connecting it with a recent attack on the Dean Street Mosque. This is my warrant card. And you are being arrested for assaulting a police officer.'

He goes through the statutory statement of rights. Vince the Prince could probably recite it himself, he's heard it all that many times.

They're coming down the stairs now, Vince in front, the two biggest officers just behind. He's wearing a vest and what looks like a set of tracksuit trousers. His hands are drawn up behind his back.

He sees me standing at the bottom of the stairs and his upper lip curls back on one side. I feel my stomach muscles tense up even more than they were before, and I'm suddenly desperate to pee. His well-muscled arms and broad frame do make him look like my attacker. Like enough. But his movement is different. He gets to the bottom, and I'm waiting for him to lash out at me like he wants to. I'm ready for him. But instead of kicking out, he says: 'I never forget a face.'

I hold his gaze for another second. Then all I can do is step out of the way and let him pass.

Paresh stomps down the stairs. The fight is over, but he's still pumped up. 'Van him!' he shouts. And Vince gets pushed out of his house through the remains of his front door.

Paresh rubs a hand over his cheek, and I notice for the first time a fresh red weal. 'Let's take this place apart,' he says.

From upstairs I can hear the sound of a woman sobbing. It's fifteen minutes before the search team will let me use the toilet.

These things I can tell you about the downstairs part of Vince's house. First the smell, lemon air freshener over stale cigarette smoke. Then the décor – the wallpaper has an oppressively heavy pattern, making the place look rather smaller than it is. There's a big wide-screen TV in the lounge and a new-looking three-piece suite.

I'd have expected racist pictures everywhere and Union Jack flags. Instead, there are twee posters on the wall, china dogs above the fireplace and a battery-driven pendulum clock that looks just like the picture in the Argos catalogue.

Then we get to the video cabinet. *Sleepless in Seattle* and

Titanic belong to her, I guess, together with a couple of dozen similarly romantic titles. A boxed history of the Second World War – this must be his – together with lots of videos of football matches and a few old films: *Kelly's Heroes*, *Dirty Harry*, *The Terminator*.

The back garden is a strip of uneven paving with a rotary washing line. The hound, thankfully chained, appears to be some sort of Doberman–Aberdeen Angus cross. There's the skeleton of a greenhouse against the rear fence. On a workbench within the glassless aluminium frame someone, presumably Vince, has placed half a car engine.

I walk upstairs, squeezing past an officer on his way down who carries a large plastic evidence bag full of men's shoes. The landing has doors leading off to three bedrooms and one small bathroom. I look through the door into the largest bedroom. A woman sits on the floral quilt, clutching her pink dressing gown around her body with both arms. She looks up at me, her face bewildered. The two female members of the search team are pulling drawers out of a dressing table, upturning them on the floor, picking through their contents with gloved hands. There's a grey haze in the air. A thread of smoke rises from an ashtray on the bedside cabinet.

Then I hear a shout from one of the other bedrooms. 'Got something here.'

I turn to see another officer stepping on to the landing, holding up a stack of boxed CDs.

Paresh comes up the stairs at a run. He takes the box from the top of the stack and reads the cover for a moment.

'They're all the same, boss. Five of them. They were wedged down the back of the desk with a load of junk. Biros, paperclips – all covered in dust.'

I step across the landing, and Paresh taps the CD case

with his finger. 'Incitement to racial violence. Thrash-metal with race-hate lyrics.'

'Illegal?'

Paresh puts the CD back on the pile in the other officer's hands. 'Illegal. Let's hope we can get him for selling the stuff.'

I watch for another hour until they finish searching the house. It's still dark when the team pack up, leaving a lock-smith working on the door. I walk away with Paresh. A curtain in the house opposite shifts, and I see a man's face looking out at us. A white face.

'We've got him on assaulting a police officer,' Paresh says, still on a high. I'm feeling it too – walking on air, not concrete. Not that we've got much, but right now it feels enough that Vince is in the cells.

Paresh unlocks the car, and we both get in.

'What about her?' I ask.

'Incitement to racial hatred.'

'No! She was *that* pissed off with Vince when she saw the CDs. She never knew they were in the house.'

Paresh shakes his head. 'Who cares? Having her inside will rattle him – even if it's just overnight. That's what counts.'

We're moving through the city now. I watch the street-lights sweep past overhead, enjoying the comfort of just being driven.

'We know Vince is a member of the Scalpers,' Paresh says. 'We get a tip-off that he was in on the Dean Street job, which gives us the excuse to turn his house over. But there's nothing to find. It all looks too clean for a crook like Vince. The man isn't stupid, though. He's got the house clean for a purpose. Some big project?'

'It was almost clean,' I say. 'Not quite.'

'But the CDs were down the back of a desk, covered in dust. My guess is they slipped down there months ago and got forgotten.'

We should be turning left at the next traffic lights, but Paresh steers the car towards the right. That's when I realize where he's taking me.

'This isn't the way to the station.'

'You're going off duty, aren't you?'

'And you aren't,' I remind him. 'You've got a desk load of paperwork to do after that search.'

He shrugs. 'It'll wait five minutes.'

Working with Paresh has gone well tonight. The excitement, danger, curiosity – they've drowned out any anxiety I might have felt from being so close to him. I've been proud of myself. But now, sitting in the car, I get a sudden and unexpected panic jolt. And I find myself panicking about the fact that I'm panicking. Of course.

I force myself to slow my breathing. I deliberately tense then release my shoulder muscles. *I am a professional. This is a professional relationship. I am a professional.*

He turns the car into my own street, slows, pulls up next to my house. Then he turns off the engine.

I'm sitting next to him, looking straight forward, not showing my emotions. It's exactly what I used to do at the height of our relationship. Him too. Pretending to be nothing more than fellow officers. Keeping the secret.

I feel my heart do a back-flip inside my chest as I fumble to undo the seatbelt. 'Thanks for the ride. I'd better . . .'

'Mo?'

I reach for the door handle.

'Mo. Everything that happened . . . you and me . . .'

Damn, but why does he have to start talking about that

right now? I say: 'I've got to go.' But I don't open the door.

Paresh says: 'It meant something, you know? It meant something to me.'

I'm still looking away from him. 'It's done. Finished.'

'I never wanted that,' he says. 'Never.' He puts a hand on the back of my neck and I'm dying inside. I'll hate myself whatever I do now. And I'm wondering if I shouldn't try hating myself for doing something that feels good. Just for a change. Something that'll wash me through with feeling. Leave no room for thought, for doubt.

He's pulling me closer with the gentlest pressure on my neck and shoulder. I could move away but it's easier to turn and face him.

'What . . . what are we doing?'

He shakes his head. 'Shhh.'

I find myself moving towards him and him towards me. My question gone. Everything gone. Just the pressure of my lips on his, of his hand stroking my neck. The whole world submerged by my awareness of this contact. By my awareness of his awareness.

My arms are around him. My hands trying to devour his hair and skin, each movement more vivid with sensation than the last, more urgent.

We're out of the car somehow, though I'm not aware of the kiss being broken, standing pressed full-length against each other. We scramble up the path. My hand is shaking, and I can't get the key into the lock. He's holding my waist, kissing the back of my neck.

I rest my forehead against the door, feeling the cool, smooth paintwork on my skin, knowing this is wrong, unable to stop it happening. Not wanting to. I'll pick up the broken pieces tomorrow. Tomorrow.

Then the light comes on in the hall. I tense up. There are footsteps coming down the stairs just inside.

I feel Paresh freeze. 'What . . . who?'

'I forgot . . . Sal . . . she's . . .'

'Your mother?'

'Staying, yes . . .'

He knocks his hand against the wall. 'Oh, hell!'

And the harshness of his emotion bursts the bubble. He's transformed back into what he really is, and I'm revolted by him. No. I'm revolted by myself.

A shadow crosses the hall window and I hear Sal's voice. 'Mo – is that you?'

'Look,' I whisper. 'This was a . . . I'm sorry . . . this was a mistake.'

Paresh is still facing the wall. He doesn't answer. Instead, he turns, walks back to the car, gets in and drives away. I don't see his expression. And he doesn't see mine.

PART TWO

There was this superintendent I heard about once. Down south somewhere. He was looking for connections between organized crime and the building trade. Following up nasty, greasy allegations about men in suits with seven-figure bank balances.

One year into the investigation and the men in suits were still sleeping peacefully in their luxury beds. What they didn't know was that the superintendent had finally got a warrant to search their offices. If it hadn't been for that, he'd probably be an assistant chief constable by now.

So the super mounted his raid and carried off a couple of boxes of files. You never get smoking guns with that kind of fraud. Even with all the evidence, he couldn't be a hundred per cent that there'd been a crime committed. But it looked like a good start.

Two weeks later the local rag printed a front-page spread on police corruption. The super's photo was right there under the headline, him and a bunch of underworld movers and shakers playing golf together. Apparently, he'd been given free membership of the golf club.

Nothing in the story, really. Just a grubby feeling. But it got people started – digging into the super's background. They knew that all they had to do was throw enough mud at the wall and eventually it would start to stick. I can't remember what it was that got him suspended in the end. But he never finished the investigation.

Chapter 12

We've got a secure storeroom out at Force HQ on the edge of town. That's where we keep all the old documents relating to the more serious of our closed cases. Photographs. Witness statements. Millions of individual items, too precious to chuck. The volume of material grows every year.

That's the problem with murder investigation – too much evidence. Detectives go out and interview the initial witnesses. A separate team puts the interview reports into the Home Office Large Major Inquiry System – known as HOLMES 2 to its friends. The computer trawls the reports and hauls out the names of more people to be interviewed. The detectives go out again. You might start with twenty statements. From there you get forty more names, leading to forty more interview reports. The numbers really start to shoot up after that.

A team of thirty detectives works away feeding the computer system. It doesn't take long before you've got more information than a human head-full. For the computer it's no trouble, though. If a name gets mentioned by more than one source, or if any two witness statements disagree, HOLMES will spot it. No room for a human Sherlock nowadays.

With this particular murder investigation we're already seeing the paperwork start to stack higher. It's another morning briefing. I'm sitting at the back of Room 3, trying to take in what Superintendent Alison Walker is saying. Right now she's going through a list of detectives, allotting tasks. Routine but vital.

Alison sits down, at last, and Paresh takes the stage. I slide my back a few inches lower in my seat. After last night, I want to keep well clear of the man. He must be able to see me, though he doesn't show any sign of recognition. He just gets right on delivering his briefing about last night's raid.

The bag of shoes taken from Vince's house is at the forensic lab being tested – even though no footprints were found in the mosque. The whole parallel investigation idea is looking a bit shaky. We're all still living in denial – officially at least.

'How long are you holding Vince?' someone asks.

'He's out already,' Paresh says. 'The assault was minor, they're saying provoked. What we've charged them for is possession of this . . .'

There's a portable CD player on the front desk. Paresh clicks the button and adjusts the volume control until the speakers hiss. There's a shuffling of bums on seats around Room 3. Then it starts. A fast, relentless drumbeat, a heavily distorted two-chord guitar riff. There might be a third chord – it's hard to make out much. And the vocals. A man screaming himself hoarse. The one word I can make out is 'kill', and that only because it's repeated at the beginning of each line.

Alison gives Paresh the nod, and he clicks the CD player off. The sudden silence is broken by Paresh. 'The lyrics are printed on the inside of the cassette label. I won't read them out. Incitement to racial hatred. Public Order Act, Part 3, Sections 19 to 23. No question.'

'Who listens to *that*?' someone asks.

'You'd be surprised. Stuff like this is big business for gangs like the Scalpers. They can knock the CDs up for practically nothing. All it takes is a home computer. Sell them on for, say, ten quid a throw. Straight to the customer. Music gigs, bars, football games. If it wasn't illegal, probably no one would bother. We found five CDs at Vince's place. Between fifty and a hundred quid's worth.'

'Five identical CDs?' Alison asks.

'Basically, yes.'

'Basically?'

'Same cover, same tracks. But one of the CDs has the tracks in a different order. Again, that points to someone knocking them up in a back bedroom.'

'What's Vince saying about it?' Alison asks.

'Says he never saw them before.'

'And his wife?'

'The same.'

There's an uncomfortable silence, broken by someone in the front row swearing – just loud enough for us all to hear. I guess we all know the stories of defence lawyers using that kind of thing to sway juries in the past.

Alison is trying to round things off on a high note, to keep morale up. 'Where from here, Paresh?'

'We're waiting on forensics for DNA testing on the pig and the blood. And we're still sorting through the list of known racists with farming connections. There are just a handful, but they're scattered all over the country. If we have to interview them, it's going to take time.'

Alison turns to look in my direction. 'What about Community Relations?'

I straighten myself in my chair. 'Out following CID around, trying to smooth the waters.'

She nods. 'I have one special job – for you to handle personally.'

Really, I should be flattered.

Two hours later and I'm hurrying along a basement corridor, listening to the footfalls of the small group of people walking with me. Flickering strip lights, two-tone walls and a powerful smell of antiseptic.

I'm at the back of the group, next to Miriam, Anwar's widow. Her hair is covered, but she isn't wearing a veil. Just ahead of us are Hussayn and a bearded cleric, who hasn't been introduced yet. All wear black. Striding away at the very front is the forensic pathologist, Dr Loné – a rigidly upright African man in a white coat.

Dr Loné takes an abrupt right turn. We follow him. Miriam has to throw in an extra step to keep up. I can hear her flat sandals slipping on the smooth, plastic floor tiles. Then, quite suddenly, the pathologist stops in front of a set of double doors. Just to the left is a white signboard with dark green lettering: 'MORTUARY'.

He says: 'Are you ready?'

The cleric starts speaking, stirring the air with one hand to emphasize his point. I'm guessing the language is Urdu. Miriam is keeping her face angled downwards. Then the cleric stops and clasps his hands in front of him.

Hussayn is nodding. 'The Siyyid says we must have respect for the body. He says there must be a covering always over. At least from the navel to the knee.'

The pathologist nods slowly. 'We do our best. But sometimes it is necessary to . . .' He lets the sentence hang and pulls back an imaginary sheet with his hand.

Hussayn starts to translate, but the cleric cuts him short with another burst of Urdu. Dr Loné rests one hand against the mortuary door. I glance at Miriam. This must be a traumatic enough experience for her without all the delay.

'The Siyyid says that if the body must be uncovered, there will be no woman doctor to see it.'

Dr Loné frowns. I can see a ripple of muscle movement cross his cheek. He takes a breath.

'Shall we go through?' I say.

No one speaks, but after a moment the doctor pushes open one of the doors and we all follow him inside.

The mortuary itself has a harsh functionality about it. There is a workbench and chair over on the left. Stainless-steel trolleys are lined up on the right. But it's the wall straight ahead which pulls all our eyes. There are drawers floor to ceiling along the entire length of the room, arranged like a set of giant, refrigerated filing cabinets.

Dr Loné leaves us staring about the room and steps across to the desk. He bends and runs one finger down a sheet of paper on a clipboard. 'Twenty-eight B.' He's walking along the line of drawers like a man trying to find a book on a library shelf. Then he stops and turns to us. 'If you'd care to inspect?'

Personally, I wouldn't care to. Nor, I suspect, would Miriam. She's been through the formal identification thing already. It was Hussayn who requested the visit – though I suspect he's been leaned on by other members of the community.

Dr Loné pulls on the drawer. It rolls out into the room. 'All covered,' he says, 'as you can see.'

The cleric steps forward and looks down on the shrouded body. I don't follow him. It's strange enough seeing the thing from this distance. A muffled shape, only special now because it once contained a personality. A cadaver. A few kilos of dead flesh. I know all this, but I still find myself wanting to see Anwar's face one more time.

There's been a hushed conversation going on in Urdu. Now Hussayn says: 'Has the body been harmed?'

Dr Loné's hands are still on the handle of the drawer. 'Harmed?'

'Cut? Mutilated?'

'There has been an autopsy. That is all.'

The cleric scowls.

'It's the law,' I say. Then I step forward so I'm looking at them across the width of the body. 'We need the autopsy to help find out who did this.'

'And we need to bury my uncle.'

'Soon.'

I'm trying to keep my voice calm and quiet, my posture unthreatening, but Hussayn is getting louder. He is leaning forward from the waist.

'Waiting like this – it is not good. Should be buried quickly.'

'First the coroner's hearing,' I say. 'That's where you can ask for the body to be released.'

We stand there, staring at each other for a moment. I can feel the chill from the refrigeration. Hussayn's eyes are wide now, as if he is only just in control of his anger and grief. 'This – is – not – good!'

'The body of your uncle is being respected,' I say.

'This is un-Islamic.'

'It is the law.'

'Then the law is against Islam.'

'It's the same law for everyone.'

'We'll make a complaint.'

'Another complaint?'

Hussayn's eyes are watery now. The first tears not quite

shed. He says: 'You don't care what Muslims believe. If the murderer isn't found, it doesn't matter. When he dies he'll be punished in hell. But my uncle was a good Muslim, and you are stopping him from having the burial of a good Muslim.'

I force my hands to unclench. 'And the men who did this? Before they die, how many others will they kill? Will they kill you? Will they kill me?'

Hussayn turns away. The cleric steps back from the body.

'Shall I close now?' Dr Loné asks. And it's somehow a shock to hear his quiet voice.

For a moment no one answers. It's Miriam who breaks the silence. She's still standing next to the door. Her voice is papery and hoarse. 'Close now. No more fight. No more.'

I'm sitting behind the steering wheel of the courtesy car. I've got the keys in my hand, but I know I'm too tired to drive safely out of the hospital car park. I'm washed out from the confrontation in the mortuary. Emotionally and physically. My heart is pounding too fast.

I close my eyes and see the shrouded body again, lying straight, but with feet turned outwards as if the cold air had somehow brought him complete relaxation. Anwar's shape is familiar but softened by the sheet that covers him – a landscape lying under fresh snow.

Then I see another face. Paresh, his pupils dilated, sweat beading on his forehead, light shining all around him. An angel. Like he was when we were last together. Everything in the room glowing. He mouths the words without letting them sound. 'I love you.'

I whisper back to him: 'If something had happened, you would have told me. Wouldn't you?'

He doesn't answer.

I think of the plastic yoghurt carton in the bathroom at home. I used it first thing this morning, collected my midstream sample just like the instructions said. Then I placed it in the bottom of the bath while I got dressed. All I needed to do was break open the sealed plastic container, dip the testing stick in the urine. Confirm that I'm not pregnant. But after breakfast I went up to the bathroom again and poured my sample down the toilet.

Don't ask me why. A psychology degree teaches you how to analyse other people – not yourself.

I don't want to open my eyes, but I do. I force my hand to lift out of my lap and place the key in the ignition. The engine fires and I'm away, driving out of the car park, joining the flow of traffic on the main road. I start back towards the station, then change my mind and turn off towards Waterfields.

I'm waiting at the traffic lights halfway down West Park Road, my head feeling a little clearer now. I look in the rear-view mirror and notice a car that looks like one I saw behind me a few minutes ago. The driver looks white, male I think, though there's a reflection on the windscreen so I can't be sure. The lights change and I accelerate smoothly away. After a hundred yards, I turn left on to Northdown Street, then quickly left again. I'm driving down Cornwell Street, with tall factory buildings on either side, looking at the empty road behind me in the rear-view. I get fifty yards before the same car turns onto the road behind me.

Suddenly I'm thinking fast and straight. I can feel strength in my arms and legs. A surge of adrenaline.

So I accelerate, increasing the gap to about a hundred yards, then turn off on to a side road and jam on the brakes. I'm out of the car in half a second and running back towards the corner. I've got perhaps nine more seconds before he reaches me. I'm standing with my back to the red-brick wall, counting under my breath, half hoping this isn't my attacker from the other night. But only half.

Seven seconds to go and I notice two punjabi suited women steering pushchairs down the pavement on the other side of the road from me, approaching the corner. I wave my hand, gesturing them back. They're looking at me as they stroll forward, puzzled expressions on their faces.

Five seconds. I can hear a car engine approaching at speed.

'Get back!'

They stop directly opposite.

Four. Three.

'Back now!'

There's a screech of tyres sliding on the road, and the blue car slews around the corner. Too fast. It is a white male driving – a face I know from somewhere. He sees my car, then he sees me. But his own car has slipped too far across the road already. One wheel hits the kerbstone next to the two women. The rear of the car bounces up on to the pavement. One of the women screams. The car drops to low gear and the engine roars. He's away, leaving a rubber trail on the road. And I'm running towards the women, both standing, both clutching the handles of their pushchairs.

'Are you all right?'

No answer. One of them kneels down and pulls her child from its seat, holds it close to her chest. She's comforting it in Gujerati, though it looks unshaken by the near-miss. I try asking the women if they want to make a complaint about the driver, but they have almost no English.

I look down the road in the direction the car escaped in. He's got away again – assuming it is the man who attacked me the other night. This time, though, I'm in control.

I take out my notebook and write down the registration number.

At this point I should be contacting the station on my radio. Telling them what's just happened. Alison would then get the registration number checked. She'd find a name and address. Before I was even back at the station, she'd be out making the arrest. And maybe – just maybe – she'd have caught Anwar's murderer. Assuming the car wasn't stolen.

I'm watching the two women wheeling their pushchairs away. I can feel my heart-rate begin to slow. And I'm thinking that perhaps following procedure by the book isn't always the best thing. So I take out my mobile phone and dial. I hear it ring three times before the click. 'Community Relations Office,' sings a voice. 'How can I help you?'

'Leah, it's Marjorie. Anyone there?'

'Sergeant Morris just walked out.'

'Go chase after him. Get him to call me.'

The phone clicks again as she hangs up. I'm left standing there on the street corner, thinking about the risk I'm taking with my career. I've already got one complaint hanging over me. That doesn't leave much leeway, even for an inspector.

I pace down the pavement, away from the corner. The wall next to me is too high to see over. It's topped with razor wire and tattered shreds of polythene. I look at it for a moment, trying to figure out where I've seen it before. Then I get it – I'm standing just outside the courtyard that leads to Anwar's factory. If I had a ladder, I could look over at the fire escape where he hung, bleeding to death.

What did Paresh say about the racist attacks? They all had the same flavour, as if they'd been arranged to look good in a photograph. The murder certainly fits that pattern.

I walk further along the pavement, keeping my head angled up, searching for a gap in the wall – somewhere to see through. There isn't anywhere.

Then my mobile chimes.

'Hello?'

'You all right, Mo?'

Ivor's voice. Worried, I think.

'Listen. I need you to check out a car registration number.'

'You want me to . . .'

'And keep it quiet. Especially from Alison Walker.'

He doesn't argue, but I know he doesn't like it. I read out the number and get him to repeat it back to me.

'Can you do it right now?'

He hesitates before speaking. 'That woman . . .'

'Superintendent Walker?'

'Her. She's been round here asking all kinds of questions about you.'

'Tell me later,' I say. 'Right now, get me a name and address to go with that car.'

'Where will you be?'

'Nowhere. Just waiting for the information.'

He grunts and hangs up. I turn back to the high wall and try to focus my thoughts. If the body was hung up to look spectacular, that implies an audience to see it. But with a wall this high around the back of the building, I can't think of a place where the audience could be standing – if not in the factory itself.

I end up walking right around the block without finding anywhere to view the murder scene. I turn in at the court-yard entrance and look up at the tall factory buildings around me. Even from those, there can't be many places where anyone could have got an unobscured view.

I wander across to the bottom of the fire escape and look up through the metal grille above my head. Then I look down to the floor where the blood must have pooled. There's no sign of it now. Someone has done a good job of cleaning it away. Then I look at the base of the wall and see a few spots. Dried blood splashes. I close my eyes and turn away. Suddenly I don't want to be standing there any more.

I'm halfway across the courtyard, heading for the exit, when I stop myself and turn for another look. All the incident tape has gone now. There's nothing stopping me from going up to the very murder scene.

The metal fire escape clangs under my feet. I turn the first corner and glance at the bolts that hold the metal to the wall. Rust has bled streaks on to the brick just below each point of contact. I'm on the second flight, climbing above the messy courtyard. A few feet to go. But I stop short, unwilling to take the final step.

I put one hand on the iron railing to steady myself. Then I turn and look around me. There are no windows in this wall of the factory. It's a place of old iron piping. The ugliest aspect of an ugly building. Tucked away out of sight around a corner. North facing. Always in the shadow. The closest structure is the back of another factory. A short wall separates the two properties here. Behind it are some bins, a narrow passageway, another fire escape.

And that's it – the only place close and high enough to view the murder – the other fire escape.

I'm back on the ground and running across the courtyard towards the exit. If I go out on to the road and keep right, I should reach the entrance to the next factory after a couple of turns. I don't get a chance. My mobile chimes again.

'Hello?'

'Mo, where did that car number come from?'

'Did you get a name?'

'Yes . . .'

'Well?'

'It's just . . .'

'Spit it out, Ivor.'

'It's one of ours, ma'am. It's an unmarked police car.'

Chapter 13

What is it they say? 'It's hard not to be paranoid when everyone's out to get you'? Something like that. So I don't go back to the station. Nor do I go home.

Instead, I come way across town to Abbey Park – a couple of miles from Waterfields. There are enough areas of thick planting here to give the whole place the feel of a maze. You can't see far in any direction. Right now that suits me fine. I'm standing under the hexagonal roof of the 'pagoda'. The ceiling above me is painted with pictures of Chinese children in traditional costume. Covering the artwork is a protective layer of heavily graffitied Perspex.

Looking out between the pillars, I can see the rest of the Peace Garden around me. A large pond. Ornamental bridges. I search the water for koi carp, but all I can see are a couple of coke cans and a Styrofoam chip-tray.

After that I sit on the bench and wait.

It takes Sergeant Ivor Morris half an hour to reach me. I see him walking along the path, glancing around him. I guess neither of us is used to the cloak-and-dagger stuff.

I get up and wave. 'Over here.'

He doesn't say anything until he's standing right next to me. 'Bloody hell, ma'am. This is a mess.' He's talking about my career, not the pond.

'Cut the formality, Ivor. We've gone way beyond that now.'

'I guess.'

He stands there looking at the pond, then at the little bridge. Looking anywhere except at me.

'Just tell me what you've found,' I say.

He shakes his head. 'No one wanted to talk.'

I sit back on the bench. 'Damn.'

'But . . .'

'But . . .?'

'But the secretary in the Race Crime Unit . . . I helped her brother with something a couple of years back.' He sits next to me on the bench and lowers his voice. 'I got it all from her, but don't drop the girl in it, OK?'

'God, Ivor, this is like getting blood out of a stone. You got what?'

'Everyone's been told to keep quiet. Civilians weren't even supposed to know. The secretary "overheard".'

'What? She overheard what?'

'You're one of the suspects in the murder investigation.'

'One of the . . . oh, shit!'

'HOLMES didn't like the way your name kept coming up.'

'It's just a computer,' I say. But my mind is doing a quick count of the evidence it must have seen. All the people in the factory will have been interviewed. They'll all have mentioned me. Plus the men at the mosque. My fingerprints are all over Anwar's office. The phone records show up a couple of calls from me to him. At least one of them from my home to his. My name on the scene-of-crime list. His complaint against me. It's that last one that makes the picture bad.

'Your name turns up, they have to investigate,' Ivor says.

'No, they don't. Not like this! Wasting an officer's time tailing me?'

'They're scared as hell, that's why.'

'I don't understand.'

Ivor turns to look at me, his forehead creased into a deep frown. 'You heard the news, didn't you?'

I get that stomach-clenching feeling again. 'What news?'

'Oh, hell. You don't know.'

'Ivor?'

'It was on the lunchtime news. The Home Secretary – he's ordered an inquiry. Waterfields. Police handling of the riots. Everything. Calling in some senior officer from outside the county.'

And suddenly it all makes perfect sense. They don't want to suspend me because it'll look like racist discrimination. That's the chief constable's decision. At the same time, everyone lower down is looking for a scapegoat to take the blame for the riot. HOLMES has conveniently given someone an excuse to slur my name. No one needs proof of anything. The suspicion is enough.

'Who gave the order for me to be followed?'

Ivor shuffles his feet for a moment. 'You don't need to ask that.'

'Superintendent Alison Walker.'

He stands up. 'Just pretend you don't know. That's the best way.'

'Perhaps.'

'What you going to do now, Mo?'

I stare into the distance for a long moment, chewing over the options in my mind. 'There's a photo shoot later. But before that I've got an overdue appointment at St Catherine's School.'

He scratches his chin. 'Should be safe enough.'

'And there's something else you can do for me, Ivor.'

'Ma'am?'

'Those fingerprints they found on the steering wheel of

my car – we should have heard something about them by now. Could you follow it up – ask your friend at the forensic garage if they've sent in the report yet.'

Head teacher Mr Dunbar doesn't seem surprised to see me standing in the doorway of his office. He gets up from his desk and his rosy cheeks wrinkle into a smile.

'Inspector.'

'I hope you don't mind . . .'

He beckons me inside. 'Come to take up my offer of a job?'

I share his laugh with as much sincerity as I can manage, but my own job doesn't look anything like as secure as it did the last time I was here.

'I could do with the help,' he says. 'Short-staffed at the moment. Can't get the supply teachers in.'

'I'll think about it,' I say.

He leads me over to the comfy chairs and we sit facing each other.

'Is it about Roddy Wellan?' he asks.

'No, actually. It's another of your students.'

Mr Dunbar sits forward in his chair and frowns. 'Who is it and what's he or she done?'

'Nothing,' I say quickly. 'And I only have a first name.'

'Oh.'

'Unusual name, though. Niko.'

The head sits back and nods. 'We only have one Niko. Slight build. Fair hair. Nervous type.'

I nod. 'I met him already. A couple of days back.'

'At the Majestic Hotel?'

'On the street playing football. He talked to me. Said some things . . . Could you tell me something about him?'

Mr Dunbar purses his lips for a moment. His hands are

in his lap, the fingers interlocked. 'Niko. What can I say about the boy? Family name Medigovich. One of a group of asylum-seekers housed in the Majestic Hotel.'

The headmaster pauses, his expression troubled. 'Inspector, whether or not Niko's family have a legitimate claim for asylum in this country . . . my concern is solely the boy's educational welfare. The information you are asking for . . .'

'Is there a doubt about the asylum claim?'

'Perhaps. I don't know. His family fled from the Balkans – to Italy initially. Mafia boats took them across the Aegean. Dumped them in the sea in the middle of the night – child and all. They had to swim the last hundred yards to the beach. Then they moved to Germany for a couple of months before deciding on Britain. That all makes it complicated. Is there a legitimate claim in the eyes of British law? That's your department, inspector.'

'Don't ask me about asylum law,' I say.

A bell rings in the corridor outside. Mr Dunbar doesn't react. Then the ringing stops and I hear a burst of laughter, running footsteps, the happy voices of children released from their lessons, exploding into break time.

The headmaster unfolds his hands. 'What is your interest in Niko – if not the asylum claim?'

'It's just something he said.' I look at my knees for a moment. 'How's Niko's school work?'

'Much as you'd expect. It's not easy for him. Though he has done well in picking up the language.'

'Has he seemed worried lately? Any behavioural prob-lems?'

Mr Dunbar stands up and steps across to the window. 'There were some problems with Niko's behaviour when he first arrived. Some minor vandalism. A couple of fights.

Then . . . he'd been with us about a month . . . his teacher caught him with a knife.'

'And?'

'It was only a penknife, but even so . . . School policy and all that. I invited his parents in for a chat. Since then I've tried to be more tolerant with the boy.'

Mr Dunbar raps a knuckle on the glass and then points through the window. I see him mouthing an instruction to someone in the playground outside. Then he turns towards me again.

'Sorry about that.'

There's another pause, then he says: 'It was ethnic cleansing. That's what brought Niko's family to England. They lived in a small town, from what I can understand. In a rural area at the foot of a mountain somewhere near the border. Other Serbs, Albanians, Romanies, a few Armenians. A community of communities.'

Where have I heard that phrase before?

Mr Dunbar shakes his head. 'Niko can't even have been born when the troubles reached them. First it was the Serbs – his own people – throwing out the others. Then, after the war, it was revenge attacks from the Albanians against the Serbs. Niko's uncle and an older brother . . . hacked to death. His father was away when it happened or he would have been killed too.'

I'm remembering the nightmare pictures Niko painted with his words. Wondering how old he was when all this happened. But age doesn't matter. No one should have to see things like that.

'Has he been behaving badly towards you?' Mr Dunbar asks.

'No. Strangely, perhaps.'

The headmaster nods. 'When you came to do our

assembly – I was wondering how he would react. You weren't to know, of course, but the men who came to take his family away – they were wearing police uniform. This is what his father told me. The bodies were still handcuffed when they found them. Hands behind their backs.'

Chapter 14

I've gritted my teeth and driven over to Force HQ, just outside the city, for my last appointment of the day. A photo shoot for our new leaflet: 'Welcoming Diversity in the Police Service.' It's part of the latest recruitment drive. We've got a mixture of white, black and Asian officers, all looking their best. Alison is here as well – to prove that the glass ceiling has been shattered.

Right now we're mingling in the car park, with the HQ itself as a backdrop. It should make for a good image. With the warm light of the late-afternoon sun, the building looks almost friendly.

This is very much the chief constable's initiative. He's been doing the rounds, thanking everyone for turning up, pressing the flesh. Now it's my turn.

He shows me his sharp white teeth. 'All well?'

'Yes, sir.'

Perhaps there's a hesitation about my answer. Maybe he knows something already.

'You must tell me,' he says, 'if there are problems. My job to direct policy. Can't do that without the information.'

He examines me, his intelligent eyes searching my face. I do want to tell him. But I don't want to stir things up, make them worse than they are already. He's still staring. I start to crumble.

'There is . . .'

'Yes?'

'. . . Alison will have already told you, I'm sure.'

'Then she should be here.'

He looks across to her. She's standing next to a black BMW, questioning a woman from the PR company.

'Sir . . . I don't think . . .'

But it's too late. The chief has caught her eye. She's making her excuses, walking towards us.

She smiles at each of us in turn. 'Sir. Marjorie.'

'Inspector Akanbai was briefing me. Concerns you as well.'

They're both looking at me, waiting for me to speak. I could try to back out, raise some other question, pretend it was nothing serious. If I go forward I don't know what will happen.

'It was a dangerous driving incident,' I say.

Alison's smile is looking brittle now. The chief's face is neutral.

'A car driving at speed in a built-up area. It mounted the pavement. Came within inches of hitting two young children. The two mothers don't speak much English.'

'Do we know the driver?' asks the chief.

'No,' I say. 'But I know the car.'

Alison has been teetering on the edge of some decision all this time. Now she makes her move. 'There were no injuries. The women haven't made a complaint. I think we can . . .'

'A police car?' says the chief.

'Yes.'

'In hot pursuit?'

Alison hesitates. This is when I know for sure that she hasn't told the Chief about HOLMES and me.

'It was an unmarked car,' I say. 'I believe the target was me.'

The chief's face is still neutral as he turns to look at Alison.

'Sir. I'd like to speak to you, please. Alone.'

He thinks about this for a moment, then shakes his head. 'Akanbai believes she was being followed. Why attempt secrecy?'

Alison is squirming in her shoes. There's nothing she can do but tell the story I already know – the computer turning up my name, her decision to mount surveillance. Through all this, she speaks to the chief as if I wasn't there. He gives nothing away. Not a nod or a shake of the head. When Alison has finished, he turns to me.

'Anything to add?'

'No, sir.'

He's looking at the super again. 'A narrow line,' he says. 'One side is thorough investigation. The other side and your motives can be misconstrued.'

Alison's face reddens.

The chief holds her gaze for a second. 'Question to ask yourself. What would an internal inquiry say – which side of the line have you been on?' Then he turns to me. 'Same question for you, inspector.'

'I'm sorry it had to come out like this,' Alison says. Though her hand has reached out to touch my elbow as she speaks, I know she's addressing this to the big fish. 'That line of investigation has been closed already. You're not a suspect any more.'

The chief shows his teeth again. 'Then we all understand each other. Let's try to keep it that way.'

I sleep naked. Usually. Tonight I feel more comfortable in shorts and a T-shirt. Something to do with having Sal staying with me. That and Niko's story. I think Sal can sense there's something disturbing me. She sits on the edge of my bed, chatting for a few minutes before going off towards the spare room.

She calls from the landing. 'Wake me if you need anything.'

The chance would be a fine thing. She sleeps like a rock.

I'm thinking that it should take me a long time to get to sleep after all that's happened today. I'm usually a bit hyper like that. My mind keeping me from dropping off, or waking me half an hour before the alarm is due to sound. But that's the last thing I remember thinking.

I jolt into a sitting position. The sound is fading in my mind, and I can't figure out if it was a dream or real. Everything is black. My heart pounds. I lie stiff and still, listening, holding my breath. Then I hear it again. A movement from downstairs. Outside the front door – that's what it sounds like.

I roll over, reach for my bedside table, grab the panic button. Press the switch. There's no sound, but a small red light starts pulsing just below the button itself.

I drop myself out of bed, landing softly on the floor. There's another noise – the metallic click of the brass letterbox. I crawl forward, my bare knees rubbing on the carpet. There's a faint smell in the air. Familiar, though I can't put a name to it. I'm out of the bedroom. Across the landing, careful to avoid that one creaky floorboard. The letterbox moves again.

I'm at the top of the stairs, looking down to the hall. There's a rectangle of dim orange light in the blackness of the door. The letterbox flap is open. A shadow moves across it and I hear a scraping noise. The quietest of sounds, yet harsh in the night. Plastic rubbing against metal.

I'm moving down the stairs, placing each foot. Halfway now. I can see something poking through the open slit. The smell is stronger than before.

I reach the hall. Less than two paces from my attacker, if that's who he is. I hear a new sound. Quieter still than the movement of the letterbox. The trickle of water running down the inside of the door. A wet semicircle is darkening the mat, creeping outwards from the foot of the door.

Not water. I almost choke as the fumes waft over me. Petrol fumes. And suddenly I'm not trying to keep an attacker out of the house. He doesn't even want to get in.

These are the thoughts bouncing off the inside of my skull: snatch the door open, or scream, or run upstairs to wake Sal. But as soon as he knows I'm awake, he'll throw in a match and run. Any sound will do it. Then I'm thinking of the spare bedroom. The back of the house. Wet towels under the door. I'm balancing the fire brigade response time against a pool of petrol.

He's pouring from the can so slowly that I wouldn't have heard it at all if I'd been upstairs. The nozzle is right in front of me. So close. And for a moment I'm transfixed. It can't be for more than a fraction of a second, but I'm thinking, ridiculously, that I could put my finger in the nozzle, stop the flow. Then he tips the can a few more degrees and the liquid starts to flow more quickly.

It's at that moment, frozen in horrified fascination, that I see how methodical my would-be killer really is. Organized. I'm his target. If he sees me outside, I don't think he'll strike the match.

I'm edging away. Then I run, barefoot, towards the back door, grabbing a long, pointed knife from the kitchen as I pass. I turn the key. The lock clicks. Then I'm out, my bare feet on the dewy grass of the back garden. Exhaling fumes.

Inhaling damp night air. Listening for the tread of a second attacker. I have perhaps thirty seconds before the can is empty and he lights the match.

I'm round the side of the house, feeling the stab of sharp stones caught between the concrete path and the soft skin of my feet. I'm gripping the knife handle so tightly that my fingers are aching. He won't see me till I turn the corner. I half run down the side of the house. There are sirens in the distance. I'm at the high wooden gate that separates the front from the back. The sirens are louder.

I crash the gate open, hurl myself around the corner. He's there. His balaclava-covered face towards me. The petrol can falling from his hands. I'm lunging, arm outstretched, knife-point forward. He sidesteps, grabs my forearm as it passes his chest, gripping hard, then ramming it away from his body. There's an explosion of pain as it smashes into the corner of the brick wall. The knife is falling.

The sirens are loud, but I'm not hearing them. All my awareness is focused on the two eyes staring at me. Then he pushes me, hard enough to send me sprawling backwards. He vaults over my body as he runs. Disappearing down the side of the house towards the shadows of the back garden. I'm half on the path, half in the bushes, feeling the throb of pain growing steadily in my right arm. The pounding of his footsteps is gone now, drowned by the scream of approaching sirens.

I lie still, looking up towards the sky, but all I can see is the image of my attacker's eyes. Wide circles, the whites showing all the way around. I can see emotion in them, though I can't read it. And to my surprise I can find nothing of the hatred that I'd thought would be there.

Sal does wake up in the end, though only when one of the

forensic team blunders into the spare bedroom by mistake. He was looking for the bathroom. Too much strong coffee, I guess. Sal sees this white-suited figure standing in the doorway, back-lit. I'd probably have screamed too if it had been me.

She's frantic with worry after that, of course. It's an hour before I can persuade her that she's safe to take a sleeping pill.

'They shouldn't have . . . shouldn't have let it happen,' she says between sobs. She means the police force.

'No, Sal.'

'It never used to be like this.'

I hand her the box of tissues and silently wish that Dad was still alive. He always managed to bridge the gap between Sal and me. He'd know what to say, how to calm her. She takes a tissue and smears away the tear stains.

'Go to bed, Sal.'

'When I married your dad, there were people who . . . who said things. Racist things. But nothing like this.'

'I know.'

Her hand tightens into a fist and she bangs it down on the table. 'They have no right!'

'No.'

There's a fire in her eyes now, and I'm wondering if one sleeping pill is going to be enough.

'They should bring back hanging for people like that.'

'I'll fix you a cup of cocoa.'

She alternates between sorrow and anger after that. I make soothing noises, while keeping half an eye on a scene-of-crime officer who's working in the hall. Then the pill kicks in and Sal's eyes suddenly dull. I steer her up the stairs to the spare bedroom. The last thing I hear her say is: 'Lock the front door before you turn in.' A second after that, she's out for the count.

I get the last soco to take the mat away with her when she leaves. Then I wipe down the inside of the door, till I'm satisfied there are no drops of liquid petrol remaining. The fumes take longer to clear. They've set a couple of unfortunate officers patrolling the area through the night. Even so, I keep the downstairs windows closed.

My mind is slowing down at last, so I climb the stairs and drop on to the bed. I can feel my arm throbbing under the bandage. Only a shallow cut – though I guess it's going to bruise pretty badly. The real damage isn't to my flesh.

For about five minutes I don't dare to close my eyes for fear of what I might see. I look at the patches of light on the ceiling, cast by the streetlamps outside. I look at the pattern of folds in the curtain. And then it hits me that I'll never go to sleep again unless I take the risk, so I close my eyes. No images come to my mind. I make the muscles in my arms and shoulders tense up, then let them go. Tense and relax. Relax. That's the idea I'm aiming for. Then the phone rings.

I lunge across and grab the receiver. 'Yes!'

'Mo. I just heard.'

'Paresh . . .'

'Are you all right?'

Perhaps it's the shock of all that's happened, but I lash out with a: 'What do *you* think!'

I can hear a rustling sound, as if he's passing the phone from one hand to the other. Then he says: 'You want me to come round?'

I look at the clock. 'Are you in bed?'

'No.'

'Well, you should be.'

'I'm in my car.'

That one catches me with my guard down. More concern than I'd expected. 'Well, you can . . . you can get out of the car. Go back to bed.'

'I'm parked outside your house.'

When I open the door, he is already standing on the path, waiting. He steps inside and his arms are encircling me. I don't even think of fighting it this time. He backs me into the hall until I feel the cool of the wall behind me. I'm pressing my face into his neck, breathing the gentle smell of his warm skin. I need to fill my lungs with it. I take so many deep breaths that the oxygen starts to make me light-headed, but I haven't had enough.

He's still holding me – his arms wrapped around my shoulders so closely that it seems as if I'm being enfolded within him. And he whispers: 'I need you.'

It's only now, with the tension falling away, that I know how taut my body must have been. I angle my head upwards, brushing my cheek against his, allowing the sensation of touch to flood through me.

His lips have found mine, and all I can do is drink the kiss. He holds my head in his hands and kisses my forehead, my hair, my eyelids. Then he pulls away a few inches and looks into my face, searching. 'You can't stay here,' he says.

'It's safe now.'

'No.'

'Yes. They're keeping watch.'

'They?'

'A couple of uniforms. Out there somewhere.'

Paresh looks to the door. He's frowning when he turns back towards me.

'It's OK,' I say. 'They'll think it's work. Don't worry.'

This time it's me moving my face towards his. He starts to back away, but I pull him towards me with my arms around his shoulders. By the time our lips touch, all his resistance is gone. This kiss lasts longer.

'Did you mean it the other day,' I say, 'that you still love me?'

He nods.

'Say it.'

'I said it already.'

'Say it now.'

'I love you.'

'And you still want me?'

'I want you.'

I see the words forming in his mouth. I hear them being spoken. And I'm swearing to myself that it's the truth. Whatever's gone before, and whatever is going to happen tonight, he does want me at this moment. He believes he loves me. And right now that's enough evidence to chance my dignity on.

I'm going to show him the test kit from the chemist. With him at least knowing – that has to make it easier. I won't be able to put it off any more if he's waiting for an answer. The result will be negative, I'm sure. Even if it wasn't, he'd be here to help me pull through.

But there's something else we have to deal with before we can talk about pregnancy. So I say: 'I lied to you.'

'You . . .'

I put my fingers on his lips. 'I lied when you asked me if I'd read the letter.'

He steps back, away from my hand. Then he turns his head, but not quickly enough to hide his sudden anxiety.

'I was hurting too much to look at it,' I say. 'But if what you wrote still matters, then tell me now. Does it still matter?'

'Yes.' He is still facing away from me, and he speaks so quietly that I catch only the hiss at the end of the word.

'If you want me now,' I say, 'you have to tell me.'

He steps down the hall, putting more distance between us, then turns. 'I never stopped loving you. But the longer we were together . . . don't you see . . . it was only going to hurt you more. That's what the letter said.'

I'm trying to make sense of his words. Putting the clues together. Then it comes to me that he must have been cheating, and that was why our relationship had to be secret. 'It was another woman!'

'No!'

'Then what?'

'You don't understand. It couldn't last.'

The more he holds back from telling me his reasons, the more nervous I'm getting. But I push on anyway. 'Tell – me – why!'

'My family . . . they have to agree, or I can't . . .'

'Can't be my boyfriend?'

'I need my parents' permission to marry you.'

Paresh has a way of catching me unprepared. I guess it's something to do with our different backgrounds. Different assumptions. Part of me is feeling relieved that it wasn't something terrible. And part of me is reeling because this is the nearest I've ever got to a proposal of marriage.

'It's our culture,' he says

'I've only met them a few times,' I say. 'We got on all right.'

'It won't work.'

'Invite me round. Let them get to know me better.'

'My mother . . .' He rubs a hand through his hair. 'She'll never agree.'

I take a step towards him. 'We don't know that yet.'

'I'll never be able to marry you.'

'*Never*?' He's using the word like he owns it. '*Never*?'

'You don't understand.'

'Then tell me in some kind of way that makes sense.'

He says: 'It's not a colour thing.'

That's when the alarm bells start ringing in my head, because I hadn't even mentioned colour. And suddenly I'm not sure I want to know what he's about to say. But Paresh isn't going to keep the secret any longer. It's like he's got something bitter inside him. He's tried holding it back all this time, but the taste hasn't gone away. Now he just wants to spit it out and be done with it. 'I'm their eldest son,' he says. 'They'll only let me marry a Hindu.'

I open my mouth, but I'm too stunned to do more than echo his words. '. . . a Hindu . . .'

He nods.

'Your mother told you not to marry me because I'm not Hindu?'

He nods again, but I've known him long enough to recognize this second gesture as only a half-truth.

'Perhaps I'll become a Hindu,' I say. 'Will she let me marry you then?'

His hands are clenched on either side of him.

'Or is it because my grandfather was black?'

'White or black – it wouldn't make any difference.'

'But Indian would?'

'This isn't from me . . .'

'But you're going along with it!'

Suddenly there isn't enough distance between us. I should run upstairs and lock myself in my room. Instead, I find myself advancing towards him.

'It's her culture,' he says.

'To be racist?'

'She's trying to protect her culture.'

'Keeping the races separate? Just like bloody apartheid!'

'No!'

'Just like Vince the Prince!'

'If you were Indian you'd understand!'

I'm shouting and my arm is swinging through the air. 'Racist pig!' On the word 'pig' my open hand connects with his cheek, sending his head twisting to the side. I stand there, my palm stinging, daring him with my eyes to hit me back.

Instead, he shouts: 'You never understood, did you!'

I slap him again, harder than before. The same hand. The same cheek. 'Out of my house!'

I can see the anger in his eyes. He's on the brink, only just able to hold himself back. He kicks at the kitchen door, splintering the lowest panel. 'It's her, not me!'

'You fucking racist fucking hypocrite!'

That does it for Paresh. His hand swings, and I'm stumbling back, aware that I've been slapped across the face, not yet feeling the pain. My heel crashes against the radiator.

There are footsteps outside. A fist hammers on the door. 'Police!' It's a man's voice.

I look at Paresh. He looks right back at me. There's no hiding from each other now.

More hammering. I turn away and open the door.

It's a constable. Nervous. 'Ma'am, I heard . . .' He looks past me and sees Paresh. 'Sir . . . I . . .'

I say: 'Inspector Gupta was just leaving.'

'Ma'am, you're bleeding.'

I put a finger to my chin, touch the wet streak below my lip. 'It's nothing. I slipped. Nothing.'

Paresh leaves, and it feels like this is the real moment when our relationship ends. He steps past me through the door without even his shoulder brushing mine. He doesn't look back.

Chapter 15

Friday morning. I phone in sick. In my absence, Greenway is the senior member of the Community Relations Unit. He gets to hold the reins of power for a day at least. In practice that means he makes sure everyone in the team is getting on with the jobs they've already been assigned, backing up the murder investigation. He also gets to attend the briefing. That's one job I'm glad to relinquish.

It's only at nine thirty, when Sal comes to bring me a cup of tea in bed, that she notices the mark on my lip.

'Is that a cut?'

I touch it experimentally. It feels a bit swollen. 'It's nothing.'

'You've got a bruise coming up on your cheek.'

I guess she thinks this is the result of the attack. She managed to sleep through the second instalment of last night's drama just like she did with the first. I haven't told her anything about my final break with Paresh.

She takes my hand and squeezes it gently. 'How's the arm this morning?'

'OK. A bit achy.'

'I'll change the bandage for you after breakfast.'

I take a sip of tea. She's made it sweet and milky.

She watches me for a moment. Then she says: 'He made a real mess of the kitchen door.'

'Who?'

'You tell me.' She tilts her head slightly but keeps her eyes fixed on mine. 'The lowest panel has a crack right down it.'

'Oh,' I say. 'That.'

'*That.*'

'One of the officers put his foot through it. An accident.'

It's only a half-lie. I'm sure Paresh didn't set out to break the thing.

'Well, you should complain.' She reaches out and runs a hand back through my hair. 'What am I saying? You get some more sleep. Make a complaint tomorrow.'

She closes the door behind her. I listen for her departing footsteps. I can hear the ticking of my bedside alarm clock. A blackbird calls somewhere out in the garden. And I'm just thinking that I must have missed it when I hear the creak of that one rogue floorboard on the landing as she steps away from my door.

She's gone and it's time to sleep. I turn over and look at the curtains. Leaf patterns in green and gold, made bright by the sun. I close my eyes. Alison can't have me suspended now the chief constable is on my side. I can sort out the rest of my life tomorrow. Have the kitchen door fixed. I'll even get out the toolbox and screw down the creaky floorboard. Time enough to sort out my computer and find out why it listed the files in the wrong order. To visit the hotel where Niko's family live. To ask about the other fire escape next to where Anwar died. To find out about my car in the forensic garage. The fingerprints.

I turn over again.

The fingerprints.

I prop myself up on the pillows, take the phone from the bedside table and key in the number. 'Hello? Is Sergeant Morris around?'

There's a pause, then Ivor's voice comes on the line. 'Ma'am? You all right?'

'I'm fine.'

It feels strange talking to my sergeant from bed. I swing my legs out from under the quilt and sit up straight, feet on the floor. I'm only wearing shorts and a T-shirt, so the move doesn't help that much.

Ivor sounds just about as uneasy as I do. 'They said . . . last night . . .'

'They were exaggerating.'

'And you're off sick today. I thought . . .'

'Nothing serious. I'm feeling wrecked this morning. Probably sleeping in all those petrol fumes.'

'God.'

He's having a hard time with this. So I pull the conversation back to what I think is safer ground. 'Listen, Ivor, you were going to get in touch with your friend from the forensic garage. The fingerprints on my steering wheel?'

He hesitates before answering, and I can hear the sound of background conversation in the office. Then he says: 'Something's just come up. I need to deliver the report in person.'

'Come on,' I say. 'Just spit it out. What did he tell you?'

Instead of giving me an answer, he repeats his last sentence – but this time slower, emphasizing every word. '*I need to deliver the report in person.*'

It's my turn to stop and think then. 'Someone just walk into the office?'

'That's correct.'

'Someone from Community Relations?'

'No.'

'One of Alison Walker's people?'

'Kind of worse than that.'

It takes me a moment to figure out who might be worse in Ivor's eyes than a member of Alison's team. 'Not the woman herself?'

He makes a strangled coughing noise. 'May I deliver that report now?'

I don't really want anyone from work to see me like I am this morning. I'm not sure how much of what happened has leaked out already. That depends on the constable who saw Paresh leave. He looked like a bright lad. Bright enough to work out something of what had gone on. In another twenty-four hours my lip won't be so swollen. A bit of make-up should hide the bruising on my cheek.

I say: 'Can't the report wait till tomorrow?'

Ivor says: 'No, ma'am, it can't.'

It's one of those days when a dull pain follows me around, trailing a couple of inches behind my head whenever I move too suddenly. This kind of thing usually happens when I get too little sleep, and just occasionally when I get too much.

I tread across the room to the dressing table and, very slowly, pull on a pair of black jeans. Then I worry that perhaps I should make the meeting more formal. It seems wrong to wear uniform on a day when I'm off sick, so I compromise with a pair of cream cotton trousers, passably ironed, and a dark green blouse. The clothes have helped, but not much. The woman in the bathroom mirror still has a battered face and a bandaged arm.

It takes Ivor an hour and a half to escape from the station and drive across town to see me. I'm watching out of an upstairs window, so I see his car as soon as it turns off from the main road. He comes down the avenue at about twenty miles an hour, then drives right past the front door without changing speed. It's another hundred yards before the brake lights come on and he slows to a stop. He sits tight for a couple of minutes, then gets out of the car and walks back towards the house.

I'm behind the front door when he rings the bell. I count to three before opening it.

'Got here as quick as I could,' he says.

'What was all that about out there?' I gesture towards the place where he's parked his car.

He steps inside and closes the door. 'Had to see if I was being followed.'

I hear a door open behind me as Sal comes out of the kitchen.

'Followed?' she says. 'Who was followed?'

Ivor turns to me to answer for him, but I'm not too sure what it is that *he's* got to be so cautious about.

I try a casual shrug. 'No one. It's . . . you never know . . . it's standard procedure.'

Sal gives me a look to tell me that she can see right through the lie and that she'll be interrogating me later on. 'Will you be staying for lunch, sergeant?'

'Uh . . .' Ivor looks to me again.

'You can't stay long, can you?'

'No, ma'am.'

I ease him into the lounge, away from Sal, then close the door behind us. He keeps his hands clasped in front of him, as if he's just stepped into a church or something. Through my pounding head, I'm trying to work out what's got into him this morning. The sudden attack of formality and his strange precautions outside the house are getting me worried. 'Now,' I say, 'spit it out.'

'Yes, ma'am.' He's looking around the room as if it's his

first visit. Then he turns towards me. The hallway is too dark for him to have noticed my bruised face. Now he sees it, he doesn't look too happy. It's not something I want to be answering questions about.

'The forensic garage,' I say. 'What did you find out?'

He looks away from my face then, which seems to help him. 'Right,' he says. 'My friend at the garage . . . I was going to ring him up yesterday, like you told me. But I thought I should check first – see if the report had come through already. So I went and asked Superintendent Walker. And she tells me she's got the report.'

'Good work!'

Ivor tries a smile, but it doesn't look too convincing.

'And the fingerprints?' I ask. 'Any match?'

'That's the problem, ma'am. The superintendent . . . she says there were no fingerprints found. I tell her I'd heard there *were* prints – on the steering wheel. And spots of blood. Then she goes and tears a strip off me for talking to the forensic boys without asking her first.'

'Ouch. I'm sorry.'

He shrugs. 'Race Crime have it covered. Not my business anyway. Any more of this kind of thing and there'll be serious trouble.' He's got the nagging intonation spot on.

'But your friend told you . . .'

'That they'd found prints on your steering wheel. Yeah.'

'Perhaps he got the wrong car,' I say. 'They must get loads through there.'

'That's what I thought. So I waited till I could get out of the building and phone him again – from a call box this time, just in case. I speak to this secretary – who tells me he's off sick.' Ivor raises a hand and tugs at his moustache.

'You couldn't talk to him. Damn.'

Up till now we've both been standing. I've been feeling

somehow awkward with Ivor today. I just wanted to get his report and send him back to work. But what he's done for me here is beyond simple duty. Alison would do more than rip strips off him if she found out he'd gone directly against her orders.

I sit in one of the armchairs and gesture him to the one opposite. He sets himself down, clasping his hands again – this time on his lap. My headache is still hovering around, but it doesn't seem as important as it did a few minutes ago.

'Someone must have made a mistake,' I say.

'Yes, ma'am.'

'And you can cut the "ma'am" thing. I'm off duty.'

He unclasps his hands and folds his arms in front of his chest. I'm not sure if this is an attempt at informality or a defensive body posture.

'So,' he says, 'I rang my friend's house. Thought I could say I was phoning to ask how he was, then slip in the question about the fingerprints. Make it easy for him. If he did make a mistake, he's got to be a bit embarrassed about it, hasn't he?'

'And?'

'And he's still at work.'

'Woah!' I'm sitting forward in my chair now. 'Wait a moment there. The secretary told you . . .'

'Found him in the end, though. Went round his girlfriend's place late last night. She said he wasn't there – but his coat was in the hall, so I stuck my foot in the door and kept shouting till he came out.

'He's not pleased to see me. Said that the supervisor had called him upstairs. Sent him a rocket for leaking confidential information.'

'Alison...'

'Yeah. She must have complained, the vindictive bitch. Now my *friend* doesn't want to hear from me again.'

I should be telling him not to speak about the superintendent like that, but right now I can't think of a better description for her. 'I'm sorry,' I say.

He shakes his head. 'It's this kind of thing shows you who your real friends are.'

'And we still don't know,' I say.

'Know what?'

'About those fingerprints.'

Ivor pulls a face. 'That's the weird thing. I was going to leave it at that. Couldn't really ask him about them – not after we've shouted and sworn at each other. I'm just about to step out through the door, and he says it. "Those prints," he says. "I was wrong. Your boss's car was clean."'

'He said that?'

'I don't have a degree in psychology, ma'am, but I know a lie when I hear one.'

I'm trying to balance all this in my head. The fingerprints that aren't in the report. If Ivor is wrong in his conviction – then there's nothing to this story. We're scaring ourselves with shadows. But if he's right – if his one-time friend is lying – then some of the shadows are real monsters.

I sit back in my chair and gaze up at the ceiling. 'Oh, hell.'

'Alison Walker must be lying.'

I shake my head. 'But why? Alison may be a bit . . .'

'. . . of a bitch?' he offers.

'I was going to say *ambitious*. But no way is she corrupt. Anyway, she isn't going to be the only person to read the report. If she says there aren't any prints, then there aren't – not in the report, anyway.'

We're both thinking this through when I hear the door-knob turn. Sal pushes through with three steaming mugs and a packet of biscuits on a tray.

She smiles at me and raises her eyebrows. 'Nice cup of tea.'

Ivor gets to his feet. 'That's good of you, Mrs Akanbai.'

'Call me Sal.'

She has the tray down on the coffee table before I can protest. 'Hope I'm not interrupting.'

There's a mug in Ivor's hand already. He takes a sip.

'The sergeant was just about to leave.'

Sal is sitting on the sofa, opening the chocolate Hobnobs. 'Well, I'm glad you managed to finish your business. You had finished?'

'Yes,' I say.

'Not quite,' says Ivor. He puts his mug on the coffee table, then stands up and starts searching through his pockets. 'It's here somewhere.'

Sal smiles innocently.

Ivor pulls out a white envelope and hands it to me. 'Inspector Gupta caught me just before I came over here. Asked me to pass you this.'

I'm sitting in my chair with the letter in my hands, feeling like the thing is made of white-hot metal. And I know that this time, when I drop it in the bin unopened, I won't be having any second thoughts. There's nothing more to be said.

Ivor hasn't sat down again. He picks up the mug and throws back a big gulp of tea. 'Better be off. Thanks for the tea, Sal.'

She beams at him.

'I'll let myself out.' He's stepping towards the door but pulls himself up and taps his head. 'Stupid. Almost forgot.

The inspector said I should make sure I told you that the letter is about Vince the Prince.'

I don't want to be in the house when I open it. Nor do I feel like analysing my reasons. I just get in the car and drive towards the morning sunshine, turning off as soon as I'm out of the city. I choose junctions at random until I'm heading down a tree-lined B-road with an uneven surface that makes the car's suspension bounce. I pull up next to a five-bar gate leading into a field of grass. I turn off the ignition and listen to the sudden immensity of silence all around me.

I lower the window and inhale. The air is so different here from how it is in the city. It's not just the lack of exhaust fumes and factory pollution – there are subtle smells here. Not all of them are pleasant. I take another deep breath anyway and try to let my shoulders drop with the exhalation. It doesn't work.

The letter is on the passenger seat. I know I won't be able to relax until I read it, so I pick the thing up and slit it open with my little finger. A single sheet of white A4 paper – a printout from the laser printer in his office, I guess.

Mo, I'm sending this as a letter rather than coming to tell you in person. I think that will be easier for both of us. We've still got to work together for a time.

Strangely, reading his words doesn't feel as bad as I'd feared. I know what my relationship with him is now. The uncertainty has gone. I read on:

We have been through Vince's telephone records and

done some crosschecking against the database of known
racist offenders/sympathizers. We managed to find eight
matches. They are mostly as we would have expected.
Five of them are from the Martin's Hill estate. We have
them listed as members of the Scalpers. The sixth is a
member of the band who recorded the racist CDs we
seized at Vince's house. It was only the seventh that
caused us any surprise. I am telling you about this one
because of a connection with the Dean Street Mosque
investigation.

  On Vince's telephone log there were five late-night
calls to a number registered to someone called Dr Albert
Cranmer-Phillips.

That's a name I've heard before. I stop reading and stare
out of the side window, trying to remember but failing.
Now my ears are getting used to this place, I'm noticing
that it's not entirely silent. There is birdsong. I can hear the
cows over on the far side of the field and a tractor engine
somewhere in the distance. I rotate my shoulders and try
again to let them drop into relaxation. Not quite as bad as
before.

The doctor's name is on the database because of things
he's written and published over the last 30 years. I would
classify it as pseudo-academic. He is clever enough not to
make what he writes an explicit incitement to racist
violence or hatred, so no one has ever managed to
prosecute him.

  He stood for local councils in two inner-city wards in
the early 1980s and once came close to being elected. In
1989 he stood for Parliament and lost his deposit. I am
glad to say that he got fewer votes than the candidate for

*the Monster Raving Loony Party. After that he kept a
much lower profile.*

*The address we had for him on the database was a
flat in central London. Our information obviously needs
updating because the doctor's new number turns out to
be somewhere in rural mid-Wales.*

I put the paper in my lap and look out of the window again.
Some of the cows are moving now, clearing away from a
gate on the far side of the field through which a tractor has
just emerged.

I'm used to seeing racism in an urban setting. And I'm
thinking that mid-Wales is a strange place for a racist to
retreat to. Then again, he doesn't seem to be like any
openly racist person that I've ever met. He's well educated
for starters. This isn't your standard skinhead with a
swastika tattooed on his forehead.

*I have followed up with inquiries from the police in
Wales. Apparently, he purchased a large farm out there
six years ago. I can't even pronounce the name. I talked
to someone called Sergeant Day. He was very helpful and
very talkative. He knew about the farm and the people
who live there. 'Harmless eccentrics,' was the way he put
it, though apparently there was a bit of trouble two years
ago when the doctor had some wind turbines erected.
There were complaints about noise and visual impact.
The farm also has banks of solar panels. The people
living on Dr Cranmer-Phillips's farm like to be self-
sufficient as far as possible. They grow their own food,
keep animals, mend their own machines, etc. This is the
bit I thought you would be interested in. Someone on the
farm used to work as a slaughter-man in a small*

*abattoir – before it got closed down with all the new
regulations. That means he would know how to use a
humane killer on a pig.*

I read the last paragraph a second time. It sounds like a
coincidence to me. But we've got few enough leads in the
investigation so far. I shouldn't dismiss it out of hand.

'You're blocking the way.'

I look up to see a man standing just inside the field,
starting to open the gate outwards. The tractor is idling just
behind him. I'd been so absorbed in the writing that I
hadn't noticed it getting closer.

'I'm sorry.'

I drop the letter back on the passenger seat, start the car
and try to drive away, but I'm flustered and don't give it
enough juice. The engine stalls.

'Haven't got all day!' he shouts.

'Give me a chance!'

I can feel myself blushing, but I'm not going to be
pushed into making another mistake, so I count to three
under my breath before trying the ignition again. It fires.

'Go back to the city,' he shouts.

Chapter 16

I get first contact with them in my office. When I think about it afterwards, it's obvious that the whole thing is staged. The words they use. The way they stand. Everything. But at the time it seems so natural. There I am, typing away at the computer when I hear a knock on the glass behind me.

'Come.'

'Inspector Akanbai?'

I turn and see one and a half men in grey suits. That's the only way I can describe it. The one is standing in front, tall and broad enough to fill the doorway. The half is behind, mostly hidden.

'I'm Inspector Roger Ericson,' says the tall man. 'This is Sergeant Thelps. Complaints and Discipline Department.' He smiles. 'I think we met at the annual dinner last year?'

The face does look vaguely familiar, though I wouldn't have been able to place it. We shake hands.

'I tried to reach you this morning,' he says, 'but they told me you were off sick.'

'Feeling a little better now,' I say. 'Thanks.'

Thelps squeezes past Ericson and steps into my small office. This is someone I'm sure I haven't met before. His face looks like my hands do after they've been in the sink too long. To judge by his expression, he didn't get the wrinkles from smiling.

'You understand why we're here?' Ericson asks.

'The inquiry into the riots?'

Ericson shrugs, as if apologizing for the way things have turned out. 'Nothing so grand. This is regarding the complaint of the late Anwar Khaliq. It's a small matter in itself. We've already read the statement you provided.'

Thelps is peering around the room. 'Is this it?' he asks suddenly, pointing towards my computer.

'I'm sorry?'

He takes a half-step towards me. 'Is this the computer where you typed your memo to Superintendent Shakespeare?'

It's not the words themselves, but the accusatory way the sergeant fires them at me. Ericson looks slightly embarrassed. I'm completely gobsmacked.

'I beg your pardon!'

'Is this the computer?' he asks again, his tone of voice unchanged.

Ericson looks from me to his colleague then back again. 'This hardly seems the place,' he says. 'Perhaps we could find a free interview room?'

'I . . . yes.'

'And,' Ericson adds, 'if this is the computer, then I think we may need to borrow it. Though for a short time only. An hour. Will that inconvenience you?'

I'm sitting in an interview room, waiting for Thelps to come back with a fresh set of tapes for the recording machine. This is the same room in which Paresh interviewed me. That was less than a week ago, though it feels more like a month.

Ericson is chatting about the weather and the possibility of a hosepipe ban. Apparently, he has a passion for roses.

I'm thinking that I should have pressed to know more before agreeing to have my computer 'borrowed'. I do have rights in this situation. And I'm wondering if I shouldn't even now be asking to have representation during the interview process – if that would make things better or worse.

The truth is, I was so taken aback by Thelps's insolent attitude that I just caved in to all Ericson's reasonable-sounding requests. I've fallen for the oldest trick in the book. Hard cop, soft cop. So much for the psychology degree.

'Of course,' Ericson is saying, 'it's not the amount of rain, but the overall pattern of rainfall. Not all varieties have the same drought tolerance.'

The door opens and Thelps walks in. Perhaps I was wrong in what I thought before – about his expression. There is a kind of half-smile on his face now, though not one that carries any warmth. He slots in the tapes and starts the machine going.

'Interview commencing at 14.22 . . .'

I half listen to the formalities, telling myself to be calm. This is a small matter – or it would be if it wasn't happening against the background of so much civil unrest and racist provocation.

'I just want to run over some of the key points,' Ericson says. He's reading from a typed sheet. 'The incident happened a week ago today. You entered the Dean Street Mosque in response to a cry for help.'

'It was a scream.'

'Good. Good. You entered in response to a scream.' He amends the typed sheet with a Parker ballpoint from his inside jacket pocket. 'You had reasonable grounds for believing that someone required your urgent assistance. Did you ask for permission first?'

'The woman was screaming her head off. Everyone was running inside.'

Ericson smiles at me. 'Inspector. I'm not implying any criticism. Personally, I don't see what else you could have done. But our procedure for investigating complaints is clearly laid down. I have to ask these questions.'

'No,' I say. 'I didn't ask for permission.'

'Fine. And you entered the prayer hall without removing your shoes or covering your hair.'

'The woman was covered in blood. It could have been her own. She might have been bleeding to death for all I knew.'

'Good. That's clear then. You believed there was an imminent risk to human life.' Ericson sits back from the table. 'That about covers the specific issues mentioned in the complaint. We'll have to file our report in the usual way, but it doesn't seem to me that what you did was in any way intended to be a racial or religious insult. There can't be any criticism of your behaviour in this matter. Quite the contrary.'

It takes me a second to absorb what he's saying. 'That's it?'

Ericson smiles. 'Complaint dealt with. I wish they were all as easy as that. There's just one other matter, though.'

'There is?'

Thelps leans forward. 'Why did you claim that you sent Superintendent Shakespeare a written warning?'

That abrasive edge to his voice again. The change in direction of the interview is so sudden that it takes me a couple of seconds to catch on.

Ericson looks down at the table and adjusts the position of his sheet of notes. 'Of course,' he says, 'you know that there are two discipline procedures. Dealing with complaints is only one part of the work of our department. This second issue came up during our investigation. An inconsistency.'

'Why?' asks Thelps again. 'Why did you claim that you sent a memo? To shift the blame?'

'What blame?'

'The second riot. You didn't warn anyone about the danger.'

'I did!'

'No, you didn't.'

Ericson shakes his head. 'Please. This isn't the way to deal with it. All we need are the facts.'

'I spoke to Frank Shakespeare about it on the phone. That's a fact.'

'The superintendent remembers your conversation as being rather general,' says Ericson. '"Vague" was the word he used.'

'He didn't take it in,' I say. 'That was the problem. He didn't listen. That's why I wrote the memo.'

'When?' fires Thelps.

'Friday afternoon. Almost a week ago.'

'You say you typed this warning?'

'You've seen it. I sent in a copy with my statement.'

Ericson is nodding. 'Yes. We read it. Our problem is this: your superintendent states that he received nothing of the kind.'

I can hear the quiet clicking of the tape recorder. I can hear the blood pounding in my own ears. The two officers from Complaints and Discipline are sitting opposite, waiting for me to respond. I open my mouth then close it. I try to swallow.

'Have you anything to say?' Ericson asks.

'I . . . I put it in his pigeonhole. Someone must have . . . anyone could have taken it out.'

Thelps hits the flat of his hand on the table. 'Why?'

'I . . .'

'They had no reason to!'

'The riot . . . they thought . . .'

'You claim you put it in his pigeonhole on the Friday afternoon. The riot hadn't happened yet.'

'I did put it in his pigeonhole!'

Thelps is trying to fix me with his eyes. I'm glaring back, giving as good as I'm getting. The air between us crackles.

'There's no need for this,' says Ericson. 'It's a simple question. We've asked you if you sent it. You've stated that you did. That's all there is to say.' He glances at Thelps, then at me, then at his watch. 'Interview concluded at 14.29.' He clicks the recorder off and extracts the tapes. 'One for our files and one for your own reference.'

I take the cassette. 'That's it?'

Ericson nods. 'Yes.'

'And . . .?'

'And now we examine the copy of the memo recorded on the hard disk of your computer. From that we can determine the real facts – the date and time when it was created.'

My computer is still in its place when I get back to the office. Leah fills me in on the details.

'There was this bloke, yeah? Said it was all sorted for him to go in your office. You'd said it was OK.'

'What did he do?'

'Didn't watch him really.' Leah is getting nervous. 'He just switched on your computer.'

'The computer.'

'Yeah. Messed around with it for a minute, then he tells me he's finished. Did I do right?'

'You did fine, Leah.'

I leave her typing and go through into my office. There's a yellow post-it note stuck to the keyboard. *Computer has been checked. Thank you for your cooperation.* That's it. No name. But it's too polite a message to have come from Thelps. Not his style. And I'd been with Ericson the whole time. There weren't that many others that it could be.

I peel the notelet off and stride out of my office, back down the corridor.

The computer manager's first name is Bob, not Robert. That's what he told me when we first met. He didn't mention his family name, and I've never had occasion to ask. He's got a thin face, a receding hairline and pale grey eyes that gaze off into the distance when he's thinking. He's the only civilian in the police station who has an office all to himself. Not that anyone would want to share with him.

When I step inside, my first impression is of the clutter. The walls are covered in posters advertising computer hardware. The bookshelves are full of dog-eared manuals and catalogues. A tangle of cables and stripped-down computers fill the workbench. Papers cover his desk, overhanging a couple of inches all around the edge. No one else could get away with it.

'Bob?'

He's bending over a computer base unit on the bench. The outer skin of the machine is missing. One of his hands reaches within the metal skeleton; the other manipulates a tiny screwdriver.

He speaks to me without turning. 'Come over here, will you.'

I do as I'm told.

'See the earthing wire?'

I look around me. 'Uh . . . this?'

'The yellow thing. Yeah. Put it on.'

It looks like an ugly plastic bracelet attached to a long, curling cable. I place it around my wrist and do up the Velcro fastening. Worryingly enough, in a room so devoted to electricity, I now seem to be wired in to the mass of cabling under the workbench.

'You sure this is right?'

Instead of answering, he says: 'Put your hand in here.' He's talking about the hollow centre of the computer's body. 'Hold that board in place, will you.'

I worm my hand into the cavity, through a network of wires and cables, until I can grip the thing he's working on. It's about the size and shape of the Ryvita slice I had for breakfast.

'What is it?'

'Modem,' he says. 'New spec. Can download files twice as fast with this baby.'

He's tightening the screws, fixing it in place.

'Download,' I say. 'Getting stuff from the Internet?'

'Sure. Used to take me half an hour to download a half-decent music file. With this new kit I'll be able to do it in a few minutes.'

It doesn't seem like the place to mention copyright law, so I say: 'Where's the hard disk in all this?'

He taps his screwdriver against a slim metal box. 'When I started,' he says, 'you'd have needed more than a thousand hard disk drives to do what this beauty does. And they'd have been big, ugly bastards too. But you know the weirdest thing? In a year's time all this is gonna be obsolete. Modem, disk drive, the lot. I have to pinch myself sometimes.' He straightens himself. 'There. You can let go now.'

I undo the wrist strap. 'Bob?'

'Shoot.'

I pull the yellow notelet from my pocket and hold it up for him to see. 'Did you leave this on my desk?'

He looks at it for a moment, then raises his eyebrows. 'That's Greevsy's writing.'

'Greevsy?'

'Peter Greeves. Fancies himself as a bit of a computer wiz.' Bob turns away from me and starts rummaging around his desk. Lifting handfuls of printout, searching underneath.

'Civilian?' I ask.

'Nah. One of your lot.' Bob hasn't found whatever it is he's looking for. He pulls open a desk drawer and starts digging.

'What department does he work for?'

'No idea.'

'What about rank?'

Bob shrugs. I should have guessed he wouldn't know. White or black, chief constable or new recruit. None of it makes any difference to him. Perhaps that's why he always looks so relaxed.

He opens the second desk drawer. 'Here we go.' He's found a small clear-plastic bag. When he holds it up, I can see that it's full of teabags.

'Fancy a cuppa?'

I say, 'Thanks,' though I'm not really thirsty. My mind's still on this man, Peter Greeves. If Complaints and Discipline were treating the question of my memo as a criminal case, they'd have had to bring in a forensic computer expert. But there's nothing criminal here. This is the same as any other civil procedure – for them if not for me. It's the 'balance of probabilities' that matters, rather than proof 'beyond reasonable doubt'. If they believe I've been lying to try to get a senior officer in trouble – frankly, I've not much idea what that would mean. Anything from a caution to dismissal.

Bob is kneeling by the bench, plugging a kettle into a bank of sockets on the wall. He's got a couple of mugs on the floor. Even from this distance, they don't look clean. This, like most of what Bob does, is against regulations. We're supposed to get our refreshment from the canteen or from the machines in the corridors. But no one is going to discipline Bob. Everyone from the chief constable down relies on computers. We all use them, but we don't understand how they work. They're a dark art, and Bob is the digital high priest.

'What's Greevsy been doing with your machine?' he asks.

'It's a long story.'

'Don't let him mess about with the settings. I'm fed up with sorting out his mistakes.'

'It's nothing like that.'

Bob fills the mugs with steaming water, then, getting to his feet, puts them on the workbench next to a soldering iron. There's a miniature carton of milk on the windowsill. He sniffs it once, pours, then pulls a Biro from his breast pocket and gives both mugs a stir. 'Strong or weak?'

I take the weak one, because that mug looks marginally cleaner. 'Thanks.'

'You gonna tell me the story then?'

'It's all about a memo I sent to someone. They need to check to see when I wrote it.'

Bob slurps noisily. 'No problemo. Even Greevsy couldn't mess that up.'

'It's easy?'

'Sure. Every document has that kind of information attached to it. Date created. Date last modified. Date last accessed.'

'Could someone change the creation date?'

Bob sips, then swills the tea around inside his cheeks, making a sound like my washing machine just before its spin cycle. His eyes are gazing off into the distance.

'I could do it,' he says at last, 'But Greevsy wouldn't have a chance. You have to know all about the way the data is physically arranged on the hard drive. You'd need the right software tools. It's pretty much a ones and zeros job. Real computer nerd stuff.'

Somehow I find this information comforting.

'But there's a much easier way,' Bob says suddenly.

He puts his mug down, slopping a small pool of tea on to the workbench, then steps over to the wall. There's a blank area in the corner of one of the posters. He takes the tea-stirring Biro, wipes it off on his trouser-leg, then starts to write.

'You've got your first document – let's call it MEMO.DOC. You open it up. Then you save it as, say, TEMP.DOC.' He's writing the words as he speaks. 'What you've done is make a new file, identical to the first, but with a new creation date and a different name. Then you delete your original document MEMO.DOC. Finally rename TEMP.DOC as MEMO.DOC. Hey presto, it's done.'

I'm screwing up my face, trying to think this through. 'So all you've done is make an identical copy. Same name and everything. But because you made it at a different time, it has a different date?'

'You've got it!' He tosses the Biro on to his desk. It skids across the papers and drops on to the floor on the other side. 'Easy. And better than messing around with physical locations on the hard drive. Any idiot could do it this way. Even Greevsy.'

Chapter 17

Monday morning. Relief. I put the unused test kit away at the back of my medicine cupboard, hidden behind the paracetamol and Canesten. Then I break open a packet of Lillets. I feel great. The pregnancy worry must have been getting to me more than I'd realized. But that's gone now. I'm off the hook.

I get to Room 3 early and grab a couple of chairs in the front row, right in front of the whiteboard. Ready for the briefing and all that life may throw at me. A group of CID officers come trooping into the room after me. Tutting and sulky looks. It's as if they think the front seats belong to them. They grumble to each other, but no one feels like asking me to move. Definitely wise.

The seats fill up behind me. The handsome Sergeant Greenway strides into the room, giving me a beaming smile. He takes his place on my left. 'You're looking well, ma'am.'

'Thanks.'

He wouldn't say that if he could see through the make-up. Perhaps he's seeing deeper than the bruises – sensing the energy crackling inside me. It's one of those days when I could take on the world and win.

'Enjoy your time in charge?' I ask.

He shrugs, and I think perhaps he blushes slightly. 'It was all right.'

'You'll be going for your inspector's exam next.'

I was right about that blush. I'm about to probe him more when Paresh and Alison make their entrance. Her in the lead, of course. Paresh sees me in the front row. He manages to conceal his double take pretty well. My lip is back to its normal size this morning, and the bruise is covered. But Paresh is seeing the invisible mark. I smile. He looks away.

Alison takes the stage. 'Good morning,' she says.

There's a rumble of answering greetings from the CID crowd behind me.

'It's been a week now,' she announces. 'You've all been working hard.'

Paresh has sat himself down on a chair next to where Alison is standing. While she goes over the routine allocation of tasks, he keeps one hand in a trouser pocket, the other is resting on his knee, holding a sheet of paper. His legs are crossed at the ankle. He knows enough about body language to try to cover up his feelings. But he doesn't have enough control to hide them from me. The forced openness of his posture. The slight jiggle of one foot. The man is tense.

Alison turns towards him. 'Inspector. Your report?'

He gets to his feet, rather too hurriedly. 'Yes. Right. Most . . . most of you know about the phone log. Vince the Prince and Dr Cranmer-Phillips. We've had time now to check back over the entire six years he's had that telephone account.'

Paresh seems to be reading from the sheet of paper in his hand, but I think this is just so he doesn't risk seeing my face. 'The doctor's name comes up for the first time five years ago. Not much phone traffic between them. Typically calls of ten minutes duration or thereabouts. Evenings mostly. A couple during the day. But the frequency of calls increases up to a point eighteen months ago. After that, the pattern changes abruptly. We get no more daytime or evening traffic. It's all during one hour in the early morning. Between 2 a.m. and 3 a.m.'

One of the CID officers behind me says: 'Does it stay the same when the clocks get put back and forward?'

Paresh nods. 'Good question. And the answer's yes. It's always between 2 and 3 a.m. as measured in local time rather than GMT.'

Paresh is starting to relax into the role now, his voice sounding less breathless.

'Are the calls all the same length?' Alison asks.

'Call duration between nineteen and twenty-three minutes.'

A couple of hands have gone up in the audience, and Paresh is taking the questions one at a time.

'Any chance of a phone tap?'

He shrugs. 'We're trying. Now it's up to the Home Secretary. For some reason the Home Office is dragging its feet on this one.'

'What about searching this doctor's place?'

'We're working on that. But the consensus is that we'd need a lot more evidence before a magistrate would give us a warrant. Right now, all we want to do is question him.'

Alison looks around the room, then points a finger towards someone at the back. 'Sergeant Woodgate. How do you feel about a trip to mid-Wales?'

'Yes, ma'am.'

'Good man. And to go with you . . .' Alison searches the faces in the room again then fixes on me. 'Marjorie?'

'I . . .'

'Do you have any appointments booked for the next couple of days?'

'Two days?'

She nods. 'Sort out the detail this morning. Drive over in the afternoon. You'll be back tomorrow.'

Alison's caught me on the hop here. That's deliberate, I think. She's trying to bounce me into going. If the chief constable won't let her suspend me, then she wants me out of the city. My face in the *Crusader* has been causing her a lot of grief. The articles are getting less frequent now, and further from the front page, but my presence on the investigation team is still an embarrassment. All of which makes me want to dig in my heels.

But there's another emotion here. I'll be spiting myself if I don't at least acknowledge it. Excitement. The prospect of getting out of the claustrophobic city. Far away from difficult memories. And the chance to question someone like Cranmer-Phillips under caution. I weigh up the two emotions and find them balanced.

'Appointments,' I say. 'I do have a few.'

'I'll take them if you want,' offers Greenway.

Alison smiles at him. 'Good.'

Greenway looks at his shoes.

And then I think of the little Serbian boy, Niko. I was planning a visit to the asylum-seekers' hotel later today. There's no appointment, but I just want a chance to see the place and his parents. To settle my mind. I've felt guilty for not following it up sooner.

'Better to get a CID officer on the case,' I say. 'Someone trained to handle that kind of questioning.'

Alison purses her lips for a moment. 'No,' she says. 'We'll put that psychology degree of yours to use. Mid-Wales it is.'

I guess she never claimed her investigation team was a democracy.

Harry Woodgate is still a sergeant, though he joined the

force many years before me. His hair has thinned on top since I first met him, and he's started to put on weight around the neck. There's nothing wrong with the way he does his job. He gets on with the work. They say he's competent. But I always get the feeling that the career step he's most looking forward to is retirement.

He drops his overnight bag next to mine and slams the boot. I'm about to ask if he wants to take the first stint at the wheel, but he's already pulling open the driver's side door.

We join the M6 and head west through the Midlands, cruising at eighty. Woodgate proves himself a comfortable driver. Smooth acceleration and braking. Never too close to the cars ahead. Mirror, signal manoeuvre.

But he's not much of a conversationalist, so I relax into the passenger seat, watching the open farmland on either side of the road. Huge fields – some of them green, others shades of yellow from pale straw to gold.

The city of Birmingham is up ahead and the traffic is already starting to build. I'm thinking about Vince and Dr Cranmer-Phillips. Two men from different worlds. The urban council estate and the ivory tower. Other than their racism, I can't think of anything that unites them.

Ten minutes later and we're in the outside lane of the motorway, overtaking a line of forty-foot trucks, two abreast. We're down to seventy and slowing. There are apartment blocks on either side. Run-down high-density housing. This is the kind of place where I expect to find the racist gangs, not out in the countryside.

Then I remember the fire escape next to the place where Anwar was killed. I left a note telling Paresh about it, but I haven't got round to following it up yet. He was the only person who would have understood what I was getting at. It was him who mentioned the theatrical arrangement of the unsolved race crimes. I could call him now before he goes off work – if I wanted to.

It's hot in the car. My mind feels fuzzy. I can leave it for a few more minutes.

Within a couple of miles we're bumper to bumper and crawling forward in first. Woodgate lowers his window. His face is impassive. 'Always like this,' he says.

I have my head tilted over to one side, resting against the seat-belt strap. 'Really?'

'I've driven it . . . must be a hundred times.'

'Oh.' I close my eyes for a moment.

'Busiest stretch of road in Europe.'

'Mmm.'

When I wake up, we're off the motorway. There are mountains on either side. Trees. Tall hedges. I rub my scalp with my fingers. The air feels cooler than it was. We're climbing, and there's a caravan immediately ahead of us, blocking off the view forward.

'Back in the land of the living?' says Woodgate.

'Where are we?'

'On the A44. Not far now.'

I check my watch. It's half-three in the afternoon. 'Damn!'

'Ma'am?'

'Sorry. Nothing. There's something I wanted to ask Inspector Gupta.'

Woodgate glances across at me. 'Give him a call.'

'He was going off duty at three.'

Woodgate changes down gear and accelerates past the caravan. 'You've got his home number, haven't you?' He glances at me again, and I wonder how much of my affair with Paresh is common knowledge.

I lower my window and let the air blow over my face and

arm. It feels good. I get out my mobile, check that there's a signal this far up into the Cambrian Mountains, then auto-dial his number. I let it ring nine times before cutting the connection.

We reach the police station a quarter of an hour later. It's an old building of grey stone, set near the centre of a small market town. Population perhaps a thousand. I thought they'd closed down all these places years ago. Rural police stations, I mean. An engraved stone above the front door proclaims it to have been built in 1904.

Sergeant Day is small for a police officer. But what he lacks in body weight he more than makes up for in the speed of his darting movements. He's a bird in uniform. 'Welcome indeed,' he says. 'Come in. Come in. Come in.'

I follow Day and Woodgate through into one of the back offices.

'Professor Cranmer-Phillips,' Day says. 'I'm burning up to know why it is you want to see him.'

Woodgate and I sit ourselves down in two of the available chairs. Day remains standing.

'He's a local personality?' I ask.

'Not as such. Keeps himself to himself. But a local subject of gossip. Very much so, yes.'

Day sits down and immediately stands up again. 'Tea,' he says. 'I didn't offer you any refreshments.'

'That'd be nice,' says Woodgate.

I say: 'What is it about Cranmer-Phillips that interests everyone?'

'Well, ma'am, he's English for one thing. Very English. No offence.' Day folds his arms in front of his chest, then unfolds them again. 'Then it's the fuss over the wind turbines. Not that I mind them myself. And all the land, of course. He's bought three adjoining farms in as many years. The owners were all keen enough to sell, mind. There's nothing but tears in hill farming these days.' He rubs his hands together. 'Now, how about that tea?'

'Please,' says Woodgate.

I shake my head. 'Tell me about the farms.'

'Well, there's another thing, isn't it. No one has a good word to say about the way he cares for his land. I've always put that down to him being English, mind. They'd never say it of him if he'd been born within twenty miles of Machynlleth, now would they? I came from Cardiff thirty years ago, but they still treat me as a foreigner.'

Woodgate seems to be doing an impression of a man dying of thirst.

Day looks towards the door. 'Anything else, ma'am?'

'The farms,' I say. 'Has he changed them at all?'

'Oh, yes indeed. It was all sheep of course, before. And not making a penny profit for as long as anyone can remember. Now it's forestry and wind turbines and he can afford a shiny new Land Rover Discovery for when he drives down to the post office. That caused some talk, now. And that's the other thing, isn't it – the people he has working for him. Not the sort we'd be wanting round here.'

Day glances from me to the floor and back. 'Not wanting to be prejudiced or anything.'

'Of course.'

There's a pause. Then Woodgate coughs. 'Strong and milky, please. Two sugars.'

'Right you are, then,' says Day. 'Right you are indeed.' Then he hurries out of the door.

I can hear the clatter of cups somewhere in the distance.

'What do you make of it all?' I say.

Woodgate shrugs. 'Sounds like proper crockery for a change.'

I chew on tooth enamel for a moment. 'And Cranmer-Phillips?'

'Makes no difference what I think. We'll go and question him. Fine. But he won't say anything.'

'Then why are we here?'

'You tell me, ma'am. You tell me.'

I sit thinking about that until Day returns. He sets the tea tray down on the desk.

'What did I tell you?' Woodgate says. 'Proper china. Lovely.'

'We'll just drink this,' I say, 'then we'd better be going. If you could give us directions.'

'Of course. Of course.' Day nods rapidly. 'But there's something you should know . . . about the professor.'

'Yes?'

'It's just what I've heard, you understand...'

'Go on.'

'Well, begging your pardon, ma'am, but I don't think he'll be happy about you going up there – not with you being black.'

We drive back out of town on the A44, then turn off on to a single-track road, which snakes up the steep valley side. Scraggy white sheep are dotted around the slopes in ones and twos. The rusty wire fencing on either side of us has strands of wool snagged on the barbs. The grass is thin here, and uneven. It's hard to imagine anything growing fat on a diet like this – even in the summer.

The road divides at the top of the slope. We take the smaller of the two ways. Woodgate keeps the car as far left as he can, so the exhaust pipe doesn't ground on the ridge of grass in the centre of the track.

It's here that I get my first view of Cranmer-Phillips's

land. The grassland ends at a high fence ahead of us. Beyond it is a mass of young conifers. In the midst of the trees there are industrial-looking heaps of grey stone, old mine tips by the look of them, and the shell of a building. Towering over the scene, at the very top of the hill, are three enormous wind turbines. All are still.

The first real problem we come to is a metal gate. I stand there looking at it, with a couple of flies buzzing around my ears. 'Damn.'

Woodgate gets out his mobile phone. 'I'll get him to come down and unlock it.'

That turns out to be the second problem. There's no signal up here for the mobile to work. So we leave the car, climb the gate and begin to walk. We reach the brow of the hill in perhaps five minutes. There below us is the shallow bowl of a wide valley. Unforested. Small fields and a scattering of farm buildings.

I'm standing there next to Woodgate, looking down on this hidden valley. And I'm thinking how the doctor has chosen a place to live in which he can't be overlooked by anyone. And that's the moment when I hear a small, metallic click just behind me.

'Just stop right there,' says a man's voice.

I turn, very slowly, to see a large, muscle-bound figure. His head is shaved to black stubble. A double-barrelled shotgun rests across one of his arms.

'Police,' Woodgate says, his voice remarkably level. 'Just keep that gun pointed away from us.'

The man smiles. 'You're on private land.'

'You've a licence for that?' I say.

He nods. 'How else can I kill vermin?'

The building he takes us to seems to be the centre of

activity. There are three cars outside, including a Land
Rover Discovery. Overhead wires connect it, via an out-
building, to the wind turbines on the ridge. Our escort – I
can't say our captor, because he hasn't made any real
threats – calls inside. A few seconds later another buzz-
trimmed muscleman appears at the front door.

I say: 'We want to talk to Cranmer-Phillips.'

'About what?'

'Regarding a criminal investigation.'

'He won't see you.'

'We can call him in to the station if he prefers.'

'Call him in then.'

The man with the shotgun tilts his head to indicate the
direction we came. I turn to go.

'Wait . . .' The man at the door ducks his head into the
building. After a moment he steps back into the sunshine.
'He'll just see the one of you.'

Woodgate looks at me. I can see the unease and embarrassment on his face. 'It's up to you, ma'am.'

In one way it makes no difference. We'll need to call
him down to the station anyway – two of us interviewing
him together, under caution. But the more information we
can gather now, the better. I'd like Woodgate to get a look
around inside the house, even if it means me standing out
here alone with these two thugs.

I nod. 'OK.'

Woodgate steps forward.

'No.' The man at the door is waving him back. 'Not you.
He'll only see the coloured one. Akanbai.'

All of which is a double shock, because I haven't yet told
them my name.

Chapter 18

I walk into the small room and he levers himself out of his leather armchair. That's the first surprise. The man actually stands to greet me. He's tall, lean, with slightly hollowed cheeks. Hairless but for a grey moustache and a goatee beard which exaggerates the length of his face. He wears a tweed jacket, a dark tie. I'm standing there looking at a polite, elderly gentleman. If it wasn't for the reception committee outside, I'd think this was the wrong house altogether.

'Professor Cranmer-Phillips?'

'No.'

'Not Albert Cranmer-Phillips?'

'You may call me Dr Cranmer-Phillips if you wish. The designation "professor" is no longer appropriate. I was dismissed from my university post.'

He speaks deliberately as he makes this admission, laying stress on the key word. *Dismissed*. It's as if he's challenging me to make a judgement of his past. On some level, I think he'd feel strengthened by any attack from me. I say: 'I'm sorry.'

'Are you really?'

I glance around the small study. There are two bookcases, almost as tall as the room. A window, curtains drawn. An empty stone fireplace. The air feels cooler in here than outside, as if the thickness of the stone walls has soaked up the heat. There is only one picture on the walls – an oil painting of a man ploughing a field.

'I imagine you will have read my file,' he says.

'Sorry,' I say again.

He runs his gaze over me, from head to feet. 'Stop being sorry and sit down.'

I don't want to be at ease in this man's house. But I've come a long way for this conversation. I place myself in the only other chair, wondering who else has occupied this bit of space. Only after I'm in my place does he reseat himself.

I say: 'I want to talk to you about Vince.'

'I do not believe you.'

'Why?'

'I think you have come to see what a racist looks like.' He interlocks the fingers of his two hands and rests them in his lap. 'Do I disappoint you?'

'Are you a racist?'

He sits back in the chair and looks at me for a moment. 'I am an historian.'

'I thought you were a maths lecturer,' I say.

'I *was* professor of mathematics, yes. But they dismissed me for applying my mind to the problems of social history.'

'You were teaching in a multicultural university. You wrote an article supporting apartheid. You're surprised they pushed you out?'

'You did read my file.' He looks pleased. 'Did you also read the paper that you just referred to – "Preserving Cultural Integrity"?' He examines my face for a moment.

'There wasn't a copy in your file.'

'No. Of course. Nor in the library.' He shakes his head slowly. 'Henry Ford once said that his customers could choose to buy their cars in any colour they wanted so long as they wanted black. The "freedom of speech" we enjoy in this country is much the same. You can say anything you like – but only if your ideas agree with the consensus of the political elite.'

I decide to try again. 'Are you a racist?'

'You,' he says, 'are like Vince.'

'I am not!' My words come out too quickly, betraying my feelings.

A slow smile creases his face. 'Vince would have been as outraged as you just were by that suggestion, inspector. More so perhaps.'

I take a breath. 'You're wrong.'

'You think you are not a racist. Vince thinks he is one. Your similarity comes from the way in which you treat the word itself. *Racist*. You use it like a lump of rock. A primitive weapon, thrown first one way then the other.'

Dr Cranmer-Phillips turns his attention to the nearest bookcase. He reaches out a hand and runs the back of his bony fingers along the spines of the books. Then he turns to face me again. 'Tell me this,' he says. 'You are mixed race. Would you expect to be racially abused by others the same as yourself?'

I don't answer. My teeth are clamped so hard together that they're starting to ache.

He nods, as if I'd spoken my thoughts out loud. 'It would seem reasonable to project your past experiences into the future, to judge one ethnic group less likely to attack you, another more so. But if you should do this, then you will have yourself come to a racist conclusion.'

I'm sure he's getting more out of this interview than I am. I take another breath. Steady my nerves. 'You're saying, all you do is apply statistics? Is that it?'

'The facts are all there to be read.' He points to one of the bookcases. 'Look at history. The greatest civilizations of the ancient world expanded their borders, taking in diverse races, being influenced by alien cultures. They lost their way, forgot the very identity that had previously given rise to their military successes. Each of these civilizations collapsed.'

I know what he's doing – trying to undermine my confidence. I also know that I've got no reason to get involved in any argument with him.

I say: 'Things are different now.'

He shakes his head. 'The principle of uniformitarianism forces us to accept that the processes which made civilizations collapse in the past will do the same in the future. Unless this civilization gets back to the values which made it great, it too will collapse.'

'So you want to get rid of all the non-whites?'

He holds up his hands in front of his chest. 'What I want is irrelevant. I merely observe the processes of history. I can tell you what will happen. That is all. Society will decay. But you are a police officer. You know the statistics. You can see the process for yourself.'

I look at the bookcase. Most of it looks pretty heavy going. Churchill's *History of the English-Speaking Peoples* sits next to hefty texts on number theory, encryption, steganography and signal processing. Further along the shelf there are several feet of bound doctorate theses.

'How did you know my name?' I ask.

He laughs. 'It shouldn't surprise you, inspector. You are becoming a celebrity. Your picture in the news every day. A face to recognize in the street.'

'But not here in Wales. My picture's only been in the *Crusader*.'

'For how long, do you suppose? You are a police officer. You are coloured. You have been accused of racist actions.'

'*Everyone's coloured,*' I say, '*or you wouldn't be able to see them.*'

'Is that a quotation?'

I nod, though I don't feel like acknowledging the source. It wouldn't advance my case in the doctor's eyes. Instead I say: 'How do you get to read the *Crusader* here in Wales?'

His face becomes serious. 'I may have been dismissed from my university chair, but I retain my research interests. I continue to compile statistics of events. The national media are of no use in my work. The tabloids contain little real news. The broadsheet editors self-censor to follow the line of their political masters. It is in the local press that the truth can still be detected. And yes, I do read the *Crusader* – through the Internet.'

'What does your research tell you?'

'It confirms what I knew before. There will be conflict and civil strife to a greater degree than you have seen – even in Waterfields. The only places with a chance of stability are the rural areas, where the original culture is still strong. It is from here that society has a chance to rebuild.'

It's the man's certainty that unnerves me. It feels as if he's talking about things that have already happened. There's no point in trying to argue history or statistics with him. Perhaps there's no point in trying to argue at all. But I feel a need to score one point at least, to leave him with some doubts of his own.

'Did you enjoy working at the university?'

He folds his hands on his lap again. 'A strange question.'

'Did you enjoy teaching?'

'I enjoyed teaching some of the students.'

'What about the academic debate – you enjoyed that?'

He nods. 'But I do not see where this is leading.'

'Many of the other academics disagreed with your theories.'

'There are opposing theories. This is the very meaning of

debate.'

'These other professors were intelligent men and women?'

'Of course.'

'How is it possible for an intelligent person to believe something that is incorrect?'

He looks at the floor for a moment, then nods and looks back to me. 'To accept the truth, they have to abandon some of their long-cherished beliefs. This hurts them. They use intellect to construct an elaborate logical defence. Intelligence and pride are the barriers that prevent them from accepting the obvious truth.'

'I wasn't talking about them,' I say. 'I was talking about you. Unless you believe that every one of your own ideas happens to be correct and every one of theirs is mistaken. Which has to be unlikely – statistically.'

He pushes on the arms of his chair and levers himself to his feet. 'So long as you are my guest, you are under my protection and I am bound to treat you with courtesy. But by attacking me in this way, you abuse your privilege.'

I stand.

'You should go now,' he says.

'We'll be needing you to come into town tomorrow morning,' I say, 'as you refused to be formally interviewed here. I'll have someone phone you to make the arrangements.'

I walk out of the room, through the hall, towards the front door. So much for scoring points. I haven't even disturbed his calm. My hand is on the latch when I hear his voice behind me.

'Your argument is flawed, inspector, because it takes no account of the possibility that my own understanding is simply greater than theirs – that I am intellectually superior.'

Chapter 19

It's chicken again. Kiev this time. Served with chips and a lettuce salad that looks considerably less alive than the plastic carnation in the middle of the table. I run the hem of the red check tablecloth through my fingers.

Woodgate is smiling – somewhat blearily, I have to say. I'm not sure if it's the alcohol, or me being out of uniform, but he's a lot more relaxed this evening. More than I've ever seen him. I'm starting to think that I should have worn something more formal than black jeans, and I've definitely decided that my dark green blouse shows an inch too much cleavage for present company.

He shakes out a stream of salt from high above the remains of his meal. 'You gotta laugh,' he says.

I don't see why. I've travelled halfway across the country to interview a suspect under caution, and all I've managed to do so far is give him the opportunity of trying to indoctrinate me. The formal interview is due tomorrow morning at eleven.

'We're not going to get anything out of him,' I say.

Woodgate is now using half a bread roll to mop up the juices from his plate. 'What did you expect?'

'Don't know. I guess I didn't think he'd be quite so sure of himself.'

'There you go. Smug university types like him are all the same. No offence, ma'am.'

I stab at a bit of tomato with my fork. 'He might still let something slip.' Even as I'm saying it, I know it's not going to happen.

'He'll have a bloody lawyer.'

'No way.'

Woodgate reaches in his pocket and pulls out a crumpled tenner. 'My money says he'll march in with a lawyer and we'll get nowhere.'

'Then why did we drive over here?'

'Beats me. Superintendent's orders, I guess. Now – you taking the bet?'

'No.'

'Suit yourself.' He stuffs the money back in his trouser pocket, then picks up his wineglass and empties it in one series of gulps.

Woodgate was in the hotel bar when I met up with him this evening. Even then I got the impression that he'd had a couple of glasses. There's an enthusiasm in his eating and drinking that I haven't till now noticed in his police work. He leans back in his chair and starts reading through the sweet menu. The decision must be difficult. He's biting on his lower lip and his forehead is creased with thought lines.

The restaurant is three-quarters empty tonight. A waiter watches us from the other side of the bar. I chew on my salad for a minute, wondering why I chose the chicken after all my recent experiences. At least I know now that the nausea is nothing to do with pregnancy. I give up – lay my knife and fork on the plate.

'What did you make of Dr Cranmer-Phillips's place?'

He glances up at me. 'How do you mean?'

'Barbed wire, locked gate, shotgun. All that.'

'It's legal.'

'But why does he have it all?'

'Eccentric professor.'

'And did you see the way he's got it set out? In a valley – trees growing all around the skyline? Very private.'

'So?'

'He must have something to hide. I want to see it again.'

'Walked right through the place already. Nothing to see.'

'They were expecting us.'

'Give it a break! The man's a weirdo. But he's not harming anyone.'

'What about the murder?'

He stares at his empty plate for a moment, then screws up his face. 'Can't see it. A beating gone wrong. That's Vince the Prince – or someone like him. Not an ex-professor.'

'They could both be part of the same organization?'

Woodgate splutters a laugh and has to wipe around his mouth with a paper serviette. He's shaking his head. 'Come off it.'

'What's the joke?'

He can't have noticed the cold edge to my question, because he tries to answer it. 'People like you, ma'am . . . it's just that you think everyone's against you.'

'People like me?'

'Yeah. You know.'

'Tell me.'

'You people – you think there's some big white plot against you all the time.'

You people. There's no value judgement in the phrase. There doesn't need to be. It's enough that two categories are established in the mind – all his friends and kindred on one side of the fence, and everyone else on the other.

'You don't think racism exists?'

'Didn't say that.' He gives an exaggerated shake of the

head. 'Didn't say that. There's racists, yes. But not so many. Not like you people say. If the police were racist, you wouldn't be an inspector, now would you?'

He turns his attention back to the menu. The man is infuriating. His prejudice. His defeatism.

'We were sent here as part of the murder investigation. That means asking questions with a positive attitude. Trying to find the truth.'

'Nah. We're here 'coz the computer says so. Bet you anything we go back empty-handed.'

The waiter has approached while we've been talking. He coughs to attract our attention then smiles at me, a little tightly, and turns to Woodgate. 'Is everything all right, sir?'

'It's great.'

'Just tell me when you're ready to order from the sweet menu.'

So much for the countryside being less claustrophobic than the city. I step out into the hotel car park and take a deep breath of the night air. Then another. The door closes behind me, and the sound of bar-room conversation dulls to almost nothing.

The car is here in front of me. Woodgate won't be in any state to use it tonight, and I could do with putting a few miles between us – for an hour or two at least. I have to be able to work with the man in the morning.

So I get behind the wheel and drive. All I want to do is find a lay-by out in the middle of nowhere. Stand under the stars. Get things in perspective. At least, that's what I tell myself I want to do.

I head out of the town, up into the mountains. It's the same route we drove earlier in the day. I take the same turning as we did then, up towards Dr Cranmer-Phillips's land.

I drive down the same narrow road. It looks so different now. A black, uneven horizon, a sky milky with stars. I come over the brow of the hill, within sight of the wind turbines, and turn off the headlights.

I'm sitting with my hands on the steering wheel.

'What on earth am I doing here?'

I don't have any answer at first. But hearing my own voice gives me a feeling of strength. 'Instinct,' I say. 'Trusting my instinct.'

I haven't spoken the other answer that came into my mind. That I'm afraid Woodgate is right. That we might be here on a digital whim, inevitably futile. Perhaps I'm too proud to handle the thought of going back to the Midlands empty-handed.

I ease off the clutch and let the weight of my foot press down on the accelerator pedal. I'm creeping forward, steering by the light of the stars. After a few more yards the road starts to slope downhill, so I turn the engine off and let the car roll, listening to the scrunch of small stones under the tyres and the click, click, click of cooling metal. I come to rest, slope and momentum used up, in a low hollow. From here I can just see over the rise ahead of me and scan the edge of the doctor's land. It's no more than a hundred yards away now.

When we came here earlier in the day, we were picked up within minutes of crossing the fence. They either had a guard on duty, or some kind of surveillance. But it's dark now.

I close the car door as quietly as I can manage and start walking, keeping to the left, close to the earth bank that runs next to the edge of the track. Dark hair. Dark clothes. I should be pretty well invisible tonight. Except that the bank gets lower as I go forward. By the time I'm halfway to the gate, I'm having to crawl along the ground to stay below it. There's no going forward from here without exposing myself – though any watcher would still have to be alert to pick me out. So I get myself comfortable, lying on my stomach, propped up on my forearms.

I don't know what I'm expecting to see. For now, it's enough to have got this close, to be watching, unobserved. I can hear water trickling in a ditch somewhere over to my right. I can hear the breath of the night breeze moving through grass. And other sounds, fainter still. I hear a tiny rustling over to the left. I turn my head to look, but it's stopped already. Then I see a tiny shape detach itself from the silhouette of the bank, a moth blotting out stars as it flies away.

I must have been here for over ten minutes, though I dare not press the light on my watch to check. There's nothing to mark the passage of time except the sharpening of my senses. I will have to go back eventually, but for now the hotel is the last place I want to be. Also I'm beginning to think that there can't be a guard on duty, because I would surely have been able to see or hear some movement.

I stand up slowly. I'd be a fool to walk right up to the gate. I do know that. So I climb over the low bank and head away from the track, moving parallel to the boundary fence. It's uneven ground, but soft. Pillows of moss and grass. I guess it would be a quagmire if there'd been rain any time in the last couple of weeks, but right now I can move fairly easily without even getting my feet wet.

I count a hundred paces, then turn ninety degrees and start advancing towards the perimeter fence. The closer I get, the more the ground firms up. There are some rocks underfoot. I'm climbing as well – the gentlest of slopes.

Then I reach the wire. It's twice as tall as anything else I've seen around here. Six foot, topped with some wicked-looking razor wire. I'm not going to be able to get over that without making some serious noise. Screams probably.

I turn ninety degrees again and start picking my way back towards the road. Slow and quiet. I count seventy paces then stop and listen. The gate should be just ahead of me now, though it's too dark to make it out against the young trees.

That's when I hear it – the scrape of one stone on another somewhere up ahead. It lasts only a fraction of a second, but I'm sure that I did hear it. I've got a direction to look in now. And when I stare into that patch of darkness – I must be looking under the trees right next to the gate – I can see a single orange spot. The glowing tip of a cigarette. It flares bright once, then falls suddenly down and vanishes.

I'm getting a real charge out of this. My heart pounding fast. My senses sharper than I can ever remember them being. I turn my back on the guard and place one foot before the other, careful not to scatter any loose stones. I'm counting my paces again. It's a way of gauging distance in the dark. And the sound of my own voice inside my head keeps me from bottling out. Five, six, seven steps. Each one putting more distance between me and the guard. More distance and I speed up. Twenty paces. Forty. Seventy. I'm back where I first met the fence. But now I'm moving around the perimeter the other way. I'm out of the guard's earshot and paying more attention to the fence than I am to my footfalls.

I've counted 250 paces before I find what I'm looking for. There's a huge pile of broken stones here. The spoil heap from one of the old mine workings. The fence overlaps the base of it. But the stones must have slipped since they put it up. I can feel a gap between the lowest wire and the ground. Not enough for me to get through yet. I'm down on my knees, pulling out rocks, placing them in the grass to either side of me. There's a big enough gap now, so I lie down, face up, and start to worm through. I've got sharp stones pressing into the small of my back, but there's too much adrenaline pumping around in my blood for it to feel painful.

I'm through and scrambling up the side of the spoil heap. The ground flattens out at the top. There's the ruin of a stone building here, and something else up ahead. A square hollow in the ground, too dark to see into. I step towards it, crouch down. I toss a small stone forward into the darkness and wait for the sound of it landing. When the clatter comes to me, it's no more than an echo reverberating in the throat of the mineshaft.

I don't hear anything else. I should. But there isn't a breath or a footfall to give him away – not that I'm aware of. I just feel the skin on the nape of my neck tightening as the hairs stand on end. Then it happens – too suddenly for me to react – a hand clamping over my mouth, my head jerking backwards into someone's body.

I throw all my weight to one side, but his grip around my head stays tight. I bring my arm forward, ready to let my elbow swing. That's when I feel the prick of his knife-point, pressing into the soft skin of my neck.

Chapter 20

It's dark, so I can't see his face. But I know this man all the same. It's not his muscular build that gives him away. Nor the tightness of his grip. These things are not unique. Control. That's the quality that makes his movement so distinctive. Physical power and coordination, combined with an icy restraint. I saw it on the night when he smashed the window of my car. I saw it when he rammed my arm against the brick wall of my house.

I'm sitting, now, with my back propped against the inside wall of a ruined mine building. My hands are drawn up high behind me. I've tried leaning my body forward – to stop the uneven stones digging into my back – but that only tightens the thin wire around my wrists.

He's standing in the middle of what was once a large room. There's no roof any more, so I can see the top part of his body as it moves, a silhouette against the stars. He hasn't spoken yet. The whole process – manouvring me inside, binding my wrists and ankles – all happened in silence.

He steps towards me, stoops down, takes hold of my blouse with two hands and rips. I hear the tearing cloth. I feel the cold air on the exposed skin of my stomach.

I was terrified before – in my mind. But now I can feel the attack coming, and my fear has become physical. It's like being sick, an involuntary convulsion, gripping every part of my body. I'm twisting my hands. Pulling. Working them around. Trying to reach whatever it is that's holding me to the wall. There's pain here. Lots of pain. But it doesn't seem to belong to me. My hands are slippery with blood.

He's very close. I can feel his breath on my face. One of his hands is on my chin, a finger pressed into each cheek, forcing my mouth open. Then he's working the ball of cloth between my teeth. He grabs my blouse again, tears another strip, wraps it around my head so that it holds the gag in place.

I hadn't cried out before. The knife was always near my throat. But now I do try. He's standing up, looking at me. All my muscles are tensed rigid. Then he turns and walks out of the ruined doorway.

It's when the adrenaline starts to leave me that the pain comes into focus. A throbbing ache where my teeth have bitten into the inside of my cheeks, the metallic taste of blood. The ever-sharpening nerve signals from the cut and bruised flesh around the outside of my wrists.

It's now also that my mind starts to work. I know that what I've done is stupid. I've risked my life, and everything has gone wrong. But beating myself up isn't going to get me anywhere. And there's something more here to understand. A puzzle.

We're miles from anywhere. But he gagged me all the same. The other night, he tried to burn me in my house. Now he gets a knife to my throat – yet chooses to delay the attack. And the strangest thing – he hasn't turned me over to the others.

I'd imagined Dr Cranmer-Phillips as head of a violent organization. United by a common ideal. But the doctor may be nothing more than he seems – a crackpot academic. That wouldn't stop some of the people associated with him from being terrorists.

Time passes and I watch the stars wheel above me. Half an hour. An hour. I start to lose track. The pain in my wrists gets stronger. Then begins to lessen. By the time I hear the returning footsteps, my hands and feet are numb.

He steps back into the building, moves straight to me, kneels down, unties the cloth from around my head.

I spit the soggy rag from my mouth. 'Bastard.'

He doesn't react.

He's reaching around behind me, untwisting the wire. My hands drop. Their movement is more painful than their cramped stillness was. I inch them around and rest them on my lap.

'Your car – where is it?' It's the first thing I've heard him say. His voice is level. Commanding. The accent is mild but distinct. South-east. Essex.

'Bastard.'

'I need to find your car. Is it on the road?'

'Why?'

He's squatting right in front of me, just to one side of my outstretched legs. His face is in dark shadow. All I can see are the whites of his eyes. He's looking straight at me.

'Do you want to live?' he says.

I don't answer.

'If your car's on the road out there and I don't move it . . . there'll be nothing I can do for you.'

I'm staring at this shadow man, wishing I could see his expression. I'd forgotten the car – blocking the road just a few hundred yards from here. For all he knows it could be a mile away. If it's found, they'll know I'm here somewhere. That might give me a chance. But if I try to hold out too long he's just going to take the keys and look for it himself. It wouldn't take him long to find.

So I say: 'Untie my legs.'

'The car,' he says again. 'There's no time for this.'

'Untie me. I'll take you there.'

His silhouette doesn't move for a moment. Then he shifts to one side and I see the starlight catch on his knife blade. I feel a stab of pain from my ankles as the wire tightens. Then the knife is through. I'm released.

He springs to his feet and holds out a hand for me. 'Up.'

I'm being hauled into a standing position.

'Hurry.'

He's tugging me along by the hand, leading me out of the doorway. I'm stumbling over the loose rocks, an agony of pins and needles all down my lower legs – the circulation starting to return. I could try to worm my hand out of his grip, but it would do me no good. It's all I can do to keep up with his walking pace.

We're down the bottom of the spoil heap now, next to the fence. He squats, uses his free hand to pull the lowest wire up, widening the hole through which I crawled. He gestures with his head towards the ground.

'You first.'

I'm down on my back, worming through the gap, face upwards, hands over my head. And I'm thinking that this might be the best chance I get. I'm almost clear of the wire, when I feel his hand close around mine. He comes through head first, never letting go.

'Where's the car?'

We're standing on the soft ground face to face. There's more light here than there was in the ruins. I can see his expression. There isn't any softness. But it's like it was before – there's no hatred there either.

I say: 'Tell me why.'

'No time.'

'Why?'

He says: 'Do you want to live?'

'You will kill me?'

He shakes his head. 'Not me.'

The moment stretches. Then I take the keys out of my pocket and hand them to him. He lets go of my hand. I point across the dark landscape towards the track. He turns and starts to jog across the uneven ground. I could escape now. Easily, I think. The feeling has come back to my legs, and with it my sense of balance. But instead of running away I find myself following, keeping pace with him.

He doesn't take any detours. It's a straight line from the hole in the fence to the track. I jump down from the bank. My feet hit the uneven tarmac a second after his. He's in the driver's seat and firing the engine. I'm snatching the passenger door open, climbing in as he starts to reverse.

He's half turned in his seat, peering out of the rear window at the ghost of the track, lit only by the car's reversing lights. His foot is full on the accelerator. The engine whines. I glance out of the front window. Something's happening up by the gate. Beams of light in the sky. Headlights from a car just out of view. Then I see them. Two bright points emerging from the trees. A figure passing in front of them, opening the gate. And the car moving forward again, accelerating.

Our headlights are off. And their headlights are still too distant to reach us. We'll be invisible for a fair few seconds. But I'm thinking about their five forward gears and our single reverse. I'm still not sure if I want them to outrun us or not. I look across to the driver's seat. The only thing I know is that this man had a knife to my throat and he didn't use it. Not even when he had an open mineshaft to dump my body in.

I say: 'They're coming.'

He doesn't answer.

'Turn the car around.'

'No room.'

We've climbed to the top of the rise now, the one I free-wheeled down a few hours before. The other car has halved the distance between us already.

'They're gaining on us.'

'I know.'

'Go faster.'

'Give me a bloody break, woman! How many seconds do I have till he sees us?'

I snatch another glance at him. It's the first sign of emotion I've seen. 'Not many.'

'How many!'

'Twenty. No, ten.'

'Hell! Hold on to your seat!'

He throws the wheel left, and the back of the car is suddenly lurching towards the fence. The rear wheels hit the edge of the grass one after the other in a sickening double bump, launching us upwards. Fence posts crack. Wire scrapes on paintwork. Then the back of the car drops suddenly. We're going backwards down a slope so steep that we'll never be able to drive back up it again. The wheels bounce on the rough field. He turns off the engine and yanks the handbrake full on. The wheels slide, and for a moment I think the car is going to roll. But it doesn't. We come to rest, and the sudden silence presses in on me.

Then I hear the other car. I see its lights. It roars past a few yards ahead of us. It recedes, and the silence grows again.

It's him who speaks first. 'That was never ten seconds.'

'So shoot me!' I can't help shouting at him. It's a reaction, I guess. He turns, and I can feel him looking at me through the darkness. Then he laughs.

'What's so bloody funny?'

But he's laughing too hard to answer now. It takes him a few seconds to get himself together. 'I'm sorry.'

'Sorry? You ...' I can't think of a swearword strong enough. 'You ... After what you've done to me! Who the hell are you, anyway?'

The laughing subsides. He folds his arms. 'Shit, but you've given me a heap of trouble tonight.'

'Who – are – you? I deserve some answers!'

'Ask something different then.'

'I need a name.'

There's a pause. 'OK,' he says. 'Call me Snakes.'

'Snakes?' It's a start, I guess. 'Who was it just drove past?'

'The Prince.'

That's a name I didn't expect. 'Vince . . . here?'

'He's looking for you – for your car. There's a security camera hidden in a hedge next to the road down there a way. We saw you driving up here. That's why all the guards were out waiting.'

I think about this. 'They didn't find me – you did.'

'I was downwind.'

'You smelled me?'

'Been eating garlic, haven't you. You were good, though . . . for an amateur.'

'If Vince had found me . . .'

'The man hates you. Sent us out to get you. We had to bring you back for him to deal with.'

'You were protecting me?' I can't help the scorn sounding in my voice.

'Protecting myself. Don't want to go away for murder. And I don't like killing.'

'Then why tie me up?'

'They were waiting,' he says, 'in the trees. You were

walking right into them.' There's a pause then. 'Sorry about the wire. It was all I had to hand.'

'You could have told me all this before – instead of . . .'

'You'd have believed me?'

'Yes.' I bite on my lower lip for a moment. 'I don't know.'

'If I'd sent you away, you'd have come right back. And before you died, you'd have told him about me.'

'No!'

'Yes. Believe me. And I'd have been the next one under Vince's knife.'

'I could arrest you for false imprisonment.'

'Don't like killing,' he says again. 'Doesn't mean I wouldn't do it if I had to.'

We're looking at each other through the dark. I doubt if he'll be able to see any more of my face than I can of his. 'OK,' I say. 'No arrest.'

'Good,' he says. 'Now wait here.'

He gets out of the car, and I see him in the starlight, picking his way towards the track. He's lifting the snapped fence posts back into position, arranging the trailing wires.

I'm reminding myself that this is the man who attacked me near the football stadium, who poured petrol through my letterbox. The racist who doesn't like killing. His story doesn't make any kind of sense. Why does he think that I'll believe it at all? And then it occurs to me that he doesn't know yet – that I recognize him from those attacks.

The door opens and he climbs back into the driver's seat. 'Right now, Vince is searching for your car. He knows you didn't pass the camera a second time, and there's no other road out. In a couple of minutes he'll be driving back along here, trying to figure how you disappeared into thin air. We'll wait till he's past.'

I sit quiet after that. Waiting for the right time. Sure

enough, the car – driven by Vince if I can believe what I've been told – comes back towards us up the track. I listen to the engine noise building, watch the headlight beams drawing lines in the night air. Then it's suddenly bright and he's passed. Snakes waits till all the engine noise is gone, then he turns the ignition key and puts the car into gear.

Instead of trying to climb the slope, he reverses us down towards the bottom corner of the field, where a gate lets us out on to a track – but not the same one as I drove in along.

'You're safe here,' he says. 'Just carry on down that way and you'll get to the A44 eventually. A right turn takes you into town. A left takes you back to Leicester.'

He gets out and slams the door. I shift across to the driver's seat, still warm where he's been sitting. Then I click the door lock and raise the window, leaving just an inch of air to speak through.

'See you in the morning,' I say. 'When I come to arrest you.'

He's standing there, one hand on the window, a thickness of glass away. 'You said . . .'

'I lied.'

Up till now Snakes has still thought he could wriggle his way out of this situation.

'I recognize you,' I say.

That's the bit of information he didn't have before. He carries on with the same emotionless stare, trying to bluff it out. 'I can still kill you,' he says.

'When you were tying me,' I say, 'that's when I knew who you were – knew where I'd seen you.'

After a couple of seconds he breaks off, looks away down the track.

'You were ready enough to kill me before,' I say. 'But tonight you want to release me. Why is that?'

'You think if I'd wanted to kill you, you'd still be alive?'

'You poured real petrol through my door. You wanted to kill me right enough.'

'Didn't light the petrol, though.'

'I might not have woken up.'

'Didn't start pouring till you were coming down the stairs.'

'You heard me?'

He shrugs, as if it was nothing.

Ouch. That one hurt. I'd been proud of the way I'd handled him that night. Going out to face my attacker. But even as I'm rejecting the idea that he let me get away with my life, another part of my mind is going back over it – seeing the truth.

I turn my face from him. Way down below in the distance I can see the lights of a village. A few points of yellowish white in the black and folded landscape. I want to swear at him for what he's put me through. I want to get out of the car, kick him where it hurts.

'You get off on scaring women out of their minds! Is that it?'

'No.'

I peer at him through the glass, trying to see his expression. 'Why did you attack me?' I say, 'if it wasn't to kill me?'

Snakes says: 'To prove myself.'

'What?'

'So Vince would let me inside.'

'All that – so you could play with the other boys?'

Snakes still has his hand on the window, his fingers gripping through the crack. I have no doubt that he could break it in a second – if I tried to put the engine into gear and drive away. But he hasn't done anything yet.

'Why did you want to get in with Vince?'

There's some argument going on inside him. He must still think there's a chance he can get me to keep my mouth shut. He'd be risking a lot by letting me go. Vince's anger. A charge of assaulting a police officer. Attempted murder, perhaps.

Identification. That would be the problem. A defence lawyer would shred me in the witness box if I claimed to be able to recognize him. I'm picturing it in my mind – my attacker, his face covered by a balaclava, his hand reaching into the car through the broken window. I see it gripping the steering wheel. Leaving no fingerprints. All of which is impossible.

'The Scalpers,' I say. 'If we had a man on the inside, we'd know when and where the next attack was coming. An undercover officer.'

'So what?'

'So everything. Vince would never let a stranger inside the Scalpers – not unless he'd proved himself somehow.'

Snakes is still shaking his head, but not to deny anything. This is submission.

I say: 'You're an undercover police officer.'

He bends down so his head is next to the crack in the window. 'If you breathe a word of this . . .'

'I'm right then.'

'No. Let me in the car and we'll talk.'

'First,' I say, 'tell me who you really are.'

Chapter 21

Woodgate doesn't like what he's seeing. And it's not just the hangover that has him in a sour mood. He bends down slowly and runs a finger over the long scratch in the paintwork. It's horrible what a line of barbed wire can do to a car.

'Just bloody typical,' he says.

I pat him on the back. 'Don't worry. I'll tell them it wasn't you.'

He makes a sound halfway between a sigh and a groan. 'Never damaged a police car before.'

'And you didn't damage it this time.'

OK. I am feeling pretty guilty about this. Even after the stuff he said in the restaurant last night, I'd still not want to get him in trouble. I'd take the blame if I could. But I have a good reason for keeping quiet – not just saving my own skin.

'The paperwork,' he says. 'There'll be hundreds of forms . . .'

'Kids,' I say. 'Too much alco-pop inside them.'

'Gonna have to drive back in this.'

'Marking the unmarked police car – a dare, probably. Some teenager proving he's a man.'

Woodgate bends further, though the effort does make him look a little queasy. He prods the tyre with a finger. 'All this mud. When did I drive through that?'

'Up at Dr Cranmer-Phillips's land. Didn't you see? All over the road.'

He straightens himself. I turn, in case my expression gives me away.

We've got a clear sky again today. Cool air, but a promise of heat for later. It's one of those mornings when every detail is in sharp focus. The tubs of marigolds around the edge of the hotel car park, the slates on the roofs, the mountain slopes tinged with purple. I breathe in deeply, smelling the cleanness. I've had only a few hours' sleep, but I feel better than I've done for weeks. Woodgate, on the other hand . . . The man's a mess.

'What time did you leave the bar last night?'

He shakes his head – rather slowly. 'Turning-out time.'

'Eleven. Eleven thirty?'

'Something like that.' He looks sheepish.

I'm dressed in my uniform this morning. The jacket sleeves are long enough to cover the bruising on my wrists. Those are the only marks I have to show for my ordeal. I did better than the car.

I'm leading the way along the narrow pavement. It's a fifty-yard stroll from the hotel car park to the front door of the police station. Perhaps village life does have something to say for it. I step inside. Sergeant Day is waiting.

'Good morning,' I say. 'Looks like it's going to be a hot one again.'

'Morning, ma'am,' he says.

He doesn't have the same vivacious energy that he had yesterday. His movements are slower. Looking at him again, I see that his skin has a greyish tint. I hadn't noticed that before. He nods towards Woodgate. Woodgate nods back.

I glance from one to the other, sensing conspiracy. 'Something I need to be told about?'

Day takes a deep breath. 'We were up late,' he says.

'Up late.' I echo the words, suddenly worried that they might have seen me returning to the village. But that was three in the morning. The bars would have been long closed by then.

'How late?'

Woodgate says: 'It's the way they do things round here, ma'am.'

'How late?'

'Three in the morning.'

I'm starting to panic. My blouse was in shreds when I sneaked back into the hotel. Right now, I haven't any ideas on how to explain that little detail.

Then Day clears his throat. 'It's an informal arrangement we have here, see. Between the police and the local publicans. They lock the doors – so it's not like people are coming and going. And there's always an officer inside, to make sure things don't get out of hand.'

'You had a lock-in?'

Both sergeants look down to the floor.

I laugh out loud. 'Is that all?'

'Half the town was there – so you're bound to hear it from someone. Only we were hoping you wouldn't need to mention it in your report. Seeing as no damage was done.'

So much of my work is done in interview rooms, you'd think I'd have seen every kind by now. But this is new to me. A slate floor. Whitewashed walls. It could do with a carpet to soak up the echoes. And some curtains. The window – high on the wall opposite the door – is crossed by three vertical bars.

Dr Cranmer-Phillips is sitting on one side of the table, Woodgate on the other. No one stands as I enter the room.

There's no lawyer. I sit. I should have trusted myself and taken the bet when Woodgate offered it. The sergeant clicks on the tape recorder and mumbles his way through the formalities.

I make eye contact with each of them in turn, then I say: 'Please bear with me a moment.'

After that I get out some of the paperwork that's come from the trip. Dr Cranmer-Phillips is looking at me, passive, giving the impression that time is his friend. That, of course, is true. I need to be driving back to Leicester ASAP. But I manage to hide my urgency well enough.

I've just started working through one form, ticking boxes, when Cranmer-Phillips speaks: 'I've been thinking about this room,' he says. 'No telephone connection. Have you noticed that? And the electricity cables run over the surface of the walls instead of being buried in them.'

I look up from the papers. 'A riddle?'

He places a finger on the side of his head. 'Never stop thinking, Miss Akanbai. It's the only thing that separates us from the lower animals.'

I look around the walls. He's right about the cabling. 'What's the answer then?'

'It was built before electric lighting.'

'And before telephones?'

For a moment I think that he's going to answer. Then we're back to the waiting game.

I put my pen down. 'You have telephones up at your farm.'

'Of course. But no mains electricity.'

I consider this for a moment, then put my first real question: 'There's a man they call Vince the Prince. You know him.'

Cranmer-Phillips shakes his head.

'You knew him when I talked to you yesterday.'

'I know *of* him,' Cranmer-Phillips says, 'but I have never had occasion to meet the man.'

'Have you ever talked to him?'

'Not as far as I can recall.'

I don't mind people lying to me in interview. In fact, I like them to – when there's a tape recorder running. I keep the sudden hope from showing on my face. 'And yet . . .' I pull out the list of telephone calls from my bag and put it on the table in front of him. '. . . and yet the telephone company records show that several calls were made to your property from Vince's number.'

He looks at the numbers for a moment. 'Perhaps.'

'You have received calls from that number on and off for five years.'

'Have I?'

'How do you account for that if you have never spoken to the man?'

He shrugs. 'The phone is in an open area. It is used by many people. I don't monitor the calls.'

I pull the paper back to my side of the table. 'Ever heard of the Martin's Hill Scalpers?'

'No.'

'Ever heard of Waterfields?'

'Yes.'

'Good.'

'And I've heard of you as well, inspector. You're becoming quite famous among the ranks of those interested in preserving the Anglo-Saxon race and culture. One could even say *notorious*.'

I nod – a kind of agreement – then go back to my papers. Sorting through them. Using the activity to hide my reaction to his implied threat. He sits, impassive.

'You live on a farm?' I say.

'It is more than a farm.'

'How so?'

'The word "farm" implies an organization dedicated to production and motivated by profit. Whereas we are a community dedicated to self-sufficiency and motivated by the vision of re-creating a strong, morally based society.'

He speaks slowly, deliberately – as if each word is being considered just before it's spoken. It all sounds so reasonable. I swallow my first reaction and smile at him instead.

'In which case, Dr Cranmer-Phillips, we're on the same side.'

He refolds his arms. 'Your idea of a strong society is not the same as ours.'

'You don't want disorder on the streets, do you?'

'No. But . . .'

'Then we're on the same side.'

I go back to my paperwork – ticking the last boxes. He doesn't say anything for several seconds, though I can see him fidgeting on the periphery of my vision.

'Where we differ, inspector, is in our understanding of why the streets have become unsafe. You ignore mounting evidence that certain groups have a genetic predisposition to criminality. Take recent events for your example. Were more people of colour arrested during the riots, or more of the white race?'

'Not a good example,' I say. 'There are social and economic reasons for that. *A riot is at bottom the language of the unheard.*'

'Another quotation?'

'Dr Martin Luther King.'

He smiles. 'Then take substance abuse. People selling drugs to children.'

'People on the white estates, you mean. Like Martin's Hill?'

'On the contrary, inspector. Immigrant leaders constantly bemoan the fact that prisons are disproportionately populated by non-whites. They claim a biased police force, a biased prosecution service *and* a biased judiciary. But genetics offers a single, simple explanation – *non sunt multiplicanda entia praeter necessitatem.*'

I shrug. 'At least I quoted in English.'

'Ockham's razor, inspector. The simple explanation is more likely to be true.'

I take a slow breath, steadying my nerves. 'And drug pushers like Vince – where do they fit into your world view?'

'He has nothing to do with drugs.'

I feel my pulse rate jump. 'You said you hadn't met him.'

'I . . .' He swallows.

'How can you know he is not involved in drugs if you haven't met him?'

Dr Cranmer-Phillips closes his eyes for a moment, then opens them again. 'I met Sir Winston Churchill once – did you know that?'

I don't bother answering.

'And I'd say that he didn't abuse drugs. But meeting him didn't tell me that. My knowledge of the man's deeds and his lineage – it is these things that tell me. Things I knew even before I met him.'

Dr Cranmer-Phillips is looking comfortable again. A tiny slip-up. No more than that. Time to change subject again.

'Let's not call it a farm then,' I say. 'An agricultural community.'

He likes that. There's a smile. A nod.

'Organic agriculture?'

'No. Though we are moving towards self-sufficiency. This means we use few chemicals that we cannot produce ourselves.'

'Why?'

'Because agriculture is the foundation of civilization. We cannot be said to have a true Anglo-Saxon civilization if our foundation depends on the non-Anglo-Saxon races that control the global agri-business. '

'Such as?'

'Hispanics. Japanese. Jews.'

'What about the Serbs and Germans – do you hate them as well?'

'Hate is your word,' he says, 'not mine. But the Serbian and German peoples have historically shared much of our natural agenda. That is all.'

As with so many of Cranmer-Phillips's doctrines, the further you dig, the nastier they start to sound. I have to back off again – if only to keep control of my own anger. I put my papers back into the file.

I change the line of questioning. 'Do you keep animals?'

'Native breeds – all but wiped out by the European agricultural directives.'

'Pigs?'

'Gloucestershire Old Spot.'

'Other varieties?'

He smiles. Nods slightly, as if in answer to an internal question, then says: 'I understand there was a pig found in a mosque in Waterfields. Not a Gloucestershire Old Spot, I take it. Fortunately, I am able to inform you that we rear only the one variety on my land. Now – presumably that is the end of your questioning.'

I sit back in my chair. The formality of the interview is over. To all outward appearances Dr Cranmer-Phillips has won. And that's just the way I want it. Since my conversation with Snakes I have a snippet of information that neither he nor my fellow police officers possess.

Till now I've been a victim. Pushed around. I'd have been suspended already if it wasn't for the chief constable's personal intervention. I still might be if I can't get the memo question sorted. But things have changed. For the first time in this investigation, I'm feeling like I'm in control of what happens next.

PART THREE

There was this police sergeant I heard about once. Had an informant that he kept all to himself. The informant was a small-time criminal – soft drugs, a few cars. Nothing much. The sergeant learned all the names and places he needed. Lots of arrests and convictions. The informant waved goodbye to business rivals. And he learned in advance if there was going to be a crackdown or a raid.

It wasn't what they called corruption. Not in those days. More like symbiosis. Business was good for both of them.

The sergeant became an inspector. The petty criminal moved on to bigger things. There weren't many rivals to grass up any more. As an informant, he wouldn't have been worth the risk. But there were new incentives. Fat brown envelopes that the taxman never saw.

You can earn money in secret, of course, but people see when you spend it. A house too big. Holidays in the Seychelles. Kids in private school. It all adds up. He was a chief inspector by that time, and his one-time informant shipping half the cocaine being snorted in three counties.

It was time to go for the chief inspector. So he took early retirement, left with all his medals and his reputation still intact – and all before the police Complaints and Discipline investigation handed in its report.

Chapter 22

The perfect blue sky ends just above the highest tower blocks in a layer of purple smog. It feels good to be back in Leicester.

Woodgate drops me off at the station. I hurry into the office, power up my computer and rattle off my report. I'm quick with these things. It doesn't take me long before I'm listening to the printer hum into life. Of course, there isn't much to say. There are only two significant bits of information. First, Cranmer-Phillips officially denies having met or knowing Vince. I'm pretty sure that this is a lie – but even if we could prove it, we wouldn't be much closer to unravelling the threads of the murder. Second, he denies keeping any other varieties of pigs. Again, that could easily be a lie as well. If he doesn't have any more remaining, then we have no way of checking.

That's what's in the report. A hell of a lot more interesting is the stuff I'm leaving out. Snakes. I'm still not sure if the man is what he claims to be. But he did have the opportunity to kill me. Three times. On each occasion he held back. That all adds credibility to his story. But perhaps he's just not very good at killing.

I'm burning to tell someone about it – to talk it through. There's Sal, of course. But she'd freak out if I let any of this slip. Dad would have known what to do and say – he always did. But now he's gone there aren't many people I can confide in on that level. I've not got many civilian friends – there's never been time for developing a social life. And after what Snakes told me, I don't know who I can trust within the force. Paresh, perhaps. But I don't want to have to talk to him.

So I pick up the phone and dial the only person I can think of within the building who I can be sure has nothing to gain or lose by the information. Bob. It rings twice before he picks up. There's music playing in the background.

'Yup?'

'It's Mo,' I say. 'You mind if I come down for a chat?'

'I'm kind of busy,' he says. 'The deputy chief's upgrade.' There's a pause, then he asks: 'What kind of chat?'

'Big chat.'

'What the heck. I'll get the kettle on.'

When I step into Bob's room, he's on his hands and knees next to a couple of steaming mugs. He dips the handle of a small screwdriver and fishes out a teabag. This he splats into the battleship-grey waste-bin. Then he gets up and uses one elbow to clear a corner of the desk. A sheaf of papers spills on to the floor. He places the mugs carefully on the newly exposed desk surface.

'Strong or weak?'

I go for the strong one this time – the mug looks slightly less stained. 'Thanks.'

He focuses his concentration on me then, for a moment. Those clear grey eyes probing my face, my posture. Then he turns to the workbench and slots a CD into the computer he's been working on.

'You got to listen to this,' he says, tweaking the volume control on one of the loudspeakers. There's a moment of silence then a familiar opening chord on a keyboard and the voice of Freddie Mercury.

Bob racks up the volume some more. 'It's a classic. "Who Wants to Live For Ever." Downloaded it this morning.'

'Sorry?'

'Off the Internet.'

'Isn't there some problem with copyright?'

He shrugs. 'Technically, perhaps. But I'm just swapping music files with other people. Their computers to mine. There's no company involved for anyone to sue.'

'Technically,' I say, 'you could get the sack for doing this here. Is that the deputy chief's computer you're using?'

'Yeah,' he says with a wicked grin. 'And I only get the sack if someone reports me.' He clicks a mouse and the music stops.

'I guess you're safe then.' I take a sip of my tea.

After a moment he says: 'You wanted to talk.'

I push the door closed.

'That kind of talk?'

'Yes.'

He takes his mug and parks himself on the workbench, legs dangling. 'The old ears are all yours.'

So I tell him the story. The investigation. The trip to Wales. But it's when we get to Snakes that his eyes start to widen.

'You're making this up.'

I pull one sleeve of my uniform jacket back a couple of inches. 'It's all true.'

'Shit.' He can see the dark bracelet of bruised and broken skin.

I hold it for him to see for a couple of seconds longer, then cover it over again. It feels good to have shown it. I'm making a bridge here, between the madness of that night and my everyday experience.

Bob is shaking his head. 'An undercover police officer did that?'

'He says he's MI5. An agent.'

'No way! Absolutely no way. MI5 are all spies and terrorists and stuff.'

'This is terrorists. They've firebombed places in the past. Now it's murder.'

'That's criminal stuff. Your lot, not James Bond.'

'Bond is MI6. And I'm just telling you what Snakes told me.'

'You gotta let someone know.'

'I am doing.'

'C'mon, Mo. You know what I mean. A police officer.' He points a finger towards the ceiling. 'Someone upstairs.'

'That's the problem. Snakes said there's a reason why they've kept the local police in the dark.'

'Oh, hell.'

'Someone started asking why more progress hadn't been made against racist attacks. I guess no one was interested before. But then this Multiculturalism Conference gets planned and they start worrying.'

'Not going to tell me there's a bent copper in here!'

'It does happen.'

'Really, really don't want to hear this.'

I press on anyway. 'MI5 took a look in our files. It turns out that there's a pattern. A statistical thing. Going back years.'

He's got his arms folded across his chest. He's shaking his head. 'It might be chance.'

'Half a ton of paperwork telling one story. This particular gang of racists have known what we were going to do before we did it. Every time. Property searches. Wire taps. Everything. That's their analysis of it anyway.'

'Then you got to talk to someone high up. The chief constable. The deputy chief.'

I take a swallow of tea. 'Perhaps. But there's big-league politics going on here. I'm just not sure yet. Snakes said not to tell *anyone*.'

'Then why are you telling me?'

'Don't know. I guess you have to be clean. How could you be leaking police secrets? Half the time you don't know what's going on next door to your own office.'

'That supposed to be a compliment?'

'Not just that. You're a friend. I want to know what you think.'

He looks in my eyes for a moment. 'God. I don't know. My advice – tell someone else. 'Coz I haven't got a clue.' Then he turns back to the workbench and extracts the CD from the computer. 'Here. Present for you. Queen's greatest hits.'

I pull back my hand. 'I can't . . .'

'Chill out,' he says. 'Take it. And any other track you want – I can get it for you. Any version. Original. Remix. Anything. Give me a challenge.'

'Sinead O'Connor,' I say. '"Nothing Compares 2 U".'

I walk away from Bob's room holding the bootleg Queen CD in my hand, not sure what to do with it. The lack of sleep last night is beginning to catch up on me now. There's about half a ton of paperwork waiting on my desk, but I think I'd throw up if I tried to work through it right now.

My health still isn't right. I know it can't be food poisoning. Not after all this time. And since my period came, I know I can't be pregnant. But even that was strange, because it was so much lighter than usual. Not much more than a few spots. Right now I'm thinking I've got some low-level bug, aggravated by a lack of sleep. That must be what's thrown my hormone cycle out. That and all the stress. What I really need is some fresh air and a walk in the sunshine.

I find Greenway in the Community Relations Unit office. He gets up suddenly when I come into the room. Guiltily, perhaps. I'd say he's enjoyed his stint in the boss's chair more than he'd want to admit.

'Back early,' he says.

'Sorry.'

'No. No . . . I didn't . . .'

'Relax,' I say. 'I've got a little job for you.'

The Majestic Hotel. Five storeys, sixty rooms and an ornamental turret all in the best-quality Victorian red brick. A luxury residence on the edge of the park. That's how the architect must have seen it. But since then it's gone through 130 years of decline

I'm walking down Dean Street with Greenway next to me and what I notice about the hotel is this: one blotchy green line of algae-stained brick from the broken gutter to the litter-strewn pavement. Three of the ground-floor windows boarded up. Graffiti on the walls. It's mostly tags, but there are the ghosts of some racist slogans as well – writing that the council has failed to steam-clean away.

We get to the front entrance and I can see flakes of peeled paint on the ground next to the doorframe. No one wants to come to Waterfields for a holiday. Not any more. That's why they put the asylum-seekers here.

Greenway hasn't been inside before. He wrinkles up his nose. 'What's that smell?'

'Disinfectant? Damp?'

He's not convinced.

'Cabbage?'

It's probably a mixture of all three.

There are seats in the foyer A group of black African men in the corner are conspicuously not chatting any more. Somalis, I guess. Greenway and I both try smiling towards them, but there's no response.

'Can I help?' The voice belongs to an Asian man behind the reception desk.

Greenway steps towards him. 'Looking for a Serbian family. Medigovich.'

The receptionist doesn't change his expression. 'If you'd like to leave a message.'

'They're not here?'

The man moves his head slightly from side to side. Not quite a 'no'.

'When will they be back?'

He shrugs. 'Sorry.'

I step up to the desk. 'We're trying to help them. That's all.'

The man glances across to the group of Somalis then back to me. 'Look. It's not good you coming in here. Everyone gets jumpy with uniforms.'

'I'm worried about the Medigovich family,' I say. 'About their safety.'

He leans forward and drops his voice so no one but us can hear. 'Mr Medigovich. He has this problem in his head – from all the things he saw.'

'Post-traumatic stress disorder,' offers Greenway.

The receptionist nods. 'Paranoid. Don't know what he's told you. But you can't believe it. He has crazy stories. All the Muslims are out to get him. That kind of thing. He's made a lot of trouble for us here.'

'It's the boy,' I say. 'Niko. That's who I'm worried about.'

He looks at me for a moment as if trying to make a decision, then he nods. 'I'll see what I can do.'

I say: 'I'm going to be in the park for the next few minutes. If you see any of the family . . .'

'I'll tell them.'

Majestic Park isn't much more than a steep grassy slope with a few trees around the edge – though it does have a couple of strips of green carpet-like material set into the ground that pass for wickets during the cricket season. We sit ourselves down on a bench and wait.

Down below us, over at the far side of the park, is an area marked off with incident tape strung between the trees. It's being prepared for the PM's visit in a couple of days' time. Two workmen are removing a litter-bin from within the cordon. They hoist it on to the back of a small park-service truck.

When Saturday morning comes, there won't be a scrap of litter remaining to offend the eye. The park will be full of the great and the good. Community leaders will line up to have their photos taken with the PM. But today it's quiet. The only onlookers are a small group of unshaven men fifty paces from where I'm sitting. None of their clothes look less than a decade out of fashion. They're sitting on the grass, holding cans of Special Brew, watching us. After a few seconds, one gets to his feet and pulls the others up after him. They stagger away.

'Nice here,' says Greenway.

'Yup.'

Then he says: 'That thing about The Bard . . .' He's talking about Superintendent Shakespeare.

'The memo?' I say.

'Yes. I don't believe what they're saying.'

That's what everyone's told me since I got back from Wales. The trouble is, they don't seem to be saying it to each other when I'm not around.

'Thanks,' I say.

'I didn't want you to think it was me, that's all.'

The drunks have moved to what they must feel is a safer distance from us. One drops to his knees before toppling to one side. He lies staring up at the sky. The others glance back in our direction, then sit themselves down next to their comrade. At the far side of the park, the workmen have removed the last litter-bin from what will become a security exclusion area on Friday morning.

I'm about to check my watch when I hear a voice behind us.

'Police?' The owner of the voice comes around the bench and stands in front of me. 'I am Ivan Medigovich.'

'Niko's father?'

I get up and offer my hand. He takes it.

He's not a tall man, though his shoulders are broad. He has short-cropped hair, strikingly blond, and a Turkish-style jacket of dark brown leather. His grey eyes jump from the sergeant to me and back.

'Inspector Akanbai,' I say. 'This is Sergeant Greenway.'

'Niko is make trouble?' His voice is deep, the 'r's pronounced with a distinctly Slavic roll.

'No trouble. But I was concerned about something he said.'

'Sorry. No mean for trouble.'

'He said you'd been threatened. Something about letters?'

Medigovich half turns so he's gazing along the line of benches next to the path. I'd been wondering what it was about him that reminded me so strongly of Niko. I've got it now. It's not the physical looks – though you might guess they were father and son. It's the way his eyes seem to be gazing at invisible ghosts.

'The letters,' I say, prompting him.

He blinks a couple of times, then looks back to me. 'Letters?'

'You did receive written threats.'

He sighs.

'Niko told me they said you should go back to your country.'

'I am a dentist. You know this?'

'No.'

'I treat all the people. Catholic. Jew. Everyone. Even Muslim.' He stops, shakes his head. 'I take away from their pain. You understand this?'

'The letters,' says Greenway. 'What did they say?'

'Say we go from this place. They kill us if we stay.'

'How many letters? When did you receive them?'

'Three letter. One month gone.'

'We need to see them.'

'All destroy. I burn them all.'

Greenway can't hide his exasperation. 'How can we find out who did this if you get rid of the evidence?'

'I tell everyone about letters. No one listen.'

'The police? You told the police?'

He sweeps his hands out and away from him, as if Greenway's suggestion is ridiculous. 'No one listen to me. They think I am crazy man.'

'We can't find out who did this if you don't tell us!'

'I know who do this. It easy. Like before. Like always. The Muslim do this to us.'

The two men are facing each other, both tensed up. Greenway the taller, looking down. Niko's father not stepping back, not letting any of his remaining dignity slip.

What is it with men – this pride thing? Put two of them together when they're feeling vulnerable and it always ends in a fight. I'm just about to remove my sergeant from the danger area when my mobile phone chimes. Bad timing.

'Sergeant,' I say. 'Take Mr Medigovich's statement. That'll do for now.'

Then I jab the button and put the phone to my ear. 'Yes?'

'It's me.'

Fear. That's my first reaction. Logically, I'm not in any danger – but the memory of terror is still attached to the voice. I'm stepping away from the two men. Greenway has his notebook out now and is sitting on the bench.

'Snakes?'

I can hear deep breathing, as if he's just run to get to the phone. 'Don't have long.'

'Where are you?'

'A call box. Listen. Cranmer-Phillips talked to me in the car – on the way back from town this morning.'

The fear is ebbing away now, leaving a nauseous and ill-defined anxiety behind. 'Cranmer-Phillips? You're his driver?'

'He trusts me.'

'Not so smart then.'

'Dunno what you said to him in that police station this morning. But he was fuming all the way back.'

'Good.'

'Not good. Didn't say anything out straight – you know how he is with words. But he said it'd be a good thing if you weren't around to bother us no more.'

The fear is rising again. I don't let it sound in my voice. 'So? He wants to hang me from a fire escape, or what?'

'He said you being killed wouldn't be any good.'

'Then we agree on something.'

'You're not taking this seriously! He said he doesn't want you a martyr. Best way to get rid of you is to plant something on you. In your house, your car. Discredit you. Turn you into a criminal.'

'They're going to move on me – that's what you're saying?'

But he's gone. The phone clicks and I'm standing on my own in Majestic Park. I look around me, as if Vince might be hiding, waiting to jump out from behind a tree. Greenway has finished taking the details. Medigovich walks over towards me. There's anger in his movements. Resentment.

'You people,' he says. 'You know nothing of what it is to be like this—' he pats his leather jacket with both hands '— a refugee. Only they drive you from your house, from your country. Only then you really know. And you will never give help.'

Chapter 23

I don't get to hear about the breakthrough till the briefing starts the next morning. But even before that I know something has happened. It's the tension in the room. Few people talking – and then only in whispers.

Superintendent Alison Walker, Superintendent Frank Shakespeare, Inspector Paresh Gupta. They sweep into the room together. By rank, I should be among them. But no one is kidding themselves that I'm anything more than an embarrassment to this investigation. I remind myself that it's only the chief constable's intervention that's kept me in the job. Even his support won't help me if Complaints and Discipline decide I lied about my memo to the super.

Alison has some A3 photographs under her arm. I get a side-on glimpse of the top picture as she turns, but can't make out anything.

'A week ago,' she says, 'we put out information about the murder to a number of police agencies, hoping that some-one would have seen something similar. Most of you will have heard by now. We got a response from the Internet Crime Unit.'

She turns and props one of the photographs on the bottom of the whiteboard. At first I think it's one of the pictures taken by the scene-of-crime officers at the mosque. The pool of blood. The dismembered parts of the pig. Then I notice the black cloth, still dry and folded neatly on the floor, and it hits me that whoever took the picture did it before the animal was covered.

'This comes from a news website based in America. The caption says: "Desecration of a Mosque in Serbia".'

No one in the room is saying anything. Alison drinks the silence for a moment. 'The website managers claim ignorance. The author of the article has already been questioned by the Los Angeles Police Department. Apparently, he wasn't keen to release his sources. Claimed his rights as a journalist were being trampled on. He changed his mind, though, when they told him it was a murder investigation. This so-called journalist had filched the article from a French-language news service, done a quick translation and sold it as his own work. The photograph came from somewhere else – another American website, this one belonging to a white supremacist group.'

A couple of people start to snigger, glad to see a journalist humiliated. Then Alison turns and props the remaining photographs next to the first. All laughter stops. One picture, a cemetery, the gravestones being smashed by men with sledgehammers and facemasks. The next picture, a building already on fire, more petrol bombs frozen midflight, streaked out in fiery arcs across a black sky.

'These are from the same site. Unsolved racist crimes from the East Midlands. All of them still open cases. And this one—' she props the last image against the whiteboard '—needs no introduction.'

I stare at the picture. Anwar's murder scene. And I'm thinking that this particular photograph must have been taken early in the investigation – because the body is still hanging by its wrists. So the first question I'm asking myself is how the hell a white supremacist group got hold of one of our photographs. Then I notice the angle of the picture and realize this had to have been taken from the other fire escape. The building opposite. Which means that it's not one of ours at all. And then, last of all, I take in Anwar's face. Not the peaceful expression of one whose facial muscles have relaxed in death. There is pain in his eyes and fear. The fear of a man still very much alive.

There's a muttering of expletives from around the room. I guess most of the detectives here have seen death before. But only in the aftermath. Only when the victim's life had already been stolen away. This is different. Even Alison can't bring herself to milk the moment of revelation.

'Why?' asks one of the detectives in the audience. 'Why keep evidence of your crime? Why make it public, for Christ's sake?'

Paresh answers. 'Boasting. If they think they can't get caught. Getting other racists worked up. Prestige. And white supremacist groups around the world have money to donate. There are channels we don't know about. Networks. But they've got to be damned sure of themselves to risk it.'

Most of the people in the room are still staring at the photographs.

Into the silence I say: 'Does this mean we're making the two investigations into one?'

People turn to look at me, then back to the superintendent, waiting for her response.

'This picture—' she swallows heavily '—this picture is eight days old. It must have been put on the Internet more recently than that. All the information should still exist to trace it back to the computer from which it entered the World Wide Web. And we're getting cooperation right now from the FBI – helping **us** to track down whoever put it up there. But if word **leaks** out that we're following this lead . . .' She looks around the room, as if she needs to check that everyone is still listening. 'It only takes the click of a mouse button to wipe a computer disk clean.

'The murder of Anwar Khaliq and the attack on the Dean Street Mosque remain as two separate investigations. And if anything of this finds its way into the papers – anything – then someone in this room will lose their job. Do I make myself clear?'

All of which should give you a pretty good clue as to why I don't want to see Sergeant Greenway with a copy of the *Crusader* folded in his hand. But that's exactly what happens after the meeting. He comes towards me with the paper held by his side, conspicuously trying to make it look inconspicuous.

'What?'

'A word, ma'am.'

'I'm listening.'

'Somewhere private.'

So we head back to Community Relations, go straight into my fish-tank office and close the door. He puts the newspaper on my desk, opens it on page three. 'Thought you should see.'

I scan the headline. *Conference Leak Probe*. 'Shit.'

'Read it,' he says.

Government chiefs announce an inquiry into the leaking of confidential conference documents. The Multiculturalism Conference is four days away, but the substance of announcements to be made there by the PM are already known. Controversial plans to accelerate the immigration of skilled workers into the country were leaked to the press late yesterday. They have caused an outcry from the right of the political spectrum and the hunt is on for the source of the leak.

'It's The Bard and you that have been involved,' says Greenway. 'In the conference planning, I mean.'

'Yes.' I'm scanning the page, looking for clues, trying to work out consequences.

'Another inquiry for you to deal with,' he says.

I'm past caring about inquiries after all that's happened. I'm more worried about what's going to happen now the news is out there. Our conference is going to draw in far-right protesters from all over England. Not what Waterfields needs right now. I close the newspaper. 'Why would anyone want to leak it?'

'Then it's true – that's what the PM is going to announce?'

I look at him for a moment. 'This is all supposed to be confidential.'

'It's all in the open now,' he says. 'But I guess if you don't want to say . . .?'

There's a knock on the glass. We both turn to see Bob the computer manager hovering in the outer office. It's strange seeing him here. He seldom ventures out of his own domain. He shifts his weight from one foot to the other, then back.

Greenway doesn't wait for me to answer his question. He steps past the computer manager on his way out. 'Take care, Mo,' he says.

'Thanks.'

Bob steps inside my fish tank and closes the door. He sits down at my computer. Then, in one supremely furtive movement, he pulls a disk out from under his shirt and slips it into the CD drive.

That's when I get the seed of my idea. And it's all from a stupid misunderstanding. Because I'm thinking that Bob has come up to let me in on some discovery about the investigation. Something about the white supremacist web-site. But of course, he doesn't even know about that yet.

He adjusts the volume control on the computer loud-speaker. Then I hear it – Sinead O'Connor's voice. Familiar words, but so full of grief that they always cut into my flesh – just like the first time I heard the song. 'Nothing Compares 2 U'.

'Told you I'd find it,' he says.

'What?'

'This is what you wanted, right?'

But my mind's started running off on a tangent. 'Downloading music . . . one computer to another.'

'Yup.'

'You could do it with pictures as well?'

'Sure.'

'If there was a wire tap,' I say, 'on someone's phone line. Would we be able to get hold of the pictures they were sending?'

Bob swivels the chair so he's facing me. 'Sure. It's just ones and noughts. Feed it into a computer and we could see what it was.'

'And you'd know, would you? If it was music or if it was a picture?'

He leans back so far that he's gazing at the ceiling. 'Um.'

'What?'

'Usually you'd know. But there's this thing that you can do: hide data in a digital photograph. Something to do with steganography. I guess you could do it the other way around as well, hide a picture in a music file. Might even be easier, 'coz music files are big bastards. More room to hide things in.'

Steganography. I tap my fingers on my forehead, trying to remember.

'Would you know if there was something hidden inside a picture?'

He looks down, shrugs. 'Not my thing, all this. Ask a mathematician. But I guess you'd need a before and after. A copy of the file with and without the data hidden in it. That way you'd have a chance at least.'

I'm out of the room, leaving Bob opening and closing his mouth behind the glass. Leah tries to say something to me, but I'm out of Community Relations and marching along the corridor towards Superintendent Alison Walker's office.

'Marjorie?' She must be able to see there's something up.

'The wire tap,' I say. 'Vince's house. Did we get it set up?'

'Yes.'

'Did we intercept any calls between Vince and Dr Cranmer-Phillips?'

Alison stands up and comes around the desk. 'Just one. I thought you'd been told. A data transfer. Computer to computer.'

'And . . .?'

'I really thought you'd been informed about this.' She reaches out her hand and touches my elbow. 'You were out of the city . . .'

'What kind of data?'

'A music file. If you can call it music. We could get Vince on promoting racial hatred because he transmitted it. But it's nothing we didn't know already.'

I may not know much about codes and computers, but I understand the psychology of criminal investigation. And of this I feel sure – the best possible place to hide evidence that connects you to a murder is inside evidence that implicates you in a more minor crime. If Cranmer-Phillips and Vince had been transmitting *The Sound of Music* from one computer to another, we'd not have stopped searching till we'd found what he was up to. We'd have had our people pull the files apart, digital bit by digital bit. But because they were transmitting race-hate music, we thought we'd found the crime already. We didn't look any further.

'When?'

'You were there in Wales.'

'Monday night? You need to get it looked at by a code expert. Bet you anything there's data hidden in the music.'

I don't know how I expect her to react. Enthusiasm would be too much to hope for. Encouragement, perhaps?

'I've been talking to Superintendent Shakespeare,' she says. 'Apparently, you haven't used any of your holiday entitlement this year.'

'The music files. Can't you see it? Cranmer-Phillips tells Vince what targets to hit. Vince commits the crimes. They put the pictures on the web to draw in financial support from racist groups in the US.'

'I'll pass the idea on.' She moves to the other side of the desk again, opens her diary. 'You have to take your annual leave by September.'

I turn and walk from the room.

Chapter 24

'What the hell are you doing here?'
I try to smile. 'Going to invite me in?'

'It's not a good time.' Paresh is holding the front door almost closed, and he's using his body to block most of the gap that remains. All I can see of the inside of his house is a triangle of carpet near his feet. There are several shoes just behind him, including a pair of slingbacks designed for daintier feet than mine. I can hear the muffled sound of conversation. Coming from the front room, probably.

'We need to talk.'

He drops his voice. 'This isn't going to change anything.'

'We need to talk about the case.'

A woman's laugh cuts over the murmur of conversation within.

'It's family,' he says, as if I'd asked.

I take half a step towards him. 'This can't wait.'

A door opens in the hallway. Paresh turns from me for a moment. Something is said, then he steps back to reveal his mother standing inside.

'Inspector,' she beams. 'Won't you come in.' She's wearing a pale blue sari and there's a few thousand pounds' worth of twenty-four-carat gold around her wrists and neck.

I leave my shoes with the others by the mat and follow her into the front room. Paresh's father clambers out of a plush armchair. 'Marjorie. It's been so long.' He's wearing a suit today, and looking good with it. The three people who were sitting on the sofa opposite have also got up to greet me.

'This is Inspector Akanbai,' Mrs Gupta announces. 'And these are our friends Dr and Mrs Patel and their daughter. She's studying medicine.'

What with the doctor's tie and his wife's and daughter's saris we're talking about serious overtime in the silk factory. Everyone is smiling. I do my best to mirror the happy mood.

Mrs Gupta, standing close to me, has the warmest smile of them all. Though whether this is because she's been able to show me off to the Patels or because she's been able to show Miss Patel off to me I can't say for sure. It could be, I suppose, that she's just pleased to see me.

'Sorry to interrupt,' I say. 'Police work. Always busy.'

Paresh ushers me through to the kitchen. He closes the door behind us. There are used plates and pots stacked in the sink. Someone's eaten well. Rice, prawn curry, fried chicken. There's a plate of chapattis on the breakfast bar. Untouched. I climb on to a stool next to it. I'm wondering if Miss Patel can make chapattis as perfectly round and thin as Mrs Gupta's. But it's none of my business. Not really.

Paresh has remained standing. His arms are folded. I look at him for a moment before speaking.

'Remember what you said when we raided Vince's place – that it was too clean?'

He nods.

'You said it was because he was planning something big and didn't want any police hassle in the run-up. But what if he knew we were going to do a search?'

'How?'

'Tipped off.'

Paresh unfolds his arms and puts his hands in his pockets. 'Impossible.'

'Why?'

'Is that it?' he says. 'I can't believe you came all the way over here just to say that.'

'Tell me why it's impossible.'

'Because . . .' He shakes his head. 'It's out of the question. It would have to be someone inside the investigation. Or the magistrate's office.'

'What about the similar racist attacks – the ones you told me about. Did you ever do any searches when you were investigating those?'

'Yes.'

'And . . .?'

He looks around the kitchen as if searching for something to help him to explain the obvious to me. There isn't anything, so he just says: 'This is ridiculous.'

'They were clean as well, weren't they?'

'No one would have . . . I just don't believe it.'

'You searched and you found nothing.'

'So? That doesn't prove anything.'

'But if you'd found something incriminating – that would have proved it the other way. At least then we'd know there wasn't a leak.'

Paresh turns and takes a cup from the draining board. He fills it with cold water then steps across and sits himself on the stool opposite me. 'It'd take a hell of a lot for me to believe this story.'

I don't see any way around this without letting him know something. So I say: 'I had a tip-off.'

'You had . . .?'

'Didn't believe it at first. But . . .'

'Hell!' He's shaking his head as if that will stop the idea getting in.

'. . . but then I thought about everything that's happened . . .'

'Who's your source?'

'Someone who should know.'

'Come on, Mo!'

'No names.'

'Then what? You won't tell me a name. So what do you expect me to do about it?'

'I'm suggesting an experiment,' I say. 'That's all. We apply for another search warrant. Do it tonight.'

He takes a sip of water. Swallows. He's not so troubled now that I've given him an excuse to reject the idea. 'Not doing anything without knowing who your source is.'

'I'll go to the magistrate,' I say. 'My name on the warrant. My neck on the block if anything goes wrong – if that's what you're worried about.'

He takes a chapatti from the pile, folds it and bites. 'Anyway, you won't get a second warrant. We've no fresh evidence. It'd look like we were trawling.'

'I'm not suggesting we search Vince's house. Remember the race-hate CDs?'

He doesn't answer this time, though I've got his attention.

'One of the CDs was different from the others – same tracks, different order.'

'So?'

'You can hide data on music CDs – did you know that?' He didn't. 'Data?'

'Words, numbers . . . photographs. You need two CDs – one with hidden data, one without. Then you've got a chance to decode it. I reckon that's what we've got.'

'Bring it up at the briefing. It's a good line.'

'And,' I say, 'we've got addresses for the band members. Three flats. All in the Martin's Hill Tower . . .'

Paresh takes another bite of chapatti. 'Searched them already. All clean.'

'Too clean?'

'Give it up, Mo. Go home. Get some rest.'

The idea of a police officer informing Vince's gang about the progress of our investigation is so abhorrent to Paresh that he can't even consider it. I rip myself a strip of chapatti and fold it into my mouth. It's warm and slightly salty. Mrs Gupta rubs butter on them when they're fresh from the griddle. She showed me once.

'Tastes good.'

He swallows some more water. 'Need to get back to my guests.'

'Right.'

'If that's OK.'

'Sure. Just one more thing then I'm through.'

He nods. 'Shoot.'

'I checked the search warrants,' I say. 'The Martin's Hill Tower ones. There's no mention of the three lock-up garages that go with the flats.'

'Garages?'

'Each flat has one – they're about a hundred yards away from the building. If they're not on the warrant, they can't have been searched.'

'Hell!'

'We can get a warrant tonight . . .'

He shakes his head. 'You'd need six officers minimum – if you're going into Martin's Hill.'

'There'll be no one there,' I say. 'We can do it quietly. You, me and a constable with a bolt cutter.'

He's tempted. I can see that. He drains his cup.

I reach across the breakfast bar and put my hand on his forearm. 'Will you help?'

'If I don't?'

'I'll do it anyway.'

He pulls his arm away. 'You'll never get a warrant at this time of night.'

'But if I do?'

'You won't.'

The kitchen door opens and Mrs Gupta bustles inside. She fixes Paresh with an accusing look. 'You haven't got the inspector a cup of tea!'

'It's all right,' I say. 'We've finished.'

She seems relieved. 'Will you come and join us now?'

'Sorry. I've still got a load of work to do tonight.' I fire a glance at Paresh, but he's looking away. I say: 'The chapattis are delicious.'

Mrs Gupta beams. Before I can stop her, she's wrapped the remaining chapattis in aluminium foil and placed the warm package in my hands. 'You're losing weight. Need to eat more, isn't it.'

I step out of the front door and walk down the steps, trying to puzzle out the enigma of Paresh's mother – the woman who wouldn't have let me marry her eldest son.

It's three thirty in the morning by the time I've got everything ready. The paperwork was straightforward. From my limited experience, I'd say that magistrates are never pleased to be woken up, but they're always keen to authorize a search warrant if it means they can get back to bed more quickly.

Getting officers to accompany me on this night jaunt has proved a lot harder. Asking for any of the regular night duty staff would have got me bogged down in paperwork. In the process I'd have had to let a load of people know what I was up to. So I've called in some favours – that means my two sergeants.

'Turn left up ahead.'

Morris is behind the wheel. He's already told me that he doesn't like driving the patrol car around the back of the Martin's Hill estate – not at this time in the morning.

'When are you going to tell us what this is about?' Greenway says. He's sitting in the back of the car, just behind me.

'I've got three search warrants in my pocket. Turn right here.'

Ivor does as he's told, but I can see his shoulders tensing up.

There are a few rusty cars here, parked by the roadside. The owners have probably worked out that they're worth more in insurance payout than they'd ever make on the market.

I point to the line of garages up ahead. 'Pull up over there.'

'Here?' Morris doesn't want to believe I'm serious.

We're parked on a stretch of narrow road with open space on the left, behind which is the ugly bulk of the Martin's Hill Tower, just a couple of windows lit from within at this time in the morning. On the right side of the road is a terrace of perhaps thirty identical concrete boxes, each just big enough to house a car. The sodium lamps make the whole place look even more bleak than it really is. And that's saying something. There's a pile of fly-tipped junk against the last garage in the row. A ripped and stained mattress. Part of a pushchair. A load of bin-liners – several of which have ruptured and spilled their rotting contents. I get out of the car, trying not to inhale the stinking air.

Greenway puts a hand over his mouth and nose. 'Jesus!'

A scrawny cat streaks out from among the bags, making it as far as the first parked car before stopping and looking back at us.

'Bring the bolt cutters.' I start walking down the line of garage doors, scanning the numbers. 'We're looking for 13, 15 and 20.'

The garages all have up-and-over doors. Each is secured by a padlock to a metal ring in the ground. The lock on number 13 snips open easily with a quiet metallic click. Greenway hefts the door up and I shine my torch inside. I don't know what I was hoping to find, but this wasn't it. Cardboard boxes, old paint tins and sheets of yellowed newspapers scattered across the floor. It takes only five minutes to check the place over. Nothing. The newspapers are more than two years old.

We close up and move on to number 15. The padlock looks identical to the first one. I watch Morris use the bolt cutter, snipping through the metal as if it was cardboard. And I'm thinking that this search is going to look really, really stupid if all three garages turn out to be the same as the first. I stand back. A dog barks somewhere over by the tower. Morris hefts the door up and I shine in the torch.

This time there's a car inside. A Cavalier – or the remains of one. It's up on bricks. The wheels are leaning against the side wall. There's no windscreen.

With less room to work in, this search takes longer. There are some old porno mags under a cloth in the corner of the room. Nasty stuff – but not enough to get the owner any more than a warning. We bag them anyway. The only other highlight is a shoebox of used syringes, complete with tea-spoon, cigarette lighter and a length of rubber tubing.

My anxiety level is getting higher now. I was sure I was

on to a winner here. Sure enough to risk making myself look like an idiot. But we've finished the second garage and there's still nothing to show.

Ivor closes up behind us. The door mechanism screeches for lack of oil. 'Third time lucky, eh?'

'Only in fairy tales,' says Greenway.

The door of number 20 is different from the others. Freshly painted. The padlock looks new. Sergeant Morris gets down on his knees with the bolt cutter. It takes him longer to break in this time. The metal finally gives with a sharp click. Morris is breathing heavily. He looks at me. 'Here's hoping fairy tales come true.'

The door swings up silently. I shine my torch inside, searching out the back wall, the corners. And what I see are boxes. That's all. Fifteen, perhaps twenty, fresh cardboard boxes on a clean concrete floor.

I step inside and I'm vaguely aware of the others following. There's a light switch on the wall. I try it, and that's another surprise, because it's working. I click the torch off and go to the first box. Empty but for two pieces of expanded polystyrene packing material. From the shape of them I'm guessing there was a computer monitor in here. The men are looking through the other boxes now, pulling out similar packing material.

'So much for the fairies,' says Greenway.

We're standing there at the back of the garage, me feeling like a fool, the others looking anywhere but in my face. So I only notice the footsteps a moment before the men appear in the doorway.

Two men. Both large, both angry. One has a short crowbar in his hand. The other is holding the leash of an Alsatian. The dog is straining towards us, growling, its front paws off the ground.

Rod Duncan

Crowbar shouts first. 'What the fuck!'

'We are police officers conducting a legally authorized search,' says Morris, his voice strong, level. 'This is your garage?'

The dog man steps towards us. 'Fucking right it is!'

Greenway is trying his police radio. But here in the back of the garage all he's getting is a hiss of static.

Crowbar turns away from us and shouts into the night. No words. Just anger. Then he swings himself back, his eyes wide. The Alsatian starts barking, its lips curled back so the teeth show all the time. There's no way out of here without coming within its range.

Morris steps forward anyway, no fear showing in his body language. 'Just back out of here and it'll be easier for all of us.' He's got one hand on his side-arm baton, but he hasn't raised it yet. He's got the kind of calm assertiveness that no amount of education or training could ever give you. But even with that, this is a no-win situation. Someone's going to get badly hurt.

Then I hear a car approaching. The engine stops. A door slams. The dog man looks over his shoulder to see. Crowbar follows his gaze for a second. 'Fucking Paki filth!'

It's Paresh who steps into view on the road outside. Unexpected, but oh how very welcome. He isn't armed like Greenway and Morris, but the balance of power has shifted with his arrival. Greenway is edging his way outwards down the side of the garage. He has his baton out. 'Drop the crowbar.'

The dog man turns to his friend. 'Do it.'

The crowbar clangs on to the concrete floor.

'I'm Inspector Akanbai. I have search warrants . . .'

The dog man is shaking his head. 'Should have showed it me. It's my fucking lock-up!'

I take out the papers, search through them till I get to number 20, hand it across to him. 'Here. You can read it now.'

'What about the others? You better have papers for them too!'

I wave the warrants in the air.

'Bitch! That's two. Not three!'

The dog has stopped barking now and has slunk back to stand between the two men, though it's still growling through its teeth.

'Warrants for numbers 13, 15, 20 . . .'

Crowbar cuts the air between us with an open hand. 'Not 22! They haven't got one for 22.'

The dog man spits on the concrete. 'You've looked. Now you can piss off out of here!'

They start to back out of the garage. Paresh is standing clear, giving them plenty of room. And I'm thinking on my feet. As quick as I can. I've never heard mention of lock-up number 22. Not before this. If I ask who it belongs to, they'll see I don't know what I'm talking about.

So I say: 'Fuck it. Who needs a warrant? We'll open 22 anyway.'

Crowbar goes crazy. He wants to lash out at me, but he can see the batons at the ready. 'You bitch! You fucking bitch! You can't do that.'

'Who's going to stop me?'

The dog man is more in control. He's shaking his head. 'You can't do it. It's his garage and he's telling you, you can't go in it, right?'

'Prove it – show some ID.'

With his free hand Crowbar reaches into his back pocket and pulls out a wallet. It opens to his driver's licence. Greenway copies down the name. This man is one of the race-hate band all right.

'Changed my mind,' I say. 'We'll get a warrant first. The search can wait a couple of hours.'

Everyone knows about the search by the time the final warrant arrives. We've got three patrol cars parked on the road and six officers drinking coffee poured from two Thermos flasks. I've had to phone Superintendent Frank Shakespeare. He had to phone Alison Walker. We've even wrecked the beauty sleep of a couple of City Council Housing Department managers – just so we could verify the rental arrangements for lock-up number 22.

If there is a leak in the investigation, then half the criminal underworld must know what I'm doing by now. But that doesn't matter any more. I've been sitting here watching the doorway all night. No one has gone in or out. The two thugs ran off before reinforcements arrived. Not much we could do about that.

I see the police motorbike coming from a long way down the road. It draws up next to me. The rider unzips his jacket and pulls out a manila envelope. The warrant has arrived.

We've got a proper locksmith now. Everyone stands back from the door as he works. It takes only a few seconds before I hear the click of the padlock springing open.

'There you go,' he says.

I'm not sure if it's respect for my actions, or a wish to dissociate themselves from a widely anticipated disaster, but all the other officers seem to be waiting for me to make the first move. I grab the handle and hoist the garage door up.

Inside, I see precisely nothing. Bare floor. Windowless. Then I notice that the back wall is hung with old sheets, floor to ceiling. I walk over to them, lift one hanging corner, pull it back. And there, mounted on industrial metal shelving, are floor-to-ceiling computers. I pull the other sheets clear, counting the monitors as I go. Twenty machines. And on the middle shelf, two cardboard boxes of blank CDs and CD cases.

I'm on a real high now. We've got the forensic computer expert out here, working away. And what he's told me already is enough. A result. This is a music CD factory. Enough machines to turn out a hundred perfectly copied disks an hour. The last thing off the production line was the latest offering from Madonna.

I'm not that hot on maths, but even I can do this sum. A hundred CDs going for, say, a tenner a throw. A thousand pounds' worth of illegal bootlegs an hour. Easy money.

But the story gets better. Our computer expert looks into the bowels of the hard disk drive and tells me he can work out the whole history of what they've been doing here. Something to do with log files. He gives me a list of bands, numbers of CDs copied, dates. It's all here. The source of half the bootleg CDs circulating in the East Midlands. But the bit that interests me most of all is when he tells me that this is where the race-hate CDs are being manufactured.

I'm going to make sure we get our forensic computer experts to hunt for data hidden in the music files. And this discovery should give me the clout to make sure that it's done. No one is going to be able to brush this under the carpet. And Alison isn't going to force me to take my annual leave.

I'm walking on air.

Sure, I haven't had any sleep in thirty-six hours. And I know I haven't had anything to eat in about as long – barring a mouthful of chapatti at Paresh's house. But I'm feeling great. The other thing I'm enjoying is the way the other officers are showing their respect for me. Everyone wants to shake my hand. For my lift back to the station I have multiple offers to choose from.

When I finally get back to the cop shop and walk up the steps of the building, it's at the centre of a group of proud officers. And there at the door is the chief constable himself, with Ericson and Thelps, the two men from Complaints and Discipline. I slow down as I approach them. The big fish isn't smiling.

'Sorry, inspector,' he says.

'Sorry?'

'Hands tied. You know how it is.'

My escorting posse is starting to melt away.

'Sir?'

'Full pay, of course – pending appeal.'

'Appeal for what?'

Thelps speaks now. 'You tried to incriminate Superintendent Shakespeare by claiming to have sent him a warning – which we now know was only written after the event.'

The Chief Constable shakes his head. 'Sorry. But you're suspended. I have no choice.'

I nod as if everything is fine. I'm going to walk away from here, get my strength together, come back when my heart isn't pounding so fast. I'll appeal. Threaten to drag it all through an industrial tribunal. They'll back off. Won't they?

I start to turn. The car park tilts. I get a pang of vertigo. My height above the tarmac seems wrong. Everything around me is receding and I feel myself falling into blackness.

Chapter 25

'Ever happened before?'

'No.'

His fingers are pressing on my upturned wrist. He counts the seconds on his watch. I listen to a trolley being pushed down the corridor outside. My work has often brought me down to the Royal Infirmary A and E department, but never before as a patient.

'Been keeping well?'

'I . . . a bit of sickness.'

'Married?'

'No.'

'Boyfriend?'

'I . . . Why is that important?'

He smiles. 'And when was your last period?'

'Last . . . last week. It . . . it was only a few spots, but . . . God. You're not saying . . .' I let my sentence trail off, not wanting to go where it was taking me.

'A few spots at the time of a missed period – this isn't uncommon in early pregnancy.' He turns to the desk and starts writing. 'At least we know you've not broken any bones. Your ECG is fine as well. No heart problems. You're not diabetic – though you'd better keep your food intake more level than you've been doing. And regular sleep never did anyone any harm.'

He seals up the note in an envelope and hands it to me. 'Take this to your GP. I'm suggesting you have an EEG, just to be on the safe side. And a pregnancy test as well.'

Chapter 26

It's almost two in the afternoon. I've been home from the hospital, changed out of my uniform. Suspended officers aren't supposed to go back into the police station. But I know the way they do things round here. No one has got round to disabling my swipecard yet. The security door clicks open and I'm in.

I find Paresh sitting in the canteen. There are other people eating here, but my ex has chosen a corner table by himself. I get a nod of support from one officer as I walk across the room. The others just look away. As if disgrace might be contagious. They don't want to risk any kind of contact. Right now that suits me fine.

I push my way between the last tables and I'm standing in front of him. 'Paresh?'

He gives me a nervous smile. 'Come to join me?' There's a plate in front of him. The remains of a baked potato. Some shreds of salad. He pushes it all to one side.

'I need to talk.'

'I'm sorry,' he says. He's talking about the Complaints and Discipline debacle. I guess he hasn't heard about my little fainting episode in the car park.

'I want to talk about us, Paresh.'

He looks into his coffee cup. 'Hell. Thought we'd said all that already.'

'So did I.'

Then he raises his head. It's the first time he's looked at me properly for days. He says: 'You cut yourself.'

'It was a fall.' I raise one hand to the graze on my cheek. I've got to tell him now. I'll hate myself if I bottle out. So I say: 'If it hadn't been for your mother, would you have wanted to marry me?'

'Keep your voice down.' He glances across to the nearest tables, then back to me. 'I can't talk to you, standing over me like this.'

I pull out a chair and sit facing him. 'Would you have married me?'

'If it didn't mean breaking up my family . . . God. I don't know. But where's all this coming from?'

'You knew all along, didn't you? That your mother would only let you marry an Indian girl.'

He shakes his head, but there's no conviction in the gesture.

'You knew, but you still went out with me.'

'Why are you putting me through this?' he snaps. 'You want me to grovel. Is that it? You want me to say it was all my fault?'

This is all going wrong. I'm being too aggressive. Making him freeze over. The harder I throw questions against him, the thicker the wall of ice becomes.

'I just want to understand.'

'I suppose you thought about marriage,' he says. 'That first time – when you almost ripped my clothes off. Did you – huh?' He picks up the salt pot and twists it in his hand.

'No,' I say. 'No. I didn't think of anything. I just wanted you.'

There's a long pause. Then he says: 'I'm not sure of anything any more.'

I can feel the ice beginning to melt. 'I'm not accusing you. I just need to understand.'

He puts down the salt pot. 'On some level, I must have known. But it wasn't important. Not back then.'

'What changed?'

He shrugs. 'We changed. We got more . . . I guess I started to love you. I never meant to hurt you.'

The canteen is closing now. Tables are emptying. The lights have gone out behind the serving bay across the other side of the room. I see one of the dinner ladies reaching to grip the handle of the roll-front grille. It clatters down into place. Some of the officers at a nearby table are piling their dirty plates on to a tray. Paresh fidgets where he sits.

I'm building myself up to say my bit. But the closer I get to it, the tenser I feel.

'I've got to get back to work,' Paresh says at last. 'But I want you to know – the stuff you did last night – you put yourself way out on a limb – and you got a great result. I'm just sorry everything else had to happen.'

He's half out of his seat before I manage to shake my head. 'Wait.' The word comes out almost as a squeak.

He stops.

'Don't go.'

He glances at his watch then lowers himself again.

'I've not been well,' I say, blurting the words out. 'I fainted today. And I've been sick . . . in the mornings.'

He opens his mouth and takes a gulp of air. 'Oh, God.' He's gripping the edge of the table. 'You're not . . .'

'I thought I couldn't be but then . . .' I raise my hand and touch the graze again.

Paresh is shaking his head. 'Tell me you're not.'

'I bought a test kit from the chemist... but I don't know

if they're . . . if they're a hundred per cent. I could get my doctor to . . .'

He grabs my hand. 'Are you pregnant?'

'The condoms always worked, didn't they? We'd have known if they'd split. You'd have known.'

'Have – you – used – the – test – kit?'

'An hour ago.'

'And?'

'Did a condom ever split?'

'No . . . not really.' He's squeezing my hand now. So hard that it's painful. 'What did the test show?'

'What do you mean "not really"? Either it did split or it didn't!'

'One broke. But I . . . it was OK. I hadn't finished or anything.'

'When?'

'I don't know . . . A month. Perhaps two.'

I wrest my hands free. 'You didn't tell me!'

'You were safe.'

I'm remembering a time now. Late one evening. Five weeks back. He'd turned up at the house unannounced, full of urgency, hardly speaking at all. We dragged each other upstairs to the bed. Then, halfway through, he suddenly needed to go to the bathroom. 'You didn't tell me.'

'I didn't want to spoil the mood.'

He tries to put his hand on mine again. But I push him away.

'You should have told me!'

'We were having such a good time. You were really out of yourself. I . . . I put on a new one.'

'You bastard! I had a right to know!'

'It was safe. OK?'

'It was not safe!'

I'm standing now, though I don't remember getting to my feet. Other people are looking at me, but it's like they're out of focus. All I can see is the man on the other side of the table.

'Sit down,' he says in a hissed whisper.

'I'm pregnant!'

'Oh, shit.'

He catches hold of my hand again, trying to manoeuvre me into my seat. I pull against him, take half a step back.

'You said the test isn't a hundred per cent.'

'I'm pregnant!'

'We'll get more tests. Even if you are . . .'

'What?'

The last word comes out as a shout. An accusation. I'm turning away from him. I'm crashing tables and chairs as I struggle towards the exit, blind with emotion. I'm in the corridor, running. He's chasing close behind. Halfway down the stairs, he catches me by the shoulder.

'We'll sort it. Somehow.'

'An abortion?'

'You still might not be pregnant.'

'It's your baby!'

There are people coming up from the third floor. A group of uniforms. Their conversation dies in the echo of my shout. Paresh is still holding my shoulder, but there's no strength in his grip now. I back away from him. His arm drops to his side. The other officers on the stairs have reached us now. They move past, looking anywhere but in our direction. I back away. Paresh sits on a step and puts his face in his hands. Then I turn and run.

I'm boiling over. Angry with Paresh for his stupidity. Angry at myself for expecting more of him than he had to give.

And I'm running blind across the car park, feeling exposed by my emotions. Looking for a hole to crawl into.

If the car had blacked-out windows, I'd just sit in it. I'd deal with this here and now. But it feels like I'm in a fish tank, on display. I reverse out of the bay without looking behind me. Then grind some metal off the gears, searching for first. I'm throwing the car around the corner towards the exit. The guard peers through the window at me. I look away till he raises the barrier, then I put down my foot and leave the police station behind me.

I'm motoring along, doing forty in a thirty-mile-an-hour zone. Holding the wheel with one hand, rubbing my face with the other. There are amber lights ahead of me. I'm through them on red. Oblivious. A car horn to my left. A yell of abuse. I'm thinking that if I hit something, perhaps that would bring relief. Solid. Physical pain to replace what I'm feeling now.

Another junction. A CCTV camera looking down on me. I'm passing the red lights again. Oncoming cars screech to avoid me. More blasts of anger.

What did Paresh feel? I'm asking myself. Did he suspect already? He's not a bad man. Half blind – aren't they all? I was the other way. The strip turning blue was no surprise. I knew it. It had just been too much to admit.

I'm coming down the avenue towards my house now. Pulling up by the roadside – though I don't remember all the junctions between the station and here. I turn the engine off and sit with my forehead on the steering wheel, listening to the silence.

I'd decided already – to end it. Before I talked to Paresh. I'm single. I've got a career. Just being me and being in this job, it breaks the stereotype. I look pretty white, but I'm mixed race all the same. And I'm a success. A graduate. Fast-tracking up through the police force. I'm not a single mother with a mix of kids and no hope of anything beyond cashing the next giro cheque. Anyway, I'm no good with babies. I'm afraid even to touch them in case I break something.

And the kid – what would it have to look forward to in life? Half Asian, three-eighths white, one-eighth black. To the whites it would be just another black kid. To the blacks it would be Asian. And each of the Asian communities would look at it and see a mixture. Nothing to do with them.

The world isn't ready for this child.

I'm at the front door now. My eyes are swimming and I can't get the key in. Then, when it does slot home, it won't turn. So I try to pull it out, but it won't come. The tears are spilling now. All I want is to be inside. Alone. So I leave the keys dangling and run around the side of the house, through the passageway to the back garden.

I tilt the big flowerpot on the patio, reach underneath. Sergeant Morris would go ape if he knew about this. I pull out the spare key to the mock-Victorian French windows. This time I have the opposite problem to the one at the front door. I put the key in and it turns easily. Click. Then I try the door and it's still locked. I turn it randomly back and forth until I find a position where the door will open.

That's when I hear the car draw up outside at the front. I hear the engine cut, the door slam. I hear a man's feet pounding up the drive. And I know it's Paresh. Even before he calls out to me through the door.

'Mo!'

I step over the threshold into the living room.

'Mo. I need to see you.'

I'm standing just inside the French windows, knowing

that I can't face another confrontation with him. I ease the door closed behind me. Then I slide the bolts into place.

'I know you're in there. Your car's out here. Your keys are in the lock, for Christ's sake!'

I'm stepping through to the door of the living room. There's a splash of sunlight on the hall carpet ahead of me. A bright rectangle that's found its way into my dark house through the small glass panel above the door. I can see motes of dust drifting.

He rings the bell again, then hammers on the door. I can see it shiver in its frame. The whole avenue must be listening by now.

'Mo!'

I put my hand on one of the door panels. I feel it shudder as his fist hits the other side of the wood again.

'Let me in!'

'Go away, Paresh.' I say it quietly, but the hammering stops.

When he speaks this time, his voice has dropped to an urgent whisper. 'Please, Mo. I'm sorry. I'm really, really sorry. I was . . . I was an idiot.'

'Go away.'

'You jumped the news on me,' he says. 'I didn't know what to say. I . . .'

'You want me to get rid of it?'

He doesn't answer.

'You want me to get an abortion?'

'It's not . . . No. I can't say that. It's your choice.'

'But what do *you* want?'

'Open the door.' There's a pause, then he hammers again. *Bam-bam-bam*, with his clenched fist. 'Open the door!'

'You're frightening me, Paresh.'

'I've got to see you!'

He's trying to turn the key that I left dangling out there. I can hear the jangling urgency of the movement. But the lock doesn't turn. Not yet. He's rattling the key – first one way, then the other. I put my hand on the catch. The metal feels cold against my palm. And I find that it's clicked into the 'lock' position – which must be the reason I couldn't open it from the outside.

'If you open the door, we'll be able to talk.'

'You could have talked to me before.'

'It was too sudden. I didn't have time. I . . .'

My hand is still on the catch, caught in mid-action. Undecided. So I slot the safety chain in place and click the catch over. It comes unlocked and the door rams open, coming up hard against the chain.

His hand is in the crack, fingers grasping the edge of the door. 'For God's sake, Mo. Let me in!'

'I need to know,' I say. 'You want me to get an abortion or not?'

'Let me touch your hand,' he says.

I put my fingers over his. He lets go of the door and clasps me instead. His grip is tight. 'No,' he says. 'No. I want you to keep it.'

'I can't.'

'You could.'

'On my own. I . . . I can't do it.'

'You wouldn't have to be on your own. You'd have me to help.'

'Your mother. What about her?'

'We could . . .'

'You'd marry me?'

'I . . . Yes.'

The strength has gone out of his grip. I ease my hand

free, step backwards, lower myself to sit on the stair. I cradle my face in my hands. There have been so many moments when I've felt it was finally over between us. But this time it's real. I think I needed to hear those words from him – to feel him struggle. I needed him to say he'd break his family for me and the baby. Because now I do hear it, I've got no one else to blame. It comes down to my choice. And I know it wouldn't work. We'd try. But the burden of his broken family would always be there.

Paresh must be able to hear me sobbing, because he's clawing at the door again.

'Open it,' he says. 'Please.'

I will face him. But I have to be strong. 'Wait.'

'For God's sake!'

'I need to . . . let me get cleaned up.'

I'm climbing the stairs towards the bathroom. Turning the cold tap, smelling the water as it froths into the sink. Cupping it, splashing it over my face. God, but it feels good. I straighten myself, ready now to face him.

I'm not ready, though, for the creak on the landing. That one squeaky floorboard that I still haven't got round to fixing.

I whip my head around and catch sight of his back slipping past the doorway in the direction of the stairs and the spare bedroom. And my first thought is that it's Paresh. But I know that can't be right. He's still locked outside. Then I remember Snakes saying he'd find a way of contacting me.

I'm stepping on to the landing. The toolbox is still here waiting to be used. The lid is open. I'm groping inside for something sharp. My eyes are fixed on the two doors just ahead of me. I grip the wooden handle of a chisel, then stand.

'Snakes?' It's a whisper, no more than that. I can't have Paresh find out about him.

There's no answer.

All I have to do is take five steps along the landing, then I'll be at the top of the stairs – within reach of safety if it turns out to be someone else. I have to pass two doorways on my way. He could be in either.

I step forward. Placing my foot to one side of the squeaky board. Then forward again, bringing me level with the study bedroom. And there he is. Not Snakes. I'm looking straight at Vince, and he's looking back at me. Behind him I can see my filing cabinet, the upper drawer pulled open. He's got one of my boxes of computer disks in his hand. He'd go for me if it wasn't for the chisel. I'm sure of that. I move backwards, getting closer to the top of the stairs. He more than keeps pace with a single forward step.

Then I shout: 'Paresh!' And with the same exhalation, spin myself around to run. The box of disks clatters to the ground behind me. I hear Vince grunt with effort as he throws himself forward in a flying tackle. His hand catches my leg and I'm falling, crashing heavily on to the landing. My elbow knocks hard on the floor, but I don't let go of the chisel. I'm gasping to get air in my lungs, and I'm trying to crawl, but Vince's hand is tight around my ankle.

Paresh is hammering on the door downstairs. Going crazy. Crash. Crash. He's shouting my name.

I try to kick out at Vince, but he catches my free ankle and starts pulling me backwards over the floor.

'Fucking bitch!'

Another crash from downstairs. Louder this time.

I twist my body so I'm half on my back, then I bend and lash out towards his face with the chisel. He pulls himself clear of the blade. I've twisted one of my legs free of him. I bring back my arm and slash the air again. He dodges, but his grip loosens. I'm scrambling to my feet, holding the chisel in front of me, sweeping the air with it, left and right, making an invisible shield.

The front door crashes with another impact but the chain doesn't come free.

I'm on the stairs, backing down, hoping that someone out there has dialled 999. Vince is moving forward, matching me step for step, his hands poised on either side of his body. Suddenly, he's shifting his weight towards his right. I lurch away from the expected attack, but it's his left hand striking out towards me. He's got my wrist. He beats it against the banister. Once. Twice. The chisel is clattering down the stairs.

Crash. The doorframe is splintering. Screws being ripped from wood.

But Vince has shoved me and I'm falling, tumbling down in a sickening sideways roll, curled up, feeling the blows of the stairs on my head and arms and back. Somewhere above, my attacker is leaping towards me.

Then the door bursts inwards. Sudden daylight. Paresh screaming my name. Vince roaring, more animal than human. Shadows flashing over me. A shriek. A gasp. Then feet running back through the house. The French windows rattling. Crashing closed. Then silence.

I open my eyes. Paresh is standing over me, looking down. He's holding the chisel in one hand. He's out of breath. Panting. 'You're . . . you're all right?'

'Don't know. I . . .'

'The baby . . .'

'I don't know.'

'I'll ring the ambulance.'

'No. I'm OK. We're OK.'

For a moment Paresh looks relieved. He drops to his knees beside me. It's only then that I see that there's blood on the chisel. It's smeared over his hands. He shakes his head. 'Oh, God,' he says. 'Oh, my God.'

'What happened?' I'm scrambling on to my knees.

'I . . . he must have . . .' Paresh half collapses to one side. His jacket falls open and I see the bloodstain on his shirt. It's growing in front of me, spreading. '. . . must have caught me.'

'Oh, shit.'

I take the chisel, throw it to the ground. Then I place his hands over the wound. 'Press here. Keep pressing.'

I've got the hall phone in my hand. I'm jabbing the buttons. I can hear myself telling them the address. Shouting at them to hurry. Then the receiver's dangling and I'm hauling Paresh onto his side. Recovery position. His hands have fallen limp to the ground, so I press down on to the wound myself.

'Paresh, you stay with me.'

There's a siren in the distance now. Getting closer.

'Stay with me! Stay with me!'

The siren stops outside. There are footsteps. Shadows of policemen blocking the light from the doorway.

The ambulance takes another seven minutes to come.

Chapter 27

We're in an interview room down at Charles Street police station. I guess it's supposed to be quiet in here. They keep bringing us cups of strong tea. Frank Shakespeare is drinking them all. His bladder must be bursting by now. I'm still on my first one.

He's shaking his head between sips. That's what he's been doing on and off since we got in here. 'Try to calm down,' he says.

'I need to see Paresh.'

'The hospital said they'd call. If there's any . . . you know . . .'

I pick up my cup – two hands to hide the shaking. The tea is cold.

'He'll be fine,' Shakespeare says, though it sounds as if he's talking more to himself than to me. 'His sort always are.'

There's someone being hauled down the corridor outside. A drunk, by the sound of it. A snatch of song, then a shout, then he's getting further away. A door slams and it's quiet again.

'That business,' says the super. 'The computer thing. I didn't complain, you know. It wasn't me.'

This comes so far out of the blue that it takes me a moment to understand that the subject has changed.

He runs a hand back through his hair, tufting it up at the front. 'It was them. Complaints and Discipline. They asked me if I'd got a memo from you. I hadn't. That was it.'

'I did send it.'

'Sure,' he says. 'Sure. I believe you. Like I said – nothing to do with me. You're a good officer. Don't want to lose you.'

I hide my face in my tea. Pretend to drink.

The super gets up and paces across the room. 'The longer this goes on, the better. The hospital not calling, I mean. He must be doing OK.' He turns towards me. 'Is it true what they say about you and him? I mean, none of my business, I guess. But it's bound to come out with all this . . .' He lets his sentence hang.

'What are they saying?'

'You and him. You know. Together.'

There's no point in trying to hide it now. Not after our little scene over the remains of Paresh's lunch. That's going to be retold across the county for years to come. I nod. 'Not any more, though.'

'Right. Good. I mean . . . I'm sorry, of course.'

'Me too.'

I don't feel like speaking after that. The super paces back across the room, then drops himself in his chair and takes another swig of tea. 'This really is filthy stuff. Tastes like piss. Don't know how I drink it.' He squeezes the cup in his hand, making the thin plastic crinkle.

'There's something I can't figure,' he says. He waits for a couple of seconds, but I don't take the bait, so he carries on. 'Vince the Prince. You say he was turning your place over. But . . . well . . . what is it he was looking for? It's not like you keep police files there or anything. What did he hope to find? If he'd gone there to attack you – I guess that'd make some kind of sense. But the way you said it in your statement – it sounded like a burglary gone wrong.'

I still haven't told anybody about Snakes or his warning – that Vince was planning on paying me a visit so he could plant incriminating evidence in my house.

The super shakes his head. 'Your neighbours. The ones who called the police. They must have seen him, I guess. You're OK on that score.'

'On what score?'

'Well . . . they did see him, didn't they?'

The door opens before I manage to get my answer out. Two CID officers step inside. Both men. I've met them before – though they aren't based here at the central police station. They wouldn't have sent two men if it were to break bad news. I'm on my feet anyway.

'Yes?'

The fatter of the two is an inspector. 'Sorry to trouble you.' He angles himself to address Superintendent Shakespeare. 'If you don't mind, sir.'

'Right. Of course.' The super gets to his feet. 'Mo,' he says. 'If there's anything I can do . . . you know. You'll ask. OK?' He leaves the room without waiting for a reply, easing the door closed behind him.

The CID men take the chairs one side of the table and gesture for me to sit on the other. The thinner officer, a sergeant, moves the empty plastic cups to one side, then he unwraps two new cassette tapes and slots them into the recorder. I think that's the moment it really hits me. My situation.

'I'm sorry about this, inspector. But you know the procedure. We're going to have to interview you under caution.'

'How's Paresh?'

'Stable.'

'I need to go and see him.'

'Of course. But first ... Do you wish to exercise your right to legal representation?'

'I ... no ... I haven't done anything wrong.'

I'm sitting here, looking at the fat man's lips moving, knowing I'm not taking any of it in. The cassette machine is rolling. The room suddenly feels unbearably hot. I take a swallow of tea. When I look up again, they are both looking at me. Waiting.

'Are you refusing to answer?' the inspector asks.

'I'm sorry. Say the question again, please.'

'Did you have a conversation with Inspector Gupta in the canteen earlier today?'

'Yes.'

'What did you talk about?'

'I ... it was private. Personal.'

'Was it an argument?'

'No. It might have looked ... But it wasn't ...'

'You shouted at him.'

'I ... it was loud maybe, but ...'

'You ran out. He chased you.' He drums his fingers on the edge of the table. 'You can see our problem. If you could just tell us the subject of the conversation.'

'We were ... it's over now ... but we were seeing each other.'

'Who ended it?'

'We both ... I don't know. Perhaps it was him.'

'He dumped you.'

'I didn't say that.'

'How long had you been having this affair?'

'It wasn't like that!'

'What was it like?'

Up to this point it's been the inspector asking all the questions. Now he sits back and the sergeant takes over.

'What you call it isn't really important, I guess. Hard to put labels on this kind of thing.'

'Yes.'

'But it was a sexual relationship. Conducted in secret. And he ended it. Is this right?'

I nod.

The other one says: 'Inspector Akanbai indicates agreement.'

'Then we get to the argument,' says the sergeant. 'Let's take the subject as personal for now. We can come back to that if it's important. But it was a row. You ran from the room, knocking over some chairs. He followed you out. You drove home. With me so far?'

I nod.

'Is what I've said accurate?'

'Yes.'

'Excellent. After that there's a gap of some fifteen minutes that we can't account for. But presumably that's the time it took for you to drive across town. And the next we know is a string of 999 calls reporting a disturbance at your address. A man – Inspector Gupta – breaking down your front door.'

'He's going to be all right, isn't he? He'll be able to tell you.'

The sergeant sits back. 'Don't worry. There'll be forensic evidence . . .'

'Forensic?'

'Fingerprints. Hairs. Maybe witnesses. Even if the inspector doesn't . . . There'll be something.'

'Am I under arrest?'

'No,' says the inspector. 'This is just questioning.'

'Then I can go if I want . . . to see Paresh.'

'Let's just get the questions over for now, shall we?'

There's a knock from outside. The sergeant looks across. 'Come.'

The door opens. In the gap I can make out Superintendent Shakespeare and a female officer. The super nods towards my interrogators.

The sergeant reaches for the tape machine. 'Interview suspended at . . . 16.28.' He clicks it off. 'Sorry about this. You'll have to excuse us for a couple of minutes.'

I try to smile. They get up and leave.

If I were an ordinary witness in a murder investigation, they wouldn't be leaving me alone right now. It's against all the regulations. But suspended or not, I did wear a uniform once. That makes them treat me differently. I sit here thinking about Paresh until I can't bear it any more. Then I get up, walk across the room, stand at the door, listening. Someone walks past outside. I can hear an angry conversation – a member of the public shouting at the desk officer in the front lobby. Nothing unusual.

I try the door. Unlocked, of course. I step into the corridor. There's no one to stop me walking away from the interview room, so I do. Then I just carry on walking, out past the argument, through the front doors, out on to St George's Way. Then up towards London Road and the railway station. I don't look back. It takes me three minutes to reach the taxi rank.

I get into the cab at the front of the line. There's a small picture stuck to the dashboard just above the radio. A blue-skinned figure playing a flute. The driver, an Asian man, turns in his seat. 'Where to?'

'The Royal Infirmary.'

We're heading out on to the road when it hits me that I don't know which ward he's in. I get out my mobile and start dialling. Directory Enquiries first, then the Royal.

'I'm enquiring about an A and E case brought in earlier this afternoon. Paresh Gupta.'

There's a click as they put me through. I hear my question being relayed. Then a new voice comes on the line. A man. 'Are you a family member?'

'I'm a police officer.'

'We did inform the station already.'

'Inform . . .?'

'You haven't been told yet? He died an hour ago.'

'He died . . .'

'Severe blood loss,' says the voice on the other end of the phone. 'There was a lot of internal bleeding.'

'. . . died . . .'

'I'm sorry.' There's a slight pause, then he says. 'Could I have your name, please. I have to keep a record.'

I cut the connection.

The taxi pulls up at a set of traffic lights. 'You have lost a friend?' It's the driver speaking now.

'Yes.' I can hear my own voice. It sounds so empty, emotionless.

'This is sad for you,' he says. 'He was a good man?'

'Yes.' Again, one word is all I can say.

'Then he will go to a better life.'

The lights are green again and the taxi is moving.

'I need you to turn back,' I say. 'At the next roundabout. I've changed my mind.'

We get to Sal's house and I try to pay the driver. He won't accept the money, and I haven't got the emotional reserves to argue the case. I try a smile instead. 'Thanks.'

'We all have work to do in this life,' he says. 'When it's done, then we go.'

I leave him, run up the path, put my finger on the bell and keep it there till I hear her coming. She appears at the door, pale. She's been crying.

'They . . . they said on the news . . . an inspector killed. I thought . . .' She wraps her arms around me.

'What are they saying?'

'A murder investigation . . . no name . . .'

'I need to borrow the car.'

'To borrow . . .?'

'It's still working, isn't it?'

'Don't know. I haven't . . . not for a couple of months.'

'Get me the keys.'

'What's happened, Mo?'

I can't tell her yet. There's no time to hang around coaxing her through. They'll be searching the police station for me by now. It'll take them a few minutes to figure out I've left the building. Then what? The hospital. My house. Sal's place will be pretty high on the list if they're bothered to search. And I've got something to do before they question me again.

I wait in the hallway listening to Sal rummage through the chest of drawers. She returns and hands me a heavy bunch of keys.

'What's wrong with *your* car?' she says.

'It's at the police station.'

'Then why . . .?'

I take her hand, lead her to the driveway. Then I start working my way around the key ring, trying to find which one fits the garage padlock. I get it third try. The doors are heavy, wooden things. I haul them back and breathe the smell of oil and creosote from inside.

It was an old car even when Dad bought it. A VW Beetle. Yellow. He wasn't a sentimental car owner, my dad. It was just that the thing kept on running. And after he died, Sal couldn't bring herself to get rid of it.

She says: 'There won't be much petrol in the tank.'

I'm not even sure it's going to start. I take a can of WD40 from the shelf, open up the boot and give the engine a good spray. Then I get behind the wheel and sit myself down. There's a smell of damp in here. Mildew, perhaps. I try the ignition. The starter motor manages to turn the engine a couple of times, then stops.

'Damn.'

'I need to know what's happening,' calls Sal from outside the garage.

'Go and get your purse,' I say. 'And lock the house.'

I'm alone now. Sitting in the car. Ideas and emotions tumbling around inside me. Chaotic. I'm scared, confused, angry. But not sad. *Sad* is too small to cope. I should be crying. I dig my nails deep into the soft skin of my forearm. But the pain seems so very distant – as if it is happening to someone else.

The logical part of my mind seems to be working. I've got a plan in my mind. I've also got questions. Is what I'm doing common sense? Is it madness? But I'm so far off the beaten track that I've got no way to give an answer. I'm not even sure there's a difference between the two. Not unless you know the end already.

I glance at my watch. Five on the dot. I've been out of the station for over half an hour now. I'm wondering if they've managed to track Vince down yet – and what he'll let slip under questioning. Right now that has to be my main hope.

I try the ignition again. This time it catches. I coax the

accelerator, listening to the engine beats even out and strengthen. Sal clambers in beside me and slams the door.

'You have to tell me what's happening,' she says.

I tell her now. I hear the words as they leave my mouth. 'Paresh is dead.' But still I can't feel.

We're tucked away in a corner of the supermarket car park and Sal's got her face in her hands. Tears are running down her arms. I watch a drip form on the tip of her elbow, then fall. And that's how we stay.

In the end we lose a good hour like that. Sal's grief flows through her so easily. And when it ebbs, she's left looking as if she's at peace with herself. I'm sitting there, holding her hand, wondering why I felt more anguish when I believed Paresh was still alive.

'What are you running from?' she asks.

'I'm not running.'

She gives me a look. 'Then why not go and get your car from the police station? Why borrow mine?'

I don't offer any answer, so she says: 'Where are you going?'

'There's someone I need to talk to.'

'Who?'

'Someone who can tell them I'm innocent.'

'Innocent?' She hasn't seen this angle before – that I might be a suspect. She can't accept it. 'That man, Vince, they'll find his fingerprints or something. They always get them in the end. You told me that. And . . . and running makes you look . . .'

'I'm not running away!'

'Take me with you then.'

'I just need a few hours to sort things out. On my own.'

*

We're in the filling station. I've put some air in the tyres and petrol in the tank. Sal's in the shop paying with her credit card. I get out my mobile. It's been turned off up till now. I key in the number of the Community Relations Office. No one is answering. I hang up and try Ivor's mobile instead.

'Hello?'

'Ma'am? Where the hell are you?'

'I'm suspended, remember? I can go wherever I want.'

'That's not what I meant. There's a murder investigation going on. It looks bad if you're . . .'

'I've not gone anywhere.'

'They're saying . . . I don't believe it, but . . .'

I don't want to know what they're saying. 'Where's Vince?'

'They've had him in for questioning.'

'And?'

'Holding him in the cells. But he's saying he was playing pool all afternoon – in the White Ox. He's given some names. They all check out. Even the barman remembers him paying for a round of drinks.'

'The Ox – that's right in the middle of Martin's Hill. The Scalpers practically own the place. No one's believing them – are they?'

Ivor doesn't answer at first. I listen to the hiss growing and fading on the phone. Then he says: 'Vince's . . . he's not got reason to be in your house. Doesn't sound like a planned attack – not the way you described it. Wasn't a burglary. Why was he there at all? Doesn't make sense.'

'Any news about that race-hate website?'

'I'm sorry . . .'

'They must have been able to track down where the pictures came from.'

He doesn't answer.

'Ivor. Will you do something for me?'

'Yes, ma'am.'

'Not as a police officer. I'm asking as a friend.'

'Anything . . .'

'Keep your ear to the ground for me.'

'Shall I tell them you called me?'

I think about that for a moment. 'Yes. That way you'll be safe. And tell them . . . tell them I'll be back tomorrow. Or the next day. They can question me then.'

I hang up before he can object or ask questions I'm not ready to answer. Sal gets back into the car. I fire up the engine and drive. She doesn't say anything until we reach her bus stop. I pull up by the side of the road. She puts her hand on the door, then seems to change her mind. She turns towards me.

'You're not going to . . . I wouldn't like to think . . .'

'I'll be fine.'

'. . . nothing dangerous?'

'Don't worry, Sal.'

She examines my face for a moment. Not believing, I think. But knowing me well enough not to try to change my mind. Then she bends forward and kisses me on the cheek.

I'm following the M6 west. There are other people here. Hundreds of drivers passing. Thousands. Each one alone. Separate. Thinking only of their separate destinations.

I'm struck by their blindness to the things that matter. The world has changed and they don't understand it. How impossibly strange that they never knew Paresh – that they don't even know of their loss now he is gone. Crazily, I feel a pang of second-hand grief for them – though I can't yet feel any on my own account.

The tempest of emotion that has led up to this moment – it has suddenly died away to nothing. I am at the centre of the whirlwind. Waiting for what must come on the other side.

Chapter 28

It's past eleven at night by the time I pull into the hotel car park. In coming here I'm gambling that Sergeant Day hasn't been informed about the details of the case. The murder of an officer will be top item on the national news. But they won't be reporting the details yet.

I get out of the car. There are lights in some of the windows of the houses. I see the flicker of a television behind one curtain. I can hear a murmur of bar-room chat from the hotel. I walk across the car park and try to open the door. It's locked. I knock, then wait. No one comes. I knock louder. Someone inside is shushing the others. The sound of chatting dies down and a voice says: 'He's closed.'

'I need to get a room for the night.'

'Sorry. But it's locked up, see.'

The other voices have hushed to nothing now. I knock on the door a third time. 'I am a police officer.'

'You can't be,' says the voice. 'He's in here with us.'

After that there's a slight scuffle and low urgent voices in some kind of argument. The bolt clicks back and the door opens. Sergeant Day is standing just inside.

'Ma'am. They were just closing up. I'm seeing to it, you can be sure of that.' He half turns to indicate the crowd inside – some thirty **men** and a couple of women. 'Weren't you, lads?'

Nods from all.

I take a breath of the beery, smoky fug.

'You want a room, ma'am – is that it?'

'I want a word, sergeant.' I'm keeping my voice severe.

'Yes, ma'am.' He darts a warning look around the bar. 'Outside.'

People are holding their beer glasses under the tables, hoping I can't see. The barman gives me a nervous nod and the briefest of smiles.

I turn and walk away from the hotel. The sergeant follows. The door clunks closed behind us. He walks up to me and glances around, looking for my car. He's sufficiently unnerved by my unexpected arrival that he hasn't started asking questions yet. But he's a bright officer and it won't take him long.

'Another lock-in?'

He nods. 'And I'm guessing you'll have to report it this time.'

'Not necessarily.'

I don't think he'd noticed my lack of uniform till now. Suddenly, there are questions in his eyes. I speak before he has a chance to voice them.

'We're all doing the same job. Sometimes we bend the rules to get the right result.'

'That's the very truth,' he says. His eyes are busy, jumping around from me to the parked cars, then to the hotel and back to me again.

'The people in the bar,' I say. 'They're less trouble like this than they would be if you turned them out at closing time.'

'And you?' he says. 'Do you bend the rules ever?'

'Perhaps.'

There's a sparkle in his eyes now and the anxiety has

gone. 'I'd be more than delighted to help,' he says, 'if that would be of any use to you.'

I'm wondering how someone as quick as Sergeant Day has missed promotion all these years. 'I want to see Dr Cranmer-Phillips again. But this time I don't want to arrange it through my office – or yours.'

His hand goes up and strokes his chin. 'Well, there's a story I'd dearly love to know more about. You don't want people to know, is it? Your office or mine.'

'I'd like you to drive me up there first thing in the morning.'

'And you think he'll see you?'

'Perhaps.'

'Or perhaps not,' says Day. 'But then, sometimes it's enough to just turn up on someone's doorstep.'

'One more thing,' I say. 'I don't want you to contact any other police officers about this. Will that be a problem?'

Day flashes a smile. 'No, indeed, ma'am. We'll neither of us say a thing. And now,' he says, 'shall I be turning them out of the bar?'

I shake my head. 'Safer where they are, don't you think?'

First thing means first thing in the countryside. Sergeant Day comes round to the hotel at 6 a.m. I'm guessing he didn't stay up drinking with the lock-in crowd.

'Good morning, good morning,' he says. 'And a very fine morning it is.'

I nod because that's easier than disagreeing. I feel hollow and fragile and the light is uncomfortably strong. I went through the motions last night. Stripped out of my clothes, washed, lay in bed with a sheet to cover me. Then I looked into the void, asked the same questions over and over. Waiting for sleep to come, or tears.

'You've brought a car?' I ask.

'We're not going in yours then?'

'No.'

'Only I was just wondering about the yellow Volkswagen parked outside.'

I don't offer any information on that count.

'They don't make them like that any more.'

'No.'

He quizzes me with his eyes. 'If you were wanting to keep our little visit between the two of us, then it would be better to go in yours. No paperwork – if you take my meaning.'

Which is how I get to be driving the animated Sergeant Day up towards Dr Cranmer-Phillips's land. Two police officers in an ageing car, climbing the mountain road in second gear. It must be somewhere around here that the security camera is hidden. I scan the hedges as I drive, but can't see any sign of it.

'Marvellous,' says Day. 'German engineering.'

I'm still wondering if I'm going to make it up the hill without the indignity of changing down into first. We're passing the place where Snakes drove us through the fence that night. One of the fence posts has fallen. The wires are on the ground. Then it's over the top of the ridge and the edge of the doctor's land is in front of us.

Even Day stops chattering now. We both look at the scene. The perimeter fence. The ruined mine workings. The wind turbines. We drive up to the gate. I pull on the handbrake.

'Here we are then,' the sergeant says. 'What now, ma'am?'

'Now we wait.'

*

It takes five minutes for the guard to arrive, a shotgun broken over his arm as before. He strides up the track between the young trees. I'm standing on the other side of the gate.

'You again,' he says.

'Me again.'

'He won't see you.'

'That's what you said last time. But if you want to risk sending us away without checking first . . .'

He spits on the ground, then gets out a bunch of keys and unlocks the gate.

The guard won't let us in unaccompanied. Nor will he get in the car with me at the wheel. So he goes in front, right in the centre of the track, deliberately slow. It's more of a swagger than a walk. Like a general leading home a pair of captives.

We pull up outside the farmhouse.

'Wait,' he says.

He goes to the door, speaks into the darkness. I'm looking around. There are others here. Big, muscular men. All cut from the same block of oak. A private army, perhaps. One man is washing down the Land Rover. I can see another by the door of the electricity building. There are three more in the distance. Bare-chested. Shorts and running shoes. Jogging around the edge of one of the fields.

I get out of the car. Day does the same. Then I start walking along the track towards the runners.

Day coughs. 'Ma'am?'

'Just stay put.'

I'm halfway to the field now, and they've seen me. Two of them are showing me faces of anger and disgust. The third is wearing an emotionless mask. That's Snakes. They stop running ten paces from where I'm standing on the track. There's sweat streaming off their faces and chests.

'Hello, boys.'

Snakes takes half a step forward. 'Piss off, bitch!'

I need to get him separate from the others – even if it's just for a moment. But I can't afford to single him out.

'You shouldn't speak to a police officer like that.'

He snorts a laugh. 'I'm so scared.'

Then he turns and continues his run around the edge of the field away from me. I'm thinking that he's an idiot. Can't he see what I need him to do? Insult me more. Take a swing at me. Anything like that and I could have Day haul him away to the cells.

The other two are running after Snakes, playing catch-up. They're fifty yards behind, gaining on him. He's on the opposite side of the field now, and the distance is opening up again. They've spent their energy. I may be imagining it, but it seems that Snakes has lengthened his stride. Suddenly, I know what he's doing. But there's activity down by the car. The guard has come back out of the farmhouse and he's shouting at me:

'Get back here!'

Snakes is coming down the last straight towards me now. The others are behind but out of earshot. Just. His feet are pounding on the turf. He doesn't slow. He doesn't even look in my direction. But as he passes, he speaks one word: 'Tonight.'

'Get back here!' shouts the guard.

I turn and walk towards the car.

The guard is incandescent. 'Told you not to fucking move!'

'Can I see Cranmer-Phillips now?'

'You are out of here, woman!'

It's late afternoon before I bring myself to phone. I'm sitting on my bed in the hotel, keying in the number on my mobile.

Leah answers, singsong as always. 'Community Relations. How can I help you?'

'Is Ivor there?'

That's when I know things have got really bad. 'Is that . . .? Oh, my God. I . . .'

'Is Ivor in the office?'

'I . . . he . . .'

There's the crash of the receiver being bumped about.

'Ma'am. Is that you?'

'Ivor . . .'

'You said you'd come back.'

'It'll be tomorrow. I promise.'

There's a noise in the background. Leah's voice. A door closing. Then Ivor speaks again, a breathy whisper, his mouth very close to the receiver. 'They searched your house.'

'So?'

'They found cocaine.'

'What?'

'An ounce and a half.'

'Vince. He must have planted it there! You believe me, don't you?'

'You've got to come back.'

'I will. I . . .'

'Now.'

'Tomorrow. And I'll have someone to testify for me. Someone who knew Vince was going to try to frame me.'

I sound more confident than I feel.

Friday night. A few hours to find Snakes and persuade him that he needs to testify on my behalf. Finding him could be the problem. He told me 'tonight'. He didn't say where or exactly when.

I've come dressed for the part. Black jeans. Black track-suit top. Not stylish, but functional. There's only one clothes shop in this town. I leave the car in a lay-by and set out to walk the last mile to the doctor's land. I don't know where the camera is hidden, so I slip over the track-side fence and make my way along the edge of the fields.

There's more light than there was on the night I met up with Snakes that first time. The moon highlights the uneven ridges in silver and leaves the hollows as black. It's as if someone's turned up the contrast on an old black and white TV. On another day I might say it was beautiful, but I'm still running on emotional empty.

I pick my way carefully, placing each foot. A twisted ankle up here on the mountain would make a serious mess of my plans. At first the going is unbearably slow. Then I fall into some kind of rhythm and my mind starts to flow. I'm not thinking about the past any more. That's gone. Burned out of me. I can see Snakes in my mind. And Dr Cranmer-Phillips. They're both up ahead somewhere, hidden below that black skyline of young trees.

And Vince – sitting in a police cell. If I had to bet, I'd say he'd get released first thing tomorrow. After that, where will he go? Back to the Martin's Hill estate, probably. To be among his people.

I can see the heaps of mine spoil among the trees now. Light splashes surrounded by dark. That's where I'm head-ing. I have to guess that's where Snakes will be waiting. The mine building is the only place that means something to both of us. Just within the perimeter. Balancing the danger for each of us.

I come to the fence, skirt around it until I find the place.

I'm down on my back and worming underneath. The sharp angles of stones are pressing through my clothes. Then I'm through. Inside. I stand, close my eyes. Slow my breathing. Listen. I can feel the night air passing into my nostrils, the warm, moist breath flowing out. I hear the rustle of a small creature in the grass away to my left. Then nothing. Silence.

I open my eyes. Check my watch again. Half-past eleven. Fifty-five minutes gone since I parked the car. I place a foot on the loose scree and start to climb. Stones move over each other, whispering, loud in the silence. Another footstep. More slipping fragments. Anyone ahead in the shadows will be able to hear me coming. I climb on anyway, scrambling with hands to the ground, feeling the sharp, cold rocks with my fingers. Then I'm looking over the top, at the dead walls of the roofless building. And I can smell something human in the air. Cigarette smoke. Very faint, but unmistakable.

I smile now. This has to be a joke from Snakes. A very private joke between the two of us. When he tracked me down the first time, it was smell that gave me away. Now he's giving me the chance to play the same trick on him. I clear the top of the ridge and walk towards the doorway of the building.

'Snakes?' I voice the name more as a breath than a word. There's no answer. I step into the blackness of the doorway. The smoke is a little stronger here. 'Snakes?'

My eyes are adjusting to the dark. I see the dull orange tip of a smouldering cigarette butt on the floor in the middle of the room. But no figure of a man. I'm peering into the darkest corners when it happens.

A hand clamps hard over my mouth, pulling me back. I'm struggling. Flailing elbows back into the body of a man.

His grip doesn't give. Then his head is close to my ear and he's hissing an order through clenched teeth.

'Quiet!'

He turns me, slowly, my head in his two hands, until I'm facing him. Then he lets go.

'Snakes, you bastard!' I want to shout it, but the habit of silence keeps my voice to a whisper.

He shakes his head. One finger goes up to his lips. Then he pulls me clear of the doorway so I'm in the deep shadow of the room. He's next to me, flattened against the wall. My heart is hammering against the inside of my ribcage. I stand, leg and arm muscles locked with tension, trying not to let the breath sound as it rushes in and out of my mouth.

The seconds slip past. Snakes doesn't move. I can smell him from here. A fresh sweat on his body. My breath begins to slow. Then I hear a noise outside. A small animal. That's what I'm thinking. Then it comes again. And again. Each time slightly closer. And I know that I'm hearing feet being placed. A person advancing towards us as quietly as he or she can manage. The shadow of a head and upper torso moves into the splash of moonlit floor just inside the room. It stops there. Snakes hasn't moved, but I can sense a new tension in his body.

There's a scuffing sound outside. The man – I'm sure it's a man now – turning around where he stands. Three hundred and sixty degrees. Then he steps through the doorway and it happens. Snakes explodes from his hiding place. There's the beginning of a cry, which ends in the voiceless exhalation of impact. The two bodies are falling together. Indistinguishable. A grunt of pain as they hit the ground. They're rolling as one. Snarling. Panting. Suddenly, an arm breaks free. I see it blink through the moonlight on a descending arc. I hear the smack as it hits home. The struggle stops.

One of the bodies rolls clear and stands. It's Snakes. He's gasping for breath. 'The wire. Quick.'

He's pointing to the wall. I step over to it. Feel blind until my fingers touch the thin metal strands that he used on me. The man on the floor is beginning to move, trying to push himself into a sitting position. Snakes has a knife out now. He's waving it in front of the man's eyes.

'Don't,' he says. 'Don't even think it.'

I'm standing behind the man, out of his view.

I watch Snakes work, trussing the man. Hands first. Then ankles. Gag after that. The same as he did with me. Finally, a strip of cloth to cover his eyes. That's when I move from my hiding place. Following Snakes out of the doorway. He leads me along a path through the trees. We walk perhaps a hundred yards before he stops and squats down.

'Need to talk,' he says.

I kneel down facing him. 'What's just happened?'

'He was standing in the building. Having a fag. Must have heard you. He stalked off into the trees. So I got to you first.'

'And what now?'

'I'm out of a job. Cover blown as soon as Rat gets to speak to anyone.'

'Rat?'

'Don't like killing – like I said before. Gonna have to let him go.'

'Then why did you tie him up?'

''Coz that buys us a couple of hours.' He turns his head and spits into the trees. Then he looks back and says: 'Who have you told about me?'

'I . . . I haven't . . . nothing official.'

'Who?'

'There was one ... but he's just a computer programmer ... a friend.'

Snakes holds my gaze for a few more seconds after I finish speaking. Then he sighs. 'Something's happening here,' he says. 'All the security's been racked up. No one's allowed to use the phone. And the way they're talking – the glorious day is coming up.'

'The glorious day?'

'Yeah. The people taking power back from ZOG.'

'The white people?'

'I guess.'

I'm thinking about the things Paresh told me all that time ago. The race war. 'They're going to provoke the ethnic communities again?'

He shrugs. 'It's the big conference at the football stadium. That's what they've been talking about.'

'Multiculturalism in the Twenty-first Century. It starts tomorrow.'

'There's gonna be everyone there in one building. All the people they hate. The PM. Loads of government suits. All the racial equality crowd. I saw something I shouldn't have. Yesterday. In the workshop. A stripped-down mobile phone and something that looked like a mercury fulminate detonator.'

'Meaning . . .?'

'Meaning someone's making a bomb.'

'Shit. You reported this back to MI5?'

He nods. 'There's a public phone box on the roadside four miles from here. Slipped out and used it last night.'

'What will they do?'

'MI5? They don't tell me that kind of thing. But there'll be a big security operation. None of this lot will get within a mile of the stadium.'

Neither of us speaks for a few seconds. Then I say: 'Vince killed a police officer – in my house. A friend. He made it look like I did it.'

'Hell!'

'And he planted drugs. If you'd testify for me . . .?'

'I'd do anything to nail that bastard!'

Up to now, I've had a real anxiety that he'd refuse. I'd hoped I could lever him into doing it. But I hadn't expected his enthusiasm. And this is the first genuine emotion I get to feel since I knew that Paresh was dead. A wave of relief. It's so intense and unexpected that I find myself gasping for breath.

'Are you all right?'

I manage a nod.

'Will you do something for me,' he says, 'in return?'

'Anything.'

'You could say no. I'd understand. But I've worked on this for months. Tonight's my last chance.'

He takes me on a path through the young plantation woodland. The trees are perhaps ten feet tall here, and dense with side branches. From the way we're curving around to the right, I'd say we're skirting the perimeter of the property. We're definitely climbing. Snakes doesn't make any attempt to walk quietly, so I guess we're well clear of the main buildings.

It's all I can do to keep up with the man. Twice I catch a rock with my foot and go sprawling. Each time he helps me to my feet then hurries on as though time were chasing us down the rough path.

We're still deep in trees when I get the first sound of what's ahead. A slow, rhythmic throbbing. Each deep beat overlain by a breathy whisper. Then I see them. Strangely beautiful. Immense. Alien. The thick, metal columns of three wind turbines rising out of the uneven ridge.

We're perhaps a hundred yards short of the first column base when we reach the end of the plantation. Now Snakes slows, keeping his head low as he walks. Then he stops and gets down on the ground. I drop down next to him. We're shoulder to shoulder. There's a clear view from here – the wind turbines ahead, the valley down to the right. Lights in the farmhouse windows.

Snakes points to the furthest wind turbine. The silhouette of a man shows up against the silvery column base. 'See?'

'A guard?'

'He won't stay long. There's no kettle up here.' He points down into the valley, along the line of power cables. 'Five minutes and he'll be back down in the transformer room.'

'Why does Cranmer-Phillips have these things at all?'

Snakes turns towards me and grins. 'This is nothing. You wouldn't believe what he's got down there. Food. Enough to last years. Water. I'm guessing they've got weapons too. Haven't seen 'em, though. Never got in that far. Another few months – maybe they'd have trusted me enough.'

'Where do they keep it?'

'The old mine workings. There's a maze of tunnels right underneath this mountain.'

The guard is moving now. He walks towards us as far as the middle turbine, then turns and starts back down into the valley. I lose track of him after a few seconds, but Snakes continues to stare, raising himself first to his knees, then to a crouching stand. At last he gets fully to his feet.

'We're clear.'

I follow him along the track to the first of the turbines. At the very base is a square, concrete foundation block. Out of that rises a circular metal column, perhaps five feet in diameter. There's a door in the metal, secured with a heavy padlock.

'These things are Cranmer-Phillips's babies,' Snakes says. 'One would've been enough for all the power we use. But he loves 'em too much.'

He takes a key from his pocket, removes the lock, drops it to the ground. Then he hefts the door open.

'There's a light switch just inside. And a steel ladder. All you got to do is climb. At the top there's a big metal box with a lever on the side. Push the lever up and you break the circuit.'

'That's all?'

'No. The important bit comes next. You get down the ladder and leg it double time 'coz the alarm's gonna be sounding down in the transformer room and they'll come running to see what's up.'

'How many?'

'One. Then lots – when he finds the door unlocked.'

'And you?'

'I'll meet you back at the old mine building.'

I step through the portal. Snakes clangs the door behind me and all is black. The echoes die and I become aware of a mechanical sound. It's not the same as it was outside. All the hiss of turbine blades cutting the air is gone. The low notes seem much louder. And there's a faint smell. I sniff, trying to place it. Concrete dust and galvanized metal. Like a builders' yard.

I feel around the walls till I get to a plastic-coated light switch. Click. I'm looking down, so the first thing I see is the ring of anchor bolts around the outside of the circular floor. Then I follow the steel ladder with my eyes. Up. Up until my neck is stretched taut. There are four lights – spaced evenly up the height of the ladder.

I look to my watch. Ten minutes to wait before I push the lever. There's no point in climbing up there yet. But I do anyway. Rung after rung clanging under my feet. The walls get closer as I climb and the column narrows. It's very high – though I don't get any feeling of vertigo. The metal walls are so close that it feels as if I'm wrapped around by them. At the top of the ladder I find the circuit breaker box. I close my hand around the lever then release it again. I check my watch. Eight more minutes.

The plan works like this. Snakes goes back down to the valley. He hangs around in the shadows until I pull this lever. Then he watches the fun. He knows how many people there are on site. He knows where they're stationed. He counts them out as they hurry up the hill to investigate the alarm.

If he counts them out and there's still one left – even if there's a doubt – then he comes back empty-handed. That's the agreement we made. Neither of us wants to take any more risks than we have to.

But if all the heavies do leave the farmhouse complex, then Snakes goes inside for one last snoop around. He doesn't have to be so careful this time. He can empty drawers. He can steal files, disks, whole computers if they're small enough to carry. He hasn't got a search warrant. But, hey, this is MI5.

Cranmer-Phillips will be there. Apparently, he never leaves the farmhouse if he can avoid it. But the ageing doctor isn't going to be any match for Snakes.

So I wait, both elbows linked behind the rungs of the ladder, listening to the low rumble of the bearings just above my head, glancing every few seconds at my watch to see if the minute hand has somehow jumped forward. And then, at last, the moment comes. I grip the lever. It takes a big push to make it move. But when it does, it goes all the way in one snap. There's a loud bang as the circuit breaker springs open.

I get to the bottom of the ladder, click the light off, then heave the door open. It hits the side of the column with a clang. I'm running back down the path. I don't slow till I'm back among the trees. Then it's a ten-minute walk back to the old mine building.

I don't go inside this time. Rat should be fully conscious now. Somehow I don't want him to know I'm here. I circle the building, keeping to the level ground, making sure that my feet don't betray me. I go as far as the black square of the mineshaft. Then I step away from the building, backing myself into the young trees. There are too many side branches to walk between the trunks, so I get down on hands and knees and crawl backwards over the pine needles, edging my whole body into the deepest of the shadows. Snakes isn't going to creep up on me this time.

I wait for another ten minutes, and while I lie there these things happen. First there's the car. The sound of a distant engine. Gear changes. Getting closer. A pause. Then engine noise again, but now getting fainter. Second, I panic. Someone is arriving. Snakes's numbers are going to be out by at least one. Third . . . there isn't a third – because there's nothing I can do except lie in the pine needles and feel my heart pounding inside my body.

The first of Cranmer-Phillips's men arrives then. He runs in along the path from the wind turbines. Boots pounding the soft ground. He's got a torch in one hand. He sweeps the beam around trees. It passes over me, then back. Not stopping. He's moving around the outside of the building. A complete circuit, then he steps inside. There's a half-cry of surprise. Then, a moment later, a roar of anger from Rat as the gag comes out of his mouth. A burst of electrical static and a distorted voice sounding through the speaker of a two-way radio.

The two men come around the building into my view. Rat is in pain, rubbing his right shoulder with his left hand. He's swearing under his breath. There are other voices in the distance now. A group tramping along the path from the main entrance. They emerge into the clearing. Four men. The two at the back have shotguns. The one in the middle is Snakes. He's limping. And at the front, eyes wide, pumped up with manic energy, is Vince the Prince.

It's taking two of them to hold Rat back. They have him by his arms – but he pulls himself free anyway and lunges towards Snakes. I'm thinking that Snakes is done for, but Vince steps in the way, snaps his knee up. Rat goes down, doubled up on the floor, gasping for air.

Then Vince turns towards Snakes. 'Why?'

Snakes doesn't answer.

'Didn't believe it. I fucking didn't believe it!'

Rat, still winded, has got to his knees. 'Believe it!'

Vince steps up close to Snakes. His voice drops and it's all I can do to hear the next words. 'We were brothers. Brothers in arms. You betrayed the cause.'

'You're wrong,' Snakes says.

Vince takes a half-step back. His fists are clenched, and I think he's going to take a swing. But instead he shouts: 'You were reading the fucking files! You beat up on my man Rat! You're a bastard agent of ZOG.'

'Just wanted to know.'

'It's need-to-know only. You did not need.'

'You'd kept me in the dark.'

This time Vince steps forward. He gets so close to Snakes that it looks as if he's going to kiss the man. Then, very suddenly, he rams his forehead into Snakes's face. The MI5 man goes down clutching his nose. The man behind hauls him by the armpits back into a standing position. Snakes is groggy, wobbling on his feet. There's blood running from both nostrils, dripping from his chin.

I can feel cold dread creeping into me.

'Give me respect,' Vince says. 'You stab me in the back. OK. But now I catch you and you have to give me respect!'

Snakes wipes his forearm across his mouth, smearing the blood.

'You know what's gonna happen?' Vince says.

'Yeah.'

'Tell the truth and I make it easy. Hold out and I leave you to Rat.'

'He's mine!' Rat shouts, scrambling to his feet. 'By right he's mine!'

Snakes looks around the clearing, searching.

'Nowhere to run,' says Vince.

But Vince is wrong. Snakes isn't looking for escape. He's searching for me. My stomach clenches. I feel like I'm going to throw up.

'Went into the study,' Snakes says suddenly. 'Saw the files.'

'Which files?'

'A file marked "Dean".'

Vince turns his head and spits a gob of phlegm into the open mouth of the mineshaft. It's as if he's disappointed with Snakes for giving in. 'And . . .?'

'Operation Dean. That was the Dean Street Mosque, right?'

'You tell me.'

That's when the understanding comes to me – complete and horrifying. Snakes isn't talking to Vince at all. He knows there isn't any way out. He knows he's going to die. And he's making his final report – to me.

'There was a file marked "Honour",' Snakes says. 'Operation Honour. That was you beating up the Asian businessman.'

'You read the file?'

Snakes shakes his head. 'Didn't read. No time. But there were photographs. The dead man hanging from the fire escape.'

Rat steps forward then back again, as if caught between fear and hatred. 'He died easy. You fucking nigger-loving bastard!'

Vince spins, lashing out a snap-kick to the stomach that sends Rat sprawling. Then he points to one of his other men. 'He tries to get up – you stand on his face. He speaks – you stand on his balls. Understand?' Then Vince whips back towards the captive. 'Who you working for?'

Snakes wipes the blood from his mouth again. 'There was another file. No pictures this time. No writing neither.'

'Who – are – you – working – for!'

'A file with a name. But nothing in it – what's that about?'

Vince steps forward and brings up his knee. 'I ask the questions.'

Snakes is bent double, hands on knees, gasping for air.

'I'm gonna count to three,' says Vince. 'Tell me who you're working for or I give Rat a pair of pliers and a soldering iron and let him do what he wants. Understand? One . . .'

But the MI5 man can't speak. It's all he can do to breathe.

'. . . two . . .'

Snakes topples, as if in slow motion, falling to his side. He's lying foetal on the ground.

'. . . three.'

At last Snakes has enough air in his lungs to get out two words. 'Operation Majestic.'

'Too late,' says Vince. 'I'm a man of my word.'

Rat is on his feet, grinning. He clears the distance in two strides and with the third kicks Snakes in the ribs. I see the man on the floor roll as if pushed back from the impact, then roll over a second time – definitely by his own volition.

Vince shouts a warning, but it's too late for anyone to stop Snakes rolling a third time to the lip of the mineshaft. Then he's gone. He doesn't cry out as he falls. I don't even hear him hit the bottom.

Chapter 29

I hammer on the iron knocker until the light comes on inside. The door opens and a bleary-eyed Sergeant Day is standing there in front of me, adjusting the cord on his dressing gown.

'You,' he says.

'I need to talk.'

Day scratches at his arm for a moment, then nods. 'Better come in then, hadn't you.'

I step past him into the narrow hallway. There are small, framed pictures on the wall here. Steam trains, mostly. Some paintings, some photographs. Day locks the door behind me and gestures towards the front room. 'How did you find me?' he says.

'The hotel landlord. I woke him up.'

'There it is then.'

The room is small and low. Overfilled with a plump three-piece suite. A ceiling of exposed beams and uneven plaster. A large television. More pictures of trains. I don't sit down.

After a moment, Day says: 'Shall I get you some tea?'

'There's been a murder.'

He doesn't react – which is strange. 'A murder,' I say again. 'And I've got information … about the Multiculturalism Conference. There's going to be an attack.'

'I think you'd better have that cup of tea. Calm you

down, isn't it.' He steps to the doorway. 'You just make yourself comfortable.'

I'm left standing there in the space between the sofa and the television, listening to him clatter cups in the kitchen. And I can't understand what the man's doing. I call after him through the door: 'This is urgent. The conference. There's a visit scheduled. The delegates going to Majestic Park. The Prime Minister as well. That's where they'll attack. They're calling it Operation Majestic. The name on the file gives it away.'

It's gone quiet. He isn't answering. I step out of the front room, a couple of paces down the corridor and into the kitchen at the back of the house. He isn't here. The back door is open. He's out there in the back yard. He sees me and drops his arm from where it was – but not before I see the mobile phone in his hand.

'We can sort this out,' he says. 'You'll have a proper chance to put your side of it all.'

That's when I know that he's been contacted about Paresh. Suddenly, it's obvious. I phoned the Community Relations Office on my mobile. CID will have been able to find out which transmitter my call was relayed through. That's how they knew I was here in Wales.

'Don't you understand what I'm saying? Another murder. Up at Cranmer-Phillips's land.'

He's coming back towards the kitchen door, not trying to hide the mobile phone any more. 'They'll be here in half an hour. You can tell them all about it. Clear it all up, eh?'

And suddenly I see it from Sergeant Day's point of view. I arrive in the middle of the night, muddy and sweaty, pumped up on adrenaline. I must look more than half-crazy. He's actually scared of me.

He hasn't moved from the middle of the yard. I step

towards the door. There's a high wall all the way around at the back. No gate that I can see. No way out for him.

I hold out my hand. 'The mobile.'

He hesitates before answering. 'Why?'

'Let me talk to them.'

He steps forward. Puts it in my hand.

'Sorry,' I say. 'I'm really sorry.'

Then I step back, pull the door closed, and slide the iron bolt home.

I hear his voice from the other side. 'There's nowhere to go.'

I hear but I don't answer.

These are the things going through my mind as I drive. In nine hours' time the PM is going to be walking through Majestic Park with the head of the Equal Opportunities Commission and all of Leicester's community leaders. If there is a bomb, it must already be prepared. Perhaps that's why Vince turned up at Cranmer-Phillips's – to take the thing back to the East Midlands.

I figure that Sergeant Day will pass on my warning about Majestic Park. He's sharp enough to do that. The only question is: will anyone take it seriously? If they do, then the best thing I can do now is turn myself in.

They'll question me. I'll tell them about the body down the mineshaft. That will stand as proof of Cranmer-Phillips's guilt. But even as I think of that, I know it won't work. So what? One of Cranmer-Phillips's men has fallen down an uncapped shaft. Cranmer-Phillips will say he knows nothing about it. And how, he'll ask, did I know Snakes's body was down there?

Could forensics sort it out? I'm not sure. Would they find my hairs and fibres from my clothes on Snakes's body?

The answer has to be yes. Even if the courts eventually pronounced me innocent, that would take how long? Months. I'd be stuck in a cell, more visibly pregnant every week. And all the while Cranmer-Phillips and his thugs would be out there trying to start their race war.

And there's another thought. A question. Which of these would be worse: to have the baby in a prison hospital or to have a termination there?

The sky is starting to pale ahead of me. I glance at my watch. Half-past four. I left the sergeant's house ten minutes ago. If what he told me was true, reinforcements should reach him in another twenty minutes. Will he break his own back door down and call them before that? Hard to say. But one thing is certain. He knows what kind of car I'm driving.

I turn off on to a single-track road, open a gate, drive into a field and park behind the high hedge. It's light enough to jog back to the main road.

I hadn't passed another car as I drove. But now one does come towards me at speed. Heading back towards the town. Headlights on full beam. I step into the long grass of the verge and crouch down. The high pitch of the racing engine Doppler shifts low as it passes. Only from behind do I see the roof lights and police car markings.

The next vehicle is heading the way I'm going. I can see it's an HGV well before it reaches me. I walk to the roadside and stick out my thumb. At first it doesn't look like it's going to stop. But it's slowing as it passes. I'm running before it's come to rest. The sixty-yard dash. There's German writing on the truck's side panels. The door opens above me and I haul myself up into the cab.

The driver is a man. Perhaps thirty years old. Balding on top. Black. His belt holds in an overhang of stomach.

'Where you going?' he asks.

'East.'

He winks. 'Dresden far enough?'

He isn't much of a talker once he's driving. For that I'm grateful.

I'm starting to think that I should trust the police force to sort out conference security and that I should trust forensic science to clear my name. And I'm imagining myself walking into the central police station and turning myself in.

'Uh-oh,' says the truck driver.

I turn to look at him. 'Problem?'

He's slowing down. 'Up ahead.'

I'd been wrapped up in my thoughts, not paying attention to the road. Now I look and see a blue and white flashing light in the distance. 'Hell.'

'People you don't want to see?'

I don't answer.

'Behind you,' he says. 'They won't look in the bunk.'

I'm unbuckling my safety belt, clambering back over the seat.

'Hurry,' he says. 'Almost there.'

There's a bed here. I drop myself flat. I hear the gears change down. Second. First. Stop. The hiss of the brakes. The window is humming down. A smell of night air.

'Officer?'

'Sorry to bother you . . . sir.'

The over-polite words. I'm wondering if the police officer knows he's speaking in a patronizing voice. I'm certain the truck driver does.

'You seen a yellow VW Beetle on the road in the last half-hour?'

'No.'

'Or anyone walking?'

There's a pause.

'Who you looking for?'

'You have seen someone then?'

'A couple of people in that last town.'

'Description, sir?'

'Didn't notice much. Who you looking for?'

'We're looking for a woman. A police officer.'

'Nah. Sorry. I'd have remembered that.'

'Thank you, sir.'

The window hums up and we're moving again. First gear. Second. Third. I clamber back into the front and strap myself in again. I'm waiting for him to ask, but he doesn't speak.

'Well?'

He glances over at me. 'They're looking for a policewoman.'

'And?'

He glances at me again. 'You are so *not* a policewoman. And I'm not asking nothing more.'

I feel my shoulder being nudged. I don't want to wake.

'You're here, love.'

'H'm?'

'This is your stop.'

I murmur some thanks and stumble out on to the roadside. My watch says eight thirty. Four hours till the PM's Majestic Park walkabout. I stumble to the nearest bus stop then ride into the city centre. It's standing room only. Stop–start through the morning traffic. Suddenly feeling faint with hunger, I get off the bus and head into the first coffee shop I can find.

The man behind the counter brings my order –

espresso and a round of toast. There's a copy of yesterday's *Crusader* on the table. I unfold it to see Paresh smiling at me from under the headline, *'Find His Killer.'* It's an old photograph – from before I met him. He's still in uniform. I scan the article. *'Inspector Gupta was killed at the home of another officer . . .'* They don't mention me by name. That's something, anyway. *'He had been investigating a series of racist attacks, but police say they are keeping an open mind and continue to pursue several different lines of inquiry.'*

I take a swallow of my coffee, feel the sugar and caffeine kick in. The man who served me has come out from behind the counter now. He has grey hair and a face that's sunburn red. He lifts the ashtray on the table next to mine and wipes underneath with a cloth. I get a waft of disinfectant smell as he sweeps his arm around.

I look back to the paper. The second front-page headline is in smaller type: *'PM's City Visit'*. For the full article I have to turn to page three.

Controversy comes to the city with the visit of the Prime Minister to the Multiculturalism Conference being held at the football stadium . . . Police warn that organized demonstrations planned by far-right groups will not be tolerated. Neither will they give permission for counter-demonstrations by the Asian community . . .

I feel an involuntary shudder run from my shoulders down my arms and back. How many demonstrators will turn up from each side? Hundreds? After all the race tension of the last few weeks it's more likely to be thousands. The city feels like a tinderbox. One spark would be enough to set the whole place burning. It wouldn't stop here either. Within days there'd be riots in cities all over England. I rub my fingers over my scalp. 'Hell.'

The man pauses in the middle of wiping a table. 'Cheer up,' he says. 'Worse things happen at sea.'

I put the last corner of toast into my mouth and hurry out.

The first thing I do is get out Sergeant Day's mobile phone and start to dial. I'm halfway through the number when I realize I'm being stupid and cancel the call. They know I've got this phone. They'll be waiting for my call, ready to trace which area I'm calling from. So I walk to a public phone box instead. They can still trace the call – but only if Ivor tells them he's received it.

I try the work number and get him first time. 'Hello?'

'It's me,' I say.

He doesn't answer for a moment. 'Where?'

I say: 'You don't want to know that.'

'They're looking for you in Wales.' This is said in a whisper.

'I was at Dr Cranmer-Phillips's place.'

'Shit.'

'I found something.'

'You need to turn yourself in.'

'This is important. There's going to be an attack on the conference.'

'That's not news! You know all police leave's been cancelled? They've got a quarter-mile exclusion zone around the stadium. Go to your nearest police station. Give yourself up.'

'Ivor. You have to listen to me. The attack isn't going to be on the stadium. It's going to be in Majestic Park.'

'Then go in and tell someone.'

'They won't take me seriously.'

'And staying on the run – they're going to take you seriously like that?'

'I want you to do something for me.'

'Mo . . .'

'Find out what the security arrangements are for Majestic Park. Please.'

Another bus ride takes me into Waterfields. I'm looking for roadside barricades, or at least a police presence along the route the PM's excursion will take. But there's nothing. Not one officer. I glance at my watch. Twenty past nine. There's a feeling of dread building up inside me. I turn the corner on to Dean Street and start to jog down the pavement. I shouldn't be attracting attention like this, but it's half a mile to the park and the minutes are slipping away.

By the time I reach the mosque, I've lengthened my stride into a steady run. There's a big crowd of men here. A few of them I know. One, at least, recognizes me. It's too late to worry about that now. I race on past, heading for the trees at the end of the road.

Halfway there and another big crowd of Muslim men are emerging from a side street. The line from the newspaper flashes into my mind: *'counter-demonstrations by the Asian community'.* They're gathering, ready to march.

I cross the road with only a glance at the traffic and run through the park gates. I'm right at the top end, the grassy slope spread out below me. Three hours to go before the PM's procession and something is definitely wrong.

The incident tape is still there, strung from tree to tree along the line of the planned walk. But there's nothing else. No police cars. No police officers. No people. The place is empty. My breath is coming in ragged gasps now. I stop running, bend my back and rest my hands on my knees.

This time I don't even bother to find a call box. I get out Sergeant Day's mobile and key in the number, praying that Ivor is still in reach of the phone. It rings three times, then I hear the pick-up click.

'Sergeant Morris speaking.'

'There's no security in Majestic Park.'

'Mo . . .'

'This is urgent, man! What's happening?'

'It's been cancelled.'

'It's been . . .'

'Cancelled. The PM isn't doing a walkabout.'

I drop to my knees on the grass, faint with relief. Suddenly, I can feel all the bruises and lost sleep of the last two weeks. And the real pain. The loss. I've got tears running from both eyes.

'Mo? You still there?'

I'm weeping freely now. 'Y . . . yes'

'There's a big protest march,' he says. 'Close on six hundred fascists trying to march to the football stadium. We're expecting double that number to be marching against them.'

I lie back on the grass, looking up at the sky. The salty drops are running into my ears now. I'm half laughing, half sobbing. It's funny and tragic all at the same time. The racist march has kept the PM away. They've done my work for me.

'You're in Waterfields?' he says.

'Yes.'

'I'll send someone to pick you up.'

'Can't you come . . .? Don't want it to be a stranger.'

'We're fully stretched here. I . . .'

'Please?'

There's a pause before he answers. 'Can you stay put for a couple of hours?'

'Thanks, Ivor.'

The real crying starts here. It's like I had some kind of dam wall holding the feelings back. But now the emotion is pouring through, widening the breach with every second. I can hardly catch my breath between sobs. I'm awash with feeling. No space in me left for thought. The world is blurred with tears. Minutes smeared.

Time has passed. I'm sitting on the grass, staring at the rooftops in the distance. People have been walking past, glancing at me. Concerned, I think, to see the sorrow. They can't understand what relief this flood has brought me. I've got everything to face still. Arrest, questioning, remand. But I will get through it. Somehow. And the pregnancy – I'll even be strong enough to face that decision.

There is a tree above me. A poplar, I think. Its shadow on the ground reminds me of a moment six months ago. Late afternoon on a weekend in February. There were tree shadows on the wall of my bedroom. The fingers of bare branches shifting with the wind outside the house.

I was lying next to Paresh, looking at the last of the thin sunlight on the wall, enjoying the cold air of the room on my face and the warmth under the quilt. Even back then, I'd been aware that something had changed between him and me – though I couldn't have put the feeling into words, even for my own benefit.

He put his hand on to mine. I turned and saw that he'd been looking at me, examining my face.

I searched his eyes, trying to read him. 'What?'

He smiled. 'Nothing. It's just . . .'

'What?'

'I don't know.'

Then he laughed and the strangeness of the moment was gone. I laughed with him. Then I rolled on to my side and put an arm across his chest. 'Mmm. Give me a man in wintertime.'

'You only want me for my body,' he said.

I winked. 'Cheaper than an electric blanket.'

Instead of coming back at me with some witty riposte, he sighed and looked up to the ceiling.

'You're moody today.'

'Just thinking, that's all.'

I traced his shoulder with my fingers. The sun must have dipped down behind the rooftops, because the light faded from gold to grey and the twig shadows blurred into each other.

'My sister's going down to London tomorrow,' he said. 'She's leaving the kids with me.'

'Lucky you.'

'I'm no good with kids. You got any suggestions?'

'Take them to see the elephants at Twycross.'

'You'll come with me?'

I pressed my teeth on to my lower lip. The pact of secrecy was always with us – even when we didn't give it voice.

'It'll be all right,' he said. 'The zoo is miles away. And it's February. No one will be there.'

We drove in separate cars the next day. Him with his sister's kids. Me on my own. Then we met up next to the Prairie Dog Village. Feigning surprise. At first we kept the distance between us as we walked.

What he'd said about not being good with children – it wasn't true. He was at ease in their presence. Some of the time it seemed like he was letting them lead him where they wanted. But other times I caught glimpses of the way he was directing their enjoyment. Perhaps it was a skill that came with experience. His younger sisters were all married. All had kids.

We strolled a little way behind the children as they scampered off towards the Lake Baikal Seals. And I found that we were holding hands. An ordinary couple on an ordinary weekend. The first time.

I realize now that this was the only time Paresh and I were able to be a normal couple. A single day. And I weep some more, allowing myself to wallow in the thought. Indulging in my grief.

The tears are still running on my face, but I'm breathing smoothly now. I'm lying back on the grass of Majestic Park, looking up at the huge poplar tree above me, its leaves trembling in the breeze. The dappled shadows are playing over me, and I'm suddenly aware of the exquisite beauty of the moment. A perfect day.

Then a heavier shadow falls across my face. I lift my head to look.

'Police?'

Standing by my feet is Mr Medigovich, still in his leather jacket in spite of the sun. My face is streaked and wet, but he doesn't seem to be seeing that. There's a wild, distant look in his eyes, as if his ghosts are more real today than the grass and trees.

I'm about to tell him that I'm not really a police officer any more, that I've been suspended. But I hold back.

'I don't want this,' he says. 'Not for The Troubles to come like this.'

I push myself into a sitting position, wipe over my cheekbones with the heel of my right hand. 'It'll be all right,' I say.

But he isn't hearing me. 'We are the same people, this what he say. But I am not the same as him.'

'Who?'

'The man who come.'

Mr Medigovich has got both of his hands in his fair hair, pressing down on the top of his head – as if that will be enough to keep the thoughts from spilling out. I push myself to my feet. We're the same height now. Eye to eye. But he's looking through me.

'This man threatened you?' I suggest.

He shakes his head. 'Come to save us. To protect.'

'Save you from what?'

Medigovich puts one broad hand on my shoulder, as if I were a man, and he my comrade. 'He say Serb people are like brother to him. But all the rest – all the Hindu and the Muslim, this he will kill. I am not brother to this man!'

I can feel the skin tighten on my cheeks and arms. The tiny hairs standing. My tears have dried now and the remaining salt is prickling my skin.

'When did you see this man?'

'Before.'

'How long before?'

'One hour. Two, maybe.'

'And what did he tell you to do?'

Medigovich is silent for a moment. Then his eyes come into focus and I know he's seeing me at last. He removes his hand from my shoulder, suddenly embarrassed by the contact. But I don't want the spell to break. I keep my gaze steady.

'What did the man say?'

'To take my family out of Majestic Hotel. Must go today. But Niko I cannot find. He should be here.'

The Majestic Hotel. I'm cursing myself for not thinking of it. *Operation Majestic*. Not the park. Not the PM – though timed to coincide with his visit. A bomb at the asylum seekers' hotel.

'Niko isn't here?'

'I wait for him.'

'And the other residents?'

'They laugh when I tell them,' Medigovich says. 'I say all to go out, Muslim, Hindu, everyone. They only laugh.'

I hadn't noticed it till now – the sound of the crowd approaching. They must be a fair distance down Dean Street, but they're getting closer even as I listen. I can't make out individual voices. They're churned together to form a single noise, like an angry swarm of bees.

I've got the mobile phone out. It's ringing and I'm waiting for Ivor to pick up on the other end.

'What did he look like – the man who told you this?'

'Not like you. White skin. Hair short. Big muscle.' He bends his right arm, by way of demonstration, as if flexing the biceps.

I give up on Ivor, cut the connection and dial 999.

'Emergency. Which service do you require?'

'Police.'

'I'm putting you through.'

The crowd is much closer already. There's an abrupt whine of feedback followed by a single voice crackling above the rest, distorted with amplification. 'Fascists out!'

The crowd echo the chant. 'Fa-scists-out!'

On the other end of the line, I hear the operator passing on my call. I don't wait for them to ask for details. 'This is Inspector Akanbai. Calling from the Majestic

Hotel. There's a bomb here. I'm going in to evacuate the building.'

I've thrown the phone to Mr Medigovich and started running. A straight line. Vaulting the park fence. Dodging between the cars. Up the front steps and into the hotel lobby.

It's the same man – the one I saw behind the reception desk on my last visit.

'Police,' I say. 'Evacuate the building now.'

He opens his mouth, then closes it again and shakes his head.

'Now!'

'This is about the bomb?'

'I have reason to believe . . .'

He hasn't stopped shaking his head. 'Medigovich told us and I . . .'

'Clear the building!'

'I searched already.'

I'm reaching for the small, metal hammer dangling below the IN CASE OF FIRE sign. I bring it back till the chain is taut, then I ram it into the alarm, shattering the glass disc and slamming into the button underneath. Bells start clanging. There's one on the wall above us. Others deeper into the building.

He's really angry, swearing, I guess – though I can't hear the words. But there's nothing he can do. There are people running through the lobby already. Africans, Arabs, Chinese, Turks. Young and old. All on the edge of hysteria. I position myself in mid-stream, slow the tide so none of the children get crushed in the front doorway. I'm hoping the bomb is on a timer. Because if it's set to be triggered by radio and if the bomber is watching what's happening – then he'll set it off in the next few seconds.

The man from the reception desk is next to me now. He's put on a big smile, and he's shining it at anyone whose eye he can catch. They respond to him. I can see some of the panic leaving their faces. The flood is turning into a trickle.

I touch him on the shoulder, then shout over the bells. 'Go out. Keep them together.'

He nods and follows the last of the asylum-seekers out through the door.

I charge for the stairs. Take them three at a time. Up the floors to the top. It's quieter here away from the clanging bell in the lobby. I run along the passageway, banging on doors. Nothing. Now down one level to the next floor. A mad scramble around each corner of the corridor, checking every door. Right at the end I think I hear a noise through the wooden panels. I try the handle. It's locked. So I hammer again. This time I'm sure. A child's voice.

'Open the door.'

The child is crying.

So I stand back and kick. Once. Twice. Three times. It's solid. There's no way I'm going to get through it. I look around me, pull a fire extinguisher from the wall. It's one of the old metal ones. Heavy as hell and tall as my knee when I rest it on the floor. I hoist it up and ram it at the door near the handle. The first time I don't get much of a swing, but it's got enough weight and I'm thinking that it's going to work. There's sweat running down the sides of my face now. I pull it back a second time and ram it forward. This time something in the doorframe cracks.

The child is crying still. As frightened by me as by the fire alarm. I swing the extinguisher again. The lock rips free from the wood and the door shudders open. It's Niko. He's backed up to the window on the far side of the room. I've dropped the fire extinguisher and I'm holding my hand out to him. Smiling.

'Come. You're safe now. Get you back to your dad, eh?'

I nod. He nods back and steps towards me. Then I see him freeze over with fear. He opens his mouth to scream again and someone grabs my arm. I'm struggling, pulling. But there's a sudden cold steel ring around my wrist.

'Marjorie Akanbai. I'm arresting you on suspicion of murdering Paresh Gupta.'

'No!'

But he's got my other arm. He's pulling it behind me, fitting the other cuff to my other wrist. He puts hands on my shoulders and turns me. He's a uniformed constable. Thin. But strong enough.

'There's a bomb in the building!'

'You do not have to say anything, but it may harm your defence if you do not mention when questioned something which you may later rely on in court. Anything you do say may be given in evidence.'

There's a second uniform coming along the corridor now. This one is older. A sergeant.

I turn to him. 'I'll go with you. But for God's sake get this boy out of here.'

He's shaking his head. 'Any way we can get those bloody bells to stop?'

'I've not cleared the ground floor yet.'

The sergeant looks uncomfortable with what he thinks is his duty. 'The bloke downstairs says it's a hoax.'

Suddenly the bells stop. The silence is even more intense than the alarm was.

'This is for real.'

'So you say.'

'Clear the building,' I'm pleading. My eyes are stinging

where sweat has run into them. 'You can blame it all on me if it turns out to be nothing.'

He teeters on the edge, in no hurry. I'm thinking about the bomb. I'm seeing the floors collapsing in my mind. Seeing white-hot shards of metal flying through the air.

'It can't hurt you if I'm wrong. But if I'm right . . .'

At last he beckons to Niko. 'OK. Let's go.'

The boy doesn't move. So I say: 'Will you come with me?'

Then he bolts across the empty space of the room and puts his small hands around my cuffed arm. The constable is pushing me down the corridor and Niko is clinging tight. Then down the stairs and across the lobby.

We step out into the sunlight. I feel disorientated. The police car is parked on the double yellows right outside. There's a crowd of perhaps sixty hotel residents on the pavement, around the car and spilling half across the road. Too close to the hotel for any kind of safety. I'm trying to figure out why none of the crowd are facing the building. They've got their backs to the entrance and are looking out over the slope of the park. Then I become aware of the noise and I understand.

It's the angry buzz of the protesting crowd. They must have moved past the hotel while I was inside. They've moved on to the park now, massing halfway down the slope. I can just see them from where I'm standing. Close to a thousand. Two-thirds of them are Muslim men and boys. But there are whites with them. Anti-fascist protesters. I see purple hair, and green, and skinhead cuts. Placards and fists punching the air.

There's a group of five police Tactical Support Units parked on the grass. Officers in riot gear are clambering out of the back of the vans, hurrying into formation. And there's a second crowd moving on to the park from the lower end. All white this time. As individuals they'd be hard to tell from the anti-fascist protesters. But as a group it's easy to recognize a racist mob. Two ad hoc armies spoiling for a fight with a small peacekeeping force to one side. And suddenly I understand why the sergeant wasn't so keen to keep the residents out of the hotel.

That's the last thing I get to see. Then there's a hand on my head, and the constable is pushing me down into the back seat of the patrol car. Niko doesn't want to get in, but neither will he let go of me. He's standing on the pavement, grasping handfuls of my blouse, pressing his face into my shoulder.

The sergeant stares out over the park. Then he crouches down next to Niko and looks me in the eyes. 'I'm sorry. We can't keep the residents out here.'

'There *is* a bomb!'

'You can't know that.'

'Search – do it for me.'

He glances at the building, then back to me. 'Five minutes. That's all I can give.' Then he springs back to his feet and instructs the constable, pointing out over the massed armies on the park. 'If that lot get any closer, send everyone back inside.' Then he runs into the hotel.

The sound of shouting from the park is closer now. Clearly audible taunts being thrown from one mob to the other. Police sirens. More TSU's arriving at speed. It's twelve twenty by the clock on the dashboard. The PM would have been arriving in the next ten minutes – if plans hadn't been changed.

They've left the police car door open, so Niko can still cling to me as he crouches on the pavement. The constable who arrested me is standing next to us, trying to look bigger

than he is. The crowd of residents have all moved across to
the top edge of the park now, to watch the standoff below
them.

Then I see Mr Medigovich. He's stumbling towards us. I
can't even imagine what memories this is reawakening in
him. There are beads of sweat on his forehead. His eyes are
wide. He tries to push past the constable to get to Niko. The
constable pushes back. Medigovich lashes out with his fist,
catching the policeman under his eye. Niko screams and
dives across my lap into the back seat of the car.

'It's the boy's father!'

But the constable isn't listening to me. He's got his side-
arm baton out already. He uses it to parry Medigovich's
next blow, then goes in with a counter to the stomach.
Medigovich stumbles back and then turns. I don't believe
he'd leave his boy for anything, but he's in the middle of a
waking nightmare and his eyes can't tell what's real and
what's memory. He runs. The constable is after him. We're
suddenly alone and I'm feeling very vulnerable. Niko has
his face buried in my chest. I want to hold him, but my
hands are cuffed behind my back.

'Niko,' I say.

He presses himself into me.

'Niko. Pull the door closed.'

I feel him trembling.

'We'll be safer then. You and me.'

He shifts from my lap, pulls the car door closed. Clicks
the lock.

I can still hear the sound of the fight. It's closer now and
the hotel residents have all dispersed. I'm hoping they're
walking away from the trouble, though some are probably
hunting around for glass bottles to throw.

A white van pulls up on the road and reverses into the

parking place immediately in front of us. The driver gets out and slams the door. He's wearing a black T-shirt. There's a mobile phone in his hand. His head is down, so the brim of his baseball cap covers most of his face. He strides away across the road and on to the park. There's just one moment, when he glances back towards the van, that I catch sight of his face. It's the same moment that I know where the bomb is hidden, because the man is Vince the Prince.

Chapter 30

I'm thinking casualties. Trying to work out some course of action. And I'm doing it all in that telescoped time that comes in moments of acute danger, when you're seconds from probable death. We're going to lose some passers-by when the bomb detonates. The police sergeant in the hotel is dead for sure. There's Niko. And the baby inside me.

If Vince doesn't know the hotel is empty, he's going to want the explosion to happen as soon as he's out of range. The longer the van is there, the more chance of discovery. He might know. He might not. It could be a timer or radio-controlled detonation. Too many variables. There's a police radio in the front of the car. I can't reach it with cuffed hands. Niko could press the buttons for me. But no one has believed me up to now.

That chain of thought has taken perhaps a second. Too long.

I hear the sudden boom of something bouncing off the roof of the car above my head. A glass bottle lands on the pavement, smashing into razor shards. The screaming roar of the fight has come suddenly close. People are vaulting the park fence. Whites and Asians together. It's one or two at first, then a flood. They're sprinting across the road. Missiles are following them. Bricks, iron bars, more bottles.

'Niko. The door. Open the door.'

But he's whimpering into my side, not even hearing. I turn my back to the door, try to reach the lock. It's too high for my cuffed hands.

The fascists have reached the edge of the park now. White men with axe handles and bottles. There's an Asian man caught on the wrong side of the fence. He's swinging a metal bar, trying to fend them off. He lashes out catching one of the skinheads full on the chest. Then he gets a bottle smashed over his own head and he's down. They close around him, kicking at his body and head.

There are sirens wailing. They seem to be in all directions, but there are no police vans here. I slide my body down low in the seat, getting my head below the view-line.

Some Asian men have regrouped. They surge back across the road, haul on the fence, pulling it down towards them. But the body of their comrade lies still on the ground, and there's blood on hands and clothes. A fresh wave of fascists are arriving, fighting hand to hand. They're fewer in number, but they're experienced fighters. They push the Asians back towards the hotel. Towards us. And suddenly the fight is around us. A brick smashes into the windscreen, sending out a spider's web of cracks.

It's all whites around the car. A skinhead face leers in through the window. It sees us. It grins. Then it's gone and the car is rocking. Another man joins him. First it's two men, then twenty. Then the car is tilting. Rolling. I'm falling towards the door. Then on to the roof. Niko is underneath me, crying and screaming. Incoherent.

There are faces peering in through the upturned windows. A hand waving a cigarette lighter, making sure I see it. Then the faces are gone and the feet are running away. I can smell smoke already. Acrid. Burning paper. And petrol fumes. Someone's lit a fire.

There are a few seconds now, for us to live or die. But I've got nothing left. Not enough energy or emotion to break free. I close my eyes. I think of Paresh. Of Anwar. Of all the people who have been left in hell. And I want death to come quickly. Then I think of Niko and the baby.

I twist over so I'm lying on my back, hands crushed underneath me. Then I bend my knees and summon up everything I have left into one final effort. I lash out with my feet at the side window. It cracks, shattering into tiny fragments.

'Niko!'

He looks at me, eyes wide and unseeing like his father's. I don't know how I'm going to get him out of the car.

So I say: 'I need you to save me.'

There's a trickle of blood running from the side of his head. He doesn't answer.

'Climb out of the window. Then pull me through.'

He still doesn't move. The smoke is thicker now. It's harder to breathe.

'I'm pregnant, Niko. There's a baby inside me. Help me to save it. Climb out of the window.'

His head trembles, more shudder than nod. But he's crawling over the shattered glass and out on to the pavement. There's something else in the air now, as well as the petrol and burning paper. The smell of teargas. There are more feet pounding past on the road just outside. Sirens. Niko is clear. I worm my way to the window.

'Run, Niko. Run.'

But he stays. I feel his hands on my legs, trying to pull even though he is too small to make any difference.

'Run!'

Then there are other hands on me and I'm being dragged over the shattered safety glass. Feeling the fragments cut into my skin. I'm out. I'm being pulled to my feet, hoisted over a man's shoulder. A policeman. He's running. Niko is with us. The car is well alight. There's a small explosion. Then, a second later, a larger one and a ball of flame. The men who tried to burn us to death are off down the road now, a knot of flailing clubs and limbs.

'You OK?'

The constable who dragged me free is the one who arrested me. He's trying to unlock the handcuffs, but his own hands are shaking so much he can hardly get the key in place.

'Take the boy,' I say

My hands are free at last. I run towards the white van. If Vince is still around, and if the bomb is remote-controlled, then we're in trouble. Because the racist thugs have been all around us for the last couple of minutes. Now they're gone and police reinforcements are coming along the road around the edge of the park.

I try the back door of the van. Then the passenger door. Both locked. So I take a brick that's lying on the road and I climb up on the front bumper and start pounding the windscreen. It takes three hits and a bloody knuckle before the glass shatters. I'm clambering in, over the front seat into the windowless back.

I've found it. And if it goes off now, they'll never even find my body. I'll be vaporized. Five large, plastic barrels. Wires trailing from one of them to a mobile phone on the floor of the van. I get a flashback image of Vince carrying a mobile a few minutes earlier. I grab the phone, pray that there are no booby traps, then rip the wires out of the back of it.

My heart is hammering. My breath is coming too fast.

Hurting my throat. I have the phone in one hand. Then it rings. But the bomb doesn't go off.

I press the 'receive call' button and speak: 'You lose!'

I can hear breathing through the phone. But no words. And I know I've got him hooked. I've made his great statement come to nothing. He's wildly angry. Animal rage. Dangerous – for me and also for him. He could escape right now if he wanted to. Go to ground. He's got money and contacts. He'd come back and get me if it took him years to do it. I put my free hand on my stomach and I know that I have to end it here.

'Vince,' I say, 'I beat you. A mixed-race woman beat you.'

'You're nothing!' He hisses the words.

'Nice little firework. Shame you didn't have the balls to stick around and light the blue touchpaper.'

'Gonna kill you, bitch!'

The line goes dead.

I'm out of the van now, through the back doors. I'm turning, scanning the road, the park, knowing he must be near. The constable who rescued me is still with Niko. The sergeant is here as well, giving first aid to a woman lying on the pavement.

There's a group of about fifty racist thugs away down the road, facing off against a group of Asians and whites. I see a figure break through the crowd of anti-fascists, running full pelt towards me. Vince. An angry bull. He's across no-man's-land and among his fellow racists. Charging through them and towards me.

But these thugs don't recognize him. He's run at them from the wrong side of the line. For all they know he's a white anti-fascist. One swings a pickaxe handle, catching him on the back of the head. Vince is down. Others are going in with kicks and punches. Someone pours liquid from a bottle. Suddenly Vince is alight and the crowd is scattering. Running from the flaming, twisting body. It rolls, over and over. The arms beat the ground. But the flames won't go out. Then he stops moving.

Chapter 31

'It works like this,' says Bob. '*The quick brown fox jumps over the lazy pig.*' The keyboard chatters as he types the words. Then he clicks to save the document. 'That'll do for our memo.'

'Nice line,' I say.

He turns to me and winks. 'How about we make it even better?' He deletes the end of the sentence and types in a couple of new words. Then he sits back so I can read the amended version.

'*The quick brown fox jumps over the lazy detective superintendent.*'

I say: 'They used to hang people for treason. You know that, don't you?'

He saves the file again. 'You like?'

'All very witty, Bob. But I don't see where it's getting us.'

'OK,' he says. 'OK. There are two bits of information attached to the document. The creation time . . .'

'Today?'

''S right. The third of October at 10.28 a.m.'

'And the other bit of information is . . .?'

'The modification time.'

'But you only just modified it.'

He nods vigorously. 'So the modification time is the same – give or take a few seconds.'

'And . . .?'

'And now we wait a couple of minutes. Let the clock tick forward.'

He pushes his chair back from the desk, then spins himself around. When he's rotated to face me – a three-quarter turn – he puts his feet down to stop. I'm thinking that he should be working in a toy shop, not a police station.

He grins at me, then nods towards my stomach. 'Boy or girl?'

I shrug.

'They can tell, can't they? Ultrasound or something.'

'I don't want to know.'

He thinks about this for a moment. 'I guess it'll be like unwrapping a present at Christmas.'

'Something like that.'

'They're giving you maternity leave and everything?'

I don't offer an answer. Right now I don't even know if I'm going to have a job next week. My appeal against suspension hasn't happened yet. Bob's attention has wandered off again. He's spinning his chair, looking up at the ceiling as he rotates. I take a sip of weak tea from the mug in my hand. No tannin stains today. He cleaned it especially for me.

'Have we let enough time pass yet?' I ask.

He jerks back to the business in hand as if waking with a start. 'OK. It's now 10.35 a.m. We're going to change the creation time of our memo.' He's got the mouse in one hand and he's tapping the keyboard with the other. 'Works just like I showed you before. I make a copy of the file. Delete the original. Rename the copy back to the original name. So it looks like nothing's changed,' he says. 'Except the creation date.'

Now he clicks the mouse to brings up a list of the file's properties on the screen.

I read it. 'Created at 10.35. How does that help me?'

'Created at 10.35. But look further down the screen. Modified at 10.28.'

'That's impossible.'

Bob punches the air. 'Yeah!'

'How can you have a file modified before it was created?'

He's off in a world of his own. 'I never thought I'd hear myself say these words – but God bless you, Microsoft.'

'Bob . . .?'

He's wearing a grin the size of a slice of watermelon. 'It's a bug,' he says. 'A bloody beautiful little bug in the Windows operating system. The modification date never gets changed when you make a copy of a file.'

Now I know why I didn't do computer science at university. Trying to understand this kind of thing seriously messes with my head. 'How does this help me . . .?'

'It helps,' he says, "coz your memo was created some time on Sunday night – that's what the computer tells us. That's why you got in trouble. But it was modified two days earlier – before it was created.'

'I'm in the clear?'

'Sure. As far as the computer evidence is concerned – someone tried to frame you.' He looks sideways at me for a moment, then says the thing that's been running through my mind these last few days: 'It had to be Shakespeare, didn't it? When you sent the memo, no one knew it was going to end up being important. Who'd have bothered to take it out of the pigeonhole except the person it was addressed to?'

I've followed this logic myself – I've lost count how many times – and always got to the same answer as Bob. I still don't want to believe it, though.

'Was he a racist, then?' asks Bob.

I shake my head. 'It has to be money. He never seemed . . .'

'Seemed what?'

'I don't know.'

'Perhaps that's why it's so hard to take.'

Chapter 32

I'm lying in a hospital bed feeling bruised. Everyone's sent cards, of course. The bedside cabinet is cluttered with them. At the front there are two big ones – from Sal and from the Community Relations team. There's even one from Mr and Mrs Gupta.

I see Ivor's face at the door. He waves. Very sheepish. I beckon to him with the arm they haven't connected up to the drip.

'How did you get in? Up till now they've let no one see me but Sal.'

He coughs, then speaks in what's almost a whisper. 'Told them it's police business.'

I laugh, then wince when the stitches pull. 'You old fox.'

He hovers by the bedside with his hands clasped in front of him. He looks around the ward, taking in the other beds, the newborn babies in their bassinets. Then he looks at the empty space next to my bed.

He clears his throat. 'Did you . . . hear the news?'

'For God's sake sit, will you?'

He does as he's told.

'What news?'

'Jury returned their verdict on Cranmer-Phillips. Guilty on all counts.'

I close my eyes and sigh as deeply as I can manage. There wasn't any doubt really. Not after we found the coded photographs and unravelled the network of his supporters in America. That's where his money had been coming from. It all connected in to the racist website. But it's good to hear it confirmed.

'Alison's been speaking to the press. She had a couple of minutes on TV, so she's dead chuffed. And everyone from the Race Crime Unit have had a big pat on the back from the chief constable.'

'And Shakespeare?'

'Resigned yesterday. Gone before the leak inquiry even starts.'

The big fish should be happy about that. No one wants a corruption scandal. Kickbacks and racism. Not inside the force. It makes for bad headlines. We want our racists rabid and explicit. That way we can chuck them in prison, throw away the key, and the politicians can make believe they've got everything sorted.

Perhaps they have a point. Calm returned to the streets after the riots, which does prove something wholesome. In the end, the people who were prepared to live side by side vastly outnumbered the ones who weren't. That should make me happy. It's just that I've always looked for something more than tolerance between the communities. Like my dad used to say – *if meeting someone new doesn't change you, then you've never really met them at all.*

I don't speak my thoughts, and Ivor seems for a while content to sit and stare at the empty space next to my bed.

Then he says: 'Greenway is doing OK.'

'Enjoying his time in charge?'

'Too much.' He rolls his eyes.

I laugh again. 'Stop that. It hurts.'

The ward doors open. We both turn to look. A nurse arrives, pushing a bassinet on its trolley.

'This is what you've been waiting for,' I say.

Ivor gets to his feet, hands clutched in front of him again. The nurse parks the trolley next to me. 'All clean and changed,' she says. Then, with a half-smile: 'Police business over yet?'

Ivor peers at the swaddled bundle, asleep now. The palest brown skin, sprouts of straight black hair and a round face that's no particular race, but somehow contains every race at once.

'She's so beautiful,' he says.

Disclaimer

This novel was inspired by Leicester – a city where diverse communities coexist in peace. Some of the locations are real and specifically identified. Others are composites. But all the characters and events are fictional, as is the local newspaper. Any resemblance to real individuals is coincidental and unintended. This is the case, even where the characters are identified as holding positions within real institutions such as the Leicestershire Constabulary, Leicester City Football Club, Leicester City Council or the Home Office. They inhabit the world of what might be rather than what is.